THE LADY IS TROUBLE

LEAGUE OF LORDS, BOOK 1

TRACY SUMNER

THE LADY IS TROUBLE

Copyright © 2020 by Tracy Sumner

All rights reserved.

Edited by: Holly Ingraham

CHAPTER 1

There is nothing stable in the world; uproar's your only music.
~John Keats

London, 1865

*A*llowing the lady to lure him into her carriage had been a brilliant idea.

Julian Alexander stared at a spider crack in the ceiling of his Mayfair townhome and wondered *when* he might start to believe it. He could presume encountering a former lover outside Hatchards on an otherwise lonely evening was a fortuitous event if there weren't the niggling—*familiar*—pinch of regret the moment his cock settled.

A faint sense of having erred, gone off the path, and into a twilight woodland where one could be easily lost.

As lost as he'd felt stepping into her dimly lit carriage.

Julian watched Marianne wrap herself in his silk

1

dressing gown, her chatter lulling him into a state of satiated distraction. Only the first and third word of each sentence filtering through, he found the conversation definitively complete. Earl, garden, tryst, scandal. Titles and the men who held them occupied her undivided interest. Each day spent investigating a riddle that had no solution.

It was not, in fact, worth the attention she devoted to it.

In all fairness, Julian could not judge.

His mystical gift separated him from a normal existence and made the world he'd been born into at times unrecognizable. Out of a sense of duty, he played the part of the gentleman for the sole purpose of propping up the viscountcy, adhering to society's rules while struggling to preserve his secrets and the secrets of those he protected. Of course, he tendered his title when it benefited himself or the League. But a barony would have profited as well and knocked him down a notch, perhaps enough to slip beneath the waves and be carried from view.

He closed his eyes and let the waves crash over him.

Then Marianne mucked it up by kicking the door to the past wide open.

He rose to his elbow, knocking the counterpane aside. Dragging his hand through his hair, he asked, "Repeat that, will you?" Alarm vibrated through his belly, like swimming in the sea and realizing a massive wave crested behind you. *No, it couldn't be.* "Come again?"

Marianne's gaze settled where the sheet hung low on his hips. "So, you were listening." She reached to touch, a stroke on air. Licked her lips in the event he didn't register her appreciation. "Jules, with you, I never know."

He slid high in the bed, suppressing his annoyance. *Jules*. He'd asked her to refrain from calling him that. *Too. Many. Memories.* "Marianne, the clairvoyant?"

Her smile grew luminous, her delight underscoring the scant attention he offered. Without trying to be a disdainful cad, it seemed he was precisely that. "Oh, darling, it was the most farcical evening! Ashcroft arranged for a fortune teller to entertain, and you know him. For a duke, he pushes the boundaries of propriety while always staying within the limit." She leaned in, clutching the lapels of his dressing gown to her bosom. "I heard there was absinthe served to the men. Why the festivities were enough to make a stuffed bird laugh!"

Julian hummed low in his throat and rose from the bed. He didn't know but could imagine. *Hell's teeth*, he thought and reached for his clothes, which lay in a tidy pile next to the chiffonier. Taken off without haste, neatly folded.

He frowned. How *little* had he wanted this encounter?

"I didn't glean any outrageous tidbit about my future. Though I tried." She lifted a delicate shoulder beneath silk. "More the delight just being there."

He buttoned his shirt, slipped his braces over his shoulders. "You mentioned the woman had an unusual accent."

Marianne crossed the room, slippers striking the floor in an eager rhythm. "It was dark, too dark to see anything. Very mysterious. Madame wore a veil, and there was candlelight. The ideal setting. Although Ashcroft seemed oddly anxious the entire evening, adding nothing to our merriment." At Julian's impatient look, she rushed on, "Madame's accent came out on one word. She sounded almost..." She twirled her hand in a languid circle, finger pointed toward the plaster ceiling rose. "Ad-ver-*tise*-ment. That's what she called the sheet she handed me. She sounded, can you imagine, *American*? Would that not be a vulgar surprise?" She laughed it away, swept beneath the Aubusson at her feet. "Although I'm sure I misheard. Doubtless, an upstart trying to hide cockney."

Julian's fingers twitched, missing a button on his waistcoat. He moved too forcefully across the room as she took a stumbling step back. "Where is it?" He drew a breath laced with the scent of Marianne's perfume and the acrid aroma rolling in the open window. Soot, sewage. That damned river. *Christ*, he hated London. "The advertisement." He extended his hand, controlling the tremor that wanted to travel from his fingers to his heart.

Could. Not. Be. Piper was tucked away in Gloucestershire. Under armed guard. Protected. *Safe.* Their enemies had been searching for her since she'd arrived from New York all those years ago. But they wouldn't look in Gloucestershire. She knew this. He'd cautioned her more times than he could count. Had been advising her for years, it seemed.

Marianne regarded him through eyes the color of fresh cow dung. "Why, darling, I fear I've not seen you react...to *anything*. Appetites fed but the heart untouched." She waved away her discomfiture and a statement she likely wished she'd kept to herself. Turning in a crimson whirl, she moved to rifle through the reticule sitting atop the chaise lounge, one just the shade of emerald eyes Julian had tried with little success to forget. "Lucky for you, I saved it. As proof, I experienced such an evening. Who would believe otherwise?"

Julian flexed his fingers, preparing for the transmission. His gift didn't marry well with a lack of sleep. Touching an object and being pulled into the otherworld of someone who had touched it previously was brutal enough. Stepping into that world when exhausted was reckless and allowed the experience to control him.

Maybe it wasn't Piper, and this endeavor would be nothing more than supernatural experimentation. He'd sent Finn to visit her last month. Or had it been May? A headache moved to the base of his skull. Lifting his hand to his brow, he pressed hard.

Blast it, had they not visited since the spring?

Marianne thrust the advertisement at him, and he hesitated. Taking time to notice she'd only secured an ear bob, and it dangled there without a partner, bouncing as she did. Her lips canted, though he'd bet a half-sovereign the smile would disappear if she fathomed the source of his reluctance. If she had any idea who he truly was and how his gift of sight forever separated them, she would run screaming into the misty night. "If you're interested, Julian, and I'm shocked you are, Madame DuPre is doing a reading tonight. The address is listed."

His breath seized. *Madame DuPre*. The name conjured forgotten summers of youth. Running through fields of grass so tall the blades hit his thigh, swimming in shallow lakes on moonlit nights, climbing trees until he was breathless surveying all that fell below. Laughter and foolishness—even love by some arcane definition—on a scale he and Piper could no longer afford.

Julian huffed a sigh and grabbed the sheet before he could think better of it. Or stop himself, which he would *not*, because it appeared Piper had jumped off another goddamn ledge.

And he was her rescuer. Her caretaker.

Her warden.

I'm going to throttle her, was all he managed as he crushed the foolscap in his hand and stepped into the otherworld.

Shadow and candlelight bathed the room. The curious combination of burnt ashes, spice, and lilac. Piper was settled over a desk, her gown as golden as the Kingcup scattered along Harbingdon's riverbank each spring. Moonlight carved a path along the floor, and Julian followed the dazzling footpath of silvery blue. The walls surrounding her were covered in tattered wallpaper, peeling at the ceiling and seams. The furniture was scuffed, the rug threadbare. The dwelling was nothing like Finn's description of the modest but opulent manor in Gloucestershire.

His heart thumped desperately against his breastbone. She was more vivid than any model he'd ever painted, and he had *tried* to recreate her, a thousand strokes of brush to canvas.

Her vibrancy eluded him.

Stumbling back, he tried to step out of the trance. It was a problem lately that he had trouble doing so. The otherworld had a voracious claim on him. Through eyes drawn to slits, he observed Marianne's lips moving, but he was too entrenched in another space and time to respond.

Too entrenched in *her*.

Independent of his gift, Piper Scott had a stronger hold over him than any woman could ever hope to have.

Muttering a harsh oath, he dropped the advertisement like it burnt his skin, and the image of Piper spiraled away, water down a drain. Forcing him from the room with the tattered wallpaper and the girl he'd sworn to protect with his life but never touch again to preserve hers.

The woman for whom he hungered.

Dear God, Piper, what have you done?

He was through the door and into the hallway before another breath had passed, ducking as a vase accompanied Marianne's shriek of rage.

～

She could only determine events had gotten out of control rather quickly.

Piper lifted her veil as she stumbled along the smoke-filled hallway, drawing a breath tasting of charred wood and scorched velvet. Baron Audley's aura had been so startling. An unusual shade: darker than lime, lighter than moss. Jealousy? Envy? Questions she would have asked had she not shifted rather suddenly in her excitement, bumping the table and sending the candlestick to the floor. She should have known better than to use such a tall taper, but they were very atmospheric.

Now the modest parlor in the hotel where she'd held her readings was ablaze for the second time in one week. *Both* could not be due to her negligence, could they?

She tripped over a crease in the runner and halted in place. *Was this the way out?* She focused on calming her mind and placed her hand on the wall to steady herself. The wallpaper felt a bit sticky, and though she realized time was limited, her mind returned to the Baron's aura. Determining the emotion associated with the color took deliberation; it was not a simple process. She needed her research journals, which were upstairs in her room.

Damnation. The papers would be of little use if she burned to a crisp trying to retrieve them.

A strip of light marked the floor at the end of the hallway. Piper's lungs stung, her vision graying as she dashed toward the exit. This would win the grand prize as her worst blunder yet. Frankly, dying would be the easier option. Because surviving this debacle to find herself, Lady Elizabeth Piper Scott, daughter of a viscount and granddaughter to an earl, exposed as a clairvoyant would be bleaker than any previous error in judgment.

And Julian...

Julian would, quite truthfully, kill her.

She could admit to fleeing Gloucestershire to gain his attention. She'd not had contact in *months*. Four, at least. Running hadn't worried her, even with the danger to her person, because Julian, the most prudent man she'd ever known, would eventually find her. Before their enemies, she trusted. Naming herself Madame DuPre was like waving a cape before a bull. And although he wouldn't believe it, posing as a clairvoyant was for her research.

For the most part.

The other reason was loneliness, which she would never, *ever* admit to feeling. Not when Julian had enforced their separation after explaining why hiding in Gloucestershire was the most judicious plan *for her protection*. Always choices provided for her protection, not her happiness, until she became so disheartened and experienced that little jab of rebelliousness that made her do silly things.

She nodded her head—*go with research when he asks why you did it*—and shoved against the door at the end of the hallway with all her strength. The garden was spring-lovely and blessedly vacant, moonlight splashing the brick path she dropped to her knees upon. There was a shout from inside the hotel, the screech of windows being raised to invite fresh air.

She coughed and hung her head, bowing close to

8

the ground, brick biting into her palms. No matter how hard she tried to contain it, chaos followed her as closely as a beloved family pet.

The polished Wellington entered her vision before she sensed his presence. A knee hit the ground beside her, fingers skimming her cheek and lifting her face into the light. She felt the veil being slipped free. Thought scattered as she curled into the contact.

Forever since anyone had touched her with even the slightest regard. All at once, she felt as diaphanous as the smoke surrounding her, dissolving in his arms.

"We have to leave this place." His hand tensed, fingers trembling against her jaw. "Open your eyes, Piper."

Julian's voice. Rich, deep, captivating. To look in his eyes would break the spell. Disappointment. Censure. *Evasion.*

His aura, however, would be *magnificent.*

He swore beneath his breath and lifted her into his arms.

"A mistake," she whispered, her cheek settling against fine wool with a sigh of surrender. "The papers. My research."

As he strode through the garden, she breathed, dismissing smoke and summoning Julian. He was surprisingly luminous, the feel, and scent of him. Memories swirled, years and years of them. She couldn't shake the calm that settled over her, the *completeness.*

How utterly foolish.

Nothing had changed in her heart.

When *everything* had changed in his.

"You have no idea how much rests on my protecting you," he hissed in her ear, rage vibrating from him like ripples from a pebble tossed in a pond. On an oath, his arms shifted, bringing her closer. She crumpled into him, his heat warming her to the depths of her soul. This was all Julian, a gridwork of contrasts. Resentment and tenderness, irritation and concern.

He wanted the lines clearly drawn when they were muddled, every last one of them.

"You have no idea," he repeated.

Actually, she had quite a fine idea.

Other little girls had gone to sleep listening to stories of fairies and princesses, gods and knights, towers rising amidst fields of lavender. Her stories had been filled with mystics and the supernatural, magical gifts that set her apart.

And those who sought to use those gifts to destroy her.

CHAPTER 2

There is no instinct like that of the heart.
~Lord Byron

A steady intake of London's stench began to
clear Piper's mind. Damp earth and foul
river, and beneath it all, the alluring scent of the man
holding her without a hint of compassion. Citrus and
bergamot, wonderfully enticing, though she wished
she hadn't noticed.

Julian had them cornered between a flowering
hedge and the garden wall, near an entrance to the
street. A street bustling with a horde either watching
the pandemonium or helping eradicate it. Their
auras pulsed like a dawn sun, one merging into another in their excitement. It lit the street, and she
lifted her hand to shade her eyes.

The movement caught Julian's attention. Bracing,
he shoved his arm against the brick. "You think
they're glowing now? Wait until they see us step out
of the garden of a hotel known for trysts, in a state of
dress that tells a very debauched story. Or worse, the

revelation that one of their own is a spiritualist who has a penchant for starting fires. If you keep this up, my next mission will be retrieving you from Bedlam."

She wiggled her chilled toes, realizing she'd lost a slipper. She surely looked a fright. Or at least, not as she *should*. Madame DuPre dressed for informal consultations and did not have the sartorial expectations of the granddaughter of an earl. And everyone expected a little grandeur with a spiritual reading.

Her gaze sought Julian's, an explanation, *some* explanation she was sure, on the tip of her tongue. But shadows and obstinacy kept them silent.

Temper lighting, she shoved against his grasp.

He shook his head, lips pressed. *No.*

The warmth of Julian's skin seeking hers through layers of cloth, his breath scalding her cheek with each uneven exhalation, combined to bring all those awful, beautiful, forbidden hopes to life. His touch still had the power to obliterate, as well as the fire raging around them.

Damn him.

"You, too, Yank," he whispered.

Mortified by the nickname and her thoughtlessness in speaking out loud, she struggled. "Let me go." She jabbed her elbow in his ribs. "I won't run. I promise."

With a sound caught somewhere between a laugh and a snort, he shifted enough to let her slide down his long body. He gave her no more than a second to catch her breath, then captured her wrist, the strength exerted conveying how, due to promises broken in the past, he held little trust. She inched back, gathering her equilibrium. In the years since she'd last seen him, he had cast aside the too-lean, scrappy young man. His broad shoulders blocked the moonlight; his thickly muscled arms tensed against hers. Combined with his height, which had presented attraction and annoyance when it arrived, he created a daunting picture.

He caught her staring, and his gaze skipped away. Back to the street and whatever it was he searched for. It was too dark to see the color of his eyes, but she remembered—slate, like a morning fog over the Thames.

They were without question the most beautiful eyes she'd ever seen.

And she'd long wished for another set to come close.

As if he read her thoughts, his lips curved— nothing near an actual smile. His hair, longer than fashion dictated and still holding a gentle curl, lifted in the breeze, the mahogany strands shot through with auburn firing in the gas streetlamp. As she studied him, an expression she could not measure crossed his face and was gone so quickly she was forced to question its existence.

The sound of a disturbance on the street had Julian holding his finger before his lips.

Seconds later, Finn, *dear Finn*, dashed into the garden. He held her valise under his arm, packed in a rush as it was not fully closed, with what she hoped were her papers escaping on all sides. "I cleared the room of anything incriminating. And the fire is contained." Breathing heavily, he glanced up, shrugged. "Mostly. The hotel isn't going to come down around us anyway."

Julian shoved her behind him, his lock on her wrist firm. "The carriage?"

"Dalton's brougham. All I could locate since we can't risk a hack or your coach. It's waiting on the northwest corner." Finn did a sidestep and caught a sheet of foolscap under his boot that tried to flee.

"Away from the horde on Bolton. You brought an audience for this one, Pip, you really did."

Julian swore soundly and jerked her along behind him as they left the garden.

Piper frowned at Finn over her shoulder. *Why say that?* she mouthed. She drew her finger across her throat, slashing to declare *no more*.

Finn grinned and offered his free hand as an apology, a typical response, so drolly delivered one forgot to be vexed. How she'd missed him, this boy, nay almost a man, who in her heart of hearts was her only sibling. *My, he's getting as tall as Julian*, she concluded in wonder. And still so beautiful it made her heart squeeze. Julian had taken Finn under his protection years ago when he realized the orphaned boy had a mystical gift as powerful as his own. Julian had been little more than a boy himself when he'd begun to lie about their relationship, planting subtle innuendos like a seed in the soil until the ton assumed Finn was his father's byblow and his half-brother.

She contained her smile as Finn danced about for another sheet. If Julian noticed amusement on her face, he would twist her in a knot with those clever fingers of his. Justly, none of this was the least bit laughable. It was her worst transgression in a life littered with them.

Julian gave a sharp whistle when they met the northwest corner, and the carriage pulled into place, bouncing off the curb in the driver's urgency to reach them. Piper wondered how Finn had managed to borrow Lord Dalton's carriage with such haste. Perhaps it only took a snap of his fingers to gain such a simple thing as emergency transport, for Finn was a born trickster, able to bend the truth seven ways to tomorrow and come out clean.

And, if gentle manipulation didn't get him what

he wanted, he read your mind as cleanly as a copy of *The Times,* and that was that. He would have made a brilliant partner—and been the genuine clairvoyant in the room— for Madame DuPre's readings.

Julian hustled her up the brougham's single step and into the dim interior. The coachman's lamp illuminated his visage, and she drew a clipped breath. He seethed without a word, though it was hard to assess his expression through the soot. *Oh, dear.* She sank to the seat.

He looked as dreadful as she imagined she did.

With Julian's hard thump on the trap, the carriage jerked into motion. Finn dumped her valise to the floor as he scrambled for purchase on the foldaway seat in the corner. She felt certain he would like to remove himself from the storm brewing inside the brougham's confines, and the boot might have been a better spot for the two of them, even battling the raindrops that had begun to pelt the windows. To her mind, enduring a thorough soaking seemed more enticing than Julian's stinging ire.

"The storm should help put out the fire," she said and traced a rip in the seat. "Although the blaze did seem rather insignificant when last I checked."

"So bloody insignificant they looked to be evacuating every building on that side of the street," Julian snapped and settled as far from her as he could get without crawling outside. His voice, raw from smoke, sounded like it had been hauled across jagged glass.

And his aura…

His aura fragmented in every direction like a spectacular sunset. Crimson bleeding into velvety blue bleeding into ginger, an imbalance she had come to understand meant one struggled to hold opposing emotions in check. She'd have liked to gather her papers from the carriage floor and record the hues, but that would have been a dreadful impulse to follow. Not while Julian sat there, brooding. An irate, brooding lord, fresh from a gothic novel. She'd wager a halfpenny in her father's favorite gaming hell that this utterly masculine display appealed to every woman in London, seamstress to countess.

It certainly appealed to *her*.

Julian yanked Madame DuPre's veil from his waistcoat pocket and threw it at her feet. The carriage's springs squealed as they rounded a corner, and she switched her attention to Finn's struggle to hold on to his perch rather than take a chance on catching Julian's gaze.

"You've put yourself, and the League, in a horribly dangerous position. Humphrey will need to spend a month in this damned town bribing everyone from bellboy to laundress to forget anything and everything they witnessed. Any of us could be placed in an asylum tomorrow if our gifts are revealed. You've met the people we've saved from that very fate. And you know about the ones we've lost. So, what do we do about the people we can't bribe, Piper? Can you tell me?" His eyes, when she finally gathered the courage to look, were silver orbs glowing amidst inky soot. He yanked a hand through his hair, leaving it wild about his head and enhancing his feral appearance.

She pressed her bottom against worn velvet while holding Julian's gaze. *Steady, Piper.* It would not do to cower. Anyway, she wasn't sure she knew how.

Julian frequently displayed anger, at least with her, but he was rarely unhinged. She wasn't frightened of him. Well, not much.

Finn laid his handkerchief on Julian's knee. At Julian's hard look, Finn circled his finger about his face.

"Might want to address the…" His words trailed off, and he slumped back in the darkened corner.

"Undoubtedly, I look like I stuck my head in a hearth because I followed an implausible vision into a smoldering hotel. Only in one's wildest nightmare, right?" Julian managed the handkerchief with violence, blending the grime in deeper.

"How—" Her cough cut off the question. She patted her chest, swallowing hard. Julian passed her a flask she presumed he'd filled with water. The gin burned a path from teeth to toes. "Oh, heavens. That is *horrid*."

With a sigh, he slipped a sheet from his trouser pocket, unfolded it with care. Even in the muted light from the coachman's lamp, she recognized the advertisement before he spun it around on his knee for her perusal. Without comment, she took another sip, her reaction controlled this time. She could come to appreciate the taste. If the choice was gin or being held at the mercy of Julian's rancorous gaze, she chose gin.

"Well?" He plucked the flask from her hand.

She sat back, out of the lamplight, formulating how honest—*at this moment*—she wanted to be. A better time to discuss her research strategy would present itself with the benefit of a night's sleep and a decent meal. Surely—

"Oh, no, you don't. Sitting there, figuring out the best path to take." Her tactical hesitation held all the strength of gauze, and he saw right through it. "A medium? A mystic in an age of cruel fascination with the spiritual world? Is this your idea of exhibiting caution and prudence, per our agreement? You nearly burned down a bloody hotel!"

Her heart skipped as the streaky moonlight filtering through the window highlighted the shadowed crescents beneath Julian's eyes. He looked weary and

defeated, for which a good night's sleep would do little. Wordlessly, he folded the sheet and slipped it
back in his pocket.

She curled her hands into fists to keep from
reaching for him. Piper had not played the healer in
many a month. Madame DuPre told fortunes but
saved no souls. That, too, had been part of their
agreement. *Wait until we know how to manage your incredibly singular gift*, had been Julian's final words before sending her to Gloucestershire.

She could draw his exhaustion from him as
quickly as venom from a snakebite, but he'd rebuff
her. So, she stared until he sensed it. Until his aura
gurgled like a brook about him. "It wasn't entirely affected. Not swindling like you and Finn did in the
rookery. I can take an aura and a few personal
queries and turn it into something quite representative. I wasn't touting myself as a conduit to their deceased Aunt Prudence."

"Not affected, huh?" He regarded her steadily, his
somber gaze razor-sharp. "Like the accent?"

Her cheeks flamed, and she hoped the dim confines protected her pride if nothing else. For all his
scrupulous nature and moral rectitude, Julian could
play in the gutter when his temper shoved him there.
This was a sore spot, and he knew it. She'd worked
hard to let the long vowels and lilting tones of the
aristocracy filter into her speech after a youth spent
being dragged into every gaming hell in New York
City while being told to sound very *un*-English. For
all her diligence, when her mind wandered, certain
words popped out with the flat undertones that gave
away her indecorous upbringing. In truth, her accent
was a complete and utter muddle. Like her *life*. "The
proper accent is simply giving them what they
want."

He laughed, genuinely amused. "When has Piper Scott ever given *anyone* what they wanted?"

"Once. Quite well and gladly, as I recall."

With a curse, he swiped his brow with the handkerchief and hurled it to the seat. "Don't. Go. There."

For the first time in three years, the sting of tears pricked her lids. Turning away, she blinked into a foggy night. Judging by the star's alignment, they were heading north, out of London and into the countryside. She had no idea where and didn't have the energy to inquire. She'd shed copious tears over a passionate instant of recklessness from a man who was never reckless. She understood and understood it well: Julian Alexander, eighth Viscount Beauchamp, took his promises very, very seriously.

And he'd promised right in front of her to never touch her again.

"Let me enlighten you, Yank. There's someone in the ton interested in us, in *you* specifically. They're getting closer if Finn's dreams are any indication. And you've possibly thrown yourself right in their path." He popped his fist against the carriage wall. "You don't think before you jump." Another fist thump. "*Ever.*"

She rolled her head to look at him. He dodged the scrutiny, his gaze seeking the onyx twilight from his window. "How could I possibly know that? You left me with an aunt we located in some dusty tome she was so distant a relation, a letter arriving once a month if I was lucky to update me on your progress establishing the League and defining my place within it. I couldn't walk to the village without a footman with a pistol shoved in his boot trampling on my heels."

"*Burke's Peerage* is hardly a dusty tome, Piper." Julian propped his arm on the window frame and dropped his head to his hand. His shoulders lifted and fell with what she assumed was a repressed sigh. "Gloucestershire was a temporary solution. Fashioned under duress, I might add. Your grandfather's death sent us into a spiral. I was only trying to get you the hell away from London until we understood who wanted you badly enough to commit murder. Our reality is far from the entertainment the ton envisions from spiritualism. You'll be trying to levitate next, is that what I'm to assume?"

Her temper overrode the logical end of the discussion, which would be to share her research and the reason for her activities in London. Julian would be interested. After all, the League was *his*. Piper's grandfather had started the society years ago as a place for those genuinely afflicted with a mystical talent to find shelter because to be afflicted was nothing short of a cruel fate, which he knew firsthand because his wife had been a healer, just like Piper. In the last moments of his life, her grandfather had laid the responsibility for the League's future —*her* future—on Julian's shoulders.

An honorable man, he'd not been able to say no.

She'd felt a burden ever since.

"I'm not certain why Gloucestershire was so demanding a situation. Why an impetuous escape was even necessary."

"Because your *temporary solution* chose to pass in her sleep last month, Jules," Piper said. "Her heirs were cleaning out the manor around me and asking how long I intended to stay."

Julian turned at this, his head lifting. A lock of hair slipped over his eyes, and he knocked it away. "She *died?*"

"Yes. So, I forged a communiqué from my dear family friend Viscount Beauchamp inviting me to stay in the family home in Mayfair with a maiden aunt as there was no longer an adequate chaperone in Gloucestershire, etcetera, etcetera. Another option would be found and so forth. Although, at twenty-three, I'm far too old to require a guardian, but try telling that to anyone in the ton."

"What maiden aunt? How did you—"

"I pinched a few sheets of your letterhead in the event an opportunity presented itself."

He blinked. "I'm afraid to ask how closely your signature resembles my own."

Piper rapped her knuckle on the windowpane, then repeated the action for good measure. She'd actually grown quite fond of Aunt Hortense and her crooked wisdom—such as the enormous biological burden Piper faced having an American actress for a mother. "Gloucestershire wasn't so bad."

"I visited as often as I could. Between classes," Finn added, trying to placate when she imagined he wanted to climb off his tiny seat and out the window. "Quite the calm setting. Much better air."

Julian waved away the sentiment with an exasperated growl. "I needed time to find an estate completely separate from the viscountcy that could house what is coming to be a rather eccentric group of people. Time to raise funds to purchase it because most are flowing into the titled estates." After a long pause, he continued, "Harbingdon is secure and quite perfect for our needs. But before I acquired it, we"—he shook his head—"weren't ready."

"You weren't ready, you mean," she whispered. She left it unsaid but wished Julian could read her thoughts while praying Finn did not. *I know why you hid me away.*

As that was not Julian's gift, he read her expression. "*Fine.* Any way you would like to interpret." The scent of him drifted to her, subtle, woodsy, close to the ground but not rooted. Like something earthy your boot released as it hit a patch of moss in the forest. Enticing without effort. So like Julian, it physically hurt.

Dashed, she could get lost in that scent.

Julian swiped the flat of his hand across the expanse of velvet between them. "You're the crown jewel in our tiara, Yank, whether any of us like that fact or not. And one must protect what is most valuable."

With a huff, she turned to face him, preparing for battle. His gaze swept her body, lingered, then returned to capture hers. Heat lit his eyes, and his aura blazed like a brilliant sunrise splitting the horizon. The wash of color nearly made her forget her point. She placed her curled fist, gloveless and soot-stained, next to his without touching him. "Send the crown jewel back to Gloucestershire. I can beg to be housed as a destitute relation, sharing that no unentailed properties or assets flowed from my father as they were all gambled away. That my cousin inherited my grandfather's title and cleanly abandoned me without provision." Grabbing the filthy handkerchief on the seat, she tossed it at Julian's head. He ducked, and it sailed out the open window. "Or, leave me at the next coaching stop. Or back at the charred hotel!"

"And be the responsible party when they find you?" He sat back with a muttered oath, his stained linen shirt still tucked neatly in his trousers and straining over muscles she didn't remember him having. His silk waistcoat lay open, the dangling ends brushing his hips. Her crisis had sent him fleeing without the benefit of a topcoat, cravat, or gloves. Her stomach tensed to imagine where he'd been in such a state of undress.

Masculine fury had never looked so magnificent.

His gaze held hers as she studied him, his tightly leashed intensity sending his aura rippling from his body in waves, like a stone had made a disturbance on its calm surface. Awareness pulsed between them, the same she remembered from long ago.

"*Jules*," she whispered without thought.

His gaze dropped as his expression shuttered. Ignoring her plea, he brought his hand to his brow, rubbing hard. Headaches apparently still beleaguered him. "I think you've forgotten what happened to your grandfather in the quest to find his chronology. To find *you*. How very precarious our existence is."

Piper turned to study the pinch of sky visible above the treetops. The air in the carriage crackled with tension and, as usual, her temper and impulsivity had trumped good sense. She swallowed past the apology she wanted to make.

Oh, how she wanted to be *different*. Prudent. Capable. Composed. Like Julian. Only, she didn't know how to rise above the Scott predilection for trouble.

She heard the strike of a match as Julian lit a cheroot, and the scent of sulfur drifted through the carriage. How could he desire this when the taste of burnt wood and fabric must be stinging his throat as it was hers? Rather rude in the confines of the brougham, too, but with the mess she'd created, she couldn't complain about a minor bit of indelicacy on his part.

She slid lower in the seat and chanced a glance at him as a shaft of moonlight highlighted his face. Piper wished he looked more like the gentle young man of her remembrance and less like one set on fighting a tiger with his bare fists. The tip of the cheroot glowed, bobbing with his inhalation.

When the silence had grown unmanageable, he

said, "Bizarre coincidence that Marianne Coswell, of all people, ended up with your advertisement." He gave the sheet peeking from his pocket a firm tap.

She kept her expression composed even as her stomach pitched. The advertisement making its way to Lady Coswell meant every salacious tidbit whispered in polite and not-so-polite drawing rooms was true. She *was* Julian's mistress. That he'd introduce this topic was dreadfully cavalier. Not for Piper Scott, but certainly for Julian Alexander. "Coincidence? Yes, very." Which it wasn't. Piper had tucked that sheet in Lady Coswell's hands with every intention of letting Julian know she was back in London.

"You know what, Yank?" His shoulder flexed as he flicked the smoldering cheroot out the window. Air blew up his sleeve, puffing the material like a sail above his broad forearm. "Honest to God, I'm feeling inclined to leap from this borrowed carriage just thinking about the mess you've created. I could locate Finn's discarded handkerchief in the process. A two for one victory."

"Leaping from a swift-moving vehicle? That's your plan?"

"No, my *plan*"—he slouched, long legs stretching the length of the interior—"was to keep you safe, albeit hidden, in Gloucestershire." His clipped words drifted like snow, chilling her. "*Temporarily.*"

She blinked away another salty tear-prick. "I think the gossipmongers have it right, Jules. You're quite terrifying in your fury. What is it they call you?" She clicked her tongue against her teeth. "Beauchamp the Lionhearted. My, having a sobriquet doesn't exactly speak to lying low."

He kicked one foot atop the other, closing his eyes and his mind to the conversation. "Well, Scandalous

Scott, the half-dozen attributed to you are extremely flattering."

"Enough!" Finn came halfway off his perch, his boots slapping the carriage floor.

Piper flinched, in all honesty forgetting Finn sat on the foldaway seat.

Slumping back, he continued in a resigned tone, "Truce, please? You've both earned everything you have, including your legendary reputations." He threw his arm over his eyes as if to block out the light from the coach lamp and their inane argument. "Somehow, we'll make a plan. We always do. We're a team, remember?" Finn's temper blistered when it flared, but it startled due to his carefully crafted façade. He'd polished himself as sharply as a jewel, and by some odd circumstance, a ruffian from London's roughest rookery fit in their world better than Piper or Julian could ever hope to. "Let's get to the inn, and we'll discuss this in the morning."

Piper perked up at this. "Inn?"

"The Cock and Bull," Julian said, his voice a fatigued rasp. "Workingham. Back entrance with a healthy monetary bonus, because you and I look like something a cat with his tail on fire dragged in. And unless you have a chaperone hiding beneath your skirts, you're already compromised." He added in a low voice, but she caught it: "Like that would surprise anyone."

So, they *were* headed north. "Where—"

"Harbingdon."

"Harbingdon," she repeated, confused, and hoping someone would enlighten her. Perhaps this was the estate Julian had found for the League. She looked to Finn, but he avoided her gaze, the coward. "I'm not to be dropped off? Hidden away? Tucked out of sight? I'm going with you and Finn?"

Something in her tone must have alerted him. "Don't smile, Piper Scott, don't you dare smile," Julian grit between clenched lips.

But she did.

After she turned to watch the scenery pass as if pitch-black English countryside was the most exciting thing imaginable.

CHAPTER 3

We look before and after, and pine for what is not.
~Percy Bysshe Shelley

The next morning found Piper awake before dawn, hungry, uneasy, and humiliated over the debacle the prior evening. Tipping aside the faded floral drape, she peered through the lone window in what was a modest but very quaint room, one Julian had, without comment or expression, escorted her to after they'd arrived. If she pressed her brow to the glass and looked hard to the left, she could just make out the back of Dalton's brougham parked near the horse stable.

She released a breath. *They had not left her.*

Since there was no more sleep to be had, and she did not want to vex Julian further by delaying their journey, she called for the maid, Adelia, who arrived with a neat bundle of clothing acquired from the owner's daughter. Seeing as Piper was 'hardly bigger than a grasshopper,' she said no one else's garments would do.

Suitably presented, Piper headed downstairs and, upon finding an empty common room, popped her head in the kitchen and bargained for a slice of cheese and bread, which she took with her into the gardens behind the inn. From corset to stockings, Adelia had given her a wonderful oral tour of the property. There was even a secret tunnel leading to the village priory, but Piper could imagine Julian's reaction if she asked to see it.

Kicking dirt off her slippers, Piper reentered the inn to find Julian seated in the dining room, gazing into his teacup as if he would find answers there. A folded newspaper lay unopened by his side. Bathed in the sunlit shimmer, he looked both younger than his bearing and older than she re-called. Time had changed him. Still heartbreakingly handsome, there was a sharpness to his visage that had not been there before, a cool detachment she felt sure he used to measure, rebuff, renounce. As she stared, his aura sparked like a phosphorous match strike, an effect she wasn't sure how to in-terpret. Tangling her fingers in her borrowed skirt, she shifted her attention to the horrendous painting of Queen Victoria above his shoulder and let his aura fade to a low hum. She needed a steady equilibrium if she was going to deal with Julian and make it out alive.

To pull him from his contemplation, she gently bumped the table when she reached him. Julian swal-lowed hard, braced his hands on the scarred wood, and came to his feet. Eyes the color of tarnished silver met hers. His regard was restrained but wel-coming enough. At least he no longer seemed spoiled for a fight.

"May I sit?" She indicated the empty chair. Any-thing to lessen her feeling like a rabbit to his hawk, partly due to their disparity in height. With his nod of assent, she shook her skirt and settled in.

Julian sat, unfolded *The Times*, and ironed it flat with his hand. "The clothing is suitable? I, myself, leave a case here for the unplanned outing."

Of course, he looked suitably magnificent in superbly tailored black. She smoothed her hand over her bodice, each borrowed button a jolt on the way down. "Yes, very."

He gazed at the newspaper, but she had a feeling he wasn't reading it. "I don't suppose we're so fortunate as to have your maid, Ebba, waiting in the"—he glanced at her over the top of the broadsheet—"hotel you almost burned down? Finn couldn't locate her last night, but I can send for her. One possible reprieve from the Madame DuPre madness should we need her assistance in getting you out of this mess."

Hmm…Julian did throw a dart near the bullseye. "Ebba left Gloucestershire after Aunt Hortense joined the great beyond."

He put the newspaper aside and took a thoughtful sip of tea. "Footman?"

"Groom. Daniel. Very young, very handsome." Piper traced a jagged nick in the table. "I tried to talk her out of running off with him."

He snorted, more ruffian than viscount, a hint of the boy she'd loved sending a tremor through her. "I'm not even going to imagine *that* conversation."

She opened her mouth to tell him she was fully capable of giving sound advice; her problem was following it. Except, blast the man, he reached inside his coat and extracted a pair of spectacles. Executing a neat loop behind each ear, he blinked and settled back with a rapt perusal of his newspaper. When she didn't comment, he glanced up. Stilled. His hand rose to touch the bridge of his nose. Then he shrugged and dropped his arm. His only comment, "Headaches."

Piper's toes curled inside her slippers. The lenses enlarged his eyes, emphasizing the amber flecks swimming in silver. As if something so lovely needed amplification.

Breaking the silence, the serving girl halted at their table to take their breakfast request. Soon, a cup of coffee, dark and pungent, sat before Piper. She stirred in cream and risked a glance at Julian, who was staring sullenly at her.

"May I ask why you're fixing me with such a vexed expression?" She lifted the cup to her mouth and practically purred as the warm liquid hit her tongue. "Didn't you flay me to within an inch of my life last night?"

Sitting back, he drew his hand to his lips, silent. Raised one finger. "Trip to London, alone, no chaperone." Two fingers. "Masquerading as a medium." Three. "Going—"

"*Stop.*" She set her cup on the saucer with a clatter. "I did *not* travel alone. Not exactly. There was a third cousin of a footman who—"

"Good Lord," he interrupted, dropping his head back to stare at the ceiling.

"Well, if you'd like to know what I did and why..." She let her words drift, doing a quick mental calculation. Honesty versus more chicanery. The new, mature Piper Scott took the courageous, *truthful* route. Even if mature Piper had to lock her knees together under the table when facing the intimidating man sitting across from her. Clicking her nail against her cup until Julian's impatient glance made her seize the motion, she finally admitted, "Rest assured, I operated completely in darkness, veiled at all times. The typical attendee: half-foxed, wealthy, well-placed in society. Not able to give more than a scant description of me, if one at all. I was never in danger, Julian. No one knew who I *was*. Except you, when you heard the name Madame DuPre. Which is, honestly, exactly as I'd planned." *No more lonely Piper*, she could have added but didn't dare.

"Brilliant," he muttered, his voice still strained from the fire. He blinked at the ceiling, the rims of his spectacles winking in the sunlight. What in heaven's name was he looking at?

"I'm sorry for this misadventure, truly." She twisted her cup this way and that, then forced her hands to her lap. Piper Scott did not fidget. "But this time, Jules, I have, well, what you like. A *plan*."

His gaze slipped to a spot just over her shoulder. Finally, with a sigh and an adjustment of his spectacles, he looked her dead in the eye. His forceful regard seared her to the tips of her toes and back, kicking her poise down by at least two notches. "I'm not sure my heart can take it but enlighten me."

Flustered, she fought to gather her words. She wasn't sure why she was so tongue-tied when she and Julian had *always* sparked like two pokers struck against each other. She brought her bottom lip between her teeth, mentally composing her rationale. A fleeting expression crossed Julian's face, causing him to shift in his chair and his aura to widen about him.

"Well," he prompted with a sharp edge.

"When you first dumped me—"

"Settled you," he cut in.

She gave a mock bow over the table. "When you first dumped me in Gloucestershire, I began to make notes about the auras I witnessed that had any *validity* to them. Such as, I understood the person's circumstances and was able to infer how this may be affecting their aura. For example, one man, a baron as I recall, lost his family home to creditors. It was the most appetizing morsel of gossip that week. I didn't speak to him, but from across the village green, the air surrounding him smoldered, the same color as the earl's old pistol."

A hint of a smile touched his lips. "I remember that pistol well."

She pointed to the ceiling. "In my valise, I have five journals detailing credible encounters matching mood, circumstance, or personality to color. Madame DuPre's included. All listing variations affecting one's aura. With validation, I could add this research to my grandfather's chronology." She rested her chin on her palm. "The missing link is how to recreate the various shades and hues. I've tried, but I'm not a skilled artist. One governess left over my lack of talent in that area if you recall."

"You've been tracking patterns with colors," Julian whispered, stark interest she couldn't discern the meaning behind shaping his words. He slid high in his chair, his curiosity sparked. A flash of delight streaked through her, knowing she had finally, *finally* done something to please him. "You have data."

"Mounds from even my short time in London. You see, Madame DuPre can ask probing questions that Lady Elizabeth Scott cannot. And at some point, if you had not located me, I would have located you." She forced her gaze from his because she wasn't sure that was *entirely* true. The absorbed young man, her friend from summers past, had proven quite hazardous to her heart.

"Piper, I can help."

She looked up to find his wistful expression clearing. He slid his hand across the table, halting before he touched her. If illuminating sunlight had not bathed him, she would have said the tint sweeping his cheeks was a figment of her imagination. *Julian, blushing?*

Rolling his lips in, he reached for his tea and sat back. "Colors. Hues. I'm passably proficient. An interest." A puzzling expression, almost what she would call bashful. "No." A quick shake of his head. "It's more of a diversion."

The table bit into her ribs as she leaned closer. "I don't understand."

He placed his cup in the saucer, the look on his face similar to hers while she decided whether to be truthful or float a lie like a toy boat across a lake.

The serving girl interrupted the conversation with the arrival of their breakfast. Quite lovely, she appeared to have a rather healthy attraction to Julian. Her aura projected yearning in vibrant shades of deep plum. When he glanced her way with a smile, the edges flared crimson.

Piper accepted her plate as her stomach gave a hard twist, wondering how frequently Julian stayed at the Cock and Bull. And exactly how solicitous their service to a handsome viscount was. Oblivious to the scene playing out before him, he thanked the serving girl, his aura shifting not one wit.

Piper drew a relieved breath as the delectable aroma of eggs, beans, and black pudding dove deep, eliciting a stomach rumble she hoped he didn't hear. She settled her napkin in her lap, watching Julian, plainly, struggle.

He glanced at her, shrugged a broad shoulder. "I left the townhouse too quickly to take my utensils. As you know, I try to limit confronting items that are not my own." Releasing a resigned breath, he grasped the fork, fingers clenching, knuckles going white. "Delightful company, hosting everyone who has touched this recently."

Startled and intrigued, she recorded his aura as it lit with not one color but a brilliant array. It would take weeks to decipher the explosion surrounding him.

"Quit reading me," he said on a hard rasp, his dark lashes sweeping up to reveal a wondrous, leaden shimmer behind spectacle glass. His brow creased, and he inhaled on a rapid gust.

Going on instinct, Piper slid her hand across the table and gently covered his. Surprisingly, he didn't push her away. Encouraged, she rubbed her thumb over his wrist in slow circles as his pulse raced. He exhaled, fingers flexing.

She stilled as a fragment of a scene, grainy and indistinct, intruded upon her mind. A barrel-chested man, rotten teeth, lips peeled back in a roar of laughter. The dank scent of ale and crisped meat. The glow of a gas lamp.

The hairs on her nape lifted as her heart lurched.

The image wrapped around her—smell, taste, touch—pressing as closely as her lace-edged chemise. The tenseness in Julian's shoulders eased, and his breathing fell into a regular pattern as the vision flowed out of him and into her.

She resisted the urge to expel it as her skin tingled, and her vision blurred. Healing often felt like the sudden pinch of a needle sliding beneath skin before she wrapped her mind around what she was taking from another person. Twisting her hand in her skirt, she held her mind steady as the image dimmed to a glow she could accommodate. It frightened her, this...*transmission* because it wasn't a common occurrence.

But she said nothing because she knew it would frighten Julian more.

She opened her eyes to find his glassy and settled

on the uneven plank floor. "Tell me about the walks in St. James Park you used to take with your mother," she encouraged. Redirection had worked well in the past to lessen the intensity of a vision when he touched an object. "What was the toy you carried along? A wooden horse?"

"A valiant effort, Yank." His hand shifted, tensed in hers, released.

"Are your visions getting stronger?" Her grandfather's words rang in her mind. *A healer must heal, Elizabeth.* "The League is my inheritance, Julian, my *only* inheritance. I should be a part of it. A working member. You should have summoned me back to—"

"You were *protected*." His tone held no room for negotiation. "Which was an overwhelming feat to accomplish in the days following your grandfather's death."

"His estate—"

"His manor proved to be the least battle-ready in Cambridgeshire, and we never saw them coming. Our enemies stormed right in, past the fortifications the earl had erected. They knew what they were looking for, too, if you have any doubt. You and the chronology. They got neither, but we may not be so lucky the next time. It was a convergence of bad tidings. Finn less able to decipher his dreams, the League in complete disarray, scattered about England, powerless to do anything more than share the odd morsel of information. I had to spirit you away, without hesitation, and that is what I did. Find a secure location for the League while organizing our efforts as more than an old man's diversion. Which is what I'm *doing*."

"The *visions*, Julian."

He glanced around the room before letting his gaze slide back to her. "They're getting stronger, is that what you want to hear? It's not bad on door-knobs, railings, dishes. Things touched repeatedly. They create only this semblance"—he circled his finger around his ear—"a whine, like a bothersome fly. Muted colors, like watching someone run through smoke. I can almost ignore those."

"But, today, you had trouble with a simple fork."

The spectacles left his face to be deposited on the table. "Too little sleep. One drink beyond what was advisable last night. And my throat feels like someone lit a fire in it." He grasped his teacup, regarding her over the rim. "The visions are going to have control this morn, not I. I'm strong enough to bring them in." He tapped the teacup to his temple. "The trouble is getting them out."

"I'm always apologizing to you, but I am sorry for making everything more difficult." Taking a deep breath, she met his gaze and forged ahead before he could stop her. "We could work on controlling the visions as we did years ago. A healer must heal, Julian." She paused, wetting her lips, and trying to ignore how his regard stripped her bare. "I no longer have a place in the League. You must return this to me. No matter the danger, you *must*. And it seems as if you need me to return as much as I need it."

He held her gaze as the sounds of a busy dining room surrounded them. "Gifts often shift with age, Yank. Mine is not wholly what it once was. Regrettably, it's stronger. Where I go...it's almost a trance."

"Control can be had with practice, was that not your motto?"

He managed a tight smile. "It was." His lips, bottom fuller than the top, pressed in on one another. "But now I know better."

Piper controlled the urge, the *compulsion*, to touch him. There were no better means of driving Julian away than to let him know their long-ago kiss lingered in her mind like a tender wound.

Maybe he had forgotten, but she had never been able to.

"Jules, you don't have to be disappointed in me." After a long moment of silence, she completed the statement, "I can do that very well myself."

He grimaced, dragging his hand across his mouth to hide it. "Piper, you misplace my intent. Maybe you always have."

"Since my grandfather's death, I've misplaced everything. My place, my purpose." She moved her eggs around on the plate, her appetite spent. "As a Scott, society has to accept me. And they do, in part. But we both know I don't suit." She tapped her fork against china. "My father never cared for anything resembling well-bred behavior, and after he died, the earl's wishes were paramount. I had no one else. Every fleeing governess brought another round of angst as he realized that not only my gift but my unusual upbringing, set me apart. The one season in London was pure agony, the auras an eruption before my eyes. I couldn't maintain a steady stream of inane conversation while colors bloomed around me." She lifted her shoulder, a shrug one of those governesses would have brought low with the business end of a book. "So, I am left somewhat aimless unless you're going to let me back in."

"Let you in? You've never been *out*." His tone, thick, vibrant, and full of meaning, called to her as soundly as his touch. The emotion shaping his handsome face was too much for her to catalogue and keep her wits intact. "After I was cast out by my own father because of a gift I didn't want but could not control, can you imagine my disdain for everything, and I do mean *everything*, he believed in? I manage the viscountcy only to protect the tenants who have spent their lives dedicated to it." He braced his hands on the table, urgency in his stance. "Like your grandfather found me, and I found Finn, there are more with gifts they cannot manage, people I am welcoming into the League, welcoming to Harbingdon. We are stronger in number. If I have any purpose in life, it's to make sure no one suffers the way I did, the way Finn did."

"They need a healer, Julian."

He brought his fist to his lips, pressed hard. "You're right, they do," he admitted.

"Partners," she said.

"Partners." The word teased from his lips, a gentle whisper.

"I work with you on controlling your gift. You help me catalogue mine."

Figuring it was honorable enough to take advantage of a man's bewilderment, Piper extended her hand, and God help them both, Julian took it.

Julian backed down the stairs, three to be precise, until the dining room, with a modest lean of his body, came into view. He'd been headed up at a swift trot, the better to end a negotiation he had no chance in hell of winning.

Her soft laughter had slowed his progress.

He grasped the railing as if his life depended on staying connected to the pitted wood. Thankfully, the visions were muted and manageable, while the riot in his brain was not.

He had agreed to be her partner. *Piper Scott's* partner.

Was he bloody cracked?

Balanced on the tip of his boot in the event he had to spring into action to avoid being caught observing, he recorded Piper's interaction with the inn's owner, Warren McAlister. A conversation about gardens and what bloomed best in sun versus shade. How much water did this plant require and which ones could go without. She was buoyant, vibrating with youth and loveliness. So petite, and this Julian had failed to recall, her head barely reached the man's chest.

Or his.

She sounded genuinely interested in horticulture, gesturing enthusiastically as she absorbed the advice of a man enthusiastic himself. A man, by the by, whom Julian had never seen rise above a bland smile in two years of frequent stops at his establishment. The exchange made him question how much he actually knew about the woman currently soaking up all the oxygen and sunlight in the dining room below. If he drew a breath, he imagined he'd catch the trace of lilacs radiating from her skin, stronger even than the scent of his breakfast sausage.

He stood there, suspended, and watched her captivate.

Asinine fool, he resolved and continued up the staircase. How could he have forgotten this?

Piper Scott loved to set people on their ears.

Especially him.

Maybe it barely registered, the vibration she projected, tilting the world around her while *he* tried to retreat to the background. Hard for the tallest man in the room to do. Especially one with a moniker or two, as Piper had so agreeably pointed out. *Beauchamp the Lion.* He cursed as he slapped his bedchamber door open. What foolishness from a group of people with nothing better to do. With nothing more to *worry* about.

While he had the entire world on his shoulders. Or so it felt some days.

He scooped his soot-stained clothing from the carpet and into his battered valise. This bag he kept at the inn, stocked with a fresh change of clothing, allowing him to leave Harbingdon or London at a moment's notice and rest at the midpoint. It was his favorite bag, one he'd retained from what he considered his *other* life. Too battered for a viscount, surely, which is likely why he felt affection for it. At one time, a boy, nearly a man, had run from an affluent but brutal existence at the hands of his father and disappeared in the bowels of London's mean streets with nothing but that valise in his hand.

It now showed its age in a very inelegant way.

Perhaps they both did.

He slumped to the bed, dropped his head to his hands, and tried to massage away the ache. He wasn't sleeping well. Controlling the visions was getting harder as they matured along with him. Images that had once made little sense now rang clearly, twisting his mind and his body into knot after knot. He was damned sick of looking into lives and being repulsed by what he witnessed. Repulsed and unable to expunge.

In actuality, he *did* need Piper.

She was buoyant, effervescent. Nothing, not even being a healer and pursued because of it, weighed her down. How did she manage that? His gift brought him low, scantly off the ground—his promise to protect the League even lower.

A ragged laugh tore from him as he imagined what she'd been up to in the past month. Fear mixed with fury inside him, but he still laughed.

Good God, she had guts.

A part of him, never to be revealed, envied her

daring, her *joie de vivre*. Her bloody lack of concern even as someone, usually him, stayed close behind, sweeping up the mess. Strangely enough, at one time, freshly installed at her grandfather's estate and not sure of his direction, Julian had wished to be more like her. Outspoken, animated, *vivacious*. But his objectivity held steady even in light of his wish that it not.

He pressed his palm to his chest. Through layers, he could feel his uneven heartbeat kicking. *Shit.*

Touching Piper Scott still made his pulse race.

Her body had filled out, curves deepening, on the verge of voluptuous for such a small frame. She should have looked drab in a borrowed dress, the bodice too tight, the hem already sporting a muddy border, when instead she looked nonchalantly enchanting.

God above did a title do anything *but* solicit magnificence, women thrown by eager mamas at your feet like rose petals. Very little were luminous without effort. Piper's deep green eyes haunted him, reminding him of the emerald earbob he'd pinched from the gaming hell the first week after he'd run away, when food was so scarce his belly ached. An impulsive decision he'd taken a sound beating for because, unlike Finn, he'd never made a good thief.

Outside of those wondrous, glittering eyes, her mouth had always been her most arresting feature. Much too large for her face, he had been correct in assuming she would grow into it.

The enormously distressing element of this accounting, which was making his head pound and his cock stiffen, was the fact that Piper would crawl all over him if he let her. Sink inside him and grasp his heart, his body, his mind, all in one effortless, dazzling swoop.

He knew this. Had always known it.

She'd quite truthfully told him about her attraction, and once, at his weakest, he'd been unable to deny his own.

How was he to handle occupying her sparkling world again, when she would, without curbing any impulse, block him as he struggled to curb every one of his?

A forced distance between them was required because he was more dangerous to her than their enemies. Her grandfather had made him promise because he recognized the danger. It was written in the pages of his chronology, laid out rather brashly for those who chose to heed its warning.

An unforeseen merging of gifts can be catastrophic.

Of late, Julian had trouble leaving the otherworld once he entered, and he had no idea if someone going in with him would also have difficulty leaving. But he feared it was so, as her grandfather had feared. *She's not yours*, he'd whispered in Julian's ear with almost his last breath.

Piper had proven the combined power, crossing into the otherworld this morning when she grasped his hand. For one moment, he had *known* she was there with him. And he'd never been more terrified in his life.

The grave possibilities when their gifts converged were inescapable, it seemed.

So he would stay away.

No matter how fervently he desired her.

CHAPTER 4

To begin, begin.
    ~William Wordsworth

*L*ater that morning, after dragging Finn from his bed, they left the Cock and Bull, seated together in the carriage, until for no reason Piper could determine, Julian's aura began to flare, and he moved to ride alongside on a horse procured at the inn. He rode with a natural rhythm, reins dangling from slim fingers, muscular thigh digging into the horse's flank. When he caught her watching, he held immobile, then, with a hoarse command, urged his mount to the front of the path, outside her view.

Nothing had changed.

One-sided, their fascination.

With a quick glance at Finn, Piper pushed the thought from her mind. Finn needed contact to read someone, or he had before, but maybe his gift had strengthened as Julian's had.

As it was, the poor boy sought to ease the strain of the past twenty-four hours by regaling her with stories of Harbingdon and the village that lay beyond it, his smile only slightly brittle. The countryside changed as they entered an area of gently rolling hills swathed in dense expanses of woodland. The air thickened with the scent of moss, decay, and pine, the fragrance drawing like a shawl around her.

The rhythmic groan of the carriage wheels circled her ears as notions of what lay ahead circled her mind.

She admitted to being nervous when she was not a nervous person.

In the afternoon, with crimson and teal darkening the sky, the carriage halted at a drive flanked by two massive stone pillars. Julian's deep voice filtered through the open window as he spoke to the gate-keeper and what appeared to be four guards. With a lurch, springs squealing, they passed between the pillars and continued along the gravel drive.

Piper considered waking Finn. She should have listened to his hours-ago ramblings about Harbingdon. Instead, she knew nothing about the place Julian called home with such longing. *Home*. When had she, Julian, and Finn ever had a place to call home? Memories of the errant childhood after her mother's death came to her, as pronounced and choking as smoke from the hotel fire. By the time she'd made it to her grandfather's estate at the age of twelve, her sense of family, security, love, shelter, anything resembling *normalcy*, was as distressed as the leather carriage grip she clung to. Only after Julian and Finn had arrived a year later and shared with her their paranormal existence did her life start to settle.

Leaning to get a better view as they pulled in the circular drive, the arched entrance of a lovely manor glided into view above a line of Yews in desperate need of pruning. She released a sigh, her hand rising to her lips to hold it in. *Oh, this house was Julian's in every way.*

Elegant, restrained, *beautiful*.

Each window was in proportioned balance to the whole, each chalk stone uniform, identical wings jutting from the main to steady the scale. This house, unlike so many others, hadn't been ruined with additions.

No line of servants stood to greet them, instead only Humphrey, scowl sitting like a lump of wet dough on his face. She sniffed. Naturally, his aura shone the color of mud. He was Julian's man of *everything*—friend, manservant, valet, personal assistant. As wide as two men, though Julian topped him in height, he intimidated with just the glower, which rarely left his ruddy face. He'd arrived on her grandfather's doorstep, bruised and dressed in rags, mere days after Julian, and he hadn't left his side since. They were as close as brothers—had saved each other was Julian's only explanation—and aside from Finn, Humphrey was his only confidant. She'd always felt jealous of their relationship, which was senseless and said a lot about how hopeless she'd always been about anything connected to Julian.

She knocked her knuckle against the window. She didn't imagine Humphrey was going to be thrilled to see her.

Julian rode past and slid gracefully from his mount. A groom appeared with prompt efficiency and ambled away with the beast. Julian and Humphrey conversed, and her anxiety shifted to irritation as Julian gestured to the carriage with a beleaguered expression. Humphrey glanced her way, ran his hand across his mouth, then raised his shoulders with a shrug that clearly said, *she's your problem*.

Prepared to defend herself but wondering how

TRACY SUMNER

she'd make it out without the step lowered, Piper had her hand on the door, ready to bolt, when her breath caught in surprise. A dog—small, wiry, and truthfully a little pathetic looking—bolted from the side of the house and ran straight to Julian, who dropped to his knee, words lost but affection clear as he stroked the animal from nose to tail.

So, this was part and parcel of home: Humphrey and a *dog*.

Her heart gave a slow, aching thump. A permanent residence had not been possible with her father's itinerant lifestyle, much less the ability to house an animal, even though she'd asked, begged, on occasion.

She had *survived* by pushing aside longings for unattainable things.

Julian entered the manor without a backward glance, the dog at his heel, leaving her with a slumbering Finn and a scowling Humphrey. She readied for battle as the step clicked into place, and the carriage door swung wide. Humphrey's arm, the one with the pitted scar running its length, shot into the interior. She straightened her spine and placed her hand in his, refusing to cower.

Piper Scott did not cower, even if she'd made a terrific mess of things and likely should. "Humphrey." She met his gaze but tucked her shaking hands in the folds of her skirt. "I hope you're well." She fashioned a wilted curtsey.

"Could be better, Scamp," he replied and turned with a nod that implied she best follow.

"That nickname"—she stalked after him—"we've discussed in the past."

He snorted. "Grow up, girl, and you'll not hear it cross my lips again." His accent, as rough and uncultured as he was, certainly suited the rebuke.

She jerked off her gloves in place of the comment she'd like to make. *And she was in deep enough, wasn't she?*

He glanced back as they crossed the shadowed portico and entered the house, the forlorn tilt of his lips possibly counting as amusement, as if he recognized she restrained her vitriol. She couldn't determine if Humphrey liked her or not, and she'd always believed he enjoyed her uncertainty. And with as many hurdles as she'd made Julian jump, she guessed she couldn't blame him.

Halting in an entryway bounded by haphazardly placed benches, she gazed up and around. "How extraordinary." She stood at one end of a spectacular vaulted hall, a curved bay window at the other end spilling sunlight in a swath across marble. A floating staircase climbed the first and second floors, providing an enchanting viewpoint. "I've never seen the like in a country home," she said, thick Savonnerie muffling her step.

"Aye, this place is like a woman in a plain dress hiding a lacy, red chemise underneath."

Piper lifted her hand to her mouth to suppress the gust of laughter. An inappropriate but correct statement. With the restrained exterior, the interior of Harbingdon was a breathtaking surprise. She fell entirely in love as she turned in a measured circle. "Charming, truly, but stark." Her echo confirmed the statement.

Humphrey lifted himself from the door. "Ah, it needs a touch, for certain. Other things, like leaky roofs and functioning cook stoves, took the first."

"So, aside from all your other *duties*, you are also housekeeper and butler?" Keeping pace as he moved along, she managed to catch sight of an exquisite

Adam fireplace holding reign in a brightly lit sitting room. "My, you are busy then."

He grunted and started up that incredible staircase. She followed without a word, her fingers trailing the flutes of a column as she passed it.

"We have staff. They were instructed, as happens with delicate"—he halted, darting a look over his shoulder—"situations to make themselves scarce."

She just kept herself from running into him and had to grasp the railing for support. "I'm a *delicate* situation?"

He sighed and continued, climbing another level. Goodness, they were hiding her in the upper reaches. "Scamp, you've never been anything *but.*"

"I think I'm insulted," she murmured, which gained a muted grouse in response.

He gestured to a bedchamber at the end of the hall, then turned to leave. The least ceremony imaginable, but what could she expect from *Humphrey?* As he passed, he ticked off information like a soldier. "Your maid, Minnie, will be up shortly. Bath. Fresh clothing. All the frippery. She's scrambling now to gather it. She'll also bring a tray. With the jumble, a proper dinner isn't on the docket." He scrubbed his hand over his face at the top of the stair, evidently unimpressed with her latest *jumble.*

"I appreciate I'm not being housed in the attic." She pressed her palm against the door. "Nor as far as Gloucestershire."

Shoulders stiffening, he glanced back, ire showing in eyes so dark they appeared black. His aura flared, golden sparks lighting the muddy edges. "Julian's had this one ready for a while. Thought you would enjoy the view. It's the best to be had."

He left her with that, feeling foolish, petty, and wholly put in her place.

Piper sighed and entered the chamber. Fading sunlight rolled in the window, one note of welcome. The room, no matter the state of any belowstairs, hadn't been neglected. Subtle shades of yellow and mauve: walls, bedding, and the canopy topping the mahogany tester bed. She toed the carpet. Usually, the ones making it to a bedchamber had been through the paces on the main floor first, but this looked new. Aubusson, unless she missed her guess. Did Julian have funds? She assumed his estates had left him desperate for cash, as was the case with most saddled with centuries of titled obligation.

The view was indeed breathtaking, overlooking a vast lawn centered by a fetching stone fountain, clusters of trees and shrubs dotting the expanse willy-nilly as far as one could see. Formal gardens spanned the western border, looking overgrown and untended. She pressed her fingertips to glass with a sudden burst of longing.

She had never been invited to tend a garden.

Dropping her gloves to the ledge, she rested her brow on the cool pane.

Unshakable loneliness, a boon companion since her first night in Gloucestershire, pulsed through her with as steady a rhythm as her heart. Tears again threatened. With a very American oath, she ran a knuckle beneath each eye when she *wanted* to weep, throw herself on the bed and let the English half of her succumb like a vapid fool.

But Minnie, the maid, could not arrive to find her mistress beset by misery the likes of which would send her running for her master. Piper's gift, her wretched familial situation, her exile from society, were *her* misfortunes to manage. Humphrey was right. She needed to grow up, take responsibility, accept what was and what was not.

Because her hopes too often focused on the *not*.

Julian, an absurd desire, the biggest *not*.

It was no wonder he found her exasperating to the point of banishment. Her grandfather's murder had sent them fleeing in a state of panic. That the earl's dying words claimed the intended target was the healer, *ah, well*. Julian had no choice but try to find a place far from London where she'd be safe. Although their separation hadn't mattered one whit to him. He was occupied with his title, a seat in the House of Lords, managing the League.

Lady Coswell, she thought blackly.

Fine. Piper now had a purpose, too. Her research.

A cardinal dropped to a branch near the window, and she tapped the glass to get his attention. Julian had agreed to be her partner. Promised with a handshake, a binding contract for a man with honor.

And Julian was a man with tremendous honor.

This time, she must separate her feelings from the endeavor.

The word *partner* had many meanings, and the potential to flare like alcohol tossed on an open flame. Attaching herself to the wrong one would drive Julian back in his rabbit hole. But this time, he needed her. The dark crescents beneath his eyes and slumped set of his shoulders said more than he ever would.

She'd always needed him. It was part of the troublesome groove she'd dug for herself. One she could not escape.

Piper exhaled, clouding the glass but not her resolve.

Scamp, Yank, Scandalous Scott.

For once, she planned to do something aside from living up to her hideous reputation.

50

CHAPTER 5

I am—yet what I am none cares or knows.
  ~John Clare

Lyon, France

Sidonie paced the length of the cavernous dining room in her family's estate, her skirt tangling around her legs with each step. Her breath came so rapidly black edged her sight. She clutched her throbbing head and studied the crude paintings on the wall through muted perception, the plush carpet her bare feet sank into providing no comfort.

Everything was a grotesque blur, a moonlight-and-shadow nightmare.

Nothing could ease the chill. Not the roaring fire in the hearth, or the fur cloak wrapped around her. The frost was bone-deep. Unrelenting and merciless. The visions arrived without any promise of containment. Ghastly, with sharp teeth and glowing eyes, they nipped at her in vicious little bites. She was unable to sleep more than an hour at a time. Unable to eat. Her life had ground to a halt while her contemporaries married and had children, things she had once longed for.

Desired.

Her former friends and lovers feared her after the tragic incident at the theatre. She would never be allowed to return to French society. That horrible night, the crimson wash beneath her feet, spiraled through her mind. She halted in the middle of the room, her shout echoing off the castle's stone walls.

She drew a soothing breath that did little to soothe. The scent of spices—ginger, cardamom, thyme, turmeric—stung her nose. *Putain d'enfer*, those had not helped.

Opium, absinthe, prayers.

Her only hope for a future without the visions was the girl.

The healer. The granddaughter.

A whisper floated through her mind. *Piper.*

Sidonie snaked her fingers through her hair and yanked the snarled strands until her scalp tingled. Desperation drove her to recall the latest vision— when she never wanted to step into that world again —and examine it for clues to the healer's location. Sliding to the floor, she let the images carry her away as if they were a river and she flotsam. Flames, smoke, *chaos*. A girl, *no*, now a woman, dropping to her knees on a brick path. Strong arms encircling her, offering protection. The force of emotion— fondness, exasperation, attraction—flowing between the two was deep-seated. A compelling force when joined, they would pose a test if challenged as one.

But there was danger in their joining as well. She lifted her head. A vulnerability. She would have to strike when they were at their weakest.

Sidonie's men had failed three years ago, finding

the earl when she wanted the *girl*. Killing him in their stupidity and getting killed themselves, which had sent the healer into hiding. Even if he had lived, the earl's knowledge was useless. Had he not proven this at their first meeting, when Sidonie was little more than a child? Her father believed the earl could cure her madness, but his chronology proved to be simply the scribbles of a man fascinated with the occult. He'd been fascinated with *her*, a true dreamer he'd called her, a curse that had consumed her entire, miserable life.

She'd not wanted to know what she was—she'd only wanted to rid herself of her curse.

She wanted the dreams afforded others in their thoughtless indulgence. Lovers, family, a future. When all given to her was death, destruction, and terror. Blood dribbling down the steps of a Roman theatre while the world watched. While *he*, the man she had once thought would be hers, watched.

She groaned and dug her nails into her scalp. Another vision intruded, this one bringing the scent of pine, earth, woodsmoke. A forest set around a shimmering lake. Stones the color of fresh cream. Protection, unease, yearning. *Love.* Heart thudding, she stood on unsteady legs.

The healer was no longer in London. The man was with her, a protective force, but their vulnerability, the crack in the façade, remained.

With a sudden mental tug, the vision was yanked from her mind.

A theft.

Someone else close to the girl with considerable skill. Someone expendable should they stand in her way as death was becoming commonplace. *Everyone* was expendable. Even the healer, should it come to that.

The vision had been clear, and even with the interruption, she'd seen enough. She could identify the trees. The lake. Those milky-white stones. She would remember enough this night or another soon to get close to the girl.

Or, expendable herself, she would die trying.

~

Finn gasped and yanked himself from the dream. A bead of sweat tracked his cheek, and he dashed it away. His breath shot from his lungs as if he'd taken the stairs at Harbingdon at full speed. Kicking at the damp counterpane, he palmed his stomach and swallowed past the queasiness. *Damn.* He could feel the woman's desperation, her *madness*, thrumming through his mind like hammer blows. Whispers with a cat's-claw bite.

The stench of spice and decay pushed him over the brink.

Stumbling to the washstand, he heaved until his body had no more to give.

Sliding to the floor, he dropped his head to his knee, throat working. His heart continued its staggering rhythm as he struggled for control, struggled to gather the memory. Bracing his palms on the worn planks, he focused on the woman as if she sat close enough for him to trail his finger across her skin.

Julian's advice whispered through his mind: *gather the details.*

Heavily accented speech. French. Tapestries on the wall. A castle. Jewels on her fingers and strung around her neck. A fur cloak. Wealth. Terror and desperation—and a willingness to *harm*. To destroy without thought, without guilt, without concession.

He watched a river of blood washing down stone steps and knew killing was not beyond this woman.

The most disturbing element she'd left him with was a chilling sense of *awareness*. He squeezed his eyes shut and shoved aside his dread. She'd been rummaging through his mind like one would a drawer for a stray sock. What if he'd inadvertently provided a clue to their location, to Piper?

Thank God he'd managed to block her, but he needed Piper's assistance to get stronger. Which, in turn, would protect her. Protect the League.

The endgame was to *steal* thoughts, not give them away.

Peeling himself from the floor, Finn stumbled from the room, preparing for a discussion with Julian neither of them was going to enjoy.

CHAPTER 6

*How little do they see what is, who frame their hasty
judgments upon that which seems.*
    ~Robert Southey

"*C*rack of sparrows, miss!"

Piper stuck her head beneath the feather
pillow, praying for mercy and more sleep, but the
curtains were thrown wide, and the window opened
with a screech. The smell of rain and gardenias circled, a welcome reminder she was no longer waking
to the soot and stink of London. Or the wretched
seclusion of Gloucestershire.

"Mr. Finn is headed to the mercantile and asked
me to wake you as you arrived with a valise packed
with scraps of paper and not much else. It's sitting at
the end of the bed when you want to attend to it. I
don't know what to do with that clutter." Piper heard
the clunk of a washbasin being filled. "Not the first
odd arrival here, I tell you. Nor the last. I'm not belit-
tling, mind you, as I was one of those arrivals a few
short months ago."

Piper peeked from beneath the pillow to see a stout woman nearly the same age as she, standing arms akimbo, expectation—for what Piper had no idea—stamped across her rubicund face. As Piper stared, her aura flared, a mix of colors not unlike a tattered quilt. She looked sturdy and fearsome, while Piper felt like a wilted flower. She'd fallen into an exhausted slumber the previous evening, missing the promised arrival of dinner, a chance to bathe, and her first encounter with her maid.

"Minnie?" Piper asked and laid the pillow aside.

"That's me," the woman replied, moving to the bed. "Mr. Julian doesn't like anything formal unless we've a guest who requires, but if you don't like using my Christian name, what with your upbringing, Miss Dunbar will do in a pinch." Minnie straightened the counterpane, a nervous movement that made Piper wonder if this encounter was unsettling to them both. "Though no one in my life ever called me Miss Dunbar."

Piper clutched the sheet to her chest. Out of necessity and fatigue, she had slept in her chemise and drawers. "Clothing, perhaps? A fresh set?"

"Ah, that dunce Humphrey! Showed you nothing, did he? Telling us to stay away when you arrived and then doing a piss-poor job. Men shouldn't be given certain duties, but here, we're all topsy-turvy. You'll find that out quick enough. Not one soul I've yet to meet trained proper for any position they hold." She darted a glance over her shoulder, staring down the wardrobe doors as they popped open with a dull click. "Mr. Julian had this filled for you months ago."

Piper collapsed against the headboard with a gasp of delight. What a wonderful addition to her readings Minnie would have been! "So, this is your parlor trick?" she asked. "Fascinating! I've never seen the like, though I read of this gift in my grandfather's papers. You can move objects with your mind, am I right? You must let me record your aura and what changes occur during the process."

Minnie turned to Piper, her cheeks blazing. "I figured I'd get it out there, because sometimes, foolish woman that I am, I shift things without thinking." She tapped her temple with a stubby finger. "I've had people faint, truthfully, over nothing more than a floating saltshaker. Can you believe that would upset anyone in this cruel world? Mr. Julian calls it influencing a physical"—she pulled at her lower lip— "system without a physical interaction. Now isn't *that* fancy? When my ma just called it misfortune."

Fancy. And terribly keen. Piper scooted higher in the bed, wishing anything connected to Julian did not interest her so. "That sounds like him," she said, the words holding a tartness she'd hoped to conceal.

Minnie halted in place. Piper instantly recognized the look and the aura framing it.

Bother. Julian had gained another devotee.

"M'lady, Harbingdon be the first place in my life I've felt safe revealing my wee talent. Why, I was being forced into an asylum when Mr. Julian offered to employ me instead. Those with a true gift, not the swindlers at high-flying séances and such, don't find the mystical world all that entertaining. It's an awful heavy burden." She gave the counterpane another tug. "I was brought up in a special place, my ma a lightskirt, to put it plainly, but I'm not suited for that employ as you can see." She executed a little sidestep, the cage crinoline beneath her mauve skirt giving a rattle of protest. "Assumed I was daft because such peculiar things happened around me. So, a lady's maid I be."

Piper blinked, appalled and enchanted.

Minnie, the mind-shifting daughter of a prostitute, was Julian's idea of a proper companion for the
most wretched excuse for a lady in England. Her
smile bloomed. *This* relationship might actually
work out.

"Minnie, please, no lady, no Elizabeth. Just Piper.
And I, well—" She slid off the bed, gaining her feet. If
frankness were part and parcel of living at Harbingdon, she would fit in quite nicely as being blunt had
never been a problem. "My mother died in Phil-
adelphia when I was three, leaving me with a father
with a disturbing penchant for gambling, not parent-
hood. I grew up above or near whatever gaming hell
he was frequenting that month, minded by a hired
attendant who often cared even less for children than
he did." Walking to the wardrobe, she stroked the
sleeves of the dresses hanging there, the scent of
starch and lemon drifting to her. Her heart clenched
to imagine Julian ordering clothing for her.

"Oh, miss," Minnie lamented. "My mother,
strumpet she is, has a heart of gold. Pure gold. I was
loved, no doubt. And protected as much as a woman
in a man's world can be. But my talent was causing
such problems at the brothel. Then that awful Mr.
Tupps, a regular client of my ma's, the bootlicker,
wanted me committed because I sent a glass flying
into his face after he made a grab for me when he realized I was not on the menu. I may have sent a
drawer flying at him, too. I can't quite recall." Minnie
fluffed the pillows, snapping and tucking until the
bed looked pristine. "Anyway, Mr. Julian heard of me
and my specialness, so here I am."

Piper turned, dress in hand. "How did he hear
about you?"

Minnie glanced away as her aura dimmed. A cardinal's call sounded, the rustle of the curtains as a

gust ripped in the window. Finally, she whispered, "Men be men, miss."

Piper turned to the wardrobe lest her face reveal too much. Jealousy shot through her before she shoved the senseless emotion aside with the dress.

The world was unjust.

Men were encouraged to obtain what they wanted, confess desire, yearning, *attraction*, while women were left to ache and burn, forced to hide their feelings where no one could see them.

And she had never been good at hiding anything.

Finn waited by the servant's kitchen entrance, slouched against a coster cart piled high with vegetables and fruit. When he saw her, he took a bite of his apple and pushed off the cart with an agile kick and a jaunty wave. Piper marveled that a boy abandoned at a rookery orphanage managed to carry himself with the grace of a duke. His innate sophistication worked to his advantage as his existence as the bastard half-brother of a viscount was a figment of Julian's imagination. They no more shared a drop of blood than she and Humphrey did. Although the heartfelt love that flowed between them was brotherly in every way.

A kitchen maid lingered by the cart, a head of cabbage held forgotten in her hand. Piper smiled into her gloved fist. There was no denying, Finn's magnificent looks staggered.

When she reached him, she noted his sagging shoulders, the lines of exhaustion streaking from his eyes. His aura shone the color of chalk. "Finn, are you well?"

"Of course," he murmured. But he turned to lead

them across the carriageway before she could reply, two hulking footmen falling into step behind them. At the end of the drive, a pebbled path was tucked between a swath of high grass, meandering away from the house and down a gently rolling slope. "This way to the village, my lady," he said and gestured for her to go before him. "Don't mind our chaperones. You know Julian. He won't allow us to explore without them."

She smiled and shot Finn an amused side-glance only to find a similar smile aimed at her. She had missed him, missed them both, her only family. Maybe she'd even missed Humphrey a little. Not knowing how long they'd allow her to stay at Harbingdon brought all the old abandonment issues to life.

She, Julian, and Finn had exhibited disparate reactions to being deserted.

"You've finished at Rugby?" she asked to change the subject, remembering that with Finn, her thoughts may not be her own.

"Thank Christ. *Adieu* to Warwickshire." He sent the apple in a mock salute. Covering a yawn with the back of his wrist, he continued, "But Julian wants more. Education, knowledge." Finn kicked a bleached stone that sat in the middle of the path. "*Oxford.*" The word dropped like a lead ball between them.

She smothered amusement that would go unappreciated. "You could say no."

He shook his head and took a resigned bite. "You say no enough for both of us."

Stung, she halted. The scent of hay and turned earth came to her on a fast inhalation. "Are you saying I can make it easier on Julian with my compliance? By following every one of his rules, the thousands of them! When he forced me from the League, created because of my grandmother's gift, a gift I *inherited*, by the by. When I should be a part of it. You know it, and so does he!"

Finn paused just ahead, sighed, then took a tentative step back. Another bite of the apple was his only reply.

"Because, if you're advising acquiescence, Finn, I must tell you that I know going along with Julian's plans without dispute is the easiest course of action. But maybe not the best. Has anyone ever considered that? Or not the best for *me*." She scowled at one of the footmen, and he turned away. "He doesn't trust me to make a sound decision. He never has. But then, history has proven that I make horrible ones, so I almost can't blame him."

"Pip, I'm not sure he trusts *anyone* to make a sound decision. Having control calms him. So everyone who loves him goes along with it for the most part. And with the danger surrounding you—" Finn took a fast breath and grasped her hand, pulling her with him as he continued down the path. "It's a simple theoretical principle. If you didn't cause such trouble, I could cause a little. Julian only has so much patience for that sort of thing."

"Why, you rascal!" She tucked a strand of hair that had come loose beneath her bonnet. "What trouble could a young man of eighteen possibly want to concoct?"

Finn laughed, but it was forced, laborious. The fingers laced with hers quivered.

"Finn." She stopped, squeezed his hand. "What's wrong? Should we consider resuming our sessions? I'm being brought back into the League. Julian promised—and it's his decision to make."

"Do you wish your grandfather had bequeathed the League to you instead of Julian? I sure as hell don't." Taking another bite, he let his gaze drift, blue eyes, blue sky, absolutely striking. "I'm exhausted. A bad night." He circled the apple in a loose loop. "The whispers were strong. My gift has gone beyond reading the mind of someone I touch. If I'm connected in some way, I have vivid dreams. It's often so tangled up, I can't quite bring meaning to them. But they feel unspeakably real while they're happening."

"Does Julian know?"

He glanced at her, then away. Color seeped from his cheeks as a muscle in his jaw flexed. "He knows."

She fought to recall where they'd been with Finn's coaching when she'd fled to Gloucestershire. Closing her eyes, she placed her thumb over the pulse at his wrist. Her heartbeat raced to match his, a bracing rhythm in her ears and behind her lids. His aura came to her, a wash of blue and gold. His skin burned, flooding her with heat.

Then all slowed as *she* set the pace.

The images weren't clear. As indistinct as gazing through a windowpane covered in ice. However, the vibrations were vibrant. Dread, terror, *insanity*. Blood on worn stone steps. The scent of turmeric and smoke.

She swayed and heard Finn's apple hit the ground.

He jerked her close, his sweet breath batting her neck. Then, with a groan, he wrenched his hand away. The impressions evaporated like mist, but her lungs felt tight and airless. Grasping her shoulders, Finn shook her. "Piper, *stop*." Another shake had her bonnet slipping from her head, her hair spilling from the loose chignon neither she nor Minnie had known how to fashion. "Come back!"

She blinked to find him leaning over her, his cheeks rosy, the dark slashes beneath his eyes no more. He cursed and dropped his hands, throat working as he swallowed. It was at that moment, she guessed, when Finn comprehended the compulsion her gift demanded.

With a nod to the footmen, who stared at them as if nothing strange had occurred, Finn turned on his heel without another word.

They continued the walk in silence, the path spilling out into the village green. To recover the ease of the morning, Finn gave a brief tour in a strained voice, pointing out a sarsen stone King Alfred blew through to summon the Saxons and the bricked public house occupying the western corner. They halted at the mercantile, where he burrowed in the pocket of his waistcoat and produced a miles-long supply list. "We can have everything delivered to Harbingdon later today. Shop all you'd like."

A parade of activity was reflected in the mercantile window. The market town was prosperous, nothing like the decaying little village in Gloucestershire. She gazed around the green, anxious to explore. "No shopping. Can I meet you back here in a bit? I'll take my protectors."

"No shopping," he repeated as if he'd never heard a woman utter those words.

Piper crossed her arms. A member of the house staff could have arranged for supplies. The proposed walk had been nothing but a ploy to separate her from mischief until they could figure out what to do with her. Minnie had practically handed her off to Finn.

This was *not* a suitable start to her partnership with Julian.

Finn raised his arm in supplication. "Now, Piper, calm down."

"Where is he?" Hardly cricket to skim her

thoughts, but Finn was welcome to these. "If you're spying, you know you better tell me."

Finn's face took on the cast of the sarsen stone at her back. "He's helping thatch the church roof. Leaked last month, coming down on Mrs. Gladstone like a sieve. Nearly washed her into the aisle, and that's saying something. Julian's placed responsibility for this village on his shoulders, along with his family seat and the entailed properties and everything else."

She searched, catching sight of a steeple. Her skirt spanked her ankles in time to her heartbeat as she stalked in that direction.

"Devil take it," she heard Finn utter as he fell into step behind her.

She caught sight of Julian as she turned off the square, her step slowing with her catch of breath. She placed her hand on her stomach to contain the beating pulse, but it overtook her. *Block,* she warned herself in desperation, a version of self-healing that sometimes worked.

The carnal thoughts entering her mind were not ones Finn could witness.

He stood next to a secured bundle of Norfolk reed, stripped to the waist save for a thin linen shirt. He gestured to the men pegging the reeds in place as he took notes in a leather folio, muscles in his forearm shifting beneath his bunched sleeve. With a smile, he jammed the pencil between his teeth and the folio in his armpit, grasped a thatch, and demonstrated to a towheaded boy standing by his side. After the transfer of the rod to the lad, Julian's hand came out to tousle the boy's hair, the affectionate gesture melting the little of her unaffected at seeing him.

Shadowed jaw. Cheeks dented to hold the pencil. Hair a dark twist about his head. More mister than lord. Closer to the boy she'd fallen in love with while watching him exit a carriage in her grandfather's drive than the man he had been forced to become. Prying her gaze away, she spotted Julian's coat and waistcoat folded neatly over the railing of a spanking-new fence. Freshly whitewashed cottages and an industrious village on the mend surrounded them. She suspected the man standing twenty paces away, face streaked with dirt and sweat, was part of the reason.

"He only shipped me off when I was close to getting what I wanted," she murmured.

"What was that?"

Heat lit her cheeks as she waved Finn away. "Nothing."

"Everything we were building was ruined that night, Pip, and he's just trying to create something secure. For us, for the League, for himself, I guess."

That night being her grandfather's last. She recalled it well, often in nightmares. The shouts and the mayhem, the smell of blood, the gumminess of it beneath her slippers. Their desperate race into a new future, a new life.

Apart from each other.

It had been an unclimbable mountain of loneliness, at least for her. And here she was, hoping Julian would solve that problem as well when he had no intention of getting near her again.

A burst of panic hit her square in the chest. "This was a mistake, Finn. Let's go."

And that's when Julian noticed her.

His words fell away, mid-sentence, his lips going slack. He took a step forward, and for a brief unguarded second, she swore on everything worth a damn to her—basically, the two men standing in the churchyard—those remarkable eyes of his filled with pleasure.

Please, let it be.

The folio slipped from its home beneath his arm. Julian bent to pick it up and was grossly recovered on the return, his expression stark, determined. Like a flame cut by the wind, his aura deepened to a hue that, if she were smarter, would have had her running in the other direction.

Five long strides and he reached them, his open collar dancing with the movement. Instead of meeting his gaze, she focused on the taut line of his trouser brace, a dark slash holding his billowing shirt to his chest. Shifting the folio, he dragged his hand through his already disheveled hair and said something beneath his breath. Weakly, she wondered what it would be like to have his fingers trail over her skin, delve, record, take.

They had not made it that far before but, *my*, how she'd wanted to.

She flushed in places profound and hidden as he towered over her. Julian was fearsome on a good day, but on *this* day, with perspiration adhering mud-spattered linen to the defined muscles of his chest and belly, and his long, slim fingers repeatedly flexing about the folio, he was impressive for reasons only a woman fascinated could appreciate.

Before her stood a very tall, very handsome, deeply aggrieved man.

The changes since they'd last been together made her stomach do a little flip-flop, a rather unwelcome reaction when she'd found him tremendously attractive *before*.

His gaze, dispassionate as frost coating a winter heath, swept her from head to toe, then shifted to Finn. "You're doing a dashed good job, boyo."

"Impossible mission," Finn muttered and crossed

his arms over his chest. "I brought the bloody footmen."

She opened her mouth to unleash a scathing retort, but Julian chose to respond by catching a lock of hair escaping her dejected chignon between his fingers. Her scalp tingled at the gentle tug, a flurry of goosebumps sprinkling her arms.

Oh, to be touched again by him, even as incidentally as this.

His aura flickered as he studied the strand before releasing it and turning to Finn. "What happened?"

The scent of sweat with an overlay of citrus carried to her, diminishing her temper and her focus. Julian always, always smelled good. But now was not the time to let his tantalizing aroma derail her objections to, well, *everything*.

How could she think clearly when he'd stepped close enough for her to see the flecks of amber in his eyes, his lashes so thick she could almost count them? He had a shaving nick on his jaw, and she forced her hand into a fist to keep from running her finger over it. Being this near brought the brief taste she'd had of him years ago roaring back, sending her heart on a race.

Again, he asked with more impatience, "What happened?"

She glanced at Finn, ticked her chin. *Respond.* Finn tightened his arms, giving a one-shoulder shrug. Guilt rode high in the pea green shimmer framing his aura. As sheltered as any lad due to Julian's highhanded management, he'd abandoned his gambling face when they left the rookery and had not gotten it back just yet.

With an irritated exhalation, Julian adjusted the folio, exposing a streak of paint on his forearm. A pale blue, it brought to mind the hydrangea bush sitting beneath her bedchamber window. Entirely without design, she reached to touch.

Startled, Julian stepped back, drawing his arm to his side and rubbing it over his ribs.

Piper met his gaze. *What is this, Jules?* Secrets, when at one time, he'd held little from her.

A bead of sweat rolled down his cheek, and he shouldered it away without removing his focus from her. If he thought to intimidate her like one of those silly paragons of virtue who cowered and stooped, hoping for a crumb of his lordly attention, he was going to be disappointed.

Unlike Finn, she'd been raised in a gaming hell and had an extremely trustworthy poker face.

And layer-upon-layer of clothing to hide her trembling knees.

"We'll talk. Later. And don't think of losing your guards, not for one moment," Julian warned, then presented his back in an unmistakably aristocratic dismissal.

"She stared me down as boldly as a longshoreman, daring me to cross her," Julian said, descending the ladder leaning against the masonry wall of the gardener's cottage.

He flipped the hammer to Humphrey, who placed it in the dented toolbox at his side. Using his tools lessened the visions, and Humphrey had been kind enough to deliver them as Julian had come straight from the church to review the cottage's aging slate roof. Another structure on the estate for which modest maintenance wouldn't hold much longer. The corresponding slate came from Wales by train, then cart, as the village had no station.

Bloody expensive to purchase and a lengthy wait, too.

Julian gave the toolbox a hard knock when he met the ground, due more to the way Piper had looked this morning in crisp yellow silk—lovely and untamed—than the damned roof. "Only as high as my chest and eight stone, or I would have been utterly disconcerted."

A gust whipped across the field, pressing damp linen to his back and cooling his blistered brow. Sighing, he tilted his face into the welcome caress. Exhaustion rode hard, and a storm was brewing, one he hoped this roof and the church's new one could withstand. The leaden air held a wrathful promise when his own tempest raged. Since their rash encounter, visions of Piper—hair unbound and lit with streaks of sunlight—had tormented. After all this time, she still made him feel like he stood on the edge of a cliff and was deciding whether to jump.

"You're taking on too much. We could bring in more men. Faster repairs." Humphrey held his silence a beat, then suggested, "We have funds, what with the successful investments. And your titled estates are sound."

Julian turned to find his friend loading cracked slate into the rather pathetic field cart that had come with the property. "My thoughts haven't changed on this subject. We risk exposure if anyone living or working at Harbingdon lacks a supernatural gift or at the very least, a direct familial connection to the occult. It's the easiest method to ensure we protect each other. Julian frowned as he remembered Finn's dream and how shaken the boy had been. "Security is paramount. Much due to your efforts, our reach is growing with new contacts in Wales and Scotland. I'm not a patient man,

but we're building a foundation, and the simple answer is, it takes time. My dream to have an under-
ground network for those in need is still years
away, let's be honest. A place to harbor them is the
first step."

Humphrey stepped away from the cart and
mopped his brow with his sleeve. "You saved my life
by pulling me out of Seven Dials, Jule. Giving me a
future, a path to follow when I never had one, not
once in my life before I met you. So, you'll have to
pardon me for worrying like hell about the breadth
of what you're taking on, building the League beyond
what Piper's fool grandpa thought it should be.
Though I admire your strategy and on my life will do
anything to see it prospers."

Humphrey had saved *him*, not the other way
around. But it was an old argument between friends
—one he'd never win. "Tomorrow's arrival?"

"Pickpocket. Maybe mudlarking, too." Humphrey
grunted as he shouldered a decaying timber they'd
removed from the cottage. "Mighty dangerous business, that."

"Mud-what?"

Humphrey dumped the timber in the cart and
propped his hands on his hips, stretching until his
back cracked. "Mudlarking. Stealing from the barges.
The boy was living with a gang above the flash-house
where they sold their goods. Silk scarves, reticules,
the like. Maybe a pocket watch on a blessed day. We
were unable to find any family, and we searched
every inch of St Giles. Not a single soul caring for or
about the poor bugger." Grasping a piece of slate the
size of a washbasin, he tossed it in the cart where it
landed with a thud. "Word of caution. He's an angry
little bastard. Shrewd enough to realize a warm bed
and food from those you can't trust is better than

living in squalor with those you can't trust. Will likely steal us blind."

Julian hung his bootheel on the wheel's spoke and gave his aching shoulders a roll. "Who better to deal with a furious gutter rat than me, you, and Finn?" No one had been angrier than Julian in those days. Both when he arrived in Seven Dials *and* when he left. The time in between had simply included a multitude of brutal learnings.

And he was an incredibly apt pupil.

"I reckon there's truth to that." Humphrey climbed atop the cart's warped seat and grasped the reins. "The boy's hand trickeries, I tell you, I've never seen the like. A magician could do no better."

Julian dusted his hands on trousers now sporting a jagged tear in one knee. "His gift?"

"A new one around here, all right. He sees people."

"People?"

Humphrey slapped the reins on his thigh. "Dead ones."

"There's a section in the chronology—"

"Oh, not that thing, please," Humphrey groaned.

Julian tilted his head toward the gardener's cottage. "We can't house him here like we usually do with new arrivals. A boy alone…" The words faded as he realized he had no idea what to do with a vagrant urchin whose skills were so astounding that in a city of a thousand pickpockets, he'd garnered undue attention. "The bedchamber next to Piper is vacant."

Humphrey had the good grace to check the smile, bringing the hand holding the reins to his mouth. The swift movement sent the horse into a nervous sidestep.

"Two hellions with only a wall separating them. Just bloody wonderful. I can't imagine what trouble she'll create with a willing, and dreadfully young, participant." He rubbed his temple, a headache surging. The visions—touching tools and supplies in the village—had completely drained him.

Humphrey turned on the plank seat, the setting sun casting him in shadow. "Move her here. Two bedrooms are livable." He clicked his tongue. "Mostly."

"And have to secure this outbuilding like we are the main house?" Julian flicked away the suggestion like an errant fly. "She's unhappy with the amount of protection trailing after her already."

Humphrey paused, a muscle in his jaw tensing. *Uh, oh,* Julian thought, *here it comes.* Humphrey didn't like to give advice, which was vital to their friendship, because Julian didn't like to take it. "Maybe, uh…you could approach her in another way. Soften her up for what you want by giving her something *she* does."

Julian slipped on his waistcoat, buttoning slowly. "I'm listening."

Humphrey withdrew a cheroot from his coat pocket and twirled it between his fingers. He insisted on Burmese-made, ridiculously expensive, and even harder to obtain. A sugary tang stained the air, overwhelming the match's sulfur. "I only provide advice because I've years of diligent observation, watching the two of you circle like bleeding prizefighters since you were in the schoolroom." He blew out a blue-black gust, gestured to the walled gardens surrounding them. "Give Scamp a project. One she accepts in coordination with any protection you chose to place on her. Make it a negotiation. Remember those? These gardens are of little importance but in need just the same. Dump it on her and have her manage. She seems to like flowers and plants and what-all if you recall."

Julian did not recall, likely because he recalled everything *else*.

He could still smell her scent from this morning, a singular blend of floral and spice, honied and at turns biting. Just like her.

This might work. The gardens needed care, and aside from bringing her gradually back into the League, she needed something else—besides *him*—to occupy her time. Their current gardener, Mr. Knotworth, a retired professor of horticulture with a vast knowledge of the occult, was revising the earl's chronology one deliberate page at a time.

Hence abandonment of the gardens.

"Let her rejoin the League." He stabbed his cheroot at Julian, the crimson tip glowing. "With responsibilities this time. Make her grow the hell up. You making the path so smooth for her has only made her unable to walk a less-than-smooth path."

"I already did." Julian shrugged into his coat and settled the lapels to rights, which was ridiculous as filthy as he was. "It's her legacy. I'd gladly give it up, but it's far too late for that."

"I know, I know," Humphrey said, smoke snaking past his face. "We're set to conquer the world, one soothsayer at a time."

Julian motioned Humphrey over on the seat and climbed up beside him. A ride to the house was welcome. His brain was screaming inside his skull. "With her stepping back in, who's in grave need of healing?"

Humphrey flicked the reins, and the horse fell into a trot. Julian caught the concern that shot across his friend's face as he studied him with a critical eye. "Aside from you?"

"Next, please."

Humphrey chewed thoughtfully on the cheroot. "The new footman. Come from Lady Northhampton's household. Lucky us, the first person we've employed actually trained for their position. He dreams one night, whatever he dreams happens the next. He tripped over a wrinkle in the carpet today and sent a serving dish to the floor. Cook looked ready to beat the life from him." Humphrey stubbed the cheroot out on the seat and released a final wisp of smoke. "Took about a month to get him past thinking he was losing his mind, so he's made progress. But still shaky."

"It's a challenge to ask Piper to solve anyone else's dustup while she's so busy creating her own." Julian didn't want to consider the feelings she aroused in him. He *positively* didn't want to consider his compulsion to strip yellow silk from her body while standing in a churchyard of all places.

The urge to show her what he'd failed to that long-ago summer was powerful.

"A person with no purpose invites trouble. And you gain no loyalty without accountability." Humphrey tightened the reins around his fist and urged the horse into a canter. "The waffle bit is your problem."

Julian sprawled against the cart's rough backing. The sun had bled into the horizon, layering Humphrey in silhouette, but Julian saw him smile. This from a man who did not smile often. "Waffle?"

Humphrey cleared his throat. "Minnie said you look at Scamp like something you'd pour over a waffle. And that, my friend, is your dilemma to overcome. Or not, should it come to it."

Julian looked to the sky, the stars like diamonds peeking from a twist of black silk. He could just make out Canis Minor, the small dog, two bright winks he'd gazed upon often as a child. Celestial happenings had been of comfort to the boy living in a filthy warren, driven out by an atrocious excuse of a father and making his way from nothing. The universe was steadfast. Unaffected by a sound beating, hunger tearing through your gut, and fathers who loathed you because of strange abilities you couldn't control.

The universe was faithful. Secure.

He was tempted to tell Humphrey this chatter was silly, inane, simply untrue. Instead, he dug a flask from his pocket and took a healthy drink. "The waffle can sod off," was all he said.

Humphrey sobered, too honorable to beat a man when he was down. "Don't take offense. Minnie was a good choice for added protection. The woman has skills. When we were practicing, she closed her eyes, and that knife hit dead center from ten paces. Just slipped out of her boot like a ghost and whack, no hands. It was damned amazing, though she put a decent tear in that painting of your father. Got him right above his ear. I guess her aim isn't completely true."

Julian took another drink, brandy burning a path to his belly. He wished it'd complete its mission and cloud his mind. "Rey, please don't share that information"—he tapped the flask on his thigh—"if you have a care for me. The added protection part. If Piper knew Minnie was guarding her bedchamber after hours, she'd have my head."

They fell silent amidst the clip of the horse's hooves and the creak of the cart. Julian drew a breath laced with the earthy, dense aroma he always associated with Harbingdon, with *home*. Wondering if he was going to regret this, he took another sip and agreed to Humphrey's suggestion. "Start her with the footman. We don't want more broken dishes or sleepless nights. I'll handle proposing the garden project." He also needed to help categorize her auras, as promised, but this involved exposing a part of himself he'd kept hidden when she'd gotten too close and was learning too much about him.

A decision based on survival, then and now.

"Are you sure?"

"My good man, where Lady Elizabeth Scott is concerned, I'm not sure of anything."

Humphrey halted by the side of the house, a lantern in the morning room spilling light on the lawn. "The plan is, we pick apart everything in Finn's dreams. Every piece of furniture, every tapestry, even the rings on that crazy bitch's fingers. Something will lead us to her, Jule."

But they both left this unsaid: if Finn's dreams didn't lead her to them *first*.

Julian braced his hands on the cart and vaulted to the ground. The wind blew his hair in his eyes, obscuring the apprehension he'd seen cross Humphrey's face. A sharp crack of thunder shook the ground, and his heart stuttered as he imagined those he sought to protect. Those he'd come to love. The knife in his boot was a welcome presence pressed against his skin.

"We must prepare," Humphrey whispered and circled the cart away from the house.

Julian stood transfixed under the kitchen eave, watching Humphrey fade into the night. The guard patrolling the back lawn nodded, their only communication. Something brushed his ankle, and he looked to find Henry sitting by his side. The dog had appeared one morning, and he, like many Harbingdon sheltered, now seemed a natural part of the household. A most mixed-up family. He dropped to his knee, searching the sky until he located Canis Minor. "Do you hear that fella? We must prepare."

∽

Sidonie trailed her finger over the lines of text, London's incessant clamor oozing through the window of her hotel room—a modest dwelling in a mundane neighborhood where coin bought silence. And every room on the floor. Her condition required isolation. Should she be drawn to companionship, because loneliness was its own kind of madness, she only had to recall the blood on the steps of the theatre in Lyon. The look of scorn and revulsion on the faces of those she had once called friends.

Lovers.

Frenzied, she flipped pages of the geological survey, searching for the small stone edifice she'd seen in the boy's mind. He'd been traversing a country lane, and an intense surge of longing had swept her when she gazed upon the edifice through his eyes. It was the same sensation she felt when she returned to her family's estate after being away. Shelter, security. *Belonging*. There would be no sleep until she located the town.

Because, she'd felt the presence of another at his side.

A formidable presence, sedative. Healing. Jamming the heel of her hand into her eye until she saw stars, she kicked the discarded pile of books, sending them tumbling across the carpet.

Her father had taken her to Stonehenge years ago, and she would never forget pressing her palms against moist sandstone and imagining those who had come before her seeking divine intervention when none was forthcoming. Raising their faces to the heavens and demanding deliverance. For one breathtaking moment, standing there in a ring of towering rock, she'd felt invincible, powerful, healthy.

Normal.

When normalcy had never been hers—would never *be* hers.

Unless the healer was able to cure her, as those towering stones had been unable to. She'd walked beside the boy on that country path, the two of them joined in protection and love. Sidonie was sure of it.

The edifice had also been made of sandstone. Filled with pock mocks and worn etchings. Prehistoric. Unusual, although she hadn't been able to look long because the boy had shoved her out of his mind quite violently when he realized she'd taken hold of him. She would know it if she ever—

She turned a page, and the air ripped from her lungs.

Sarsen stone. King Alfred. Saxons. Danes. She traced the sketch with her ragged thumbnail. The Blowing Stone.

Kingston Lisle. Oxfordshire.

"Rebirth will be mine at any cost," she vowed and dropped her head as tears soaked the bodice of her dress.

CHAPTER 7

Those who make us feel, must feel themselves.
~Charles Churchill

*P*iper woke with the sun and shoved aside
the bed curtain to find her maid prowling
the chamber like a restless feline. Disconcerted but
forced to suppress it—after all, this relationship had
been forced upon them both—Piper asked Minnie
for assistance with dressing. It was just as well as
she'd left her front-fastening corsets at the hotel.
Piper refused a breakfast tray, deciding to face Julian
and the discussion he'd threatened her with in the
church courtyard. Why hide under the bedcovers or
in scented bathwater when he'd run her down soon
enough? She grabbed her folio in the unlikely event
the conversation moved to her research and headed
from the room with Minnie's keen gaze heating her
back.

Her luck did not hold, as she found only
Humphrey in the dining room, patrolling the mahogany sideboard with a menacing expression. They

exchanged the requisite hello-good mornings, then settled across from each other at a table seating fourteen by her count. Family portraits lined the wall opposite her, a morose group Piper guessed had come with the house.

They looked on disapprovingly.

Unsurprisingly, Humphrey finished eating quickly, as if a master stood behind him with a pocket watch and a whip. He instructed her to wait for Edward to arrive, a footman in need of a healer. After their mystical consultation was complete, Julian would fetch her.

She wrinkled her nose in displeasure. *Fetch*, as if she were his wiry little dog.

Directive delivered, Humphrey strode from the room, ducking at the doorway to avoid hitting his thick head, leaving her to snap her mouth shut lest this morning's well-prepared eggs fall from it.

Julian was fulfilling his promise to bring her back into the League.

From a polite distance, of course.

While Piper pondered the change in strategy, Edward stumbled in, slumped shoulders and bowed head, little more than an overgrown boy. A *large* boy, as was typical for his position, another absurd fixation of society when most did nothing but open doors and serve meals. She observed the dark crescents beneath his eyes when he fixed his gaze on her as if searching for a miracle and expecting to find none.

Piper made notes as he told her about his dreams —ones that foretold truths. Like most, he had begun to disclose his abilities when he was too young to understand he should hide his gift. Because, sadly, no one but another forced into their world understood. His parents, servants in a modest household in

Portman Square, had gained him employ with a baron's family through a connection. Partly to remove him from their residence. They feared Edward's condition could infect his seven brothers and sisters. He'd come to Julian's attention after a minor incident in a public house, emphasizing how the organization's network had grown since her grandfather's death.

Piper grasped Edward's hands and focused her entire being on his rasping inhalations, the pulse skipping beneath her fingers. "Calm your mind. Learn to control your gift and redirect," she whispered. Her heartbeat leapt to match his, so she struggled to calm her own mind, visualizing a mantle of snow blanketing a sallow field. The verdant woodlands bordering Harbingdon bathed in a foggy haze. Julian's face, which always, even if she denied it deep in her heart, quietened her. Although she didn't *see* Edward's dreams, his terror flowed through her, pricking her skin like she'd run through a patch of nettles. A rainbow exploded behind her closed lids, the scent of oranges, cinnamon, vinegar.

She absorbed his discomfort until her lungs felt near to bursting. A roar, like a wave crashing over her, filled her ears. "*Enough,*" she gasped and dropped his hands.

Blinking hard and coming back to the present, she found Edward sitting straight and tall across from her, the crescents beneath his eyes expunged. His scarlet cuffs matched the startling rosiness of his cheeks. His eyes were as wide as her teacup's saucer. "M'lady," he murmured and swallowed.

"Every morning at this time, meet me here. You have the strength to manage this. I'll help you find that strength, the ability to channel and release.

You're letting your gift govern you when *you* must govern. Or face being torn apart at the seams."

She pressed her hand to her chest at the sudden thought: Like Julian was being torn apart.

With a mumbled agreement, Edward bowed and exited the room with a lively step, much restored.

Piper groaned and dropped her head to her hand. No wonder sleep had been difficult as traveling the boy's mind had been like trying to cross a crowded London thoroughfare while blindfolded.

An iridescent shimmer of awareness slipped past like a warm sigh.

She lifted her head to find Julian propped against the doorjamb, light from the window high above his head waterfalling over him. Attired for the country, his open collar revealed a patch of sun-dusted skin; his informal breeches clung to his muscled thighs. He dressed with purpose, with subtle restraint. From their first encounter in her grandfather's study, when he'd worn tattered cast-offs but still looked the part of a young man not to be taken lightly.

He flipped a wide-brimmed hat between his hands as he studied her. There was a coiled stillness about him today. His jaw clenched, and she suspected he kept himself from crossing to her.

"Healers must heal," she said, each word deliberate like she traversed a ballroom floor littered with shards of glass.

Their gazes locked and held. The hat stilled in his hands. Desire sparked and erupted as his aura brightened to a crisp, sharp blue. She clasped the back of the chair to keep from accepting her body's challenge, a ridiculous impulse to finish what they had started years ago. An impulse Julian would soundly reject. A clock somewhere in the house ticked off the seconds as she slipped under a spell she knew he didn't seek to cast. Her blood rioted through her veins, and she marveled that he could still stun and enthrall.

She came to her senses first, gesturing to the chair and the hulking footman no longer there. "I must do it. If I'm to be accepted in the League, I must."

Shoving off the doorjamb, he sent her an enigmatic look. He beat his hat against his thigh in a tight rhythm. "I'm not going to fight you."

She sat up straighter. "Well, good...because I'm not going to fight you, either."

"That, Yank"—he jammed the hat on his head—"would be a first."

"One of those for everything, I believe." Hiding her trembling hands by clenching them in her skirt, she rose. Sought his gaze, which had turned from her to an inspection of the dour canvases at her back. Only a gossamer of yellow—caution—lit his aura, so he had not blocked himself off yet. Not completely. And his lips held a tilt she could *possibly* consider a smile.

With a mental handshake, she accepted the truce.

"Yours?" She gestured to the painting he perused, a father and son in ceremonial attire from a century prior.

"No," he said with a low laugh. "But I'd rather house them than my own, so here they remain." He cupped her elbow and led her into the hall. It was a veiled touch, familiar, relaxed. Yet it sent a whisper of cognizance through her as if he'd trailed his fingers along the nape of her neck.

She questioned them occupying the same space if he continued touching her.

"Would you like to ride?" he asked, breaking the charged silence.

Her step faltered. "Astride?"

"In that skirt?" He turned to walk backward, one step, then another. His hands rose in entreaty as he noted the stiffening of her shoulders. "Get a proper habit. Then we'll talk. Put it on Minnie's list." Light snuck beneath his hat brim, revealing eyes the color of mist rising off a cobbled lane, and her heart gave a powerful squeeze. "I'm quite happy if you rip around Harbingdon like a hooligan—as long as a guard accompanies you. Unpretentiousness should be considered a benefit of country living. Though who would be surprised were you to play the hooligan in the middle of a London ballroom," he added and turned to cross the terrace with a purposeful stride.

"I heard that," she said and hurried to catch him as he took the steps two at a time.

Julian angled down a narrow footpath with a glance to ensure she followed. An enchanting blend of hardwoods dotted the trail: crack willow, Scots pine, field maple, wych elm. She stumbled over a root as she craned her head to see through the needled canopy. A governess once gave her a book on dendrology, the study of trees and shrubs. Knowledge contained mostly in her head, as she'd had no chance to explore, but she'd taken a liking to the subject.

The terrain was a lush, mossy-olive spill. A dense forest closing them in on all sides, as strong a defense as a moat.

Julian had planned well for his community of misfits.

The path ended abruptly at a building constructed of chalk-white brick, where a groom was leading two horses through a stable doorway streaked with sunbeams and shadow. His trouser leg caught on the rounded edge of the knife concealed in his boot as he handed Julian the reins to a gorgeous thoroughbred.

"Thank you, Murphy," Julian said and swung a leg

up, settling effortlessly in the saddle. The horse took note and began to sidestep, where he delivered a calming word and a stroke to her neck to reassure. Piper frowned as Minnie's comment squeezed between the sharp smell of hay and the humid splay of sunshine: *Men be men, miss.*

Apparently, Julian was very good at soothing females.

His little dog sat by the stable door, his coat a perfect complement to the brick. Piper squatted, extending her hand with a whispered appeal.

"Henry," Julian said from atop the black.

"Henry," she called, deciding he looked quite like a Henry. Arrogant, a bit cunning. "Come."

The dog tilted his head, thoughtful, then sauntered into the stable.

"Smart boy," Julian said.

Turning her back on dog and man, she grasped the reins of the magnificent beast Murphy presented to her. The saddle had two pommels, thank goodness, which allowed freedom while still maintaining her blasted modesty. "Medieval torture," she said with a sharp look at Julian, his muscular thighs gripping the horse's flanks like he owned the world. She had learned to ride in America, where all was shocking and indecorous, she supposed, but where one learned to ride *correctly*.

With a leg thrown over each side of the horse.

The English method for women, in almost every aspect of life, chafed.

"M'lord," Murphy whispered with a back-step toward Julian. "Stewart be spirited, and he can smell rain in the air. Be he perchance too much for the miss?"

Piper huffed a breath and indicated Murphy assist her up. Grasping the pommel and settling into the saddle, she crossed her right leg in front of her and shoved her left into the stirrup, which hung low. Frowning, she wiggled her boot, and Murphy rushed to adjust the strap, something she should have done before climbing atop her mount. Once again, temper caused carelessness. "I'll have you know I'm as good a rider as he. Better even," she added, though Julian's burst of laughter crowded out the comment.

Murphy nodded when it was clear he fathomed little. He likely believed her crazed. Henry objected, after all.

Julian didn't look too sure, either.

"Thank you," she said when Murphy presented her with a pair of butter-smooth leather gloves. She turned to find Julian tugging on his own, rich black, matching his horse and his pressed breeches perfectly. She suspected he concealed a smile beneath the brim of his hat.

She felt her temper stir. *Bloody happy I amuse.*

"Lunch be in the saddlebag, sir. As requested."

Piper glanced at him as they rode from the stable yard. Lunch. With Julian. A pleased glow lit, and she looked down to hide it, though Julian's eyes had not strayed from the path.

He lightly tapped his mount's flanks and moved into a trot, those impressive shoulders flexing, one hand holding the reins, the other resting on his thigh. He rode as he lived and breathed, with artless, measured elegance. Nevertheless, she *was* as good a rider. As natural a seat. She claimed this without conceit because it was a simple fact. She had learned to ride beside a man with no allegiance to propriety, no allegiance to anyone. Her equestrian skills were a gift, the only her father had given her.

Julian knew this. They'd raced across her grandfather's estate many times. Not sidesaddle, which was intolerable. An excellent way to show off trim ankles in Hyde Park, but absurd for a seasoned horsewoman.

"Quit sighing," he called back. "We'll get the habit."

"Anything you say, m'lord," she murmured and pulled Stewart in line with him. Julian glanced over, but his hat shaded his eyes and his expression. Tilting his head in thought for a long beat, he then looked away without comment.

She slowed and let her gaze linger, examining him freely as her heart raced. It was a wretched spot of luck that Julian Alexander was the only man who had ever fascinated her. There had been other kisses aside from the one they'd shared—precisely two. Men of interest, or men *interested*, during the horrid season her grandfather had pressed upon her.

She had tried to find someone else who lit her up, phosphorus to her sulfur. Find another person who made a room blaze when he stepped into it. Because with Julian, it was hopeless. His defenses were stronger, his reasoning in place and firmly protected. He had, mallet to stone, crushed every entreaty.

Heedless to her internal debate, Julian pointed out areas of interest as they traveled a well-worn path through the meadows. He identified something note-worthy about each section of his property. A herd of muntjac lived here, a pack of fallow there. Fishing was excellent in a series of lakes below the house, duck hunting possible along the parkland drives surrounding.

"Is Harbingdon profitable?" she asked as they passed through what Julian called a conifer plantation.

"If managed by a titled fop, it wouldn't be. Although I'm still looking for a steward to join the League, to shoulder the management. Until then…"

He slowed, bracing his hands on the pommel. The black sidestepped at the sudden halt, and Julian tightened his leg at the flank. "I'd been saving, keen investing, and some luck. Funds unconnected to the viscountcy, on principle not committed to being funneled back in. Mismanagement forced Harbingdon to market and my attention. I knew from the first moment that it was perfect for my needs and those of the League. Rife with opportunity, if one was willing to put in the work, which the former owner was not. A piece of the estate closer to the village was let under a fruitful farm years ago, and plans are to explore the property's timber and mineral rights, again, when I locate a steward. If I'm to have others live here, we need a self-sustaining model." He drew a breath and sighed it out in a gust. "Takes time to untangle the mess created by the foolish young baron who sold me the place, but I'm learning as I go along."

"Repairs?" she asked to his back, as he'd turned to study something over the rise. There was evidence of restoration to the ceiling and floor in her bedchamber.

"Substantial. And the cash flow from my titled properties is locked up keeping those relics afloat." He lifted his hand to his neck and rubbed as if it pained him to discuss the viscountcy. "It takes an astounding amount of cash to keep a five-hundred-year-old family seat propped up. We have faithful retainers connected to the estates for centuries, thank God, or I would be up a muddy creek with the rest of the ton."

They continued, the wind picking up as it raced across the open savannah, tugging at her skirt and sending tendrils of hair into her face. She caught a hint of precipitation, as Minnie and Murphy had suggested. "The other buildings I see in the distance?"

"Gardener's cottage."

"Hmm...yes." She took a brief inventory of the surroundings, profuse with rose bushes, flowering shrubs, not a pruned specimen among them. The air was dense with various fragrances. "I'm guessing it sits empty."

"Actually, it does not. But the gardener, well"—Julian shook his head, issuing a brief shrug—"he's quite knowledgeable about the occult, and his work with the chronology has occupied most of his time."

Piper wanted to laugh. *Of course.* "The smaller building, lovely brick and ivy?" she asked instead.

His brim lowered, a hesitation. "The lodge."

"That one is—"

"Mine."

She waited for him to elaborate, but he moved on.

"I thought to ask you about assisting with management of the gardens. As for the gardener's cottage, we've been lodging the newly arrived League members there. The main house is too active for a restless mind, and often, those arriving are troubled. You'll be able to help them, I hope." He shifted in the saddle, slowing to a walk and allowing her to come alongside him. "Minnie stayed there, as did Murphy. We placed Edward, the footman, too soon in the main house." He smiled sheepishly. "You see, he's the only arrival to date trained for his position, so I assumed it would be an easier transition. He should have stayed here first, a calm setting. Instead, he's losing his mind, or thinks he is."

"I'm going to help him. I could have before—"

"You were too busy playing Madame DuPre to help."

She ripped off her glove and threw it at him. It hit his chest exactly at the tantalizing open point of his shirt. "You abandoned me. Left me to fend for myself.

I had no idea you were building the League into an organization my grandfather never envisioned. Healing and support and assistance. Why, a place to live should one not have any other options. Why not bring me in sooner? Why wait until I'm hunted and have to be guarded within an inch of my life?"

He halted his horse and considered her glove as it fluttered to the ground. "Residing with a failing old woman certainly didn't curb your temper. And you were *never* left to fend for yourself. I was close, even if you didn't think I was."

"No one trained for their position." Her gaze fell to the leather embarrassment resting on the stalks of golden grass. "That explains Minnie, who is no more a lady's maid than I am a lady." It also explained the scattered Harbingdon household, so unlike the lock-and-key discipline of a typical aristocratic one.

Julian dismounted with a resigned air, going to his knee to retrieve her glove. Grass brushed his thigh, drawing her gaze to the shifting muscle as he knelt. "This is not a country home for hunting season, Yank. Here, we live and work together. Sadly, abuse and denigration are our familial connection." He glanced up, regarding her through eyes gone quicksilver in the sunlight. The faint lines drifting from them as he squinted were new to her. She was fascinated. Entranced with a mere look, as always. An intense look that crawled inside, softening her against her will. "Most shared their gifts as children. You know this. Such honesty is a lovely aspect of being a child but horrible for someone, anyone, *different*. I'm untangling more than finances on these lands. I'm sorry if my mission is a surprise, but if I'm devoting my life to this, giving up so much, it's going to mean something."

She was speechless as Julian stood and extended

the glove to her. His undertaking seemed exceedingly benevolent and amazingly naïve. Her grandfather had only wanted to complete his research, keep his granddaughter safe, and understand why the gift of healing had traveled through their family like a big nose or a particular eye color.

Julian sought to right wrongs and build a community on an entirely singular level.

And what, exactly, did he mean by *giving up so much*? Did he include her in what he had to give up? She folded and refolded the glove, afraid to ask. "How democratic," she finally said for lack of a candid comment.

"Democratic." He laughed softly and came around to assist her dismount. His touch was offhand, and he immediately moved away, but the heat of his body had transferred at each point she'd grazed on the way down, tiny patchworks of fire lighting her skin.

"Your glove chose an adequate spot for lunch," he said, his moist breath crossing her cheek. Then he surprised her as he'd never surprised her before. With a gentle, easy smile, he lifted the hat from his head and settled it on hers. It sank low on her brow, held up by her ears. When she continued to stare, dumbfounded, he said simply, "Your cheeks are freckling," and turned from her as if nothing earth-shaking had occurred.

She was left standing in a field with his tantalizing fragrance drifting from his hat to her nostrils, the lingering warmth of his body dissipating, carried away on the breeze.

It was heaven and hell.

Julian gathered her bay and his black, giving them apple slices with murmured appreciation for their patience. From his saddlebag, he removed a tightly rolled blanket and a leather satchel. Ripping off his glove with his even, white teeth, he settled the blanket on a patch of grass beneath a towering black-thorn she imagined to be as old as Harbingdon.

She crossed to the picnic spot with uncharacter-istic hesitation, pressing her glove between her palms until she noticed Julian studying her with a muted, yet challenging smile. Her hands stilled, her chin lift-ing. "Strangely, I feel tested."

His movements slowed, long fingers neatly tucked under the corner of the blanket. His gaze met hers, then fell back to his task. "Perhaps I test myself," he replied, then turned to unpack the bounty con-tained in the satchel, negating any explanation about a comment she was sure to spend a sleepless night puzzling over.

Silent, she turned a full circle in the shaded clear-ing. A cushion of discarded blossoms littered the ground, a lacey, white border surrounding the blanket Julian had secured as neatly as if it were nailed down. Piper lifted her hand to her brow and peered into the distance. "Is that Murphy sitting atop the rise?"

"Yes."

"Groom or chaperone?" she asked as she knelt, wrapping her arms around her knees in an indelicate perch.

"Guard," Julian replied, a container of strawber-ries balanced in his hand.

He opened the container as she removed the oth-ers, placing them on the sea of linen. Sliced chicken, asparagus, walnuts, cheese. Stilton, she guessed from the aroma. Lastly, he pulled out a corked bottle. With a turn of his lips, he shrugged. "I worried I might need reinforcement."

"How ridiculous." She twisted her legs to the side, doing a visual check to ensure she was, except for a minute glimpse of stockinged ankle, covered. Ripping her remaining glove off, she brushed him aside when he would have served her and reached for a plate. "So, that's why Murphy had a knife in his boot."

"And a pistol in the other," Julian said, slipping off his coat and making a neat fold of it, the gloves dangling from the pocket the only hint of disorder. He squatted, knee pressed to the blanket, the other rising high in delicate balance. His waistcoat, a somber but very fine pewter, played off his eyes as if a well-paid valet had planned it when she understood this was not the case. The wind, picking up as wrathful clouds moved in, pressed silk against his muscled upper body, and she again marveled at his physical maturation.

Repairs at Harbingdon were evidently not sourced to workmen.

Taking a bite of a strawberry, she licked at the crimson streak on her palm as the puzzle pieces fell into place. "They're coming for us." The hat brim slipped over her eyes, and she knocked it back. "For me."

Julian's gaze lit on her effort to clean her skin, and she watched his aura spark at the edges. "What happened between you and Finn, before you arrived in the churchyard? Your hair was unbound as if you'd run a race, and Finn looked"—Julian grabbed the wine bottle, uncorking it with a flip of his thumb—"Finn looked stunned." He drank deeply, his throat pulling. Plainly, Cook had neglected to pack glasses. "That smile he never leaves home without hidden deep."

"I have no idea what you're referencing," she whispered, the denial as fragile as one spun with gossamer thread. She could hear the lie ringing between them like the village's church bell.

He laughed, razor-sharp, an uncharitable retort. Tapping the bottle against his forearm, he took another sluggish pull. "Your bravado is admirable. I know few men who possess it, but you scare the hell out of me with the risks you take. Leaving Gloucestershire the latest in a string of them."

Piper squeezed her hand into a fist, found she still held the half-eaten strawberry and tossed it to the grass. Juice ran down her wrist, staining her sleeve. "You hide me away when I cannot deny *who* I am, any more than you or Finn. Maybe the risk, to you, is acceptance. When there is no choice *but*."

With a curse, he jammed the cork in the bottle and tossed it aside. Before she read his intent, he palmed the ground alongside her hip, his long body looming over hers. His intimidating stance shocked even as she leaned into it. Julian rarely moved close enough for her to study him. "The healer's gift is so rare, scholars suspect it's illusory. The chronology lists only three in our world since the 1500s. Only the power to arrest one's gift completely, something your grandfather crudely called a blocker, is rarer. Power like yours in the wrong hands...I'll die before letting them possess it. Possess *you*." His eyes flashed, catching like dry kindling.

And his aura...*glorious*.

Resting back on his heels, he dragged his hand through his hair, sending the strands into disordered coils. "I'm simply trying to protect you. Protect them." He nodded in the direction of the house. "But you make it very difficult, Piper. You always have.

"Why, then? Leave it. Leave us."

His gaze snapped to hers. "Do you think I haven't considered running? Going to one of my estates and hiding behind this blessed title? I tell myself I stay because of the promises I made to your grandfather when I know"—he thumped his chest—"I stay because it's my destiny. My *choice*. I couldn't leave you, Finn, anyone I've asked to join the League if I tried. I wouldn't make it to the end of the drive."

"Is that what you promised the earl? What he died whispering to you? Is that why—"

"*One time*," he grit through clenched teeth. "We'll discuss this one time, then never again. It hurts us both to remember."

Hurts us both. She swayed, her hand sliding off the blanket, her fingertips sinking into moist earth.

All this time, she had assumed it only hurt *her*.

"I touch a ring, a cup, a bloody fork, and suddenly parts of a life, someone's *life*, are flashing before me so furiously I fear for my sanity. I step into another world, one I'm connected to and not. It's like being pulled by each arm in vastly different and painful directions. It feels impossible even as I'm living it." He lifted her hand from where it lay nestled in the stalks of grass. "When one touch from *you*"—he circled her wrist—"has the ache in my head seeping away like steam shooting from a kettle. The visions dissipate, as if they were never there, though my gift remains. I gain control. I seize your strength and am stronger for it." Releasing her, he backed away in a graceless shift so unlike him, his gaze lifting to the branches above their heads. "Do you realize I was practically going mad, begging for an escape from my *mind*, until your grandfather found me and brought me to you?"

"I know this, Jules. But—"

"*No*," he whispered harshly. "You don't know. There were times you healed me when…when I couldn't let go. I couldn't physically release you. Like coercion, a momentary lapse, not allowing you to come back to yourself. I wanted to *keep* you. Have

you purge the images running through my mind forever, not just the transitory slice of healing you'd offered. Your grandfather warned me away on his
dying breath because he *knew* I wanted to use your
gift to lessen my own. Which makes you incredibly
vulnerable, Piper, because it's what *everyone* wants
from you. He knew I was equally compelled." His
gaze sliced through her like a hot knife through
butter when the emotion propelling it was cold resolve balanced on a razor blade. "And for all the
wrong reasons."

Her breath arrested in her lungs. "The wrong reasons," she repeated, three hammer blows. *The wrong
reasons.* Wrong meant *right* was not part of the equation. It made their age-old kiss seem contrived, trivial, her feelings before and after an impassioned
instant of feminine nonsense or worse yet, misper-
ception. Like a sandcastle washed away by the sea,
what she hoped she had with Julian or could have in
the future was, in reality, no reality at all.

She had waited years for absolutely nothing.

Reaching blindly, she grasped the bottle, popped
the cork as he tried to snatch it from her and took a
long drink, the wine scorching a path down her
throat. The. Wrong. Reasons. Dropping her brow to
her hand, she began to laugh, sending Julian's hat
tumbling from her head, releasing her hair about her
face like a funeral shroud.

"Stop it, Piper." He wrestled away the bottle; it hit
the ground with a thunk. "Would you rather I continued letting us get closer when I couldn't interpret
my motives? Confusing my desire for you with my
desire to be *free* from this bloody curse? My need for
you muddled with my need for your *gift*." He gripped
her chin, tilting her head high. When she refused to
open her eyes, he gave her a gentle shake, but she

only shut them tighter, the suppressed emotion in his quivering fingers flooding her with sorrow. "I feared consuming you. Until there was nothing left."

Breathless, he released her, a storm-promise breeze sliding in to widen the gulf between them. A gulf she'd thought she could breach if she tried hard enough. If she *loved* him enough.

"I still do," he said, voice breaking.

She dragged her hair from her face, singed from his touch and his words. Clouds had gathered in anticipation of the approaching downpour, cloaking the day in a leaden stench. Julian rose to his feet, his back to her, palm flattened against the tree trunk as if it held him up. The wind tugged at the dark strands curling over his starched collar. She denied the urge to straighten his twisted waistcoat ties, dust off the blades of grass clinging to his trousers. Those were things a wife might do, a lover perhaps, not someone connected for all the *wrong reason*s. She closed her mind to his aura, healing herself. Watching him struggle only brought her lower.

For the first time since Julian stumbled from her grandfather's carriage and into her life, she had absolutely no entitlement.

A strange sensation settled over her as she rose unsteadily to her feet. Strangely, it felt like strength. Breaking the charged silence, she released an admission that created an impenetrable barrier between them: "I wanted you to consume me."

His shoulders stiffened as the air crackled like the lightning she'd seen in the distance. As she stood there shivering, she set fire to her memories, her hopes, watched them blacken to ash, swept away by the wind. Sound finally intruded over her thundering heartbeat: horses snorting at the approaching storm, and the short rein Julian had tethered them with, grass whipping into a frenzy. A raindrop hit her cheek and rolled down her face, bringing her neatly to the bleak present. "But, of course, this comes as no surprise."

His head dropped; a punishing breath sounded through his teeth. When he finally turned to her, stark lines of restraint chalked his face. His hair lifted as a violent gust pushed her toward him when she'd decided moments ago never to be pushed in his direction again.

They stared across a grassy plain, agreeing to disagree as hell's fury raged around them.

Finn woke with a gasp, his heart racing, his body tangled in sheets drenched with sweat. The dream arrived in distorted vignettes, glistening and sharp-edged, slicing his mind as shards of glass would his skin. The woman, her body bent over a book, her hair wild about her head, her eyes…lost to madness, anger, pain. There would be no negotiating with this mislaid soul, should Julian assume there was. She had looked at Finn with hatred and disgust, plunged a knife through his chest in her hallucination and laughed as his blood pooled at her feet.

She'd linked to his feelings for Piper, his love for her. He squeezed his head between his hands. There was more…

"*Home*," he murmured on a low hush, the words coming out in accented English.

She had seen something to connect the League to Harbingdon. The village. His mind was an ingress—and a colossal breach in their security. For one panicked moment, Finn considered packing a valise and running, hiding in the rookery he knew as well as the lines on his palm, at least until the threat was over. But he could never leave his family, and Julian would go to the ends of the Earth to track him down.

Because it was quite simple.

Though she'd stepped into his mind and taken, he could fight back and step into *hers*.

CHAPTER 8

That willing suspension of disbelief for the moment,
which constitutes poetic faith.
  ~Samuel Coleridge-Taylor

Six days later, Julian lingered by the lodge's front window, watching a storm gather resources in clouds the color of graphite. The cottage stood at the perimeter of the estate's vast woodlands —carefully chosen isolation on his part—but the feeling of remoteness, usually soothing, stung this evening. The moon shone in bursts, tossing intermittent streaks across his desk and the spattered Wilton beneath his feet. He had soaked a canvas and the scent of linseed oil married with the metallic tang of paint. Bolstering aromas in his favorite dwelling in all of England, a place of creative solitude and modest expectation. A place he allowed himself to be nothing more than a humble artist, the supernatural and the aristocracy forbidden company.

Why, then, the tangle of emotion?

With a muted sigh, he cocked his hip on the ledge,

his hand dropping from the velvet sash. Piper had ruined rainy days for him—in a country with too goddamn many of them—because all he remembered as the storm gathered was *her*, drenched from head to toe, her gown clinging to her body. In the downpour that had suspended their impromptu picnic, her eyes had flooded green like the bottom of a lake in winter.

Unblinking regard. Challenging.

Her reaction to him, unveiled, raw, fierce, had been a substantial chip to the jaw.

He realized the paradox as he glanced around a room scattered with paint and brushes, remnants of his private life. He hid his secrets when Piper hid little. Her fearlessness exposed his vulnerabilities. Not even his memories of the atrocities experienced in Seven Dials held power to bring him to his knees. Not anymore. Nor those brutal beatings at the hand of his father. They visited him, yes, but in nightmares from which he awakened, choking on air, but *awake*.

He knew no way to wake from dreams of Piper.

She recognized him for who he was at his core, stripped of artifice. Even as he dodged, lied, coerced. He'd gotten so bloody used to hiding. To manipulation. To the trappings of wealth, the idiocy of society. This cerebral *knowing* they shared, combined with his desire to join his body with hers in a purely elemental way, left him no room to maneuver.

No room to hide a damn thing. Not when she owned him, mind and body.

Pensive, he rolled the hairclip he'd found jammed inside the lining of his hat between his fingers. Piper's visage washed over him, sending his blood pulsing through his veins. He'd touched it so frequently in the past week, that the visions were fading. However, one was still distinct. Minnie assisting Piper with her coiffure, a skill she and her mistress lacked. This image he was able to join like an unseen apparition. The choice was his. To step into the otherworld or watch through murky glass. A somewhat recent experience, the option to go deeper, both remarkable and frightening.

Remarkable because it represented a heightening of his gift.

Frightening because he was not always able to step *out*.

Piper could help him refine the ability to cross that mystical bridge as easily as Harbingdon's village footpath.

If he let her.

"You idiot," he whispered and tapped the hairpin against the windowpane. Tick, tick, tick like the mantel clock counting off minutes behind him. He played an excruciating game. He should return the hairpin, posthaste. It carried not only images but *feelings* that twisted his heart, clouded his mind. Instead, he kept it like some sorrowful token of Piper's affection.

When the affection between them was scarce.

They'd avoided each other in the past week, exiting and entering rooms as if connected by a pulley, which was for the best. Wasn't distance from Piper Scott what he'd always wanted? Another four taps of the hairpin. *He. Was. Not. Sure.* Astute fool that he was, he recognized the hollow ache in his gut. The enticing taste he'd gotten of her during their ride across the estate had recalled those candlelit discussions during his time home from Rugby and, later, Oxford. Conversations lasting into the wee hours, bare feet and laughter, scandalous freedom allotted due to her grandfather's advancing age, a remote locale, dwindling lack of funds and servants, and the degree of risk Piper was willing to take.

Which was much.

Nevertheless, he'd been her friend. And she his when he counted few as such.

And he'd not been a threat in *that* way, her best interests entirely at the forefront of his mind. Except for the slip up on her nineteenth birthday, he had been positively angelic, denying impulses at every turn when he'd wanted her—or felt supremely linked —from the first moment he set eyes on her. That kiss, *ah*, he thought and released a tortured breath through his teeth. A tempestuous spot of youthful abandon, that night the only instance where he'd chosen to ignore reason and consequence. Where he'd let his body rule, obstructing sound judgment and his obligation to protect.

He rapped the glass hard enough to shatter. In a mocking twist, protecting Piper also meant protecting her from *himself*.

In any event, with the transitory exception of an aged earl who had left her life too suddenly to make plans, no one cared to step in regarding her care. He was the only taker. Her cousin, Freddie, who'd inherited the Montclaire title, had proven useless, callous even.

Julian slipped the hairpin in his waistcoat pocket, questioning his promise to assist with her research. Bloody hell, if he hadn't dug himself in deep there. Relighting the lamp's wick, he returned to the desk and the stack of ledgers awaiting his attention, the joyous weekly accounting of his properties. Letters from stewards, secretaries, and solicitors cross-referenced against Humphrey's notes from recent visits; records on repairs and tenancy issues; checks and balances on bank drafts and deposits. Evaluation of his contributions to the village schools, the churches.

Knocking his spectacles high, he knuckled his stinging eyes.

It was *astonishing* they were in the black.

If he cherished any of the fading relics, felt a familial connection to just *one*, his heart would have been in the management, but most held appalling memories of a troubled youth spent hiding who he was, evading a father with a loathsome temper. With a heavy heart, Julian glanced at the corner of an envelope peeking from a stack of mail Humphrey had delivered earlier. Scented paper. *Roses*. He preferred the smell of oil, paints, *Piper*. With the tip of his finger, he edged Marianne's dispatch further beneath the pile.

Frustrated to have two women battling in his head, he pulled Lady Coswell front and center, as she'd looked the night in Mayfair, his robe hanging off her body, waiting for the coil of heat to dart to his mind, belly, or cock.

Nothing arrived aside from a faint, fond glimmer.

Conversely, all pathways tensed in anticipation when he thought of Piper, the one woman he did not *want* to want.

To say he'd placed an immovable wall between them would be a just assessment. After their heated discussion beneath that damned flowering tree, the irrational need to grovel beckoned. His words had come out honestly but indelicately. *The wrong reasons* now seemed like a crude way to express his indecisiveness. Displeasure crossing Piper's face was a common occurrence, but firm resolve was rare. And shocking.

Pride and distress had warred within him at her self-possession.

Novel in his dealings with her, a grown woman had confronted him. And he wasn't bloody sure who'd won the battle.

A knock on the door had his heart kicking as he imagined Piper coming to him. Except, she was avoiding him for the first time in memory, turning the other direction when she saw him coming. He patted the hairpin helplessly as a burst of lightning shot through the window and danced across his desk.

"Jule?" Finn popped his head around the open door. "Are you free?"

He crooked his hand to signal entrance, and Finn made an awkward bow into the room, his body having grown faster than even his enormously innate poise could account for. A paternal rush hit Julian hard as the young man took a seat, dusting raindrops from his coat and hooking one leg over the other with the cool finesse of a peer of the realm. Tilting his head, Finn nudged a canvas into view with a boot you could see your reflection in. Julian poured brandy in two glasses, managing to find a clear path between ledgers and paint supplies as he slid one across the desk.

Finn took it with a crooked smile, a raised brow. Being offered a drink was unprecedented and a signal of his approaching majority. He took a leisurely sip, his posture lowering little for the brandy's delight. An astute student since their first encounter in the rank back alley of a gaming hell, Finn had sucked in every measure of polite society and looked prepared to expel it back in their faces. Possessed of an amiable nature and a rather indolent manner, Julian suspected the world was set to write Finn off as little more than the harmless, beautiful bastard of a deceased viscount.

The League would use this lack of discernment to their advantage as the beautiful bastard read every stupid thought in their heads.

"You came out in this storm. You must have

something on your mind." Lamplight passed through the crystal as Julian turned the tumbler, sending amber facets over his trouser leg and across the desk.

Finn extracted a sheet of folded foolscap from his coat pocket. Sliding forward in his chair, he ironed the list over the desk's surface with a broad palm. "We came up with three names for those who visited Madame DuPre on both nights the hotel caught fire." Finn shook his head, a frown pleating the skin between his brows. "Piper swears neither originated in the parlor she used. It helped when she finally mentioned the earlier blaze, minor as it was."

Yes, it had. Julian rotated the list with a quick turn of his finger. A vision of Finn composing it streaked through his mind. "Why would the Duke of Ashcroft visit Madame DuPre? From the little I know of him, he doesn't strike me as a willing participant to this absurdity. Perhaps his current mistress is intoxicated with the occult, as many in the ton are." Julian settled back in his chair. "What did he ask her? Did she record his aura?"

"You'll have to actually talk to her to find out," Finn suggested, freeing his opinion and his body as it slid into an elegant sprawl.

Julian took a reflective sip, alcohol cutting a path through his resistance. Too much discussion with Piper and he'd be throwing paint on canvas, helping her catalogue auras. Then she'd know *everything* about him, and he'd be wholly and hopelessly destroyed.

"There's a benefit to having a woman around who can manage our rather pathetic group of servants, Jule. For one, the house smells better, like lemons."

Julian had noticed the changes. An unfamiliar but tantalizing scent clinging to his sheets; vases of flowers in every room; knickknacks he imagined had been packed away sitting atop once lonely mantles. It unnerved him that Harbingdon was more comfortable with her there, the close of a gap he hadn't identified as essential.

"Dinners have been on time. I think there's even a new rug in the hall." Reaching for his glass, Finn studied it as if his attentiveness would produce more brandy.

"I've given her the gardens. And a horse," he said and slammed the window at his back shut. The storm was pushing moisture into the room, which was not good for his artwork. Julian had recorded Piper's journey past the lodge this morning, Murphy at her side, her rolling movement atop the bay snagging him like a hook beneath his skin. While he imagined, vividly, her astride *him*. Releasing an exasperated huff, he bent the edge of Marianne's letter in an inelegant fold, where against his will, it still peeked from beneath a battered ledger. "And my dog," he added, laughing at his puerile reaction to Henry, who, after quiet consideration, decided he was fascinated and clung to Piper like a shadow.

Like master, like dog, he supposed.

Turning his glass in a circle on the desk, Julian studied Finn. "Let me guess what happened the other day on the footpath."

Finn dropped his head before Julian read the confidences hidden in deep, vibrant blue.

Julian's temper sparked. There would be no secrets between them until Finn came into his own, and Julian lost all control. "Is the compulsion to take her gift and keep it for yourself what you're hiding?"

Finn's cheeks bleached like the lodge's brick.

"For one glorious moment, her touch soothed, then you had to fight to release her, thinking only of deliverance." Julian slipped his spectacles off and

THE LADY IS TROUBLE

flipped them to the desk, rubbing his eyes until stars shot behind his lids. "Am I correct or close to it?"

"Imagine…" Finn swallowed, his throat pulling in a long draw. His fingers drummed an anxious rhythm on the desk. "Imagine someone who cares naught for her being caught in that tempest. I told you about the dream, how that woman killed me without thought. Without hesitation or guilt. And I let her in, somehow, drew her closer to Piper. I'm so sorry—"

"Stop torturing yourself. We'd know nothing about this threat without your knowledge, Finn." Julian poured himself another drink, and at the pleading look, splashed a modest dram in Finn's as well. "We'll protect her until she marries." He lifted his glass high and gazed through the faceted liquid, the fractured picture perfectly fitting his tempestuous mood. Imagining another man's hands on Piper made him want to put his fist through the wall. "If she'll agree to entertain the suggestion, which she never would before."

"What do you mean?"

Julian laughed when the situation had been an utter disaster. "You were too young to remember. Her grandfather sent her to London three seasons after her father's death. He sought to gain interest from a family unconnected to the League." A union with anyone *but* Julian, as the attraction between them had become noticeable. Innocent, but noticeable. "She hadn't learned to manage the auras in a country drawing room, much less a ballroom of crows wanting to ogle the earl's uncivilized, half-American granddaughter."

"And?"

"She stretched the boundaries of polite society until they snapped."

Finn slid low, knees bumping the desk. "She had admirers?"

"At first, flowers arrived daily at the earl's home in Berkley Square. Calling cards from the best families. Invitations to every event of the season." He set his glass aside, the brandy making him maudlin. It was just after their kiss that she'd gone to London, agreed to it after a vicious argument where he'd tried to tell her both how he felt and why he could not allow himself to feel it. The earl, with vicious threats and compelling reasoning, had made *his* position clear. "A dowry was believed to be in existence. Maybe it was, in the earl's mind, because it was certainly not on paper. I've always wondered if he realized the depth of his financial woes."

"And now? If she were to agree to entertain the suggestion?"

"Easy to create a modest inheritance where none existed. I created one for you as well, from the devoted, albeit reckless, deceased Viscount Beauchamp. We're blessed the old man acknowledged you, or everyone thinks he did, as it will pave your way in life." Julian removed a tiny paintbrush from a gash in the desk and rolled it between his palms. He ran his thumb across the angled tip, dots of azure spotting the ferrule. The perfect tool for creating thin, crisp lines. Control on canvas, if not in life. "Enlist the assistance of a morally-flexible solicitor, falsify a few documents, and there you are. I used Pearson. Remember him? Best goddamn forger in England." He swept the ox hair bristles across his skin and wondered at his sudden hitch of despair. It was substantial, although he couldn't readily locate its source. "I recently floated rumors as I did with you, which caught fire and spread through the ton. Her situation is not as dire as assumed; the earl prepared well, and so on. Although I can't do anything about the regrettable circumstances of her birth or her unmanageable temperament."

His gaze met Finn's. The boy's regard was a deep blue sea, scorching him where he stood. "Quit reading me."

"I can read your expression, Jule." He shrugged, polishing off his brandy in a neat move that made Julian question how often he'd practiced it. "No need to delve into your mind."

"Hell." Tossing the paintbrush atop the desk, he bounded from his chair. The wind was creating havoc outside, sending branches tumbling across the lawn. The same turbulence was churning through his body. "No matter what you and Piper think, I'm making this up as I go along." He rubbed his temple, a headache beginning to pulse. His image, partially reflected in the windowpane, looked drained, wrung out. "I don't have all the answers. I only pretend I do. My conviction seems to make everyone feel better."

"Jule..." Finn's boot hit the floor, leather squeaking as he shifted. "Piper said something the other day. About being close to 'getting what she wanted' before her grandfather died. Any idea what she meant?"

A lightning strike lit the room, thunder rolling in just after. The storm was on top of them. Julian watched the chaos unfurl, marveling at Finn's naivete. Thank God for it, however short its life. He had protected the boy like the most diligent of parents for just this sort of innocence.

He glanced over his shoulder, his lips forming what could only be a grimace. Let the boy read that expression. Or, if not, he was welcome to Julian's thoughts.

Finn bobbled his glass. "She meant you?"

"Impossible…" was all Julian got out in the way of a response. It was impossible, he and Piper, even if he wanted them to *be* more than he'd wanted anything in his life.

"Downright frightening," Finn whispered.

Exactly. Her desire combined with the blistering rush he experienced every time he saw her made for a combustible problem.

The lodge's door flew back on its hinges as Humphrey shouldered into the room, his somber expression one presented before stepping in the ring. "We have a problem," he said as he shook raindrops from his coat, pushed a sodden mass of hair from his brow. "Messenger just arrived from town."

Julian jammed his shoulder against the window ledge, bracing himself. Damned if this day was going anywhere but down.

"Crowley found someone lurking in your Mayfair office, ripping the place apart looking for God knows what." Humphrey cracked his knuckles, three slow pops. "Got him locked in the wet larder at present. Maybe someone connected to the woman in Finn's dreams? If so, this might be a good thing."

Life in the rookery had prepared Julian for conflict in a way no amount of proper training could. Rugby and Oxford had provided the sheen when everything underneath was sullied. The poor sod locked in his larder would be terrified should he know how far this middling viscount had gone to protect what was his.

"Bring him to me," Julian whispered and gazed back into the pitch night.

≈

Even amidst a violent storm, Harbingdon maintained a unique, soothing stillness. Piper stretched beneath a crisp bedsheet emitting the faint essence of jasmine, Tennyson's book of poetry slipping from her hand. Her mother had loved the scent, and one of Piper's only memories from that time was lying with her in a towering tester bed perfumed much as this one. Adding fragrance to the laundry was one of the minor requests she'd made of Harbingdon's staff, usually after a healing session, when said servant was bright-eyed and appreciative, better able to complete tasks they had no training for. The house had smelled like a gentleman's club, or what she assumed one smelled like before she made minor modifications—drapes open to let in the sun, flowers from the garden brought into the house, rearrangement of decor. Everyone knew the nicest rugs went on the main floor, every advance of a level advancing the deterioration.

She wondered if Julian would mention the changes, but so far, not one peep.

A door slammed belowstairs, disrupting the calm. *Humphrey*. No one slammed a door like that man.

She looked to the window, the drape drawn in and out as if on a staggered breath. Tucking her arm beneath her head as lightning illuminated the room, thunder shook the house hard enough to rattle the glass panes in her wardrobe. The flame from the oil lamp fluttered like a butterfly's wings, casting dramatic shadows on the ceiling. Tennyson's warm words were doing nothing to bring sleep this night.

Tis better to have loved and lost. She frowned at the plaster ceiling cap, overly ornate, and not in step with the rest of Harbingdon. What in heavens name did he know? Loving and losing, or never *securing* love, was nothing short of horrendous.

A branch struck the house with a snap, and Piper sat up, sending the book of poetry thumping to the carpet. A boy lingered at her bedchamber door, hair the color of ripe wheat streaking into his face and over his nightshirt collar. His shoulders shook, hand grasping the beveled doorknob like a lifeline. Henry, her morose but steady companion of late, got to his feet and edged closer.

"He don't bite, does he?" the boy asked. Evidently, the dog was less risk than the storm.

"He hasn't bitten me yet. But I'm not sure he wouldn't like to."

Die being cast on the baize as the boy shuffled from one foot to the other in indecision, she patted the bed, crooked her finger in invitation. "It's a turbulent night. Company would be welcome." After a week of evading Julian, this was mostly true.

The boy came forward with halting steps as if he were being pushed forward and pulled back in unison. He glanced toward the window when another roll of thunder clamored over the house. "I don't like storms." When he reached the bed, she held back from helping him as he scrambled atop the high mattress. A rush of affection hit her, a straight shot to the chest. He was a pathetic little thing, too thin by half, bony knees barely covered by fine linen that, if she looked closely, appeared to be one of Julian's shirts.

She laughed. "This bed is made for a king, isn't it?"

He slid beneath the sheet with a sniff. "Smells right like a king, I reckon."

Another chuckle burst from her, and he flinched as if a blow naturally followed sudden movement.

She breathed in and out twice, quieting her rage, then tucked the sheet closer about him with the gentlest of movements. He studied her all the while with yearning in his deep brown eyes. "It does indeed smell nice."

"And there's no one lurking," he said with a none-too-gentle nose rub. A streak of dirt trailed up the side of his cheek and into his hairline. Wasn't someone on the staff, ineffectual as they were, assigned to oversee this child's care? He needed a haircut, bath, clothing.

She settled back, her gaze seeking that silly ceiling cap. Molded roses and arrows intertwined, like an image from ancient Greece. "Lurking? Do you mean Humphrey?"

He kicked his legs, lifting the sheet high. "Lawks, no. The people. The *dead* ones." He sighed as if this were an answer she should have known, the sheet deflating to rest on them. "Was hoping they were only city toffs, but nah, in the bloody country, too. Not like folks don't expire here, same as anywhere else."

Piper turned her head, the boy's silhouette in stark relief. She knew little about him. Simon, rescued from St Giles, a pickpocket of extraordinary talent. She'd assumed he would be brought to her when the time was right. "Do they talk to you?"

Eyes shadowed from exhaustion met hers. The troubled gaze spoke of dreadful negotiations with those living *and* dead, enlightenment no boy of eight or nine should have. "You the healer?"

Wordless, she nodded.

Holding the sheet to his nose, he drew a full breath as his gaze roved the room.

"My mother loved this scent." She licked her lips, uncertain how to proceed. She'd not been around many children and had no idea how to converse with them.

"Roses?" he asked with another sniff.

"Jasmine."

Simon slid from the bed and began a casual inspection of the room. Each burst of lighting gave chronicle of his progress. His touch was tender, curious but contained, his finger tracing the inlay on the wardrobe, toe sketching the twining blossoms edging the carpet. Henry recorded the tour from his place on a discarded blanket. "My ma, she never smelled like this."

Piper swallowed, afraid to ask and send the conversation downhill but knowing nowhere else to go. "Where is she?"

He darted a look over his shoulder, reminding her of a rabid mongrel she'd once seen on the streets of London, caution and fury rolled into a very wearisome package. "Gone. Stepped in front of some bint's carriage." Crossing to the open window, he extended his arm, soaking his nightshift to the shoulder. "And don't be thinking it was any accident. Cause she told me right 'fore she did it."

Piper scooted up the headboard, hugging a pillow to her chest. She opened her mouth to reply but could think of absolutely nothing to say. *I'm sorry. What a horrible mother. You deserved more, better.* She had lived with her own very imperfect parent and wasn't sure graceful apologies were of any comfort.

Simon frowned, noting her discomfiture. What a remarkably astute child. The waters ran deep. "Guessed I was mad as a hatter, she did. Seeing all them souls. Once or twice, they were dearly departeds she'd known in the rookery. When I see 'em, I see 'em clear, right down to the buttons on their frocks. The coin was gone, so to the streets for us. The rough life proved to be too much for her." Turning, he rested his bottom on the windowsill, which she imagined was getting as soaked as his sleeve. "Tried mudlarking for a wee time."

She shook her head, not sure what this meant.

"Scrounge the river at low tide. Bits of coal, maybe a copper nail. Cut my fee something awful to threepence! So, I switched to sharping. Found out I'm a right fair cutpurse," he said, flipping a brooch he'd pilfered from her dressing table from hand to hand. It disappeared and reappeared at will, snaking through his fingers like a talisman. With a charming eyebrow wag, he lifted his hands in supplication, the brooch nowhere in sight. "But it weren't enough. Never enough." Walking on his toes to her dressing table, he returned the brooch, smiled back at her. "Then I worked for a group, weren't too good to me, truly, until the giant bloke found me. Offered me a better...hmm..." He drummed his fingers on the marble top. "Arrange whatnot."

"Arrange*ment*." Piper smiled, slipping from the bed and crossing to him. "And the giant is Humphrey."

"None too sure of me, that one." Simon lifted a piece of foolscap before his eyes, studying it intently. It was a drawing of plans for the gardens Piper had attempted to sketch. A quite poor attempt. "Spitting mad when he found me, I was. Tried to give him a good smack in the gob. But then I thought, be spoony to say no to this arrange-whatever, hey, right? Food every day, no begging. A real, actual *bed*." He looked at his makeshift nightshirt with a grimace. "Stupid attires. Stuffy. But ain't going to be good news delivered on every corner, now is it? Least no chilblains this winter, if socks be part of the bundle."

"That makes two of us." At his startled glance, she clarified, "Humphrey isn't too sure of me, either." She didn't want to admit she found much of her clothing downright uncomfortable, the multitude of layers ridiculous, thus presenting a negative example.

"This sketch is awful," he said, turning the sheet in every direction as if this would improve it.

Approaching with care, she halted at the settee and perched on the edge, as if, like Simon, she were a bird set to take flight. "Yes, my charcoal broke in the middle of the composition."

"Don't think that mattered."

Amusement she couldn't contain spilled forth. She drew her hand to her lips, leaning into her delight. "I suppose not."

His eyes, as dark as the soil she'd planted a row of winter heather in, tracked back to her. A smile, the first genuine one he'd shown, curved his lips. Returning the sketch to the dressing table, he held up a finger. "Wait," he instructed and was out the door like a shot.

He returned, clutching a battered leather satchel. Going to the settee, he turned it upside down, the varied contents spilling forth. Two charcoal pencils, a bound folio, a paintbrush, a tube of red paint, a silver fork, a folded sheet of foolscap, and a stick pin in the shape of a fox's head that could only be Finn's. Grubbing through the pile, he brought the pencils close to his eyes, selected the one with the longest lead, and presented it to her as a gift.

A gift he had clearly stolen.

"Thank you," she murmured, taking the pencil.

He repacked the satchel—one she had seen Humphrey carrying—with swift purpose. She grinned, imagining Simon robbing him blind. "Where did you find art supplies?"

"Oh, in Mr. Julian's house. Has more than he needs for years of slopping paint around. Colors were all over the floor. Like a rainbow. Like no place I've ever seen."

"This house?" she asked as if she'd stumbled into a room with no light.

Simon flipped the folded foolscap like a sharper a deck of cards. "Oh, no. He lives in the ivy cottage in the woods."

Piper did a quick mental examination. Julian the morning after the fire, his face alight with enthusiasm as he'd talked of *colors, hues, tones*; streaks of paint on his skin on two occasions; his avoidance of her questions about the lodge. *Mine* was all he said when she asked about it, his tone possessive.

Blast. There was a large part of Julian's life she knew nothing about. For all the *right* reasons, he'd kept secrets from her.

Piper blinked to find Simon standing as still as a statue before her, a talent she did not associate with young boys. Regrettably, it seemed his experiences had matured him beyond his years. "I only broke in once," he said, scuffing his toe across the carpet as he pressed the folded sheet into her hand. "I'm trying to quit the cutpurse ways, been ordered to, mind you, by the giant bloke, but it's hard to remember I don't have to anymore."

Her heart stuttered at his admission. "I won't tell." She didn't see any benefit to breaking the trust they were building, as it seemed he didn't trust anyone else. She did wonder, however, what of hers was going to end up in Humphrey's satchel.

She unfolded the foolscap with care, the yellowed creases conveying age. When she got a good look, her pulse thumped so stridently it cut out the sound of rain pelting glass.

"It's you," Simon said as if she needed him to tell her this.

"Yes." She pressed her fist to her chest to help her

draw a breath. "Years ago." The charcoal study was exceptionally detailed, a vivid representation of a young woman on the cusp of maturity. The sooty lines and smudged shadows softened features that should not have been as her expression was the penetrating one she recognized from the mirror. She brought the drawing closer. The dress she wore had unique trim at the sleeve, a double row of pearl buttons crawling up the bodice.

Buttons Julian had been unfastening, his lips pressed to hers, when they were interrupted by her grandfather's murderer.

CHAPTER 9

In short, I will part with anything for you but you.
~Lady Mary Wortley Montagu

he storm continued into the next evening, a
steady assault against the harness room's
slate roof and lone window, which was closed to
keep the discussion within the building but allowed
no respite from the scent of horse dung, beeswax,
and leather overwhelming the space. Julian rested his
elbow on a saddle tree, his hand clutching a bridle
similar to the ones they'd used to bind the Mayfair
intruder's wrists and feet to the loft's post.

Humphrey, his face marred by frustration, paced
from the wooden block centering the room to the
glass harness case, two tours there and back before
he halted next to Julian.

Julian slapped the bridle against his thigh. "Finn,
bring the lamp closer."

Finn stepped in, the oil lamp casting a golden
glow over the four men. Three in a tight ring around
another rendered helpless in what was not only an

undignified position but a painful one, his shoulders drawn to an unnatural angle to allow for his trussing to the post. The man, who had revealed the name Cookson and his position as a Bow Street Runner but little else, blinked a bloodshot eye. The other was swollen shut, currently caught in a mix of blues vivid enough to paint a summer sunset. The scar running from his temple to his chin provided insight into how hard they'd have to press to get information.

"You're going to tell us who sent you." Julian cocked his head toward Humphrey, adding a smile that didn't reach his eyes. "The next drop of blood spilled will be yours. And my friend here is itching to spill it." Cookson had gotten a swipe at him when they were hustling the man out of the carriage and into the harness room. A blade hidden in his blasted boot; one Julian wished they'd located when they searched him. His shoulder hurt like a beast and had bled quite copiously down the sleeve of a shirt newly arrived from his tailor.

Cookson's anxious gaze shot to Humphrey. "Why say a deuced word when I'm headed for a shallow grave in the miles of forest surrounding this place?"

"Dead men don't talk, true enough," Julian replied.

"A Mayfair toff was all I was told you were." Cookson yanked at his restraints, grimacing as leather cut into his skin.

"Regretfully"—Julian snapped the bridle with a crack—"you were misinformed."

"I should have known from the lock on the door." He knocked his head against the post. "None better guarding a bleeding vault."

Humphrey stepped forward, fists clenched. It had been a struggle to keep him off the man when blood started running down Julian's arm. "I'm done with this gentle line of questioning."

"Jule," Finn said, light dancing as he placed the lamp on the wooden block. "There are swifter ways to handle this."

Julian turned on him, a flare of panic sliding through his belly. "No." He didn't want Finn involved any more than he already was. *Damn Humphrey for even bringing him.*

Finn's gaze iced stark blue as he stepped around Julian. "Yes."

Humphrey raised his arm, blocking Julian's interference. "Let him," he whispered, "nearly a man, he is."

Finn moved to Cookson, who assessed him with a scathing glance—from the damp sweep of Finn's hair to the tip of his polished boots. The mocking twist of Cookson's lips told Julian the man had, for the second time in recent history, misjudged an adversary. The handsome face, the immaculate dress, the intelligence Finn stored in a portmanteau, and placed at his side during most encounters made people overlook him. It was a stout defense.

"Who sent you?" Finn asked, dusting lint from his sleeve in a veiled theatrical show. "All you have to do is think of who you're trying so hard to protect. Imagine what they'd do to you if you revealed their name." He cupped his chin in supposed thought, his thumb covering the dimple that had come to life with his slight smile. Julian had seen these moves before when Finn was trying to separate himself from a spot of trouble he'd landed in at Rugby.

Julian hid an inappropriate chuckle behind the raised bridle.

Finn leaned closer. "One name. And what you were looking for. It will save time and effort. On my part, I mean."

Something in Finn's countenance must have

clashed with the witless, glossy exterior because Cookson's eyes narrowed. "Bugger off."

"You chose the road, my friend," Finn replied and placed his palm on Cookson's brow as if assessing for fever.

Finn's lids fluttered as he staggered, and Julian stepped forward. Humphrey's hand circled his arm, holding him back.

After a long moment of silence broken only by the shaken breaths coming from Cookson and the plink of raindrops against the windowpane, Finn's hand dropped. His fingers flexed and closed in a tight fist before he spoke. "The Duke of Ashcroft," he whispered on a rough exhalation. "He wants the chronology."

The bridle slipped from Julian's fingers. "*Ashcroft?*"

"Holy hell," Humphrey breathed.

Cookson's response proved the validity of the report. "You bloody, grand bastard," he snarled. "You thieving trickster!"

"Correct on all counts." Bracing his arms on the block, Finn dropped his head to his hands. "A parade of ghastly images housed in your mind, sir. Thank you for that."

Cookson's throat pulled on a long swallow. "He read my bleeding mind, he did."

Julian advanced on the man before he had a chance to lodge another threat. He wedged Cookson's head against the post, his blood rioting through his veins. He could end this here. One snap to mitigate risk.

One snap to protect his family.

"Julian, *stop.*" Finn's plea was a dry rasp behind him. "If you," he added, directing the words to Cookson, "think my stealing your thoughts is upsetting, next time I'll scramble your brain like an egg."

"Not a word, *ever*." Julian closed his eyes, fighting the images Cookson's shirt collar was sending through him. "And your association with the Duke of Ashcroft is finished. Do we understand each other? We have people who could use your skillset on the Welsh coast. You leave tonight."

Humphrey stepped in and knocked aside Julian's hand, allowing the haunting visions to drain away. "You'd better take the offer, my friend. These two are what you would call civilized, but me, ah, you wouldn't be the first person I've killed, and you'd likely not be the last. But I'm trying to limit myself—and I'm fairly sure you're not worth going to hell over."

"Ashcroft," Cookson gasped. "What to tell him?"

Julian shared a look with Humphrey across the rank distance. "Don't worry. We'll take care of the Duke."

The undertaking was a foolish impulse.

One born of little sleep and the compulsion to return that distressing, wondrous sketch, which sizzled like a coal in her skirt pocket. Showing up at Julian's secluded quarters without escort suddenly seemed foolhardy.

Even for her.

However, she couldn't keep what served as evidence of his fascination and maintain her promise to suppress hers.

Exiting a copse of trees, she passed through two ancient stone pillars standing sentry, glancing around to ensure no guards monitored here as they did the main gate. During her morning session with Edward, he'd mentioned Julian would be engaged *elsewhere* this night—so here she was. After sneaking out a parlor window that had no sentry attached.

Moonlight splashed across the brick portico as she stepped onto it. Halting at the door, she replayed Simon's words: top desk drawer, right side, beneath spectacle case. She turned the handle. Locked. Sighing, she pulled a hairpin from her pocket, where it resided alongside the sketch. The metal felt cold to the touch, telling her the blaze emanating from the drawing was a figment of her passionate imagination.

It had been years since she'd picked a lock, but Finn had provided exhaustive lessons, and she'd been an apt pupil. Concentrating, she pressed her tongue against the back of her teeth and felt the hairpin settle in the tumbler.

The tantalizing scent hit her before the realization that she was not alone. Citrus, smoke, man. The tip of a muddy boot entered her vision as she glanced down. Oh, dear God in heaven, she was as doomed as doomed could be.

"I wasn't expecting you." He brushed her aside, his touch traveling like sunlight through her.

"Jules," she whispered directly into his ear. Stilling, he turned his head. Gazes locked, they stared as the night wrapped them in a mantle of radiant heat. "You're not going to believe why I'm here."

"Hmm…" He gave the hairpin a twist, and the door swing wide. "I just might."

She glanced at the line of trees just visible in the scattered moonlight. If she started running, she might be able to make it to the house before he caught her.

He issued an aggravated snort and took her by the

upper arm, hauling her inside, and with a swift kick, closed the door behind them. A rainbow of color, just as Simon had said, splattered the planks beneath her feet; canvases large and small—finished, blank, and somewhere in-between—were perched against the walls, the settee, the Chesterfield sofa. Nudes, landscapes, portraits. Wooden shelves holding tubes of acrylic and oil paint. Charcoal pencils, sketchpads. And on every surface lay ragged bits of cloth doused with the same colors that had hit the floor.

Shadow cloaked the bedchamber off the main room, but she noted the massive tester bed, the crimson counterpane lying in a twist upon the mattress. She tore her gaze away when her belly started to jump, her mind conjuring images it had no permission to conjure. Her senses unfurled like rose petals in the spring as she searched for equilibrium.

This was Julian's world, and the secret he had kept from her.

The urge to sink to her knees before a canvas and study the wild slashes of color until Julian made sense to her rolled over her like a wave. Because *this* man, she knew nothing of.

"I can explain why I—" She turned, her breath seizing.

Arm braced on the doorjamb, the other hanging limply by his side, Julian's aversion to this intimate examination of his life was evident in his unsettled, rippling aura. Eyes shadowed, shirtsleeve torn and bloody, he looked like a man on a precipice, wavering between surrender or a fight.

"Jules"—she crossed to him without hesitation—"you're bleeding."

His head fell back against the door. "I think bled is more apt."

He didn't stop her as she separated ruined linen

from his skin, his only response a harsh inhalation sucked between his teeth. His acquiescence alarmed her more than his bruised, torn flesh. "This is going to require stitches," she said and probed hesitantly, her stomach tightening as he winced. "At least it's a clean cut."

Like a knife would make.

Since it seemed the door held him up, Piper chose to let the presumption remain unsaid. Another time, another conversation.

"Didn't one governess quit"—he stood, lock-kneed as if the floor were undulating beneath him— "over your horrendous stitching skills?"

"Are you expecting daisies on your arm?"

He huffed out a startled laugh. "No."

She nodded, convinced enough for the both of them. "Then, my inferior skills will suffice. You need help. And for once, I'm going to give it."

He didn't seem to know how to take this, testing his shoulder with a stretch and an accompanying groan.

Had he ever let someone take care of him, she wondered?

As he calculated benefit-loss, a trickle of blood trailed down his arm and over his closed fist, and any opposition seeped away as if through a cracked teacup. With a sigh, he slid to the floor, propelling his long legs in an elegant stretch before him. His smoky eyes held hers the entire way down, daring in some manner she couldn't define.

She raised a brow. Tapped her toe on the floor, then mimed pulling a needle through fabric. Or in this case, skin.

"Desk. Bottom drawer. Left."

Much like Simon's directive for return of the sketch.

The mahogany desk would have made for fascinating study had she the time to search it. Mixed among the explosion of art supplies was proof of Julian's responsibilities: ledgers, mail, copious notes in his precise script. Silver spectacles lying by a book on Renaissance artists that was wedged open with a paintbrush. She took measure of the man, her heart breaking as she realized how little she truly knew of him.

Knocking aside emotion that did neither of them any good, she crouched behind the desk, finding needle and thread, scissors, bandages, a bottle of brandy, and an ointment that smelled horrific but promised much according to the label.

It seemed Julian prepared for a crisis.

Before rising, she hastily replaced the sketch, glad to be rid of a talisman she'd been unable to stop touching since Simon gave it to her.

Julian analyzed her with calm precision as she crossed to him, his hooded gaze having settled to the color of the mist that chaperoned her morning rides. She seethed inside but tried to hide it. That she'd not known this about him seemed a betrayal.

When it was simple.

His passion resided in this dwelling—and his passion was not *her*.

"No questions?" he murmured, breaking the charged silence.

She dropped to her knee before him, placing the supplies at her side. "Yes." Tucking back a lock of hair that had broken free of her chignon, she took the needle in hand. "How do I thread this thing again?"

He laughed roughly and closed his eyes, permitting her attendance. There were no battle lines drawn, as even a playing field as they'd ever entered. She took this discovery and held it close: his interminable self-possession could be disabled, the man beneath accessible should he allow the breach.

Piper knotted the thread, seizing the opportunity to examine him without his vigilant gaze holding her back. There were discoveries—a crescent scar beneath his nose, freckles scattered across his cheeks—when she'd once known him well enough to sketch a portrait not only of his gorgeous body but his dazzling mind.

He stiffened at the slide of needle through skin. At some point, she handed him the brandy, which he drank liberally. She wished to drink herself but worried it would affect her steady hand as she was no nurse, and this task was making her woozy. "So, this is how you can help me." She dabbed blood from the wound with a discarded paint rag, praying for an even stitch. "Cataloguing the auras."

He swallowed, his throat doing a supple pull above his open shirt collar, the slice of bronzed skin in startling contrast to the creamy linen. Peeking through the collared vee was a liberal amount of dark, coarse hair. Face flushed, she tracked back to her task. "Your little secret," she said, appalled the statement sounded wounded when it arrived.

"I was punished if the staff found paints in the house. And by punished, I mean savagely beaten and locked in my bedchamber without food or water until the viscount's temper settled. Which could be days. He thought art for the lower classes. Though painting gave me the only relief I found from the visions until I met you, so I kept going back to it, withstanding the abuse until I couldn't withstand it any longer." He gave a dismissive wave with his good hand, a release of two fingers from the brandy bottle. "It was my savior. My *normal*. Some days, my reason. When I ran, my art came with me, and my bastard of

a father didn't." His lip curled. "Although the viscountcy remains."

"Why hide it…" She tied off the thread and
clipped the loose ends with a snip, avoiding his gaze
should those soulful eyes of his slide open. "Why hide
it from me?"

His head dipped as he drew a clipped breath. She
thought he wasn't going to answer when he finally
did: "Self-preservation."

She swabbed at the blood pooling around the
slightly crooked stitches. This would not make a
handsome scar. "Absurd."

He clicked his tongue against his teeth.
"Perhaps."

Uncapping the ointment, she wrinkled her nose.
"This is putrid," she said, spreading it liberally over
the gash.

"To keep the wolves at bay, Yank."

"Am I a wolf, then?" she asked, wrapping a length
of gauze around his arm and tying it off.

He lifted his head, his gaze locking with hers. The
scent of his skin, the ointment, a tepid summer night,
and the sting of paint and turpentine swirled to form
an unbelievably tantalizing mix. Abrasive, ardent,
inviting. Wrapping her longing in an utterly per-
plexing package. Her body trembled, and she released a breath of frustration. Of torment. The flutter
in her stomach, the sensation raising the hairs on the
nape of her neck trumped sound judgment and her
promise to herself.

His lips canted, the suggestion of amusement
should she wait for it. As if he recognized what being
this close to him did to her.

She shook her head. *No.*

In response, he lifted his hand, thumb gliding her
lower lip, a silken sweep.

"What"—her words were like steam, faint and effervescent, dissolving over his skin—"are you doing?"

"Remembering."

Swaying, she fell forward, palms hitting the planked floor. He took control of the adjusted position, his fingers tangling in her hair and drawing her closer. "I can't—" She gulped the cluttered scents—hers, his, the room's. "I can't think when your hands are on me." In fact, she wasn't sure where the needle had gotten to. A jab for one of them was coming any minute.

"I know the feeling. Have always known it," he whispered, his confession a balmy caress. His lids fluttered as one of his infrequent smiles curved his lips.

She waited, breath held, letting her lids drift because, if he *were* to kiss her, it might startle less if she didn't see it coming.

And then…he did the worst, the sweetest, the most vulnerable thing she'd ever known him to do.

Like a child, he slid swiftly, silently, into sleep.

The boy's dreams had led her here.

Sidonie placed her palm on the sarsen stone and imagined those who had come before her. Wondered as her tears fell, how many tears had soaked this very spot. The village green was deserted, the night liquid, hushed, tranquil. His dreams had been filled with images of the mystical community being established in a manor across the field, the healer at its center, the earl's chronology their guiding treatise.

They were forming a society of misplaced souls without her—the most misplaced of all.

But the end of her torment was near. The granddaughter was going to liberate her from this repellant life. The healer was going to help Sidonie slay the dragon.

Before the dragon ate her alive.

"Patience," Sidonie whispered as her men circled her.

It took perseverance to win a battle like the one she and the boy—*Finn*—waged. He was taking, *oui*, but he was also giving.

He would hate to know how generous he had been.

It was quite simple: she needed to find them before they found *her*.

CHAPTER 10

*J*ulian roused from sensual slumber with Piper's voice drifting lazily through his mind. He frequently dreamed of her, but, ah, this one had been so intoxicating it would linger for hours. Possibly a day. He slid his hand over his belly to his aching cock and considered letting the notion of her rouse him in a thoroughly inspiring manner.

Yes, he resolved and stroked, sending a painful jolt through his shoulder.

What?

He blinked, puzzled, the details presented not adding up. Morning, but late judging by the sunlit strip sitting high atop the wall. His head lay on his bed pillow, but the hard planks beneath him were no bed. Shading his eyes against the spill of light, he went up on the arm not throbbing like the devil and kicked a thin woolen blanket from his body. *Bloody hell*, he thought as the night came flooding back. He was sleeping in front of the lodge's door and...

Piper's touch had been no dream.

Had she stayed? Would she risk such—

He didn't have to actually *see* her curled in a neat bundle on his sofa to feel the impact; his body vibrated like someone had teased a bow across it. As if the floor was made of ice, he got slowly to his feet.

Obviously, she would risk everything.

She lay on her side, hands folded beneath her cheek as if in prayer, hair a russet spill teasing the paint-spattered carpet. The counterpane from his bed had slipped to her waist, her luscious breasts doing a gravitational shift against the fabric of her dress.

She looked innocent, angelic even, when she was anything but.

Her invasion of his private space for some unfathomable reason called to mind that damned kiss.

Something he should have never started but wished he'd started earlier.

Dangerous thoughts, dangerous desires.

His cock hard enough to pound timber was an excellent sign he should wake her, send her back to the main house.

Helplessly, his gaze flicked to his bedchamber door. He'd never made love in the lodge; he'd only made art.

Recognition consumed him as he stood there debating. He realized the feeling was similar to one *after* sex, that instant of intimacy which, in his experience, immediately turned in upon itself and made you feel lonelier than when you'd started.

Only, he didn't feel lonely.

He felt *complete*—when he had yet to touch her.

Julian rocked back on his heels. Lifted his hand to his head and tried to rub the sensation out. *Idiot.* Seeing her thus was familiarity afforded a husband.

Or a lover.

Releasing a low hiss through his teeth, he again glanced toward his bedchamber, steps away from where she lay sleeping.

Piper let out a soft murmur, and he looked back to see a stockingless foot slide from beneath the counterpane and through a dazzling sunlit strip. Forming the drawing in his mind, he stepped in. Shadow dancing over the delicate arch, light over the bony point of her ankle. The contrast between grey silk, the golden hue of her skin, and the crimson counterpane would be extraordinary in oil. Her hand dropped from its tuck beneath her cheek, finding rest in an artistic curl that broke his creative control.

Crazy, crazy, crazy, he cautioned even as he reached for his sketchpad.

He whispered instructions to a sleeping woman. Her beauty held that kind of power. The delicate curve of her shoulder, the dainty spill of her fingers on the carpet, cupped as if asking the sky for rain. This was his lost place, where time, plans, worry, slipped away like smoke in a fierce wind. Where he forgot the title, those days in the gutter, his goddamn gift. The people he had sworn to protect.

His very life.

Here, there was nothing but light and shadow. Bone, sinew, skin. Curves, lines, shapes on paper. *Colors*. A multitude of them.

As Piper lay there, he gloried in taking her where *he* wanted her to go.

An hour later, maybe two, he came back to the present, found his hand stiff, his shoulder screaming, the sun a fierce burst outside the window.

The mental list came easily. Points that excited him; points that made him ill.

One. The house staff was aware of Piper's presence. Breakfast had been left on the stoop, as it was each morning, but the amount was doubled this morn. And included chocolate, which was certainly not for him.

Two. The sketches were only the foundation for a complete work. Oil, if he went with what best suited. Full length. In the garden, surrounded by a riot of pigment. Or, with less clothing, right back there on his bed.

Three. She was a heavy sleeper, as the day was sliding by and she continued to slumber without a care in the world.

Four—and this was the point that made his stomach knot. Made his heart pump in hard beats against his ribs.

She was searching. While he slept, she'd investigated. He noted the subtle shift of his ledgers; the movement of a canvas. Paints and brushes on a side table that had been on the floor.

What genuinely terrified—were she to go deeper —she now knew where to look.

He sipped tea, balancing the cup on his thigh as he tried to arrive at a compromise with himself. An alternative to the concept his body proposed: licking away the dab of paint on her wrist, lifting her skirt past her waist, and sinking his teeth into the supple flesh of her thigh.

She would scream when he found what she liked —and he would find what she liked.

But the deal, the damned promise and not only to her grandfather, was that he keep his hands, his cock, his cursed gift, to himself.

There were elements of his life he could prudently share. His artwork, his plans for the League. She now knew about the first and deserved to be part of the latter.

If he opened the door standing between them instead of straining to hold it shut, perhaps the influence she had over him would lessen. Friendship could flow in, friendship they'd shared before. It sounded logical, though he wasn't sure he believed it with his body poised and ready, pulse zipping through his veins as he watched her sleep.

He had never enjoyed watching someone sleep.

Moments later, Piper woke as he'd have expected. Alert in an instant, quelling an expression he couldn't decipher. The wheels in her mind whirled as she scooted to a sit, checked her clothing, evaluated the situation, surely his aura, before deciding on her strategy.

She would have made an excellent gambler, clever and fearless, able to make a bold choice when pressed figuratively against the wall.

He'd never seen someone vacillate less amidst disaster.

As she watched him watching her, her smile grew, though she brought her hand to her mouth to cover it. *Damn it.* He wanted to be a stern presence, even got so far as opening his mouth to admonish her for the inadvisable situation they found themselves in. But he couldn't come up with one reasonable statement as her delight seeped through his skin, unleashing his smile.

He shook his head, glanced at the detailed sketch, erotic in its stark simplicity, and wondered what the hell he was doing.

He did not want to be—*become*—lost in Piper Scott.

The stillness playing havoc with his nerves, he

pushed off the floor with a grunt, his shoulder stretching in protest. Placing the sketchpad on his desk, he turned to the breakfast tray, arranged a plate of food, poured tea. The visions he encountered were governable. No need to involve the healer. All the while, the intensity of her regard burned a hole through his thin cotton shirt.

Sidestepping the tempting puddle of stockings beside the sofa, he handed her the plate. Knocking aside a tube of shockingly expensive Dutch paint, he set her cup and saucer atop the table. "Breakfast, Lady Elizabeth, as your reputation takes its final bow."

Balancing the plate in one hand, with the other, she completed a quick modesty pat down her wrinkled bodice. Notwithstanding the bare feet, which she took the instance of his review to wiggle, she was otherwise covered. *Thank God*. Lifting her gaze to his, she brushed aside his comment with a flick of her fingers. "Another benefit of country living."

With this avowal, she commenced eating.

Delicate sips, poised bites, as if unchaperoned, barefooted, sleepy conversation over poached eggs, kippers, and toast was not only wholly acceptable but preferable. With a muted groan of capitulation, he flipped to a blank sheet in his sketchpad and settled back against the desk. The drawings he'd completed this morning pulsed on the pages beneath his fingers, but he was unsure if he wanted to share them. His image of her was drawn from a secluded place and likely a version of herself she didn't see when she looked in the mirror.

All she would see was his desire, chalked in every charcoal stroke. Trapping him with its tangibility.

He wanted to paint her, he thought in desperation. Sketches were a good start, although charcoal was not enough to capture the golden splash flowing through the window, the way it lit her skin where it struck her.

Not enough to capture the contradictions. Dreamy innocence and bold challenge. He shaded the stubborn tilt of her chin, struggling to portray the look. *Her* look. "Head up," he instructed, then banged his on the desk when he realized he'd said it out loud.

"So, the viscount is an artist."

He held up a hand, urging her to let him take another stroke. Releasing a tense breath, he stepped outside the sketch and looked up in time to see her slide her knuckle from her mouth, jam clinging to her bottom lip. Feeling like his brain was going to explode, he forced himself back to outlining the sweep of hair tumbling over her shoulder. "The artist is a viscount," he corrected. "He always was."

"The boy my grandfather located in the rookery…"

He didn't want to think, much less *talk* about that boy. This sketch was the *now*, taking shape in ways he'd not planned. Art calmed the chaos in his mind, and he wanted to embrace what calmed the chaos.

Only a healer's touch, if he let himself accept it, calmed more.

When he understood the silence was going to draw out like she'd placed him on a rack with her comment, he said so low he hoped she didn't hear, "A rebellious, furious young man. So bloody angry." He grimaced at the pathetic recollection. Maybe if he painted that boy, he'd retreat gracefully into the past, too.

"Your father"—she paused, twisting her skirt in her fist—"somehow, somehow you've been able to forgive him."

His heart stuttered, the pencil falling still in his

hand. If he could relieve her of the misery of having a parent who cared more for himself and had shown this deficiency quite cheerfully, he would. "Forgive is not the word I'd choose to describe how I handled ending my relationship with him."

"My anger has driven too many choices." She tapped her teacup on the table. "I don't want to be angry. I don't want him, and how little he cared for me, to matter. To shape one more step I make."

With a sense of hopelessness, he dove back into the sketch. He wasn't sure what he'd do if he touched her now, offered solace that would turn to something else. "A dart thrown at a dead man's portrait, I suppose, but I hate him for what he did to you. Or what he *didn't* do. Failed at the only significant task of his life." He tapped the pencil against his chest without looking up. Her gaze would be too open, too tempting. And his too hungry. "My father loathed the sight of me. Or rather, he was terrified." He shrugged, then swore as his stitches yanked. "I didn't know at such a young age not to trust him."

"Do you remember the Marston Ball? The first, that…my season. After my father's passing?" He heard her cup settle on the saucer, leather squeak as she shifted.

He edged a line, used the tip of his finger to shade. He needed to keep his hands occupied with this discussion pelting him like rocks, bruising his soul. He recalled more than she imagined. "Yes."

"A rainbow hit me when I entered that ballroom…" Her words died, and he wondered if she was chewing on her thumbnail as he'd seen her do of late. Another effort drawing his gaze to her mouth was not needed. "I wasn't a good reader of auras then, not yet. And I understood no specifics of these people's lives, or very little, which helps me pack them away in a valise of sorts. Everyone parroting each other, looking the same on the outside but strikingly different in my eyes. Violent slashes of red. Yellow, pure, and golden. Black." Her foot dropped into his range of vision, the toes slim and lovely, his gaze focusing on the delicate arch he'd tried all morning to put on paper.

What would it feel like to start kissing there and not stop until I hit her mouth?

"It was disconcerting, jarring. I felt like I knew things they didn't," she added.

"And…" He darted a glance at her, arousal beginning to gnaw at his restraint, when she likely had no plan to send him into a fever pitch.

"I couldn't be there." She wrenched forward, her bottom nearly sliding off the sofa. "I *can't* be there."

"You don't have to be there. You never have to be there. I've made sure you and Finn are beholden to no one. I can't protect you from society's censure, but I can protect you from being destitute."

"But when you marry I—"

"That *isn't* going to happen, Yank." He stared at his sketch, wondering what he'd done to deserve this conversation. "We've discussed this. Many times over the years."

She was silent, but he felt her gathering courage. His strokes gained in speed and intensity, preparing for the onslaught.

"Does Marianne Coswell visit you here?"

The pencil tilted in his hand, an unplanned contour going wide. "And this is your business, why?"

Her teacup clinked when he guessed she'd finished what he'd poured long ago. Feeling like a boy entering a headmaster's chamber after wreaking havoc, he found her hands joined tensely in her lap, fingers linked. And the look on her face…

She wasn't going to quit until he answered.

"Never here," he said on an irritated gust.

"But—"

"Harbingdon is my life, Piper. London is my duty."

"Well, your dutiful mistress mentioned you." She pressed back against the sofa, her throat pulling on a deliberate swallow. "At the reading."

"Brilliant," he whispered and raked his hand through his hair. He threw the pencil aside. *Fine*. Let her bludgeon him with his errant behavior. Beat him about the head and face with it. Just bloody fine.

"She said if you married, she would not deem to be your piece on the side. I believe that was how she phrased it." Piper rested her chin on her hand with a challenging look, sleek brow rising so faultlessly he bet she'd practiced in the mirror until she got the move just right. "And the ton calls me vulgar. She asked me to 'see' if you were wedded. In the future, that is." Her lovely mouth twisted in contempt, those magnificent eyes doing a languid roll to the ceiling. "If you had the chance to look into your future, gain *true* answers about life, would you waste it on that absurdity?"

Julian denied the urge to squirm as she gazed at him in expectation of what he had no clue, his temper starting to spit from being chastised over what was an entirely ordinary state of affairs for a man of his station. Guilt was not an appropriate emotion, even if guilt nipped at his heels. Thus, he took the familiar path like men the world over. "It means nothing."

"Means?"

"Enough!" He threw the sketchpad aside and rose to his feet. "You wish me to speak to you as I do Humphrey and that isn't going to happen." He crossed to an unfinished painting of the village green he was completing for the owner of the Blowing Stone Inn. He would, of course, funnel the proceeds back into the village. The main road needed assistance, and soon.

It gave him a sadistic thrill to imagine his father's reaction to the ninth Viscount Beauchamp selling a piece of art he'd created. An unflinching blow to the face, he knew without searching hard. Julian frowned and touched the painting. He had gone too dark in his interpretation of the sarsen stone in the green. Without looking at her, he grabbed a detail brush from the rusted can holding them, uncapped a tube, and set paint to bristle. "I'd have to have a stronger attachment for anyone to be anything"—leaning in, he lightened the stone with the most minute strokes —"on the side. Also, I'm careful not to transfer my gift to another generation."

He'd made that vow to himself years ago, and he damn well meant to keep it.

"Careful with your favors. It seems like an apt plan."

He grunted in lieu of comment as this was going nowhere.

"Thank goodness you're with Lady Coswell for the *right* reasons."

He stilled, turned to find Piper standing by the window, light cascading over her to settle in a butterscotch puddle on a floor dotted with a thousand colorful spills. Even in a crumpled gown that wasn't the best fit and her hair an utter mess, she was so beautiful, so flawless, he took a helpless step back. "This is beginning to feel like a lover's quarrel."

Her shoulders lifted and sank beneath wrinkled silk. "I wouldn't know, Jules."

Although he'd guessed as much, her comment

sent conflicting emotions through him. He looked away before she witnessed them. Jealousy; possession he had no right to feel. And absolute, cold, hard *relief*. "Reasoning has no play here, Yank. It's basic, god-damn *need*. A small part of me is there. The rest is elsewhere." He stabbed at the canvas as if the brush was a weapon, drops of paint splattering his fingers. "I've never given more, and I never will."

"Small part there, the rest elsewhere," she murmured. "Like your visions. A partial investment."

He frowned, this having never occurred to him. He had prodigious control in some areas, little in others. But there was *always* an element of restraint, examination. He never let go. He needed her gift greatly to do so, but he had sacrificed to protect her.

He was without options. Move forward with help, stumble back alone.

"My waistcoat. By the door, I think." His hand trembled, and he withdrew the bristles from the canvas. "Could you please...the money clip in the left pocket?"

He heard her cross the room, bare feet a soft tap over wood, carpet, then back to wood. When she got close, her scent overwhelmed the formidable one of linseed oil, turpentine, paint. Circling, ensnaring, making him question spilling his life like an open bottle of brandy at her feet.

Wordless, she waited, her gentle breaths mixing with the sound of his pounding pulse.

"I need your help. I don't want to touch that"—he pointed an elbow to the clip she held in her hand—"without you."

"Are you trying to make me angry? Jules, you don't have to ask."

Cleaning the bristles with a stained rag, he placed the brush back in the can. "Come. The sofa. Or the floor. Not here." He shook his head. "Not near the paintings."

"Julian?"

Her eyes were an extraordinary mix. Dark green, a patina you'd find in the most remote part of the forest, but upon keen inspection, dappled with enchanting specks the color of cinnamon. He doubted he could recreate them to even half their beauty if he tried. As he stood there deliberating, imagining a brush in his hand and her eyes unfurling beneath it, the gash in his shoulder began to thump in time to his heartbeat, pulling him back.

"Tell me," she urged, her fingers curling around the clip. It was an expensive piece, a lion etched in silver on its front. Possibly a family crest. Humphrey had left the runner with the bills contained within, so they had not stooped to beating *and* robbing him.

Except of the clip.

"The League receives items from our contacts in various locations. I read them to ascertain whatever I can." He dropped the rag to the floor. "I need to do that with this piece, but the visions are getting stronger. Or my gift is."

She flipped the clip between her hands, her gaze drilling into him.

"I've lost consciousness twice, once hitting my head rather hard on the hearth in my study. Scared the life out of Finn, although he knows head wounds bleed like the very devil. I woke to find him retching in my rubbish bin. Pathetic nurse, that one." With a crooked smile, he touched a faint mark on his temple. "My new motto: better to read in an open space."

She pressed her lips together, struggling to gather her words as her cheeks flushed a lovely pale pink. "If you don't tell me everything, Julian, so help me—"

"I'm getting trapped," he said in a rush.

She lifted her hand, the money clip glinting in the sunlight. "Trapped?"

"I'm easily able to step into the otherworld. The problem is—"

"Stepping out."

Leaving her, he went to one knee before the sofa. "Sharp edges and gifts"—he indicated the table as he shoved it aside—"are not a good match."

She followed, lowering herself to the carpet. "Being trapped in a dashed vision isn't cause for mirth, Jules."

Ahead of what he suspected might follow, his gut started to ache, his hand to tremble. Closing his fingers into a tight fist, he settled back on his heels. "If you start to see something, something *I'm* seeing, damn it, cut it off, let me go." His gaze met hers, defying her to look away. "If the experience transfers, I don't care how lost I am, *let me go.*"

When she didn't respond, he grasped her arm and pulled her close. "Do you understand?"

"Yes"—she yanked her arm free—"*yes.*"

He released a fast breath. "Okay."

It was a simple thing to take the clip from her, the metal warm from her grip. He closed his eyes as the vision tore through him, swift, powerful—and insistent he step inside.

With a harsh entreaty, Piper reached for him, tried to pull him back.

But he was already gone.

The room he entered was cavernous. High ceilings, tapestry-covered walls, hefty furnishings. A masculine chamber. Julian breathed in Frankincense on his first full breath, onerous, cloying. Choking. In one corner, a man huddled over an immense round-table stately enough to have been Arthur's. Books were stacked on every surface, volumes discarded topsy-turvy on the floor. The man turned pages rapidly, searching with an urgency born of terror. Julian felt the fear, pulsing as intensely as the wound on his shoulder. He moved closer, his gaze locking on a signet ring on the man's pinky. A ruby centered on the crest of a lion with bared teeth.

The Duke of Ashcroft wore just such a ring, Julian recalled and curled his fingers around the money clip. If he could just get a good look at the man's face. Piper shouted to him, beseeching. Along the narrow tunnel of his vision, he saw her, ghostly, an apparition.

"Go back," he screamed, but no sound traveled from his lips.

Julian watched in fascination as the man held out his hand, a tiny flame flickering to life a digit above his open palm. It wavered like flames caught in the wind, then ruptured with a wondrous, sparking burst.

Against his will and with it, Julian stepped closer, entranced, mesmerized.

∽

Piper ripped the money clip from Julian's hand and tossed it aside. His eyes fluttered as the hint of an odd fragrance filtered to her, then he broke their connection, shoving her from the otherworld.

A tear traced her cheek, sorrow she scrubbed away. He wasn't denying her that effortlessly.

Leaning over him, Piper cupped his jaw, a touch as gentle as if he were made of glass. The abrasion from his unshaven skin sent a dizzying rush through her, reminding her what she risked by touching him in this way.

He was not hers to caress, to want, to *love*.

But he was hers to protect.

His heat seared at each touchpoint where skin met skin, the slide of air from his parted lips a tantalizing sweep across her cheek. She fought a cascade of emotion, none stronger than yearning long contained. "Come back to me," she whispered, running her thumb along his whiskered jaw. "Come back, Jules."

Frantic as the silence drew out, she tilted his head and pressed her mouth to his. Her entire focus centered on him as their long-ago kiss roared through her mind. Potent, sweet memory. She recalled how Julian had touched her in exceptional detail, however brief, and the extreme pleasure born of his touch. Having little experience to draw on, she mimicked what she remembered, placing her tongue at the corner of his mouth, tracing the seam, moving her lips over his, begging for entrance.

Begging him to return to her.

He grasped her shoulders, his lids lifting to reveal irises gone so dusky they edged to black. His aura radiated molten gold, as if she stared directly into a sun blistering her to her core. The wound on his shoulder had bled through the bandage and left a crimson trail down his arm.

Her heart broke, doomed with love.

"If this is how you're healing others, Yank, I have to object."

Somehow, she found the courage to ask: "Are you going to object now?"

His gaze lowered to her breasts, straining with each urgent breath against the bodice of her gown. Then he murmured one word—*no*—threaded his hand through her hair and brought her to him. She fell, a mad tumble, but he knew how to find the perfect fit. A skillful roll and he was atop her, pinning her in place. His other hand went to her cheek to still her movement as his lips covered hers—a rough invasion.

No gentle foray, no polite request, his need rolled over her as powerfully as a wave over the shore, ripping her feet from beneath her and plunging her into a chaotic, sensual sea. She accepted his challenge, opening like a flower beneath him. He tasted of mint and tea and felt like the answer to a prayer.

To deny him never occurred to her—and if it had —she would have rejected the offer.

With a throaty sound of pleasure, he settled between her legs, which with no hesitation, sprawled wide to give him better access. He adjusted his body, a subtle hip shift, once more, then, oh, yes, *there*. Her nipples instantly peaked, scraping against fabric, so pleasurably sensitive she sighed as the air left her lungs and entered his mouth in a sharp burst.

Desire poured through her; ablaze, covetous, she seized each new sensation. "Jules," she gasped, her head falling back. "*More.*"

In impatient fistfuls, he yanked her skirt high as he found her lips, bringing her back into the kiss. Their bodies melded beautifully, naturally, pelvis to pelvis, each peak met with a contrasting valley, hot flesh separated only by thin, damp layers.

Unlike their sweet encounter long ago, this was a frantic, erotic *battle*. His tongue engaging, delving until she had no choice but to match his rhythm. She arched into him, the swollen weight of his shaft pressing against her thigh. She should have been repelled, when instead, she realized a wild urge to grasp his solid length, memorize each single, stiff inch of him.

This is madness.

It was the last coherent thought to funnel through the carnal haze surrounding her.

Her arms rose to encircle his neck, her hands diving into the silken strands she had imagined touching in a hundred wicked dreams. The scent in the room—citrus, man, paint—lit her nose and her senses to a peak. She liquefied, melting into the wooden planks beneath her, pliable, mastered by his touch. His lips trailed her cheek, her jaw, a diverse seduction she couldn't record or prepare for.

Her pulse had centered to a relentless thump between her legs. Never, never had she felt this reckless, this consumed by need, raw, urgent, indescribable.

It was an onslaught as he took complete and utter possession of her mind and body.

"God, Piper, I want," he whispered on a rough exhalation. His lashes fluttered, revealing frantic, glazed eyes gone deep slate. "I want…"

"Then take," she answered against his cheek. Following his example, she nipped his jaw, then laved it with her tongue, deciding his skin tasted like ambrosia.

His harsh oath evaporated in the sensual mist surrounding them as he trailed his fingers along the nape of her neck, a teasing dance over her shoulder. Along her collarbone, where he dipped his calloused fingertip inside the lace edge of her gown. Her breath too frayed to speak, she bumped her breast against his palm. With a low hum of approval, he curled his fingers around the sensitive mound, taking firm possession.

His thumb brushed her nipple, once, twice, then stayed to circle, over and over until she began to lose the battle, a familiar defeat. She had touched herself in the darkness of her bedchamber many times while thinking of Julian, wanting the sensations she created to come from his fingers, not her own.

Now, maybe her dream to break apart in his arms would be fulfilled.

She expressed her hope that it would without saying a word.

Seeking a resolution to the delirious wonder of his hard length pressed against her thigh, she slid her hands down his back and helped direct his movement. His shirt was free from his trousers, her fingers tracing bare skin before she realized what she was about. His hair fluttered about his face as he pulled back to stare at her, silken strands brushing her cheek in a charged touch.

Cheeks flushed, breath ripping from his lips, he looked bewildered and famished, his gaze so savage she marveled she was able to hold it.

"Is this how you look when you lose yourself in a painting?" she asked, as his pupils flared the color of a stormy sea.

And his aura, oh, his aura was something to behold.

She'd never imagined desire could destroy. Promises, rules, plans. She now understood why he'd fought so diligent a campaign, putting distance, rationale, heavy furniture when the situation called for it, between them.

She dug her nails in his back just where it sloped to his bottom, scraped his skin as she traveled in an abrasive glide to his shoulder.

"You unman me," he said, his admission thrilling her to the tips of her toes. Which was not the kind of thing a gently-bred young lady should be thrilled by.

Incorrigible. Like everyone had always said.

Hardly knowing what she was about, she turned her head and caught his thumb between her teeth.

She liked when he used his teeth on her.

His brow dropped to hers as he released a staggered breath. "You're not helping."

"Our goals differ," she whispered and slicked her tongue over his thumb as she sucked the calloused tip. His lashes fluttered against her skin before he recaptured her mouth without finesse or any of the restraint the ninth Viscount Beauchamp was renowned for. Yanking her gown low, he drew her peaked nipple between his lips, and her world spun away. The caress flowed to the outer reaches of her body, to her toes and the pads of her feet.

She felt reborn, appreciated in a way she'd never imagined she would be.

She strained to reach him, crawl inside and gather *more*, whispered that very word, and surprisingly, he acquiesced. His hand left her breast and skated down her body: belly, hip, thigh. Locating her warm core without hesitation, his finger shot through a slit in her drawers and grazed moist flesh. She groaned and arched, her nipple bumping his teeth.

Pounding on the door brought them apart like a vase smashed against the floor. They scattered, a body-width between them as their eyes locked.

Her heart hammered in her chest. Her hair had come loose from the few pins remaining through the night and it lay in a tangle beneath her. Skirt at her waist, breasts exposed, she was utterly undone. Julian didn't look much better, breath rushing forth as if he'd dashed from the main house and collapsed atop her. She held up a finger, opened her mouth, then shook her head and flopped to her back. There were no words. She doubted she'd recover, find herself— the woman without him—after this.

"Bloody, Humphrey," she whispered and pressed

her bottom into the planks to keep from tucking into his body.

Julian called out a warning. "Don't come in! She's here. Give us a moment." Then he rolled to his back, arm going over his eyes, chest working beneath blood-stained linen.

"Are you all right?" she asked when she found her voice. He had popped one of her less-than-skillful stitches if the blood streaking his arm was any indication. His hair shot from his head at all angles, a tempting mess. A bead of sweat tracked his jaw; she was compelled to lick it off.

She tried, with minimal success, to avoid staring at the hard ridge tenting his trouser close.

"*Brilliant.*" He lifted his elbow just enough to train one irate steel-grey eye on her. "I told you to let me go! Instead, you start *this*? And damned if I wasn't set on finishing it."

"I had no other option. I wasn't going to leave you there." She worked her bodice in place as it seemed she'd lost him on this side of the world. "Heavens, the real thing is better than any description in any book. And statues, oh, Julian, they have nothing on you." She saw him stiffen, heard his aggravated snort and felt she should add, "Don't go ruining it. Not when I can still taste you on my lips."

He dropped his arm, closing off her view. "I was rough. I'm sorry. The vision. Lack of control." He wagged his fingers. "Too far, too fast. Need just about…swallowed me whole."

The steady pulse returned to her nether regions as she imagined those artistic fingers touching her slower, whatever this meant. More and at a longer interval is what it said to her. "We can go *slower*?" she asked on a breathless whisper.

He shot to his feet, trying to gather himself

THE LADY IS TROUBLE

when she could have told him it was a hopeless endeavor. He looked like he'd been forced through a keyhole, the darling man. A rumpled, bloody, sweaty mess, he cracked the door, spoke to Humphrey in an aggrieved tone, then closed it with a snap.

Jamming his back against the frame, he crossed his arms and regarded her with dismay. "You have to go. I...this..." He shrugged quite forlornly. His aura was a kaleidoscope, a mad churn, worse than the spill of color across his carpet.

He was slipping through her grasp, returning to his place as her protector, one fleeting second at a time. "Go? With Humphrey?"

He dropped his head to his hand and rubbed as if he could wipe out his thoughts. "Minnie's there, too."

"Oh, no. You're going to send me back with both of them?" She scrambled to find a better solution than a cart ride to the house with two disapproving chaperones. "Wait until dark. I'll sneak back. Use the kitchen entrance and straight up to my bedchamber without stopping."

"No chance to get you out of here without notice when you look this"—he paused, rubbed his temple harder—"compromised."

"You don't look so wonderful yourself, Jules." Although he did. Good enough to eat, *damn him*.

He raked his hand through his hair. "What do I tell them? Although I see you object, can you give us until early evening"—his head went against the door with a thump—"as I was about to have my way with Piper."

She rose on unsteady legs. When she reached him, she laid her hand on his muscled forearm and tried to suppress her intense yearning. Could she help it if the dusting of hair beneath her fingers enticed beyond belief? "*Were* you about to have your way with me?"

His gaze left its inspection of the ceiling and drilled into her. Beneath her fingers, he trembled. His eyes flashed, the amber flecks competing with his flushed skin.

Taking her by the arms, he turned and crowded her against the door. "What do you think?" Then he bent low and brought her high, allowing his long body to press into hers, as solid as the wood at her back, neither giving mercy as he reclaimed her lips. She fisted her hands in his hair and moaned, the kiss racing back to where they'd left off, tongues tangling, hips beginning to mate. *Oh*, like what had occurred on the floor but not. Without his weight, this joining felt wonderfully *different*.

"Send them away," she whispered.

Those words, spoken without intention, broke the spell.

Julian ended the kiss gradually, skimming her cheek, her ear, a silky whisper. Then his brow settled on hers as he released a sigh and her body, allowing her to do a languid slide down his. When her toes hit the floor, she sought his gaze, but long, dark lashes conveniently hid it. His hands went to the door, braced on either side of her shoulders, fingers splayed.

He appeared a man cataloging the taste of a delicacy he didn't anticipate consuming again.

After a charged moment, Julian tapped his knuckle on the wall, then peeled himself away until they were no longer touching. Their harsh exhalations were the only sound in the room, aside from the distant call of a woodlark. She wished she could say something to erase the resigned expression from his face, like a hard swipe with one of his rags across canvas. The smell of paint and linseed oil would pose an erotic challenge until the day she died.

"I can see you shutting down, turning away from me, from us, from *this*. It isn't a surprise. So Jules Alexander, it pains me."

"What isn't a surprise is your arguing with me about this," he growled, his gaze going hot, his aura flaring around him.

His scorching regard only made her burn as she recalled how skillfully he'd touched her, how he seemed to anticipate precisely what she needed and *where*, when she'd had no idea how to direct him. She'd never imagined longing this intense, hunger and hopelessness burrowing deep. The combination was horrific, a dreadful masterpiece. "This is my burden. For not letting you go, as you've begged me to from practically the first day we met."

He had started across the room, sidestepping canvases, brushes, and rags, but her comment stopped him short. The glance he threw at her was as loaded as the pistol she'd seen in his desk drawer. "That is utter rubbish."

"At least you're not proposing another trip to Gloucestershire."

He went to one knee, as dejected as the discarded stockings and muddy boots he knelt before. He toyed with her stocking without looking back, broad shoulders lifting and falling in resignation. "What in the hell do you want from me, Yank?"

She knotted her fingers behind her back. "Can I return the question?"

An emotion she couldn't decipher crossed his face. "No."

"I want you to share your knowledge, so I'm better equipped to manage the experience next time."

"My *knowledge*." He expelled a sound somewhere

between a laugh and groan. "Like we're beside the stream on the earl's estate, discussing essays from one of my textbooks. How do you even—" He flinched, and her stocking slipped from its cradle in his palm. She wondered what vision the thin wisp of silk had pushed into his mind.

"One of your textbooks," she repeated, the memory of those days distressing when she considered how much had changed. "What chapter?"

His eyes when they met hers shimmered like a rainy mist just before dawn. His hair was longer than she'd ever seen it, dusting his collar in dark twists. And his face…

At this moment, she *loathed* that she found him so beautiful.

"Chapter?" he asked.

Jealousy scorched a white-hot hole through her belly. "You completed the entire book with Lady Coswell. What chapter did we make it to?"

He went back to his study of her stockings. "I'm as likely to answer that as I am to grab a lit fuse and shove it between my teeth."

She wrenched the door open and slammed it behind her. It was only when she was to the cart, blasting by a disconcerted Humphrey and a wide-eyed Minnie, that she realized she'd left her boots on Julian's paint-splattered floor and her stockings like a shamefaced witness in his hand.

CHAPTER 11

*Who walks the fastest, but walks astray, is only fur-
thest from his way.*
   ~Matthew Prior

$\mathcal{J}$ulian traversed the uneven footpath leading to the stables, the saddlebag in his hand a sound reminder of his impru-dence. His mood was foul, best left to fester alone, although Henry trailed at his heel, sensing his master needed him most this day—the morning after Julian had made a grievous error in judgment and turned his world, his soul, upside down.

The wildflowers edging the trail brought his dis-position even lower because he knew Piper would have taken joy in the sight. Joy in the crisp scent of pollen and earth riding the air.

Joy in *everything*.

He shoved the stable door aside with a grunt, his shoulder wound stretching to an intolerably painful degree.

The stitches were as uneven as expected.

And the scar was never going away, a Piper Scott brand burned in his flesh.

As if his fevered dreams since that kiss on her nineteenth birthday had not been enough, he'd decided making love to her on the floor of his art studio might better the situation.

Bloody, bloody hell.

If only his disgrace would jettison the memory of her teeth marking his neck, her sigh of pleasure as he finally touched her as he'd yearned to. When he'd lowered his body to hers, her eyes had gone this extraordinary bottle-green, blurred and wispy around the edges, just as they would, he imagined, if he slid inside her.

She was an angel in his arms and a determined, independent fury out of them.

With a curse, he tossed the saddlebag to the floor. He was angry that she'd chosen to bring him back from the otherworld in such a manner, but mostly, he was angry with himself for wanting her so desperately.

And for so long.

At its base, greater need than any he had known existed. A primal compulsion to ease his hunger was his only excuse.

He was just a simple, stupid man, after all.

Besides, she'd goaded him. Teasing touches, the daring glint in her eyes. As if he needed encouragement to misbehave. He'd misbehaved with any number of women, and it had not mattered one whit, which Piper had pointed out as bluntly as a man.

As if anything he'd experienced without her compared to anything he'd experienced *with*.

Piper *meant* something.

No easy tangling of limbs, this situation.

If he were honest with himself, he'd been fascinated from the start. In his book, no matter the page, Piper was penciled in the margins.

From that first moment on the earl's drive, when he'd stepped from the carriage delivering him from Seven Dials and noted a golden shimmer by his boot. He'd grasped the locket, and the vision had been clear, compelling, and for the first time, *restorative*. Her lovely face came to him, yes, but also such a potent *sense* of her. Loneliness, determination, recklessness, generosity, the characteristics that made Piper so unique.

So damned maddening.

An instant connection unlike any he'd ever experienced, then or now.

She'd joined his family before she ever saw his face.

Before he ever truly saw hers.

They'd become quick friends, his attachment already in place. Those enchanting summers, home from Rugby, and then Oxford, where they'd conversed about numerous topics, forthright conversations unlike any he conducted except with Humphrey. Her wit, her fearlessness, her vitality had utterly riveted, and he'd been hard-pressed to turn away.

This before his desire began to be a hindrance.

She'd been discarded, left to her own maneuvers —which were habitually foolish and impulsive. Desperate cries for attention. When he returned to the earl's manor each summer, he found her isolated, hungry for knowledge, for companionship. He saw himself in her—lonely and struggling to make sense of a supernatural gift while stranded among those lucky enough to be deemed *normal*.

This mirror of insight only heightened his feelings.

And, for a while, he'd given her what he'd never given anyone—a view into the mind of the introspective lad. A lad who'd longed for his father's acceptance and upon receiving the opposite had turned into a very wrathful person indeed. He'd shared what it felt like to be forgotten and abused because she understood as well as anyone he'd ever known.

Then, that final summer, God, he would never forget.

She simply grew up.

He'd stepped from the carriage to find her waiting. The day disagreeable, as he recalled, stormy and dismal, but when she'd thrown her arms around him, there had been an enormous shift. Sunlight flooded his vision, dispelling those wicked clouds. Breasts clearly defined and pressing against his chest, a curious new scent layering her skin. Those details had gained his rapt attention, but the realization of how much he'd missed her, the list of things he had to tell her, collected like treasures, had acted like a mallet to the head.

Standing on that pebbled drive in a misting rain, he'd never felt more accepted for precisely who and what he was.

The conclusion had been clear: *this is my person*—the other half of my soul.

In the days that followed, to bring some semblance of control, he began to sketch her, bringing her, though she was unaware, into a very intimate space. A space he shared with no one.

Confessions on bits of foolscap.

And then the birthday kiss.

She'd caught him on the back lawn after a drunken night of roughhousing with Humphrey, the brooch he'd given her earlier in the evening pinned to her collar. The encounter had been sweetly inno-cent and impossible to deny, as she was.

He retrieved his saddlebag and hooked it in place atop his horse. The earl had presented a lifetime challenge with his dying breath.

She is not yours.

Perhaps not, but his desire hadn't abated.

And no matter Harbingdon's steadfast fortifica-tions, there were no guards posted at the entrance to his heart.

"Headed out, are you?"

Julian squinted into the sunlight tumbling through the stable door. Dashed if he wanted to deal with anyone right now, even his best friend.

"Mayfair bound, it looks," Humphrey said, settling in if the sound of his bulk perching against the door was any indication.

Julian tightened the saddlebag strap and gave it a good jerk. "The Duke of Ashcroft holds a mid-summer gala at season's end. I want to see the room from the vision before we approach him."

"Fire from his fingertips." Humphrey dragged his boot across the straw-covered floor. "That's a new one. Has to be what happened at Scamp's hotel, both times. Meaning, he can't control it for shit. Though it looks like, by breaking into your townhouse, he's trying to."

The silence lengthened as Julian adjusted his bridle and checked the stirrups. He wished Humphrey would leave him in, well, there was no way to leave him in peace, but there was a way to leave him alone. "Is that it?" he asked, darting a glance over his shoulder.

Humphrey shrugged, gaze rising to the rafters. "I don't think bolting outta here in a black mood, alone, mind you, is the best idea."

Julian thumped the saddle. "I've taken this route a hundred times."

Humphrey pushed off the door with a growl. "Not with them on our tail, you haven't. Finn's dreaming every night, telling us they're getting closer. You think to ignore that?"

"I'll watch my back. It's not me they're after. Danger doesn't place us on ice, Rey, unable to move. The League is always going to be vulnerable, and I need this information."

"My advice, take some time to think about this." When Julian failed to respond, Humphrey blew out a tense breath. "I can't leave today. We have someone arriving from Whitechapel. Blackmon. Clairvoyant. Worked on the docks. Good head for figures and likes children." He gestured in the direction of the house. "I may have him tutor Simon, the squirmy little bastard."

"I assume Blackmon can shoot straight?"

Humphrey waved the question away as if it were a fly in his face. "What choice is there on the docks? Someone gets gutted every day."

"A clairvoyant steward sounds enchanting as the position is currently vacant." Julian yanked gloves from his coat pocket and tugged them on, tucking between the fingers to tighten the fit.

"Can't be worse than anyone else we've placed in a job they've never in their life undertaken." His lips canted, the topic a familiar argument between them. "Since you insist everyone employed here be able to make magic, shoot fire from their eyeballs or something."

"I do insist. We'll be lightly staffed until we're not." Since they'd been talking crack shots and pro-tection, Julian checked the pistol in his boot, the cold metal caress relieving a little of his tension. "You're the only ungifted person I'll ever trust in this lifetime."

"Oh, ah, thank you very much, too," Humphrey snarled as he kicked aside a pile of hay littering his path.

"For?"

"Leaving it to me to tell Scamp you went running to London with your tail between your legs."

"I don't care what you tell her, you just keep her in your sight every *minute*," Julian said between gritted teeth as he led his horse from the stable. In the yard, he grasped the pommel and swung into the saddle. The black danced to the side, and Julian reined her in with a deft shift. "Her pattern is to rebel when denied."

"Denied, huh?"

"She followed me right into the vision, Rey. I looked back, and there she was." He drew a gloved hand down his face, still panicked to recall her entering the otherworld. His hell, not hers. "I don't want her there, but I don't know if I can leave without her. How disturbing is that?"

"It's a damned mess any way you play it." Humphrey squinted as he looked up at Julian. "Who knew she was going to end up being such a beauty?"

"Are you listening to me? I'm talking about *protecting* her." In any case, her beauty wasn't the main draw. It was her wit. Her nimble mind. The way she challenged him; the way she kept him off-kilter. And, if he must admit, how she'd always approached him charmed him right down to his toes, like cracking him open and looking inside was the most essential quest she'd ever undertaken.

Humphrey grabbed the halter as Julian tried to trot past before anything he was thinking tumbled out of his mouth. The black nickered in response and danced on the lead. "I saw her, Jule. I saw *you*. The chit about took my head off on the ride to the house when Minnie was the one at fault. Her idea to intrude!" He stepped back in disgust. "Did you ever consider that you're exactly what that reckless girl needs? She's exactly what *you* need? And maybe, just maybe, the earl, that old fool, was wrong about everything?"

She is not yours.

Julian dug his thigh into the horse's flank and wheeled her around. Torment to be fascinated by the one woman you couldn't have. Why, when London was full of women ripe for the plucking, did he only want *her*?

Had never wanted anyone *but* her.

Dirt and grass flew as he galloped from the yard without a backward glance.

As he crossed the windswept field, a phrase he'd learned at university circled his mind: *fuoco nelle vene.*

Fire in the veins.

Piper Scott was fire in his veins. And as he was about to consider, fire was a ruthless power best left undisturbed.

The crickets in the ragged bush edging the portico were screeching, their chirp shattering an otherwise hushed night. Even after years spent in the country, whether here or one of Julian's estates, Humphrey wasn't used to the sound, as unpleasant as a streetlamp's glare cutting through a crack in the draperies.

He rested against a column, his cheroot an orange glow across his fingertips, smoke drifting about his head and mixing with what he *had* come to appreciate about country living: air so clean and clear you could drink it. Layers of smells that made a body want to fall into them like they were a feather mattress. Flowers, grass, and something—he rubbed the cheroot between his fingertips, deciding maybe it was just good old dirt.

He sighed, tempted to leave his station and track Piper down.

Keep her in sight. Blast, what a bitter pill this girl and the calamity that followed her was to swallow.

Taking a final drag, Humphrey lifted his leg and stabbed the cheroot out on his boot, then slipped the stub in his trouser pocket with a grimace of equal parts amusement and embarrassment. Minnie complained something fierce about the things littering the ground. He didn't need two harping females, that was certain.

Another hour passed without a murmur, until Humphrey suspected he and Julian were wrong. Maybe Piper had grown out of her hotheaded decision-making.

In the end, nothing had changed, and they weren't wrong.

Thudding footfalls sounded, and his stomach fell. "Coming down the back stairs, heading for the scullery entrance," Edward whispered, his words halting, uncertain, as if he delivered information he should not. The boy had taken a liking to Piper. He was sleeping again and working on his gift, although he'd had no dreams that would benefit the League at this juncture and darn if Humphrey hadn't asked. As was the way, in the process of working with her, Piper had twisted the boy around her finger, like she did to most without exertion. Men, women, children, dogs. His call for the staff to watch her this evening had been met with more than a few frosty glances.

Waving Edward away with murmured thanks, he

rounded the house, a headache arriving in the center of his head. *Bullseye*. Damn the girl. If anything happened to her, Julian would never forgive him, a guaranteed fact no matter feelings denied on all sides.

Like he believed that horseshit.

He was responsible for the two of them and had been since the beginning, an anvil resting squarely on his chest and at times sucking up all his oxygen. Stuck in the middle, between a rock and a hard place. Piper, he guessed, was the rock. Julian, he laughed at this, because he had to do something or he'd start shouting, was the hard place.

He watched Piper's head, covered in a ridiculous, frilled bonnet, peek from the scullery doorway. *My God*, he thought, sorrowful for whoever ended up marrying her, if Julian wasn't going to accept the challenge. At least the pathetic sod would never be bored, but he wasn't likely to live long enough to appreciate his delightful existence, either. Frankly, Humphrey wasn't in the mood to pansy around. Wordplay was not his gift.

Truth be told, he was highly annoyed *and* disappointed.

"Julian sure had you pegged," he snapped as she stepped from the shadows.

She gasped, stumbled on the uneven step and propelled herself into the yard. A leather satchel, one of Julian's, was tucked neatly under her arm. Her gown was designed for travel; the boots on her feet weathered and perfect for tracking through the muck.

Humphrey pressed his finger and thumb against the bridge of his nose to hold back the headache. "You truly deemed to try this? With the danger surrounding you?"

Her head tilted, gaze seeking his. Moonlight fluttered over them, stealing through the scattered clouds, and her face became visible before being thrown back into darkness. But he'd seen enough. A fierce expression, and it was no longer a girl's face but a woman's. A woman who loved Julian more than anyone, if Humphrey's bet was sound, and one who had his best interest, no matter how senseless her design, at heart.

Oh, hell. Her eyes were that roaring green Julian told him to watch for. And he never argued with Jule over colors. *Blast it*, he swore, consigning his best friend to Hades for leaving him with this mess.

"He's going after the room from the vision," she said, tucking the satchel under her arm, perhaps preparing to run for it. As if she could make it ten paces without him catching her. Him or the ten guards posted around the house.

"I know what's he going after." Fear, rarely engaged, tunneled through his belly. Dread, because Piper had gone directly to the point without lying, which was her norm when pressed, and the bloody simple fact they shared the same concern.

He believed it insanity Julian had ridden off to London on his own, but he didn't want to admit this to Scamp Scott, of all people.

"The vision, I can't quite explain..." Her lips pressed as she struggled. Again, a spike of unease hit him. This woman had never lacked for words, not once in her *life*. "It was like being pressed between two sheets of vellum. No room to move." Stepping closer, moonlight hit her just so. Humphrey noted the desperation shaping her features, the worry lines drifting from her eyes, her mouth. She grasped the satchel like the battered leather would bring answers if she wrung it hard enough. "I had to pull him back, pull him out. And there was a hesitation, like he didn't *want* to return. I was terrified I'd have…have to leave him there."

Humphrey heaved a huge sigh, itching to light another cheroot. Or break open a bottle of brandy and guzzle the entire thing. "I can't keep him from searching for that room, Scamp." *But I can stop you.*

"Oh." She frowned, as if stopping Julian had never occurred to her. "I know that." She managed a surprised laugh, but what the heck she found amusing he didn't know. "Heavens, Humphrey, I only know I must be there when he finds it."

"You must be there when he finds it," he said, feeling as if he'd drunk the brandy, and his mind couldn't keep up. The ground tilted as control shifted to the sprite standing before him. A tiny thing, her head barely reaching his elbow, harmless if you judged only the physical, but she'd just worked him over rougher than a hustler on the streets of Bethnal Green.

Her head slanted in question: *you agree with me?*

His hand went out in a gesture of helplessness.

She danced from one dirty boot to the other, hugging the satchel close. "You hulking beast, you know I'm right. Bring the bloody battalion if that's what it takes."

With a violent oath, Humphrey brushed past her and into the house, the scullery deserted at this hour except for the lingering smell of charred meat, cabbage, and onions. She dashed after him, right on his blamed heels, knocking a pan to the floor in her haste, the dull ting echoing along the hallway as she chased him down it. The tick of a clock counted off each second, matching his irate stride. He knew what Julian would say. He'd been played, outfoxed, *outmanned*. But his gut—way, way, deep where he listened when it spoke to him—said she was right.

"Finn is coming along for the ride," he growled as he took the stairs by twos. "And Minnie. She started some of this mess if you ask me. She can *chaperone*."

"I have no idea what—"

"Let me be clear. I'm sharing the pleasure of this trip." He grasped her arm and propelled her toward his bedchamber, situating her as kindly as anger allowed in a mahogany chair gracing the hallway for looks, not comfort. The hard-backed piece was perfect for her troublesome arse. "*Stay*. Until I get back here. Or I swear…"

She dropped the satchel and lifted her head. That warning green flickered again. "I'm insulted by this tirade." She blew a strand from one of her sad little hairstyles from her face. "And wondering why we're wasting time arguing."

"Insulted?" Humphrey paused with his hand on the doorknob, glancing over his shoulder in amazement. "Julian's going to take a knife to my throat for this."

"He would never."

Humphrey laughed roughly and thumped the door against the wall. "Scamp, you have no idea who you're dealing with."

CHAPTER 12

The man that blushes is not quite a brute.
~Edward Young

Chandeliers scattered fiery prisms across the ballroom floor Julian traversed, his path blocked by viscountess, earl, baroness, marquess, earl —each an oar stuck at an awkward angle, pulling him off course through a lake of society jetsam. The orchestra played at a level allowing for conversation should he desire it, when he only wanted to make it to the veranda, imbibe his third glass of champagne, smoke his second cheroot, and wait the night out.

The tapestries in the vision had looked quite valuable—Boucher, he learned—a reasonable discussion point, viscount to duke. A footman had taken no note when he mentioned seeing them years ago and questioned if they were in *this* home, one of Ashcroft's many. The footman had been quite knowledgeable and had unwittingly given Julian the tapestries' exact location. Interestingly enough, he'd also mentioned a house fire last week and advised Julian to pay no mind to the charred area staining the drawing room floor.

Humphrey was right. Ashcroft needed help before he gutted a structure to completion. Julian wanted to laugh when the topic was as far from humorous as one could get; the rumor circling the ballroom was that the Duke liked to dabble in pyrotechnics, hence the occasional blaze at his estates.

The subdued light provided a forgiving lens with which to behold the glittering, bejeweled mob, but still, the colors stunned, making him question how Piper tolerated it in combination with hundreds of brilliant auras. It was hard enough for him; already, his head pounded from the unwanted visions even as he tried to limit what he touched.

"No need to face this horde sober, Beauchamp." Lord Holt, the Earl of Stanton, grabbed a flute from a waiting footman and thrust it at Julian, leaving him no opportunity to refuse. Holt had a fast wit and was one of the few men Julian knew who had stooped to commerce to save his earldom from insolvency—as Julian had done for the viscountcy. He gave Julian an update on his wife and his mistress, the upcoming Henley Royal Regatta—as they'd been in the same boat club at Oxford and soundly beaten Cambridge two years running during those years when Julian had tried so hard to fit in—before elbowing his way back into the crowd.

Leaning against a pillar, Julian dipped his head to avoid the interest of the ladies on the hunt. From first-season virgin to widowed countess, they were at turns wide-eyed and blunt. His attendance had drawn comment—it was rare. Strangely, the seductive glances, whispered entreaties, and bared breasts made him moody and even a bit cross, where before they'd left him bored. Chalk dust swirled with each passing group of dancers—a stunning floral design on the floor meant to keep the masses from slipping on new leather soles to their padded bottoms.

Amazed to feel so isolated in such a crush, Julian was quite simply alone with his visions.

A modest distraction, they shimmered through his mind, the champagne acting as an antidote. He felt weightless, unencumbered, able to take the cleansing breath he could not at Harbingdon. The wagers going on around him amused, though he took no part. Who would be the first to pass out in the Duke's rosebushes or cause a scandal of the first order?

A steady wash of relief flooded him. Piper would not be there to win the latter.

He wouldn't have to save her from herself.

Not tonight, at least.

Although, he thought, his hand going to the hair-clip in his coat pocket—brought for stubborn locks should he need to pick one, not because he was a man obsessed—he would have loved to take her in his arms beneath a thousand glittering candles, draw her lithe body against his while whispering sugges-tive words in her ear. Ashcroft's garden had con-cealed nooks ideal for clandestine activities.

Blistering images lit his mind. Of hiking Piper's skirt and following her down to the dewy grass; fit-ting her across his lap on that massive stone bench beside the fountain, her legs on either side of him as she rode him to completion. He could make love to her for a month, in a hundred different ways, without leaving Ashcroft's lawn.

Marianne Coswell found him moments later, as he'd expected she would, looking as beautiful as in-tended. Her hair, the color of a wheat field in bloom, was caught in an intricate knot at least two maids had assisted with. And the gown? Fit to perfection, a lustrous silver which perfectly suited her gossamer skin. He recalled her fingers tangling in his coat lapels as she pulled him into her carriage. Accustomed to being pursued, for the title and hint of intrigue surrounding him, her assault had been particularly acute.

When she reached his side, she flashed a knowing smile. Deep in his pocket, Piper's hairclip pulsed, posing strong opposition.

He questioned if his cock could rise to Marianne's occasion should his very life depend upon it. When seconds ago, fantasies he had no intention of satisfying had him considering a brief retreat to the gentlemen's drawing room until the erection pressing awkwardly against his trouser buttons wilted.

"I'm beyond delighted to see you here, darling." Marianne curled her hand around his wrist and a gemstone on her bracelet nicked his skin. A vision of her body twisting in ecstasy beneath someone flooded his mind. Someone who was most assuredly not *him*. Closing his eyes, he focused on the masculine face captured in the throes of delight, because he really couldn't help himself.

Oh. Lord Featherstone.

Julian repressed a shiver of distaste and uncurled her fingers. He and Featherstone had shared little in this life, and he wished it had remained that way.

She arched a brow, her lips sliding into a treacherous twist. "Would your indifference have anything to do with the recent arrivals?"

"Marianne, I have no idea what you're talking about."

She smiled, a genuine display that made his stomach sink. His former lover had him in some way he could not account for—and suddenly, they both knew it. "Your ward just arrived. With your devastating half-brother." She clicked her tongue against her teeth, her cheeks glowing. "Give that boy a few years, and society is going to go mad over him, by-blow or no. Almost painful to gaze upon such splendor."

Julian inhaled a startled breath of Marianne and chalk. He was going to strangle Humphrey. Then Finn.

Then he'd deal with Piper.

She hadn't come alone, but he bloody-well knew whose idea it had been to come.

"Lady Scott is not my ward," Julian said as he peeled off the pillar, "as I've stated on more than one occasion." *And Finn is the brother of my heart.*

"I see surprise beneath that tranquil facade," Marianne drawled in a voice not unlike the one she used during sex. Obviously, gossip brought her as much pleasure. "Not invited, I assume, but no one would deny them. Both amusing toys, apt to turn this into the most discussed gala of the season."

Words choked his airway as he gripped the flute hard enough to shatter glass. No matter Piper's reputation, deserved, or Finn's exceptional good looks, astounding, they would never be anyone's *toy*, not as long as Julian breathed.

"Goodbye, Marianne," he said before he said too much. With a bow, he left her to circle the outer rim of the ballroom, gaze tracking. He was taller than most, an advantage, and his target likely the next tallest in the room. Ah, *there*.

Finn lingered on the main staircase, caught in a robust tide he couldn't swim through but looking, with an unruffled mien, as if he'd like to try. Again, that weighty feeling zipped through Julian: pride, affection, apprehension. A boy from the streets, without a single drop of the blood the ton believed made one exceptional flowing through his veins, Finn looked ready to conquer the world.

Placing his flute on a passing tray, Julian side-stepped, and Piper came into view. At Finn's side, the top of her head barely striking his elbow, he feared the crowd would topple her. His eyes skimmed her length, and with the resulting burst of heat beneath his skin, he decided it best to wait until he could approach without hunger crossing his face for all to witness. Kissing the life from her in a crowded ballroom would strike the final blow to her reputation.

Stunning in a gown he wondered how she'd acquired, his hands itched to touch. The rosewood silk gleamed in the candlelight, setting her apart like a jewel embedded in dirt. What a gorgeous woman she'd grown into, he concluded with dismay, which she seemed unaware of as she smiled with apparent indifference at the men surrounding her.

Julian's purpose weakened, his focus splintering.

Grabbing a flute from a liveried footman, he took a fast gulp while studying her over the crystal rim. When she finally noticed him, a shiver streaked through his chest and down his legs. She lifted a brow, commanding him to her side. As if she expected him to rescue her from the mob encircling them.

Only, he didn't feel like being herded.

Holding her gaze, he lifted his flute in mocking salute.

Her lips thinned, then she nodded. *Fine*, he imagined her thinking, *let's play*. In challenge, she took a proffered flute from a marquess with a horrid reputation and smiled as if the man ignited the night.

Julian took a threatening step forward, then recalled his objective and, more notably, his connection

—or factual *lack* of one—to the woman holding him entranced across the scant distance of a ballroom. Close family friend, everyone knew, the story prudently circulated after his arrival on the earl's doorstep. Yet, he was not her guardian.

Or her lover. Or her husband.

Turning away, he forced himself to participate in the inane banter, the grasping indelicacies, while compelling impulses took a hammer to his fragile ramparts.

～

Her legend had grown.

Well past the girl who sent teary-eyed governesses fleeing back to London with outrageous stories to impart, the girl who'd failed to manage even one London season successfully. This newly proposed version had her not only finally accepting her unfortunate lineage but *embracing* it. Although pity was bestowed upon her because one could not alter one's biology, and her mother's was most regrettable.

Having spent the past three years among the unsophisticated but inherently interesting natives of New York—an assumption she made no move to correct—Lady Elizabeth Piper Scott was considered entirely outside the pale but cream for the cat, and everyone wanted to take part in the latest valuation of the Earl of Montclaire's wayward, half-American granddaughter. Listed in DeBrett's along with the rest of them, but with a pencil-strike through her name, she could not be *wholly* cast aside. Most were thrilled, in a season scarce of excitement, to welcome her.

Scandalous Scott had returned to the proper side of the ocean.

She could only give the curious partial attention as she had a thousand auras to contend with. A vibrant swirl transformed by the incandescent crystal chandeliers and blazing wall sconces. She longed for her folio to record the brilliance, Julian's assistance at categorizing the colors.

If a crowd hadn't surrounded Finn as he lounged against a marble column, a careless sprawl calling to the cats in the room like a putrid plate of tuna, she would have elbowed him in the ribs and request *he* assist her. But the titled flock provided no respite as they lined up before her, almost as they had when she posed as Madame DuPre, asking silly, no, *absurd* questions about her supposed travels while the world stained around them like paint streaking down one of Julian's canvases.

The rumors circled, the accounts propping them up *mostly* untrue, but they were, this mob of leering people, so riveted she felt lifted from her slippers. *It's no wonder* Piper concluded with the culmination of her second flute of champagne, *Julian wanted to leap from a speeding carriage rather than defend me from this.*

Now everyone was cross with her.

Everyone who mattered that is.

Finn, the height of elegance and ease on his worst day, was, in actuality, hiding his apprehension over Julian's reaction under layers of buttered charm. Humphrey and Minnie were sullenly awaiting the explosion, either Julian's or the Duke of Ashcroft's, in the relative safety of the carriage.

As for Julian...his glittering gaze periodically grazed her, then dusted off like a touch he hadn't meant to place. Penetrating scrutiny, it was not. Was this her future? A fixture in his life, trivial and of little consequence. *Foolish girl.* She wanted to hold the key to his heart, his mind, his soul, when she was beginning to believe she was like his artwork.

There to admire, refine, then hide away when the project was complete.

The sumptuous Lady Coswell, who Piper swore Julian gave the cut earlier in the evening, stood close by his side, no doubt waiting to wrap herself around him if given a chance. Yet, Piper knew him well enough to see he was detached and impatient, his aura measured.

Piper nodded her head in agreement with Lady Allen and Countess Clare, having no idea the topic discussed, as she watched Julian consult his timepiece for the third time in an hour.

She wanted to look away, but she had rarely seen him dressed so elegantly. She tried to ignore the pinch in her belly, the pulse between her thighs. Even Henry Poole, Julian's tailor, one of the best in London, couldn't confine the sturdy physique shaping layers of wool, linen, and silk.

Noting the direction of her gaze, Countess Clare murmured, "Such extreme height must be a gift of the Beauchamp men."

Piper hummed a meaningless reply as Finn and Julian shared not a lick of blood.

"Exceptionally diffident, Viscount Beauchamp. Such reticence drives the ladies wild, wouldn't you say?"

"Perhaps his reluctance is with purpose," she replied, this chat reminding her of running her hand over a blade and hoping it didn't draw blood.

The Countess sniffed and presented a pale shoulder in reply. If the woman had hoped to inquire about Piper's relationship with Julian, hotly debated for *years*, she was going to be wretchedly disappointed, for Piper could barely explain it herself.

Julian chose that moment to glance above the horde and lock eyes with her. The scent of orchids and sandalwood, every clink and gasp in the ballroom retreated until only her resounding heartbeat registered. Without thought, she lifted her hand to her stomach and pushed the tingle away. His gaze followed, then narrowed and skipped away. He took a long draw of his drink and swallowed hard.

Reluctant indeed.

Finished with this game, she turned to Finn, intent on raising a white flag and asking him to escort her to Julian. But her cousin, Alfred Weston, the tenth Earl of Montclaire, snuggled alongside her with a hand laid greedily at the small of her back. As if he hadn't gotten everything inheriting the title and estates—as if there was more to be gained. Conceivably, he thought to remedy the slight of her being left with nothing by extending the presently vacant position of Countess.

Repelled, she took a lurching step back.

Something about Alfred made her skin crawl. His features were pleasant, his form admirable enough, but his eyes held something quite disagreeable in their bronzed depths.

"Lady Elizabeth," he said, his voice so honied she'd wager he practiced introductions with his valet. "An unexpected surprise. I supposed you roughing it in the colonies."

She worked to twist her mouth in the correct direction. It was a struggle; she held little of Finn's natural charm in reserve. "My lord."

"Alfred, my dear." Again, the smile. "After all, we *are* family." Although he'd not offered assistance of any kind after her grandfather's death; even if she'd justly passed the age of needing a guardian, she would have appreciated being remembered. He leaned in close enough to send the scent of ambergris to her nose and a dance of unease along her skin.

Issuing a hushed sound that meant nothing but filled the silence, she took another step back.

Alfred tilted his head, his lips sliding into a lecherous smile. "It is too much to hope for the next dance? A vacancy, perchance, on your card?"

She flipped her kidskin-covered hands back and forth, a show of having no dance card on her person. Managing auras *and* a waltz was more than she could account for.

"It is too much, Montclaire, old boy." Julian maneuvered himself between them in a graceful effort no one would argue was anything but entrance into a conversation among friends. He turned to Piper, hair shooting off his brow as if he'd tunneled his hand through the overlong strands then forgotten to set them to rights. His eyes by candlelight gleamed like polished silver, the lids lowering to hide any clue to what he was thinking. "The ankle, my lady, is it better?"

She shook her head. Emphatic. Not better.

Before she had a chance to build a story around the lie, when she was excellent at highspeed lying, Julian did it for her. "Stumbled over a cobblestone upon arriving at the ball. So, dancing with you"—he paused to adjust a cuff which did not need adjustment, giving time for the words to sink in—"is not going to happen."

Alfred's cheeks flushed though his smile remained in place. "Still playing the mother hen, eh, Beauchamp?"

Julian stepped nearer than inconsequential conversation warranted. So near his aura bled into Alfred's. "An issue you should have researched more

182

TRACY SUMNER

leaned in close enough to send the scent of ambergris to her nose and a dance of unease along her skin.

Issuing a hushed sound that meant nothing but filled the silence, she took another step back.

Alfred tilted his head, his lips sliding into a lecherous smile. "It is too much to hope for the next dance? A vacancy, perchance, on your card?"

She flipped her kidskin-covered hands back and forth, a show of having no dance card on her person. Managing auras *and* a waltz was more than she could account for.

"It is too much, Montclaire, old boy." Julian maneuvered himself between them in a graceful effort no one would argue was anything but entrance into a conversation among friends. He turned to Piper, hair shooting off his brow as if he'd tunneled his hand through the overlong strands then forgotten to set them to rights. His eyes by candlelight gleamed like polished silver, the lids lowering to hide any clue to what he was thinking. "The ankle, my lady, is it better?"

She shook her head. Emphatic. Not better.

Before she had a chance to build a story around the lie, when she was excellent at highspeed lying, Julian did it for her. "Stumbled over a cobblestone upon arriving at the ball. So, dancing with you"—he paused to adjust a cuff which did not need adjustment, giving time for the words to sink in—"is not going to happen."

Alfred's cheeks flushed though his smile remained in place. "Still playing the mother hen, eh, Beauchamp?"

Julian stepped nearer than inconsequential conversation warranted. So near his aura bled into Alfred's. "An issue you should have researched more

182

thoroughly after coming into the title, no? As it is, we no longer need your assistance."

Piper recalled the heated exchanges between the two as adolescents; Alfred's insecurity and bitterness as the random pieces of life's puzzle—attractiveness, intelligence, purpose—began to fall into place for Julian. He'd viewed Julian as a rival for her grandfather's affection and imaginably for hers as well.

Alfred's hands balled into fists. "You know, Beauchamp, you have such the look of your father about you, it's quite hard to tell the difference."

Piper heard Julian's whispered oath, his posture settling into one of a man set on entering a brawl. Did Alfred not recall his ferocious temper? Julian was not a man you insulted and walked away from, crowded ballroom or not.

Uncaring who might witness the indiscretion, Piper grabbed Julian's wrist, circled warm skin and sharp bone. Closing her eyes, she focused on the rapid pulse popping beneath her thumb. *Calm. Control.* Julian tensed, then he sighed softly as his hand fell limp in hers.

Her lids swept up as Julian turned, his dusky gaze nailing her to the floor. She knew he didn't like that she had trespassed and used her gift to pacify.

Alone amid a crowd as remembrance of his body pressed to hers, the surge of his breath in her ear, invaded her senses. "Remember why you came," she found the courage to advise. "Don't let him ruin it."

"Go, Freddie"—Julian shook his hand free of hers —"before I decide to follow a wayward impulse, as I've been known to on occasion, you should recall." He blocked Alfred as the man went to scurry past. "If I hear something untold circulated this night, count on my being on your doorstep, *any* doorstep, to discuss the situation. Trust me, you don't want that visit."

The Earl of Montclaire clenched his jaw. He had loathed the nickname as a child, as Julian loathed any reference to his father. They understood how to score a direct hit. Freddie's meager bow as he left them expressed all he feared saying. *Silly fop*, Piper thought, watching him shove his way into the crowd, taking his rightful place among the vermin.

Julian studied his hands as if he questioned what he might have done with them. "Don't look so worried," he said and flexed his fingers. "If I'd intended harm, his blood would be spattered on the marble beneath our feet. Mixing quite imaginatively with the chalk."

"Worried? About Freddie?" She laughed softly. She only worried about *him*.

"Your temerity astounds," he said, angling his head and catching her gaze. Light from a sconce near his shoulder highlighted the stunning planes of his face as he frowned. The tantalizing aroma of citrus and something very earthy, Julian's scent alone, drifted to her, lighting a fire in her belly and sending a wild, hot sweep to her toes. She shifted from one slipper to another to encourage the feeling to seep out the soles of her feet.

"I don't suppose a chaperone is hiding underneath that lovely crimson skirt?"

"Minnie is waiting in the carriage. With Humphrey. Guards are posted at each entrance and in the garden. If it makes you feel any better, they're irritated, as well. Well, not the guards." Piper pleated silk between her fingers until the fabric felt as warm as her skin. "Minnie said she's never seen such brazenness, even in her mother's workplace."

Julian reached wide and grabbed a glass from a

passing footman, downing the contents in one gulp. "So you've less sense than a prostitute? Huh." He turned the glass in his hands as if it held the answer to a problem. "Methinks the glare of yonder chandelier shines much too far—or I am much too near."

Piper shook her head. This conversation was senseless. Was he quoting *Byron*? "Are you soused?"

A sputter she supposed was a laugh parted his lips. "I'm not sober."

"I'm not letting you go alone."

His hand stilled, crystal suspended between finger and thumb, an internal debate about pitching it against the wall. "I'm aware of the situation, Yank. The yin and yang of our relationship. Ashcroft's money clip is wrapped in a handkerchief in my pocket lest it encourage further visions should I touch it. Honestly, I'm scared to touch it again."

"After the other night—" *You need me with the visions*, she wanted to clarify but felt this declaration might send his glass to its death.

Another low laugh rolled forth as he shrugged in defeat.

"I'll be helpful."

He jabbed the glass at her like a weapon. "Care to wager on that?"

"What are the terms?" she asked because she'd never backed away from a dare in her life. A crowded ballroom wasn't going to be the start.

He leaned against the marble column, a shoulder perch that set his long body into a slump both arresting and exact. His aura exploded, trails of red snaking through a burst of blue. Passion, ire. She yearned for the first and wished, for *once*, there would be no demand for the second. Powerlessly, her gaze traveled from his polished patent shoes to the emerald stickpin lanced through his snowy-white cravat.

His expression was composed as his head lifted, a slow burn igniting beneath her skin as their gazes clashed. "I feel as if I'm being mentally stripped of my clothing, one agonizing piece at a time." He tapped the rim of the glass to his lips, lashes lowering to lessen the impact of his statement. "It's quite arousing, I'm sorry to admit."

Piper's breath seized, nipples peaking as if Julian had sucked them between his teeth.

Nodding to an elderly baron who called his name as he passed, Julian flipped the glass from one hand to the other. "This wager. My terms, is it?"

My, he *was* foxed.

The urge to capture the drop of champagne clinging to his bottom lip was crushing. What would he do if she slid her hands into his hair and yanked him off his always steady balance? Had the roar of a ballroom not intruded, she might have accepted the challenge her famished body threw at her watchful mind.

"If you keep looking at me like that, Yank, scrap the wager. We're not going to make it out of this ballroom."

She crossed her arms and blew out a breath: *all or nothing, Piper.* "One night," she whispered, glancing around to ensure no one heard her. Fortunately, to her left, Lord Ranier was arguing with a gentleman she believed the Marquess of Everleigh. Over a woman, no doubt. Possibly the frantic, quite beautiful one gesturing next to them. Naturally, the crowd had gravitated to the trio with a magnetic force.

Julian pushed off the column, rising to his full height. "Excuse me?"

"If I help you, and I'm going to…" She shrugged as

her hands were occupied, twisting her gown into disarray. "If you accept my help, that is, I claim one night." She tried for a smile, but Julian's gaze was as hard as the marble he rested against, and she was not an able negotiator. Deceiver, yes, negotiator, no. "Consider it payment, if you'd like." The request went well with her dress—those were *always* the terms in the establishment where Minnie had acquired it.

Julian stepped closer, but not too, a dent forming between his brows. "Payment?"

She nodded.

"For my services?"

"For one night." She looked him dead in the eye, contradicting how hard her knees were shaking. "I want to know. And I want *you* to show me."

"You want to know," he finally whispered in a tone of distinct bewilderment. His fist went to his temple, pressing against what had to be a headache. "And you want me to show you."

She thrust her hand out, a crass American tradition, and certainly not one a woman typically employed. "Agreed?"

Julian's gaze bounced to her hand. "This is no wager. It's a business transaction."

"Call it an agreement if that better suits." She raised her voice to climb above the argument between Ranier and Maitland, which had escalated to gentlemanly fisticuffs. "Between friends."

"Name them then," he bit out, the sconce's light sparking off his glass and tossing a prism on the chalked floor, "the terms for this friendly agreement."

She ticked off the points on her fingers. "The lodge. The night after we return. A full night. Oh"—she pointed—"*and* the next morning. No cheating about the time. No running out at dawn. Let them bring another round of chocolate. I want to utilize every benefit of country living."

He took her arm, gently moving her aside as Everleigh, who'd been knocked off his feet by a blow to the chest, slid to a stop between them.

"Many thanks, Beauchamp," Everleigh said after accepting Julian's help up, then he shoved through the crowd and leaped back into the fray.

"What about clothing?" Julian asked, nonchalantly wiping Everleigh's blood on his coat.

"Clothing?"

"Am I to render these services with or without clothing?" His gaze sliced through her, and her breath caught at the savage look on his face. All refuted by his steady voice, as if nothing monumental transpired. "Just so I'm adequately prepared should I accept."

She tried to recall the images she'd seen in the French text in the library in Gloucestershire, the one hidden on a top shelf behind a row of Dickens' first editions. Her cheeks stung as she imagined Julian leading her through those acrobatic poses. Had the people in the drawings been clothed? She pulled her cheek between her teeth in thought. "I would guess both are possible."

"They are." Dazed, he looked to be running through the possibilities himself.

"That is to say, unclothed and maybe—" She chanced a glance at him and slipped beneath the waves. This expression she had seen once before, when he was poised above her, his hips locked in place as he created a steady rhythm, crowding her into the floor. She'd been close to orgasm then, something she'd only experienced in the privacy of her bedchamber. Always in fantasy partnership with the brooding man standing before her.

If she told him this, they might not make it out of the ballroom, so she kept it to herself.

The scuffle concluded, and the circle surrounding the men disbanded, people scattering across and into their path. Most were laughing, champagne in hand, including the two combatants, the gala a supreme success in terms of entertainment value. Piper wished she hadn't added to the significance of the evening, but, if she were honest, knew she had. Julian nodded to those who called out to him; Piper did the same with a bland look that offered no invitation to deepen the connection. She wanted to tuck herself in a corner and hide. The color parade assaulting her was beginning to vex.

The orchestra started to play, and Mozart's haunting composition echoed through the ballroom. Julian dug his watch from his waistcoat, flipped open the case, and glanced at it with a sigh. He had done a stellar job of avoiding her gaze for the last five minutes.

"Jules," she said, question or plea she wasn't sure.

Impeccably timed, Finn interrupted, out of breath from elbowing his way through the crowd, a tumbler of what looked to be brandy in each hand. His cravat was askew, his hair a glorious tangle, his cheeks rosy, too rosy for a march across a ballroom. With a sinking feeling, Piper wondered what female had sucked him in and spit him out.

His grin spoke of an unparalleled experience.

Julian examined Finn from head to toe, his aura shredding. Piper felt a flash of compassion; she and Finn couldn't make a sound decision between them.

"What a crush!" Finn thrust a tumbler in her hand. Julian took the other and in return, presented his empty one, which Finn accepted with a scowl. "I could barely make it across the room. Gads, the

189

thoughts running through the minds of these deviants. I didn't even have to touch anyone to get most of it."

"A far easier journey if you were ugly," Julian murmured.

Finn laughed, pursing his lips. "Yes, but then everything *else* would be more difficult."

"True," Julian agreed and took a slow sip. The movement brought her regard to his mouth, along with the remembrance of him working her bottom lip between his teeth, then smoothing with his tongue just after. Awareness surged with more force than a river of brandy. Her glass shifted, and an amber drop dribbled on her glove. Adrift, she touched the damp spot to her cheek.

Lost to another time, another place.

Julian tracked the movement, and when he spoke, his voice was husky. "Meet me at the servant's staircase off the kitchen. North side of the house. Thirty minutes. Don't be late." He jabbed his finger in Finn's chest. "Not one second."

Finn jerked his thumb back as if to say: *what about her?* Piper opened her mouth to tell them she was bloody well coming—

"Bring her," he said and elbowed his way into the throng. He glanced over his shoulder before the crowd gobbled him up. There was bold promise in that look. "I can't fight us both."

Then he was gone.

⁓

Sidonie gazed from the carriage window at the theatre of society on full display. The Duke's townhouse was ablaze. Every window lit, a sea of footmen, maids, and partygoers mingling as they would not dare if they encountered each other on the street. She'd been born into that glittering life. Destined for an extraordinary existence of frivolity until her mind left her, vacated rather abruptly without notice, leaving her a quaking shell.

Her yearning to interact with the healer—*Piper*— had not abated, but Sidonie was determined to succeed where they had failed miserably before. Rushing in without full understanding of the situation had led to the earl's blood staining her hands. She was heavily armed this time—but so was Julian Alexander. "*Vicomte*," she whispered, the language of her country calming her. Harbingdon would not make an easy target, surrounded by thick forest and secured at every split in the wood. And there had been no opportunity in London. The boy, too, was proving harder to read, gaining strength, likely from the healer, who was by his side.

The time was not right, not yet.

Sidonie let the curtain fall as she collapsed against the carriage seat.

Soon, the rebellious girl would step outside her guarded world because her nature demanded it; she would do what she'd done before and create chaos.

Sidonie would be waiting.

CHAPTER 13

One man loved the pilgrim soul in you.
~William Butler Yeats

*J*ulian learned much about Piper that
night.

Intriguing, wondrous aspects of her
personality, which only served to heighten his fascination. Hammer on the nail-of-a-belief that she was
made for him.

Composed under pressure, fearless actually, and
curious in *spades*, she made an excellent thief.

Christ, he thought and observed her calmly rif-
fling through the Duke of Ashcroft's desk mostly by
feel alone, as the moonlight filtering through the
open drapes was paltry at best. They'd decided one
lamp risked enough, and it sat on the bookcase
nearest him, throwing modest illumination over the
chest Julian sought to crack.

Anyway, who needed lamplight when her vitality
brightened the room like a thousand candles?

With a twist of Piper's hairclip, he sent the rusty

tumblers on the lock spinning, and the chest popped open. She raised a brow at his implement of choice but did not comment.

It held a varied assortment of journals. Slipping his spectacles from his coat pocket, Julian held one into the light, an image of Ashcroft a shimmer in his mind. The first entries were dated ten years ago—a long time to go it alone in their anomalous world. In a faultlessly tidy script, Ashcroft had listed instances where he'd experienced his gift. Those instances where a fire had raged out of control included the damages incurred.

Setting aside the journal, Julian disassembled the chest.. Removed each drawer, running his finger along the dovetailed edges in search of a hidden compartment. If he found nothing else, he could steal the journals, but torturing a man already tortured wasn't the plan. To protect what was his—a compulsory response to the break-in—*was*.

Julian moved the lamp to the desk, the money clip he'd returned sitting atop a stack of books on the occult. Pages were folded and spattered with ink, speaking to frenzied research. The chime of a hall clock had him swearing under his breath. He glanced at Piper, but she remained relaxed and efficient, on her knees as she searched the lower drawers.

"This desk is very similar to one in the earl's library. There was a concealed partition behind the pigeonholes." She stretched, and he tried, he really did, to ignore the thrust of her breasts beneath silk. Even amidst bloody intrigue he wanted no part of, his cock gave notice where it wished this search was occurring. She pulled her bottom lip between her teeth in concentration, her hands doing undeniably marvelous things to Ashcroft's mahogany.

He felt run aground, abandoned on an island of enchantment and vacillation.

He imagined sweeping books to the floor and hoisting her atop the more-than-spacious desk. Bending her over the glossy surface and moving in behind her, sliding inside and showing her everything she wanted to know.

I want you to show me.

He'd never heard a more erotic declaration in his life.

"There was a trick to finding it," Piper said.

He shoved his spectacles up. "Pardon?" He had completely lost the direction of the conversation.

Laughing softly, she examined the adjustable drawer, giving it a firm tug. "A small spring in the earl's, right about here." She gestured for light, and Julian scooted the lamp closer, pressing his hands to the desk to keep them from following commands his mind issued at rapid speed.

Brush the lock of hair from her cheek.

Tilt her head and kiss her before she knows it's coming.

Before you can stop yourself.

She hummed low in her throat and probed the dovetailed edges. Julian pushed off the desk, rocking back on his heels. Was that the sound she would make as he thrust inside her? Her hands sliding over his skin with the same care and concentration as that drawer?

He suddenly, very urgently, wanted a drink. Or three. Piper wasn't his partner in crime, no matter the comfort he experienced working alongside her. She was wreaking havoc, creating disenchantment with his uninspired but orderly life. Understanding this, he leaned in as her enticing scent caught him in a chokehold, her breathless exhalations leading his heart on a merry chase. His erection intensified until he was as hard as the mahogany he perched on, as hard as the damned ballroom floor.

While he brooded, the spring clicked, and the bedeviling woman shook her fist in triumph. "Gotcha." She removed the drawer's false back, drawing forth a velvet satchel the color of a bruised sky. "Ah, a treasure of"—her words clipped off as she moved the bag into the light—"my grandfather's."

Julian held out his hand, and she transferred the package, the embroidered initials coming into view.

ELC.

Edward Lucien Chesterfield. The ninth Earl of Montclaire.

Julian opened the bag, his hand shaking. A vision of the earl and Ashcroft in a room he didn't recognize struck him. He made a rough sound and stumbled back.

So this was how the Duke was surviving.

"What did you see?" Piper reached for him.

Julian grabbed her wrist, arresting the movement, then releasing her before the vision spread. Even this brief touch cleared his mind like bristles across a filthy floor. With a shake of the bag, the earl's crystal rolled into his palm, cold against his flushed skin. "Fluorite." Thankfully, gems didn't transmit, or he'd have been on his knees as this one carried so many tales.

"The soul catcher," she breathed. "I thought it—"

Drunken laughter in the hallway had Julian rushing to her side and pulling her to a crouch. He held his finger to her lips, dipping his head so their eyes were level. They'd locked the door, and left Finn to guard, but the situation was admittedly precarious. The voices in the hall lingered, a thump as a body, or bodies met the wall in what sounded like an amorous collision. Finn, bless him, cajoled the couple into choosing another area with the implication he'd already claimed this spot.

Piper's gaze shifted, taking a leisurely path down his body, searing his skin as cleanly as a glowing torch tip. Even in this light, he could see desire shading her eyes the bottomless green he loved so much. She was done hiding her hunger because everything was there for him to see.

He didn't know if he could fight her when two infinitesimal letters—*no*—were all separating them. A little word, barely a breath if you whispered it against one's skin or into their waiting mouth.

He flipped the crystal from one hand to the other, tempted to forget his promise to her grandfather, an oath he no longer felt sure was the most capable plan. What would happen if he allowed his fascination free rein?

What if he let it consume them both and to hell with the consequences? Maybe his approach was more stringent than required.

Why not chose Piper's instead?

She was clever, intelligent to a fault, and she believed one night of passion would excise the demon, lessen the enthrallment between them. Enthrallment sitting there like Henry, an obstinate, glowering dog.

Why not a swift, indulgent kick to get it moving?

They could ravage each other and be sounder for it. He could introduce her to a sensual world in the way women wanted and men often ruined: tenderly, skillfully, attentively. He, in turn, could overcome his fixation.

Truly, how could touching her be as good as he'd dreamed?

Nothing was ever as good as one dreamed.

In the end, he would get over her. She would get over him.

"Have you decided?" she asked, the supple turn of her lips highlighted by a most accommodating band of moonlight. Dust motes danced in the strip, tiny glistening points in a world that suddenly seemed infinite. Leaning in, she slipped the crystal from his hand and began to roll it between her palms. She entranced, and he was held captive by everything about her.

He always had been.

"Decided?" His voice was thick with longing. If he heard it, she obviously could.

In return, her smile grew with feminine wisdom, age-old and carnal. "If you're going to accept the agreement."

There was nothing between them but darkness, moonlight, and a magical stone the earl had gifted to another. Desire warred with apprehension, but desire ruled.

Removing his spectacles, he tucked them in his coat pocket.

"So this means—"

He laid his finger over her mouth with a murmured hush. Her eyes were bright, glorious, and fixed on him. He was a fool. He couldn't look away if a thief had a knife to his back when he'd spent the better part of their relationship renouncing what she did to him. "Let me show you a better kiss this time," he whispered, sliding his thumb along the seam of her lips, gaining entrance with her soft inhalation. Her tongue touched the tip, and he questioned how long he could play this game. "One where I'm not fighting you, fighting myself."

"Yes," she said and swayed into him, the crystal tumbling to the carpet and rolling to a stop by her slipper. It flared, calming the aura surrounding them, reminding her of its proposed power.

Catching her, he cradled her face and brought her close enough to record all those treasures he had missed holding himself so far away. Parts of her he would add to his next painting. Freckles scattered across the bridge of her nose, a slight crook in her front tooth, she was stunning.

And the only person he wanted to see in this incredibly intimate way ever again.

More than the physical, this was the *soul*.

"What can I teach you, Yank?"

Her jaw tensed beneath his palm, her body trembling. Or maybe it was his, being played, an instrument of her pleasure. Her hands found his waist, slid beneath his coat, and up his back. Clothing, too much damn clothing sat between them, he agreed with her whispered entreaty.

"What can I give you?"

She answered with pure, fearless sweetness: "Everything."

"Everything," he vowed and molded his lips to hers.

Years later, she would recall the moment with perfect clarity.

Momentous, because it was the first time Julian gave of himself fully.

As he pulled her to him with a tortured moan torn deep from his throat, she comprehended, *finally*, the exceptional force of his desire.

And the overwhelming possibility of her own.

She wanted to explore his body, every swell of

muscle, every rise of sinew. She wanted all of him. *All.*

More, she thought, or perhaps it was a murmur against his lips because he reacted, pinning her to the wall as he angled her head until, ah, *yes...*

Their lips melded, faultless penetration. *This* was the wondrous connection he'd held from her.

Beneath his coat, she dug her nails into crisp linen as he growled and arched into the touch. Going on instinct, she lowered her mouth to his neck and sucked a patch of skin just beneath his jaw between her teeth. Because it brought such bliss, the taste and smell of him rushing through her, she repeated the act just above his stiff shirt collar, marking him.

He blinked, lashes fluttering. So handsome in the wash of moonlight, eyes a slate glimmer in the darkness. She couldn't stop herself from framing his face, words she wasn't even sure made sense leaving her. He groaned and lifted her from her crouched spot, swept the books from the desk and placed her bottom atop it as his lips captured hers.

The perfect fit they'd found was a robust memory, and their bodies evoked it with ease.

Julian stepped between her legs, nudging them wide, a refreshing burst of air sweeping her ankles as he yanked her skirt high. Moving in, he sighed her name, taking her bottom lip between his and biting gently. A low moan she couldn't contain slipped free, and she twisted atop the desk, grasping his shoulders, searching for deliverance. The flood of heat between her thighs should have been disconcerting when it felt like a victory.

"Jules," she whispered, her thread of yearning pitching her voice high, *"please."*

He drew back to kiss her upper lip, her cheek, a

tender spot beneath her jaw. Gentle, teasing nips, each sending her heart in a race against her ribs. The sound of a clock in the hallway, his breath in her ear. The taste of his skin on her tongue. His body shifting as she tugged on his coat sleeve. Imaginings were running riot like the blood in her veins as she sought to collect them.

He moved so purposely while she was frantic. "Quit tormenting me."

"Maybe this will help," he murmured against her neck. The same stimulating chill assaulting her lower extremities hit her chest as Julian adjusted the neckline of her gown just enough to free her nipple from her corset. Her head fell back, arms going behind to support her body, the position one he used to his advantage. Circling her nipple with his tongue, it peaked, a rigid point he then laved so tenderly it was nothing *but* the most extreme pleasure of her life.

"*Just like that,*" she said in a voice that did not sound hers, an answer when there had been no question.

As if it were the most natural thing in the world, she wrapped her legs around his hips and urged him closer, seeking to join—nothing to do with experience and everything to do with intuition.

He lifted his head, her nipple trailing across his stubbled jaw, sending another sizzling pulse through her body. A hum of desperation climbed from her throat. In response, he palmed her breast, set his thumb to the moist tip in a teasing, insistent rhythm. He was not going to offer mercy, a respite. He glanced down at their bodies, intent and focused, calculating even, so like Julian, her heart lurched.

"You are flawless," he said, his words torn, ragged. "Magnificent. But not quite where I want you to be."

Issuing whispered commands against her cheek, he slid her forward and shifted his hips until the unbelievably hard length of him met her pulsing center, chaperoned by nothing more than the thin layer of her drawers. The height of the desk pure kismet, it brought their bodies together in a most beneficial way. High desk, tall man. He rolled his hips as he claimed her mouth, the rhythm of his tongue set to their bump and grind as she picked up the challenge and met him, beat for beat. She released her hold on the desk and tunneled her hand into the tufts of hair hanging over his shirt collar. Tightening her legs around him, she helped drive the movement, showing him exactly what she wanted.

What she loved, what she *needed*.

Her skin tingled, a recognizable buzz filling her ears. The heady sensation of an orgasm calling to her.

"I'm close," she murmured. "Don't…stop."

He stilled, his mouth falling from hers. Even in the muted light, she could see the color drain from his face, his aura sparking at the edges. "How…"

Her hand dropped to his shoulder. *Oh*. Was this something she was supposed to conceal? She understood men touched themselves with predictable regularity. Were women not supposed to? Or not supposed to talk about it if they did? This predilection came from her indecent American roots, not the proper English ones. Out of step, as she had been in the ballroom two floors beneath them. As she had always been.

The pieces falling into place, she realized from his stone-faced expression that he'd misconstrued her statement. "I touch myself, Jules." *Dash it*. She may as well tell him the whole of it what with her skirt wrapped around her waist and her naked breast pressed to the rough brocade of his waistcoat. "I touch myself…and I think of you when I do."

He sighed gustily and dropped his brow to hers,

his breath a harsh symphony over her cheek. His thumb resumed its exploration of her nipple, barely-there circles, which allowed only half her mind to focus on the conversation. She trembled beneath his touch, a groan of delight flowing like a sluggish river from her lips. After a moment, where the only sound was their labored struggle for air, he laughed raggedly when she wanted his mouth somewhere, doing *something*. She arched, nudging her sensitive core against his hard shaft.

Here, Julian, *here*.

"You don't have to encourage me. I could come just by looking at you. In my trousers like a school-boy. But I'm not going to let you go so easily," he growled, then settled his mouth to hers and initiated a kiss which startled her with its force. He demanded, and she complied, meeting him with equal enthusiasm. She wanted him, begged for it, her plea taken in on his inhalation. The tender touch at her breast changed, his fingers twisting, a light pinch that drilled directly into the essence of her.

She nearly laughed at the thought: his touch was leagues above what she did to herself.

She finally understood how one could throw away everything for passion, make deals with God or the devil to possess it, as she would this very night. She wanted Julian enough to destroy reason, intention. This knowledge validated the scandals summarized in sitting rooms each season until she experienced true kinship. Sympathy. For her to feel so much when she couldn't, in the end, have him...

"Don't think. I do enough of that for the both of us," he whispered against her lips, his hands journeying over her body. One higher: along the nape of her neck, a deliberate slide into her hair, where his fingers tangled in the strands, tilting her head back just enough to deepen the kiss. One lower: over bunched silk at her hip, across her belly. His palm felt as hot as a brand, the pads of his fingertips calloused, creating delicious friction. He nudged her thigh with his hip, hand going to the opening in her drawers, wide enough to allow access without untying the drawstring closure.

A minor amount of convenience in an otherwise absurd sartorial trap.

She whimpered when he began his exploration, his touch light, skilled, focused. Never again would she curse Julian's devotion to detail. Hoping to help him, she inched forward as he stroked, circling the nub that provided the most pleasure. Once she got used to the pace, he changed it, slowed to a crawl, driving her to the brink. "*Julian.*" She broke the kiss, his name drawn out until it sounded like a hiss.

"So wet, so tempting." His gaze found hers, his eyes stained smoke. He studied her like he would one of his paintings, his thumb pressing harder. His fingers sliding along her folds, delving, seeking.

"*Inside.*" Her head fell back, her body bowing like a strap of leather snapped between two fists. He caught her, his fingertips digging into her scalp. Her lids fluttered. She *couldn't.* The way he touched her, the hungry look on his face.

She couldn't gaze upon that and survive. If this were a battle, she would lose.

His lips trailed the nape of her neck, to the fleshy pad of her shoulder, to her waiting, wonderfully exposed breast. His mouth assaulted not just the nipple but the rounded slope. Below, with a subtle shift, he slid a long finger through her folds and gained entrance.

She gasped as he angled his hand side-to-side and glided fully into her, the heel of his palm resting at her throbbing center. Then he did this delicious curl with his finger, and her vision splintered. Calm and oh-so in control, he stroked her with murmured words of passion, then reassurance as he brought another finger to join the first. His hips moved in cadence, and she understood his cock, hard and pulsing against her thigh, would someday replace his finger.

Imagining *that* brought her to the brink of climax.

"Next time," he breathed, "my mouth. Right *here*." His thumb gently circled her nub as he thrust from fingertip to knuckle.

A moist sheen covered her body, a twist in damp silk. It was too much. Uncontrollable, the feeling, her body clenching around his hand, her legs drawing him to her. When she crested, she would have released a harsh cry had he not covered her mouth with his, welcoming the sound of her pleasure. Her toes curled as the sensation traveled, making a complete tour of her body, then spilling out like light through a thousand pinholes.

He brought his hands to her face, cradling, and kissed her once more, lingering as if he did not want to leave her.

She shuddered in his arms, helpless to do anything else.

With a glance around the room, he brought his cheek to hers and gathered a ragged inhalation through his teeth. "I must be insane."

She gazed at him, her heart overflowing with unrevealed emotion. His aura sparked crimson and gold with an unyielding cobalt border. He was dazzling, absolutely wondrous.

Her favorite person in the entire world, should she ever have the courage to tell him.

But, *no*, she could not tell him—not part of the agreement, her obsession.

"Insane," he repeated hoarsely. But still, he held her, his hands flexing on her shoulders.

"Insane, but wickedly talented." She traced her nail along his jaw, trying not to imagine how he'd honed his skills. When he made a truncated sound of pleasure and tilted his head into the touch, she marveled that she was hungry for him so soon after release. One night would never be enough—but she would take it, nonetheless. "I will say this was *much* better than doing it myself."

A smile crossed his face, so ridiculously pleased, masculine satisfaction sharpening every feature. "Hmm, do tell," he said and twisted a strand of her hair around his finger.

She swatted his hand away. "You're making me admit all kinds of things a *lady* leaves unsaid."

Without comment, he straightened her skirt, his trembling hands letting her know he felt it, too. He leaned to kiss the slope of her breast before working her corset and gown into place. "Imagining you touching yourself is the most arousing—" His head lifted, his gaze blistering. "I want you to touch yourself while I watch. And"—he gestured to the short distance between their bodies as if this spoke volumes—"if you come as easily as this, I'm overjoyed in advance."

"So, this didn't count."

He smoothed his coat, his hopelessly wrinkled cravat. "Are we counting something?"

"Our night," she said, her gaze hungrily recording his weak effort to adjust the impressive bulge in his trousers. "This didn't count against it."

He hesitated, running his hand along the hard length, considering. With a deep exhalation, he looked up to find her staring. Their gazes locked, and her heartbeat stuttered and tripped. *I want that.*

I want him.

He took her in, a detailed examination as moonlight rippled over his face. She wanted to know what his naked body pinning her to a feather mattress felt like; how pleasure shaped his features when he came; what he liked best, what he *loved*.

"The way you're looking at me makes me want to take you right here, in the Duke of Ashcroft's damned torture chamber."

She shrugged, her well-loved nipple scratching against boned stays and sending another whip of heat through her body. "I don't know how"—she swallowed, having told him so much already, exposure of the highest measure—"not to want you, Jules."

He laughed, his head lowering with it. Dragged his hand through his hair until it stood in dark twists about his head. "I don't know how, either. God help me." Footsteps tapped down the hallway, and he turned, throwing the most fantastic admission over his shoulder, "And I'm not leaving this world without making love to you, so no, this didn't count against our night."

Three light taps, followed by two more, sounded on the door, bouncing off the gothic tapestries papering the walls. Finn, letting them know they needed to leave.

Julian held out his hand, invitation and directive. "You must go."

She slid to the floor, her legs unsteady but holding. "Not without you."

His lips flattened, and she understood they were set to quarrel. "No negotiation, Yank. Ashcroft knows I'm here. Likely knows *exactly* where by now. I have to bloody well wait him out." He jerked his thumb over his shoulder. "You, my lovely partner, are leaving with Finn."

"But—"

"I'm guessing Humphrey is in the carriage."

Of course, he was. No need to go there.

Julian stepped in, her skirt brushing his knee. "You're going to leave with Finn because I need my mind, every trace of it, for the conversation with Ashcroft. I can't"—he tucked a strand of hair behind her ear, let his fingers linger as they traced her jaw— "I *won't* have you here. For your safety *and* my own. I shouldn't have allowed this in the first place. Not here."

His aura flooded the color of a flawless pearl. Compassion.

"You're going to help him," she breathed.

"He *needs* help. Isn't that what my life is all about?" He crossed to the desk and came back with the velvet bag clutched in his fist. He frowned, rotating the package as he tried to solve the puzzle. "Perhaps he's part of the League, and we didn't even know it. Your grandfather recruited others long before he rescued me from the rookery, and you came back from America. I've been trying for years to marshal our community, find those he contacted, but I'm still learning. In any case, I mean to discover how much he knows. And how we can help each other."

His eyes when they found hers had softened to the color of a lake in winter. An endless stretch of crisp color hiding astounding depths. Seconds passed as they stared, spellbound. With a sudden shift, their lips met in heartfelt exploration. He clutched her to him, the crystal pressing into her back. Not the first hard object she had encountered this evening, she thought with a smile that shaped their lips and sent a shiver through her.

"I'll come for you when I return to Harbingdon." There was a plea hidden in his words, desperate and unsure, one she hadn't the heart to deny. "One night, then you must promise to let me go. And I must promise the same."

She drew his request in on a halting breath and offered agreement in its weakest form—a slight nod when the comment would not come.

Because, she could promise, but she would never in her heart agree.

~

Ashcroft's medieval chamber lost its consequence the moment Piper stepped from the room, her gaze capturing his until the door between them snapped shut. Julian's champagne euphoria had also departed, leaving a steady drumbeat in his skull and a slight tremor in the fingers wrapped around the earl's crystal.

Or was his unsteadiness a tangible remainder of pleasuring Piper? He lifted his hand to his lips, the scent of her clinging sweetly to his skin. Watching her crest had been the most gratifying experience of his existence.

He would base a thousand solitary future orgasms off just one of hers.

She'd clutched him as if letting go was a test and whispered four heart-wrenching words before departing. *Your promise, one night.* Because she knew he always kept his promises, even ones that pledged to separate him from the love of his life.

"I'm beginning to understand why my runner disappeared without a trace."

Julian flinched, the soul catcher shooting a vibrant prism over the desk as he bobbled the stone in his hand. The Duke of Ashcroft lounged against the doorjamb, his smile enigmatic, but his eyes glowing.

They were exotic eyes in a predictably English face, an unusual hue, neither brown nor amber, and reminded Julian of the fires the man was reputed to start, which was strangely ironic.

All at once, he understood the game had begun.

Reclining against the desk, he mirrored Ashcroft's nonchalance even as blood pulsed through his veins. Rarely had he offered membership to the League in this manner—and never to someone of Ashcroft's station. "A position in Wales fitting his skillset, your runner. No shallow grave in the forest, should that be your concern. Feasibly, he'll even be of assistance to us, with an appropriate amount of encouragement." He caressed the crystal, noting the way Ashcroft followed the movement, his stance having gone rigid. The stone meant much to the man, Julian realized. "I returned your money clip. I'm guessing the bastard pocketed that as additional payment. No thank you is necessary."

"The fires started when I was a child. Literally, in leading strings the first time I recall my fingertips getting hot. Then, later, the dreams. Unbelievable prophecies. Forests aflame, the world one fierce, glowing ember." He stalked to a sideboard Julian had not had time to search. He'd been too busy exploring the depths of Piper's eyes as she came around his questing fingers.

"A firestarter. That's what the earl called your gift in the chronology," Julian finally said.

The Duke's hand quivered, splashing brandy across his boot before he inhaled and resumed pouring a generous amount in the tumblers he'd set before him. "Firestarter." A rough laugh slipped past his lips. He grabbed the glass and threw back the contents. "Unfortunately, an apt categorization."

"We might help each other," Julian offered, seeing

no need to tread lightly. "There are others. More than you would think possible."

Ashcroft laughed again and swiped the back of his hand across his mouth. Bowing his head, he pressed the tumbler against his temple as if this would soothe. He gasped, and a spark shot off the hearth's brick. "Wait," he breathed and held up his arm when Julian would have crossed the room to him. In the next moment, the fireplace roared to life with a pop that sounded like a champagne cork releasing in the ballroom below.

Julian bumped against the desk, sending it skidding back, wadding carpet beneath his feet.

"Quite a fabulous parlor trick, isn't it? If only it didn't exact such a high price for the entertainment." He tossed back the rest of his drink. "Now, if you'll give me the fluorite, which helps me control my curse, though I have no idea how, I'll try not to burn down my ancestral townhouse when half of London's elite stands between its walls."

Julian crossed to the sideboard, exchanging the soul catcher for the tumbler. The brandy trailed a restorative path down his throat. "We thought the stone a myth, though it's mentioned in the chronology."

Ashcroft's gaze caught his, then skipped away. "Years ago, the earl sold it to me to save one of his properties. Quite a handsome sum I forked over. The bastard was interested in my gift but not overly sympathetic to its challenges. I suppose you're proof there is a clandestine group, one I've heard whispered about in foul places no one will admit they've been. Your name connected to each rumor as the opium swirled high above my head. The earl wouldn't admit it. My lofty title made me suspect in his eyes, as I recall." His hand closed possessively around the fluorite. "I should have asked you for help from the start. Saved a hundred pounds on Bow Street."

Julian took a slow sip. "Consider this your request."

The Duke tucked the soul catcher in his waistcoat pocket with care. "I don't suppose the chronology is for sale."

"No, but you have full access to it at my country estate. There's a woman, a healer, who also may be able to assist you." He would not reveal Piper's identity until Ashcroft was standing on Harbingdon's property. "There's no cure for people like us...but there is salvation."

"This is sounding dreadfully biblical, Beauchamp."

Julian recognized the cynical twist to Ashcroft's features. He remembered what it was like to have no one to trust, to share the madness that was this life.

"Before my brother's death," he continued, "before I assumed the title, I chose the life of a soldier to escape. Then, I found I was cursed with blood, death, *and* fires. I don't want to wage another war. I can't win another war. Not when I have this role to play. This damned curse doesn't keep me from my ducal duties. Has it kept you from yours?"

As the Duke's voice rose, the temperature in the room soared. With another cork pop, a tiny spark caught the edge of the carpet. Julian was there at once, stomping out the flames beneath his heel. The scent of charred fabric stung his nose, and he looked back to find Ashcroft with his head in his hands. "You started the fires in the hotel. It *was* you."

"I thought the medium might help me. I'm quite desperate, as you can see."

"She *can* help you."

Ashcroft lifted his head, moonlight washing over

him, throwing him into shadowed relief. "I don't understand."

"Let's consider it a gentleman's agreement. My resources for your might. You have contacts in places I can't begin to penetrate—and I've seen the men you travel with. I need an army, and you have one."

"Mercenaries are more like it. I've too much to hide and protect to travel lightly." Ashcroft gestured to the smoking carpet. "You'd invite this into your home?"

Julian felt his pulse settle for the first time in hours. The Duke of Ashcroft was going to accept his offer. "I have a lovely stone cottage at the ready."

A smile crossed the Duke's face, the first hint of the man beneath the apprehensive mask. "Fire and stone don't mix."

"Exactly," Julian said and raised his glass in partnership.

CHAPTER 14

You pierce my soul. I am half agony, half hope.
~Jane Austen

wo days later, Julian rode into the Cock and Bull's courtyard, soaked to the skin from a driving rain, grateful to see a crested Beauchamp carriage parked next to a stable that looked as if a strong gust would send it to the ground. Evidently, Humphrey had received his missive.

The mere suggestion of another second astride brought a queasy jolt to his gut.

Sliding from the saddle, he dropped his brow to the black's flank and sucked in an equine-scented breath, the reins clutched in his fist. Somewhere in the air was a fresh slice of the country, too, cut grass and wildflowers, a sensory shout telling him he was close to home, the stink of London hours behind. That alone knocked the headache down a notch. He'd anticipated fatigue this trip, but the visions had been fiercer than expected, unrelenting, and entirely too vivid. There was only so much he could do to protect himself when each turn of a corner presented mental involvements he was not always able to manage.

Unfortunately, this was not his only problem.

Piper, he thought and lifted his gaze to the sky as if tempestuous clouds could help him deal with a tempestuous woman. Beautiful, tenacious, charming, intelligent Piper, whom he wanted and feared in equal measure. *What to do about her?* She was turning his world inside out, ruining his plans, a destructive, enticing squall. Every second he'd spent with her in Ashcroft's medieval chamber circled his brain, a bloody carousel that never stopped rotating.

And now he *knew*, at least in part, which was horrible and glorious.

Details men dreamed of knowing.

Maybe he imagined with an artist's mind. Maybe another man would have recorded the images with less precision.

Her pale-pink thighs; the burnished swatch of hair between her legs; the shape and, down to a *very* specific hue, the color of her nipples; the round, faultless weight of her breast in his hand. If sculpting were his chosen passion, he'd prepare the clay and set to work. As it was, he promised to bring her to life on canvas.

And he'd not seen all.

Ah, but he wanted to.

He tried to suppress the memories, but they, like the woman, intruded. That throaty mew she made when she came apart, a silky, panting moan. Stronger than a whimper, softer than an outright groan.

The most erotic sound he'd ever heard in his life.

Too, he wanted not just her body but her mind. Conversations in the pitch of the night. Her laughter, her wit.

One night. One night to cleanse them both. He

wasn't going to drag Piper into the abyss his gift was pulling him into. A gift propelling him to the outer edges of sanity.

The black danced to the side, and he whispered a gentle plea, begging for another moment to gather his strength. He had no experience with tender emotions, and the protective ones he expressed for those he loved seemed to overwhelm. His childhood had been an experiment in survival, sleeping with one eye on the bedchamber door, a butcher knife stolen from the kitchen stuffed beneath his feather mattress. Love or anything close to it had *never* entered into the equation.

Sleeping beneath a luxurious counterpane with a face bloodied, a body bruised, had been the worst sort of torment. He'd fight until his death to save as many people as he could from the hell he'd experienced as a child. His journey had started with Finn and would end when he drew his last breath.

To fulfill this oath, he would relinquish the only woman he'd ever loved.

Because her gift gave; his *took*.

And he wasn't going to take anything more from her than one night.

The touch to his shoulder had him spinning around, the sudden move splashing black across his vision.

"Jesus, Jule," Humphrey muttered and steadied him with a firm grasp under his elbow, for which Julian was embarrassed but thankful. He didn't want to pitch face-first in the mud. He really didn't.

"I'm okay." He held up a hand that shook enough to have him deciding it might be better to have it retreat to his trouser pocket. "I have it."

Humphrey cursed, a gutted breath shooting from his lips. "Sure you do," he snarled and brushed past

Julian to gather the saddlebag from the horse. He tossed it over his shoulder without comment and left Julian standing forlornly in the yard. A young lad from the inn rushed over with a promise that Julian's horse would arrive tomorrow at Harbingdon, brushed down and fresh as a daisy. He nodded and slipped the boy a coin, too exhausted to comment.

With a sigh, he trudged to the carriage, feeling like a child reprimanded for breaking an antique vase in his mother's salon. He'd be dead, throat slit and body dumped in a gutter or the Thames, if not for the towering man guarding the vehicle with an expression equal parts annoyance and concern. Humphrey was the only person Julian had ever let protect him in the way *he* protected everyone else. It was humbling but, hidden deep where most men housed their feelings, welcome. They'd agreed long ago to total honesty in their friendship, almost like a marriage, if Julian wanted to be downright maudlin. Humphrey and Finn were his brothers, as surely as if they'd been unlucky enough to be sired by Edward Alexander, eighth Viscount Beauchamp.

In the most delicious revenge possible, because of Julian's subterfuge, all of London thought they had.

He reached the carriage and without a word of appeasement, clambered inside, keeping the pain the movement caused to himself. Head pounding in time to his heartbeat, he sought the darkest corner and prayed for the interrogation to wait until he had a night's sleep behind him. And food in his belly. Closing his eyes, he dropped his head to the velvet seat and willed the ache to perdition.

Humphrey tapped the trap, three hard knocks, and they settled into their journey. A blanket smelling of lavender landed on his lap. He wadded it

up, cushioning it underneath his cheek. *Brilliant.*
More of Piper's sweet-smelling laundry.

The bump and sway of the well-sprung carriage
would have lulled him to sleep had he not felt the
heat of Humphrey's scrutiny. He blinked into the dim
light cast from the lamp. "*You* brought her to
London."

For a long moment, Humphrey studied him.
Whatever he found during the investigation did not
satisfy. With a grimace, he tossed a leather satchel
next to Julian. "You trying to kill yourself, is that it?"

Julian opened the satchel and reviewed the contents. Cheese, bread, ham. A flask containing excellent scotch, which lit him up quite nicely. "What?" he
asked as if he'd just heard the question. He shook his
head to clear it. "What? No."

Humphrey ripped his flask from his coat pocket
and jabbed it at Julian in a violent motion. "I saved
your arse from that once. I'm not feeling up to it
again, boyo."

"That's—" He halted, the word *absurd* set to follow, but the boy in that alley had, in all honesty,
nothing to live for. Why flee a grand estate in his
family for centuries for the most crime-ridden
neighborhood in London if not to punish someone?

Abuse by his hand rather than the random cruelty
his father had dished out.

Julian observed the passing countryside, the little
he could see with rain-streaked glass and negligible
moonlight. He considered eating, but when
headaches were this bad, keeping what you put in
wasn't a sure bet.

"You're going to take her goddamn help."

He took another drink, the liquor hitting hard
with nothing to cushion it. "Says who?"

The flask left his hand to pop like a champagne

cork against the wall, liquid raining down on him. He rolled his head toward Humphrey, temper beginning to spark. "What the hell did you do that for?"

"I have responsibility in this, too, my friend." Again, he stabbed his flask Julian's way, rising from the seat. "For you most of all. And *you*"—he jerked his head in the general direction of Harbingdon—"for *them*." He settled back with a fast sip. "See how the bleeding structure works?"

Julian grunted, incapable of going rounds. *He understood the* bleeding *structure*. Sliding low, he let his legs sprawl, hoping the indelicate slouch adequately expressed his wish to conclude the conversation. He was drained, chilled to the bone, and famished but afraid to eat. His clothing was damp and sticking to him in all the wrong places. And the interior of the carriage reeked like a scotch-and-lavender prostitute.

"You've been angling after each other for years. How hard can it be to let her in?" Humphrey paused, his voice folding in on itself. "I don't care what that bastard Montclaire made you promise."

Julian fumbled for the flask, but it was bone-dry when he lifted it to his lips. Blast Humphrey and his sulking moods. "If you know so much, why ask?"

"Because I don't understand your reluctance!"

"It transferred, Rey." He closed his eyes, willing away the dizziness, which was starting to send the world into sluggish, nauseating rotations. "In the vision, she was standing in the Duke's room, right beside me. She could have described it as well as I."

"But—"

"If I'm unsure about my being able to leave," he interrupted, "what to do with *her*? Can she step out as easily as she seems to step in?" He swallowed, taking a harsh breath through his nose. "If you can guarantee her safety, or tell me a way *I* can, I'll gladly accept her help. Her *healing*. If not, I have to go it alone. At least for now."

"Your plan, then?"

Julian was too weary to lie. "One night, then she's going to release me. After that..." He lifted his hand from his lap in a meaningless motion. He did not feel well. And talking about Piper pained him on a good day.

"One night, as in—"

"*Yes.*"

A charged silence lapsed. Julian heard Humphrey take a drink. "Release you? Like you're a dog on a leash?"

"If it amuses you to think of it that way. Hell, maybe it amuses *me* to think of it that way." She could tie him to the bedpost with her leash any time she liked.

"Scamp agree to this claptrap?" Humphrey grunted beneath his breath. "Doesn't sound like her. Girl wants all of you, always has."

"She knows me too well," Julian said as if this answered the question, which it did not. We're *connected*, he could have added, but that was too private, too intimate, to share. "I think I'm inviting her inside the visions." Without opening his eyes, he reached for the satchel, took a bite of cheese, and mumbled, "If we can get past this—" *Fascination.* "Maybe then, I can accept the healing without wanting the rest."

"Isn't my place to enforce society's senseless rules, but won't your one night amount to ruining her?"

Julian laughed when he wanted to cast up his accounts on the carriage floor. "We're already ruined, Rey."

The silence stretched, broken only by squeaking carriage springs and wheels churning over packed earth. Julian drifted for a minute, maybe two, then Humphrey's voice, halting and unsure, split the calm. "Finn had another dream."

Julian peeled out of his slouch. "When?"

"The day after you left." Humphrey tapped the flask on his thigh. "The Frenchwoman was in London. Finn knew from the room, the street, something. He felt she was close, maybe to that damned party. And it's killing him because he thinks he's pulling her in, making us more vulnerable with what he can't help sharing."

"My God, the whole world was at that ball, so Piper is officially out of hiding. Ashcroft's had them, too. Dreams." He frowned, the ache in his head fair to splitting it open. "Why do they have them? And I don't?"

Humphrey pushed his flask into Julian's hand. "Drink, Jule. You're looking the color of a cow's teat."

Julian laughed, having no idea what color a cow's teat was. But following the directive, he drank while giving Humphrey a brief accounting of his meeting with the Duke of Ashcroft.

"He wasn't angry to find you there?"

"He was relieved, I think. He cast a blaze in the hearth with a flick of his fingers. He just bowed his head and *poof*! The earl's crystal has kept him from burning down the city, although we don't understand the power it possesses. More investigation is needed. As a child, he dreamed of flames engulfing him, then one day they started rolling off his fingertips. Firestarters, the earl called them."

"And?"

"He's arriving next week."

Humphrey jumped to his feet, bumping his head on the carriage roof. "*What?*"

"Hard for him to enjoy the benefits of our merry

club if he's not asked to join. Plus, reflect on this, my cautious friend. The Duke is a former soldier and surrounded by a small band of loyal mercenaries. And they're coming with him. That's protection we can use. Not to mention how much this expands our world. You may hate it, but he has influence and power we may someday need."

Humphrey threw himself into the seat with an exasperated gust.

Julian pitched the flask back to him, then tugged his coat off. He was starting to overheat in the confined space. Maybe the reason for his cow-teat complexion. "Consider it a symbiotic relationship. We help him control his gift; he shares his contacts. And his army. We'll have entry into every gaming hell, every public house, every drawing room in a way no mere viscount would."

"He can take the West End, and we'll take the East. Don't want him to dirty his velvet slippers tramping through the muck."

Julian dropped his head to his hands, minutes from asking the coachman to stop the carriage. Scotch on an empty stomach had been a ghastly idea. "No velvet slippers this one. Trained for combat when we only trained on the street."

"Fireball trained as a soldier? What, in a drawing room?" Humphrey snorted. "I could stomp his wee arse."

Julian counted until he caught a full breath. "I think that's an excellent…start to your friendship."

"Hope the village fire brigade is prepared if the flaming bastard's coming here."

"Laundry cottage. By the lake," Julian whispered, his composure slipping. He should have taken an extra night in London to sleep this off. He'd drained his reserves with the visions—and he wasn't recovering quickly. Not as quickly as he used to. But he'd been frantic to make it back to Harbingdon. Back to Piper.

"Made of stone, which is fireproof. And near the lake, should we need water quickly."

Julian bounded to his feet, rapping on the trap with a closed fist. "Halt!"

He was out of the conveyance before it rolled to a stop. Flinging himself to the ground, he sunk his fingers knuckle-deep in the mud. The scent of rain and earth rose to him on a rip of air that was a moist blessing washing over his skin. It almost eradicated the smell of lavender gliding from the carriage's interior and into the night.

Minutes passed before he was able to climb to his feet and lumber back into his transport. He sank to the seat, avoiding the censure he knew would be lingering in Humphrey's eyes.

Maybe his friend was right.

Maybe he *was* killing himself.

∼

Before she touched him, Piper reminded herself of her mission.

Because anything connected to Julian was a snarled morass of conflicted reasoning and always had been. Love, rage, admiration, jealousy. *Possession.* She'd never used her gift in an organic way for his benefit: with only the thought to mend.

But this day, this *moment*, she would touch him as a healer. Not a lover, not even as a friend.

When Humphrey had woken her in a mild panic —unusual enough an occurrence to bring life to her own—he'd demanded she direct her focus toward Julian in one way and one way *only*. Part of her 'growing up process,' he issued beneath his breath in the event she'd misconstrued his meaning.

She was to separate what had happened in the lodge, in Ashcroft's townhouse, the way Julian had consumed her in both settings with devout fervor, from what she was set to do in a bedchamber located a floor beneath hers, one Julian rarely used from the look of it. No unfinished canvases, no spattered rags, not even the pungent suggestion of turpentine and paint. Just ancestral paintings and random relics that had likely come with the house. The viscount owned this room, the artist the lodge.

She preferred the lodge. She preferred the artist.

Oh, Julian, she thought when she reached the massive tester bed. He was as pale as the creamy counterpane they'd laid him upon, his skin flushed, his hair an absolute snarl about his head. His aura alternated between restorative indigo and a blinding cherry hinting at extreme unrest. She placed the back of her hand against his brow—no fever—then snatched it away.

A healer must heal. And only heal.

Avoiding letting her gaze travel the length of his body, she glanced over her shoulder to find that Humphrey and Minnie had retreated to the hallway, thankfully taking their apprehension with them. If Julian knew how many people depended upon him, how many loved him, maybe he would take better care.

Or maybe it would only add to his burden.

With a whistle-sigh, she perched on the edge of the mattress, took his hand in both of hers and closed her eyes. The initial rush of emotion sent the air from her lungs in a burst. The images were so disparate, she couldn't credit them. Shadowy, vague, engulfing. Each a split-second review before another crowded in and knocked that one aside. She stepped into none, held herself from delving too deeply. A skill she had recently mastered, one she called skimming. A way to heal without leaving her shattered. She couldn't follow the plan Julian had developed to grow the League, participate fully as she wanted to if she didn't learn to manage the process.

To control the process.

Julian's hand flexed, his fingers tightening around hers. "Piper...*stop*," he whispered with what sounded like the last of his strength. "It's starting to hurt."

She blinked to find his gaze fixed on her, a drowsy, adorable—though she would never admit this—expression on his face. His cheeks were glowing with a healthy color.

She frowned. "Hurt?"

"Feels wonderful, like a warm bath. Cleansing. Then...too much." He swallowed, his lids drifting low. "Like being tickled."

Tickled?

A wry smile that let her know he was going to recover twisted his lips. "Forget I said that."

"So, you like being tickled?" She clicked her tongue against her teeth. "Shall I add this to my list of items?"

"List?"

"For our night."

He linked his fingers with hers, but his eyes remained closed, so he missed the scorching blush that hit her face as she imagined his naked body and what she would like to do to it.

"There's a festival in the village. In two nights."

And?

"Go with me," he murmured, his voice on the buttery fringe of sleep.

She waited for him to say more...but moments later, he was lost to the world.

Crossing the lone window in his room, she blindly searched the night sky. She was stunned. For the first time in memory, Julian had asked her to accompany him to an event. Nothing to do with the League. An invitation apart from the night she'd secured by twisting the proverbial arm behind his back.

He wanted to be with her. There had been a sincere timbre to his words, a tone he was too exhausted to hide.

Wrapping her arms around her body, she swallowed past the sting of tears and reminded herself of Julian's words: *one night, then you must let me go.*

Heavens, how was she going to follow through on her promise?

CHAPTER 15

Nothing ever becomes real until it is experienced.
~John Keats

---

*P*iper suppressed a sigh and glanced at the hulking, straight-from-the-rookery types on either side of her. Finn lagged just behind, his demeanor as vigilant as she'd ever seen it. His dreams were troubling him.

She chased away the nip of fear and marched forward, a circle of torches, their glow a stain against the darkening sky, acting as her beacon. The village celebrated on the grounds of an abandoned chapel sitting atop the highest hill in the shire, whispered to be the birthplace of true love. The surroundings were what poets envisioned, and she wasn't going to let *her* true love and his overly protective protestations ruin this night. Julian's note telling her he'd meet her as he had to help prepare for the festival, was tucked in her corset, pressed quite inappropriately against her wildly beating heart.

After her return from London, erotic imaginings

had begun to plague her dreams, nothing so melancholy as Finn's. She woke with sheets twisted about her ankles, skin damp, lungs churning. She wanted to unleash her passion in a fury, knock Julian from his feet with the force of it. No matter their conclusion, no one could take her delicious memories from her. Julian's lips grazing her nipple, finger delving, eyes locked on her as she glided over the precipice.

She returned welcoming smiles as she made her way into the boisterous crowd, vastly disparate from the leering ones in Ashcroft's ballroom. A feast of cakes, pies, cheese, and bread covered a long table placed before the highest chapel wall. Barrels of ale, bottles of brandy and scotch kept company on the other. A trio of musicians sheltered beneath a towering oak played with abandon, to the delight of those dancing in a style Piper imagined best described by Jane Austen. Nothing so refined as a waltz in this delightful setting beneath the trees. No one was waiting for scandal and ruin, waiting for her to make a horrendous mistake.

Piper turned in a languid circle, the auras of the townsfolk transcendent, more beautiful than she ever recalled them being.

Then she saw him, and her heart melted, a soft cascade of emotion flowing through her.

Julian was settled on his knee next to an ale barrel, shirtsleeves rolled to his elbow, a waistcoat of the somber variety he favored clinging to his chest. He held a mallet in one hand and with the other, gestured for the barrel to be positioned on its side. Looking over his shoulder, not in her direction, he called out to someone standing at the edge of the forest. Simon stepped shyly into the circle of men. Her breath caught at the boy's expression: equal parts hope and resistance. Julian beckoned him near, his smile tipping at the edges. Not until he extended the mallet, a peace offering, did Simon move close enough to take it.

"Give it a couple of good whacks," Julian coaxed, pointing to a spot on the barrel where a tap hung loosely. A sluggish but steady flow of ale dribbled to the ground, releasing the sweet scent of yeast. "To seat the tap, you see."

Simon pressed his lips together and dropped to a squat, his behind dusting the ground. He looked quite stylish tonight, in summer woolen trousers and jacket Julian must have had fitted for him. Twigs and dirt covered his clothing as if he'd rolled on the ground like Henry, but they were a vast improvement over the filthy rags he'd arrived in.

"Like this?" the boy asked and gave a mock jab with the mallet, soft enough to smash a butterfly.

Julian's teeth dug into his bottom lip to hold back a laugh. "Imagine someone trying to steal your last halfpenny. Right out of your pocket. Give it as hard a blow as that."

Simon nodded in all seriousness, adjusting his slim fingers around the mallet. "You wanna move yur hand, sir? I would meself."

Julian shook his head. "No, I trust you."

The astonished look on Simon's face rocked her where she stood. What would have happened if Julian had not found the boy? An example of the League's work, its *purpose*, sat perched on his grubby knees before her.

"Hey-ho, then," Simon said and swung with all his might, missing Julian's fingers by the merest measure. The tap jammed in the hole, slowing the drip to a modest trickle.

"Another strike to the halfpenny thief," Julian instructed and this time, withdrew his hand before the blow came. "The barrel can take it."

The group was turning the barrel upright, the tap in excellent placement, when Julian saw her. He rose to a stand, towering over the men surrounding him and stepped through a circle of torchlight, shadows striking his cheek and diving in the neck of the shirt held together by an impossibly loose cravat. Amber highlights streaked his hair, much like the ones shooting from the firepit to the stars.

She marveled at the wonderous contrast of him. Rough-hewn in one light, wholly elegant in another, like his divergent past. Part boy of the streets, part titled gentleman. An honorable man with an extraordinary gift he loathed but accepted. How he managed the varied facets of his life with such care, she couldn't fathom. She'd never been able to blend her conflicting halves into a capable whole, not once in her entire life.

When he reached her, eyes the color of a dawn mist swept her from head to toe, and she confessed to complete and utter fascination.

"You flaunt the saddest chignons I've ever seen," he said and brushed a loose tendril from her cheek. She must have flinched, because he pulled back, then moved in again to tuck the stray piece behind her ear. "The wonderful news is, we're surrounded by farmers and craftsmen, a tailor, a butcher, a cobbler." His gaze was warm, intimate, delighted. "You can be who you want here, that's the magic. The lord and lady disappear in the fog. Julian and Piper step out of it."

All that stood between them was shimmering, implicit awareness. His aura shifted, pale to dazzling as he watched her watch him.

Her heart squeezed. The examination aroused him as much as it aroused her.

He nodded to her guards, an unspoken command to stay behind. "Come," he said huskily and offered his arm as if they were set to stroll through Hyde Park. She slipped her hand through the crook between warm body and bent elbow, never once considering anything but agreement.

Brushing his finger along her kidskin glove, he paused when he met bare skin. Halting, he raised her hands and with efficient jerks, tugged the gloves off and tossed them over his shoulder as he led her away from the circle of light, music, people. "Julian," she whispered, unsure of his mood, watching her gloves land in a neat twist at the gnarled base of a tree.

He drew her along a pebbled path leading away from the chapel, through a thicket of nettle-leaved bellflower so dense it obscured the night, and into a clearing surrounded by dogwoods and azaleas. The music of the festivities lingered, but to her, they had entered another world entirely.

One Julian had created.

Until her last breath, she would remember this night as the most romantic of her life. Although it was a simple setting, a simple picture, one he could have easily sketched. A blanket spread over the grass, his coat lying to one side. A broad band of moonlight coloring the ground an ethereal, misty silver.

She turned to him, words taken by the gesture.

He shrugged, looking away as if embarrassed. Julian *embarrassed*. "I want to be, Piper. With you. Us. I don't care where, I don't care what. Just this night, let there be an *us*."

Feelings piled in on one another like carriages on Bond Street during the height of the season. *Us*. Julian thought of her, of them, as *us*. A fount of affection welled, shooting from her fingertips and the ends of her hair. She imagined her aura, a brilliant burst the exact shade of a sapphire.

Going to his knee on the blanket, he gazed up at her, his expression so transparent, so open, she marveled he had ever hidden anything from her. The dimple she loved so well dinted his cheek with his smile. "You're pleased?"

Nodding, she made a vague motion toward his horse, tied to a tree just outside the clearing. Silence would have to do. Her heart had not released her to speak just yet.

"When you're ready, we can be at the lodge in ten minutes." He made a graceful loop with his hand, indicating something in the near distance. "There's a back trail. Rarely used, faster than going through the village."

"My...my bay?"

He shook his head, his gaze catching hers then skipping away. His hand flexed on air at his side. "Though I may lose my mind, for this ride, I think you'll fit quite nicely on my lap."

"Ready?" She laughed, imagining another ride she would like to take. "Julian, I'm ready *now*."

"Of course, you are," he whispered, the words so soft they were almost beyond her hearing. Grasping her hand, he tugged her down beside him. She went to her knees, then her bottom in an inelegant tumble. Her shawl landed in a puddle beside her. "But maybe I'm not, my love," he added and helped her arrange her skirts in a modest circle about her.

"Am I going to have to convince you?" she asked, creating a list in her mind of ways to do just that. Starting with the removal of his sadly-folded cravat, her lips moving to the enticing hollow beneath, then lower, and lower still. She closed her eyes to the image; that or follow through.

Frustrated and vastly awakened, her sigh ripped through the night.

Julian laughed, a rare sound, magical and earnest. He closed in, and she caught his scent and the heat of his body before he touched her. Cupping her jaw, he tilted her face into the moonlight. In his handsome visage, she saw the young man she had loved from the first moment she saw him stepping from her grandfather's carriage. "Go easy on me, Yank. I beg of you," he whispered, his breath flowing over her cheek and into the neck of the simple day dress—one easily removed—she'd chosen for the outing.

She slid her fingers into the hair brushing his crisp collar and with a gentle tug, brought him to her. "*Closer.*"

With a low growl of agreement, he captured her mouth in a display rough in urgency, stunning in perfection. Sensation swept her as he worshiped her before diving in, blatant seduction she could not deny.

Had no plans *to* deny.

The sound of the festival faded as Julian uttered fervent entreaties in her ear. Her thoughts scattered until she was nothing but a roaring heartbeat, flushed skin, staggered breaths. Responding, she arched into him, her pulse convening between her thighs in a molten rush. Her nipples peaked beneath her stays, imprisonment when she wanted *release*. She shifted her hips, seeking, a low moan bursting forth. He answered her demand, pressing her into the blanket, his body moving over hers, their sculpture molding into one. He slowly tugged her skirt to her waist, allowing one brief second of refreshing relief before the long, hard length of him settled, and she reheated, head to toe.

"You taste like home," he said, his breath racing into her ear like a wave. She gasped as he nipped her earlobe, peppering her skin with goosebumps. "Like golden fields shimmering in the summer sun." He trailed tender kisses along her throat, halting at the laced-edged neck of her dress. "Exquisite, as far as the eye can see."

She skated her hand over each bump of his spine, to his lean hip, where she guided his movement against her. Her need was boundless, and she didn't care if he knew it. Tugging his shirt from his trousers, she met bare skin with a beholden sigh. Linen, cotton, and silk, neatly stitched seams, ties, and buttons were all that kept their bodies apart.

"Here, *now*," she urged, their rhythm caught between cool earth and dark sky, a rhythm as old as time. His hard length nestled between her welcoming folds, their bodies surging. Undoing strings, he opened her bodice, and she anticipated the arrival of his mouth with an excruciating surge of heat and cognizance. He nipped the side of her breast, and she moaned with approval. "Leave your mark on me, Jules."

He lowered his brow to her shoulder, his breath a rapid shot across her inflamed nipple. Edging to his elbows, he palmed the blanket, sending his hips in a tighter fit against hers, pinning her to the ground in the most delicious way imaginable. "Not here, Yank, not here."

"*Why?*"

"Ah, Piper, you unman me." His hair, lustrous and thick, tumbled in his face, the tips brushing his hollowed cheeks. "I feel a boy, completely without aptitude." His thumb swept her bottom lip and held for the briefest second. "I brought you here because I want to *know* you. More than..." With a harsh breath, he rolled to his back, his arm going over his eyes. His other hand found hers, fingers linking. "I'm trying to live my entire life in one day. I want to slow down. Record every heartbeat, every touch, every sigh."

His poetic words were not surprising, though she was surprised he shared them. Julian was the most compassionate person she'd ever known. Even when he'd hurt her, she understood his motives were honorable though, at times, thoughtless.

"Jules, you know me better than anyone," she said and squeezed his fingers, uncertain when she'd experienced the wondrously simple gift of holding his hand. Unwise to feel such possession over something so basic. "Because I've never held anything back when I'm sure I should have. From the first moment, standing on the drive outside my grandfather's manor, such a conflicted expression on your face... I've never been able to deny you."

His thumb traced a soft circle on her palm. "Then, I guess I want you to know *me*."

My, this night was presenting one astonishment after another.

Her heart soared. He was here, with her, not merely a fantasy born of loneliness and grief. Her gaze traveled over his lean stomach, his narrow hips, and lower, where his arousal made an impressive display beneath his trouser close. His aura flickered around him like a golden halo. Lifting her free hand, she trailed a finger along his chest, drifting over each waistcoat button, a leisurely glide to desire.

With a swift inhalation, he caught her hand before it reached its destination. Lifting their arms high, he pointed to the heavens. "See that one?" he asked, his voice a rough cut through the still night. "Next to Orion."

Piper trained her eyes on the sky, where stars had begun to gather like shiny pearls nestled in black silk. The night was brilliant, cloudless, a breathtaking portrait.

"The brightest star is part of Canis Minor."

"The smaller dog," she whispered.

His gaze shifted from the constellation to her as a bemused expression crossed his face, gone so swiftly she almost missed it.

"Latin was on the agenda, you know."

He lowered their arms, pressing her hand flat over his stomach, the warm hollow rising and falling with his breaths. "I didn't know you kept a tutor around long enough to have an agenda."

"See, look how much you're coming to learn about me." She turned, pressing her face against his chest. "Latin is not my only talent, I should hope." At her teasing words, his pulse skipped beneath her cheek, matching the one tapping beneath the hand he held trapped on his belly. She was caught between blood and breath, owning those parts of him. His thoughts would complete the circle. Choosing her words carefully, she cracked the box open. "You've never talked about it. Your time before my grandfather brought you to me."

He released a gusty exhalation, his hand tensing around hers. "The stars were of great comfort because they were steady, no matter if viewed from the window of a richly furnished bedchamber or the alley of a filthy warren. There was safety in the clouds. A refuge. Something I could touch without the curse of haunting, damning visions."

Tears sparked her vision, but she swallowed past the sting. She wouldn't embarrass him with senseless emotion when he was finally sharing painful memories. "Your father…"

Another exhale and a charged silence before he spoke. "He was exacting. And unkind, as I look at his actions from a man's perspective. He brought out the worst in everyone. Servants, estate managers, family. The house was run on and largely by fear. When I began to touch things and tell stories, at a very young age, mind you, oh"—Julian huffed a sound somewhere between a laugh and growl—"his tolerance was not merely low, it was nonexistent. Somehow, he believed regular beatings would keep the visions at bay." His lids dropped, lashes sweeping the shadowed skin beneath his eyes. "I'd have gladly accepted the abuse *if* it held them at bay. If the bruises cured me. But both, his loathing and my own"—he brought her hand to his lips and placed a soft kiss on her fingers —"was too much to bear. The visions were staying in my life. My father was the removable part. He was sick by then, though dying none too quickly."

She tucked herself into him, shoulder to knee, an instinctive compulsion to protect.

"So, I ran. A young boy, a titled fool. My pockets crammed with enough objects to pawn and keep me afloat for a time. A baron as a courtesy, the viscountcy sitting in the wings, I chose to wait my father out. Away from the reach of his fists. He looked for me as I was not only his heir but, most unfortunately, his only child. Except, rookeries are rather fine places in which to disappear, grimy alleys and gutters hiding many rats. I was just a well-educated one. When Shelley wrote, *hell is a city much like London*, damned if he didn't know what he was about."

For a moment, the faint rumble of the festival and their shallow breaths were the only sounds. "I tortured him as best I could, letting him know through his solicitor that I was indeed alive—and would return when he was in his grave."

"And the earl?" She'd never been entirely sure how her grandfather found Julian, only that he had.

Again, he placed a kiss to her fingertips, silent.

She tried to shy away from reading his aura or allowing herself to absorb his chaotic emotions and secondarily soothe. She wanted to comfort without her gift involved, so he understood a *normal* exchange between them was possible.

"As much as I tried to keep it quiet, there were, I don't know"—he shook his head, a frown denting his cheek—"episodes. One in a public house when I was fourteen. Another on the street later that year. Humphrey was there for both, thank God, and I wasn't using my real name, of course, but I gained a reputation for having the *touch*. People sidestepped me in the street like I held magic in my hands. The earl had established deep connections in the very communities where we sought to hide. Participants for his research complied more readily when circumstances were desperate." His eyes met hers, silver and amber sparking in the moonlight. Her heart gained speed as his emotions flowed in, against her will, drawn in by her vulnerability. "Look how long it took Ashcroft, a man with means, to come out of the woodwork. Until he had nowhere else to turn. Needier ones suffer even more and fail faster."

"But…the earl said, you weren't desperate." She wondered how long she could continue this conversation before she began healing. His open heart had, in turn, opened hers, weakening her resolve.

He blinked, his words coming out as if sliced from his mind with a razor. "Oh, but I was. Not for myself. It was clear Finn wouldn't survive the rookery. He couldn't control his readings, the dreams. Couldn't control much of anything. And I wasn't much better. Humphrey was doing his best to keep us out of trouble...but it was a disaster. Going back to my family was out of the question, so I accepted the earl's offer when he made it." Julian shrugged a broad shoulder, a brush against the blanket. "I agreed to every request, giving your grandfather pages and pages of detail for his chronology, assisting with research, anything, as long as Finn was safe. My father conveniently passed a year or so into my time with the earl, allowing me to step back into this world, even if I didn't truly want to."

Her blood rushed through her veins at a dizzying speed. Sharing his life in this way was the most treacherous act of seduction when he did not aim to seduce.

Revealing his heart, his mind, his soul.

Pieces of himself he would leave her with.

All he would leave her with.

As if he sensed her distress, he grasped her chin and pulled her lips to his. The kiss bled into chaos in seconds. Her arms flowed over his broad shoulders and into his hair, where she tilted his head and dove deeper. Their bodies locked into place until she couldn't have said where hers left off and his started. He tasted of mint, brandy, and something uniquely Julian. Nothing she could define in this lifetime.

She didn't know how to measure the taste of *home*, but this might be the classification she searched for.

When it was now or never, their hands releasing ties and buttons, their clothing a damp, unnecessary tangle between their writhing bodies, his breath hitched as he paused, his sigh batting her cheek. When he had himself under control, as graceful as one could, he rose to his feet. The midnight sky a glorious canvas at his back, he stood highlighted against the darkness; there were no bounds to his beauty or the depth of her feelings.

I'm scared of you, of this, she thought in sudden desperation.

Then he extended his hand and said the words that somehow found their way to her heart, "I've dreamed of you for so long."

With this sincere declaration easing her fear, she accepted his offer.

Sidonie lay puddled before the oak door she had bloodied her fists against. Her men had followed orders and kept her from leaving the monstrous country dwelling during one of her episodes. They had learned in Lyon the calamity going into public during one could bring.

Sidonie screamed and thumped her hands against the scarred wooden planks beneath her.

The healer was near. So near Sidonie could feel the heat of the girl's skin burning into her own. Her men had seen her in the village, too protected to capture, just this morn.

Piper. Piper. Piper. The name was a chant, a refrain, a prayer. Campfire and twilight and friendship. Love. Through the boy, she had seen this and more—before he thrust her from his mind. *Finn.* She could not wait to seize his last breath, compensation for keeping her from the answer to her invocation.

She would enjoy watching him die.

Sidonie stumbled to the window and pressed her cheek against the beveled pane. The healer was out there somewhere, beneath the stars.

Her deliverance.

Shielded, but not forever. Rebellious women never followed instructions for long. She should know.

And this one dared much.

When she made a false move, Sidonie would be waiting.

CHAPTER 16

My heart would hear her and beat.
  ~Alfred Lord Tennyson

The door to the lodge closed behind them, and Julian pressed his back to the pitted wood, watching Piper cross the room, stepping over paints and a canvas he had completed but had yet to store, heading without deliberation toward his bedchamber. A bedchamber he'd never shared with another. Never considered sharing until she stumbled back into his life.

In that space, he tossed and turned night after agonizing night as reflections of her tormented. He kicked off his boots, telling himself to go slowly.

In the doorway, she hesitated, glancing over her shoulder with a smoldering green gaze, the look a blatant invitation. Then she disappeared inside.

Piper Scott in full, glowing arousal.

He expected no less as he'd never met a more determined woman in his life.

While reiterating the internal agreement he'd

made with himself in Ashcroft's medieval chamber, he followed with a resolute stride.

Show her what she wants to know.

Overcome your fixation.

And the last, so he did not lose himself in her: *nothing is as good as imagined.*

Yet, when he entered the bedchamber to find Piper standing by the bed—feet bare, hair unbound and flowing loosely over her shoulders, hands toying with the buttons of her bodice—the feeling that moved through him with a sharp primal thrust was so distinct he almost sank to his knees with the force of it.

Love.

He had no experience, certainly no practice. His examples of romantic love were nonexistent as his childhood had provided nothing representative. All he'd learned was survival. And the connections he considered his closest had been created not through love, but under duress.

An abnormal collection of people who fit nowhere in society were his family now.

Piper is your family, his mind threw out as justification.

Yes, he decided with an inward sigh of relief. He was not *in* love. Love and *in* love were very, very different things.

He could never let her go if he was *in love*.

He watched as she struggled with the buttons, her hands shaking and making slow work of it. A smile curved his lips, and he thanked God the delightful woman showed some trepidation in this thing.

Two strides and he had his arm around her waist, his hand plowing into the dark tangle of hair and bringing her mouth to his. Her lashes fluttered as she complied with a mewling sound that tore through him. Bouncing to her tiptoes, she struggled for better reach, her fingers circling his shoulders, grasping his shirt, scraping the skin beneath crisp linen. She revealed no reluctance, no fear. A greedy response, one he answered.

The kiss was flawless, like they'd practiced a thousand times to arrive at this level of perfection. He had known, with that one, much more innocent kiss, oh, he had *known* she was his missing piece. Call him a romantic fool, but he believed there was *one* person who matched you, wit for wit, passion for passion.

A blistering fever swept him, settling in his groin, sending restraint and reason charging from him. The scent of lavender and crisp, warm earth, as if she'd been gardening and just come in from the sun, clung to her skin. There was desire, but also a powerful thread of affection stitching this experience together. A years-long bond strengthening everything he felt for her. Impatient, he deepened the kiss, hand trembling where he held her securely against his body. He angled lower, wishing he'd not grown so tall the summer after his seventeenth birthday.

The boy's height would have better suited the man's craving.

With an aggrieved sound, she placed kisses along his jaw while shoving him back a step. He stumbled, not realizing what she was about until she'd backed him into the wall. Her hands went to the buttons of his waistcoat, her fingers slick, slipping. Her need battered him like a fierce, unrelenting wind.

Stunned, he lifted his head, his gaze landing on the mirror opposite him.

The ravenous expression on his face was not one he recognized. He'd never exposed himself in such an intimate way; of this, he was sure. Emotion flooded him, admittedly some unwanted.

Longing, doubt, eagerness, compassion.

She shook her head—*no thinking*—and brought his mouth back to hers.

There were no words to describe his obsession with the woman standing before him, though he spoke nonsensical ones against her lips, her cheek, the curve of her neck where it swept like silk to her shoulder. Urgent commands and avowals bounced between them as he unsteadily loosened buttons, ties, hooks, her clothing pooling about her in a twist of watery blue silk, boned stays, and cotton.

"Goddamn all these layers," he growled and kicked her corset aside. Without a breath of hesitancy, she removed her garters and stockings, her movements languid, teasing, as she darted gazes at him throughout the unveiling until she stood naked before him.

His mind cataloged her beauty in separate dimensions.

The man captivated versus the artist. Her hair a dream-filled cloud about her face and shoulders; her breasts high, plump but not too, perfectly balanced to her slight frame; her nipples the wondrous pink of the delphinium that littered the banks of Harbingdon's lake during summer. Her hips were gently rounded, her legs lithe. And the curls nestled at the delta of her thighs brought new meaning to *exquisite*. So petite, facing him calmly, arms by her side, not reaching to cover any part of her body from his interpretation.

He marveled at her composure when he was shaken to his core. But she allowed his study, so he took his time, his gaze drinking her in as if the view presented water to a man done crossing a barren wasteland.

Her frank review in return sent a bolt of awareness pinging right through him. "Piper, love," he said, his voice gone thick, "you are stunning."

But when he moved to guide her to the bed, make her his in every way he'd dreamed, she raised her hand, staying his approach. Stepping in with a knowing smile, she trailed her finger over the notched lapel of his half-buttoned waistcoat, across his belly, following a direct path to his erection. She covered his length with her palm while he struggled to maintain control and keep his gaze trained on her. Her touch was tentative and untried—devastating.

"My," she whispered with a playful glance shot through incredibly long lashes, "that *is* impressive. I always"—her cheeks flushed a becoming pink—"imagined."

A spurt of laughter left his lips, joy he had never, *not once in his life,* experienced at such a moment. The way she looked at him then was a more exhaustive study than standing nude before her would be. He knew not how to reply, discomfited to feel his cheeks go hot. "I'm happy you think so," he finally came up with while his brain was trying to communicate the fact that her hand caressed, none too gently, his throbbing cock.

He allowed her exploration as she undressed him. Cravat, waistcoat, and shirt fluttered to the floor before she shifted her attention lower. He dropped his head back, his forearms going to the wall to hold him up. Another minute, maybe two, was the most he could take of this. Seconds if she caressed certain areas again, which with a hesitant move, she did. Already he couldn't catch a sure breath, and he was certain, *dead*-certain, he'd never wanted another woman this much.

And he never would.

Humming beneath her breath, Piper enchanted,

ostensibly delighted by the entire deed, even the awkward parts he usually tried to move quickly past. Like the trouser button that wouldn't come loose, one she sent bouncing to the floor. "Help me," she finally whispered, her mouth going to his chest and nipping a patch of skin beneath his collarbone. She went up on her toes to further encourage his assistance, her nipple scraping his, and he thought: *enough*.

His hands covered hers, making quick work of his trousers and drawers. Then he walked her back, back, until the high mattress met her thighs and gravity took her down. He scooted her across the counterpane, resolving for their difference in height before gently flowing over her, their hips brushing, shifting, melding in an absolute, hot, slick seal.

Her hushed groan echoed as he rocked against her, once, then again, her body readying, moisture coating his cock. So wet so quickly, he marveled as a surge of animalistic lust tightened his scrotum to an almost painful degree. Desiring everything, he captured her lips, his hands on a quest for hidden treasure.

He wanted to know what she liked, what made her cry out and arch beneath him.

His aim: memorize how to drive Piper Scott mad.

Circling her nipple between finger and thumb, he twisted gently. Then he followed with his breath, lips, tongue, teeth. Sucking one pebbled nub, then the other, as she moaned. A band of creamy-silver moonlight poured in the open window and across her body. One hand fisted in the counterpane, the other trapped in his hair, she curved into him, seemingly lost to sensation.

Lost to him.

No artist had fashioned any woman more remarkable. There could be no more magnificent splendor.

"Here," she demanded on a whimper, her hand falling from his hair to slide between her legs. Trapping it beneath his, he raised her arm above her head and pinned it to the mattress.

"Oh, no," he said and blew air across the damp nipple he'd just released, "that is all mine."

He followed moonlight down her body, over every sleek rise and dip as she murmured nonsensical bits of encouragement. His gaze skated up as his teeth nipped her hip, lips gliding over smooth skin and bone. Piper's head was back, her hair a dark twist beneath her. Her hands were again caught in the counterpane, so forcefully, he questioned it surviving the night.

Spreading her legs, she sought relief in the most basic of appeals. Wanting to give *everything*, wanting to drive her wild before he let himself be driven, he delved through her silken folds, gently working a finger inside until the heel of his hand lay against her.

She came partially undone in a primitive and precise transfer that drove his finger deeper. "Julian," she gasped on a hitched breath, *"please."*

"This?" he whispered, his thumb settling on her peaked clit, circling, pressing, gauging her response as he stroked. He pressed his lips to her thigh, nibbled softly, then soothed with his tongue, offering a steady river of contact. In this, he had extreme patience, even as his cock felt near to cracking open.

He planned to make her come in as many ways as he could devise.

"Kiss me," she urged, her hand going to his wrist and working to pull him atop her.

"Ah," he agreed, "a perfect plan." So, he set his lips where his thumb had been, and he nearly came himself as her moist passage contracted around the finger he stroked deep as her taste flowed into his mouth. A pulse, then another, a clench he questioned lasting ten seconds through once he made it inside her. "Tight, dear God," he mouthed against her, sucking her clit between his lips.

She gripped his hair, guiding him as he toyed with her.

He varied the caresses, circling, delving, working in rhythm until heat, sweat, desire entangled them.

Gratification he'd never experienced.

He gazed over damp skin covered in the lightest dusting of hair to find her helpless, caught in a storm. She looked as unhinged as he felt, completely unraveled. "Look at me," he whispered, his breathing ragged. He wanted, *needed*, to know the color of her eyes when she went over the edge.

Covetous, he wanted this for his memories; he wanted it *all*.

This night had been years of fevered dreams in the making.

She moaned, head twisting on the counterpane. *No*, she voiced without sound. Her hands clenched, silk trapping in her fists. With a wicked smile, he lifted his mouth from her, his finger stilling, teasing with nothing but his breath across her heated flesh. She gasped, thwarted, lashes fluttering, her bewildered gaze meeting his. Her eyes had darkened, the shadowy green of moss in the dead of the forest, her pupils wide and unfocused.

He imagined she wasn't even sure what he'd asked of her.

"There you are." He felt pleased in an absurdly masculine way. Piper Scott was, for once, under his thumb. *Literally*. In fact, she looked as baked as a cake. Generous lover that he was, he took mercy and renewed his assault.

With a tortured cry, she collapsed to the bed.

Stroke after hungry stroke, he worked her into a frenzy as her pleasure built, her body contracting and releasing, her words part supplication, part threat. A fantasy, her rampant longing thrilled. He gripped her hip, guiding her twisting body against his tongue as they mimicked the joining that would come later.

"Let go," he coaxed and slipped a second finger inside her. She tasted of fresh rain and something sharp, piquant, like a flower's nectar and was so wet she was trailing moisture to his wrist. As she closed in on bliss, he again let his gaze skate over her gently rounded belly, her heaving breasts, to find her arms thrown wide, head tilted so far back on the mattress her expression was lost to him.

Stretched out before him in the throes of release, she was the sensual answer to his dreams.

A goddess of his design—mind, soul, and body.

With a throat-deep gasp, she came apart, her carnal cry shattering the silent night. Her fingers clenched in his hair and urged him against her, harder, *harder*, then, seconds later, pushing away, begging for freedom.

Gentling his touch, he counted to ten and imagined Cook, a woman who had to be close to seventy, naked. He was honestly desperate to keep his body from erupting like an untaught boy on her thigh.

His belief that nothing could be as good as imagined evaporated in the mist.

~

Piper arrived from her tour of the universe, feeling as if she'd closed in on Julian's beloved Canis Minor only to find herself lying weakly on his bed. Choked for breath, her skin—every inch of it—covered in a light sheen, muscles she'd not known she had quivering, she was utterly destroyed. The triangle between her thighs throbbed in time with her racing heartbeat; her nipples were hard enough, she surmised as she brushed her hand across them, to snap off like pieces of chalk.

The mystery of passion was unfolding around her.

Show me, she had asked without knowing.

Blinking into hazy moonlight, she was stunned to find she held a strand of Julian's hair in her fist. Had she torn out his *hair*? Gazing down the curves and twists of her body, she watched as he lifted his head from her thigh, his gaze glowing as fiercely as his distant star when it met hers. There was an incredulous expression on his gorgeous face, as potent as what was surely stamped across hers. He gulped a breath, dropping his head once more, sweat from his skin fusing with hers. After a long moment, he laid a tender kiss on her thigh, and she, amazingly, felt desire spike.

"Stop those little mewling sounds. Or I'm going to have to imagine Cook naked for the rest of the night."

With a gust of laughter, she propped up on her elbow as he slid from the bed, heading to the lone window in the room. His body was glorious, she marveled as he entered and exited a broad beam of silvery light. The meager glow did nothing *but* illuminate the bands of muscle, the flex of his buttocks as he stretched to open the window, the give of his calf muscles as he settled back to the floor. Helplessly, she tracked the enticing line of hair trailing down his chest to his erect penis. Her body lit from within. He was flawlessly masculine, a physical specimen much like a statue in the National Gallery.

As if he tried to control himself, he braced his hands on either side of the window and leaned out into the night. A gust of air swept inside, fluttering the hair at the nape of his neck, skin she'd worshipped with everything in her.

"You *are* beautiful," she vowed across the short distance.

His hands tensed around the window frame, the muscles in his back rippling, her words disrupting like a pebble thrown in a still pond. He took a hard breath, two. When he turned, blocking the light and throwing his body into silhouette, he looked a hero crossing the moors, windswept, skin flushed, eyes wild.

Although she wanted to separate her gift from this night, she couldn't help but record his aura as it blossomed, a dazzling, sensual blue.

Her power rose as his attraction raced across the space like a bullet discharged from a pistol. Dropping her head, she trailed her hands over her body, touching each spot he had, neck, shoulders, breasts, nipples. With a muttered curse, he was there, flowing over her, pinning her to the bed before her exploration made it any lower. She gasped as his weight landed fully atop her, his hips pressing as his indescribably hard shaft found a welcoming home. The area expanded and throbbed in preparation for ecstasy.

For invasion.

"Wider," he urged, bringing her leg alongside his hip.

Oh, she thought and lifted it high and around, her heel digging into his firm buttock. The other she locked in place around his calf as she curved into him. Incredible leverage, trapping him within the circle of her limbs.

"I feel the pupil," he murmured, then kissed her deeply, tilting her head to better enable his assault. Any sensation that drifted away following her orgasm circled back, escalating, pulse points thumping along every inch of skin he touched.

"You taste of me," she whispered against his lips.

Julian cupped her face, his heavy-lidded eyes deepening dark as gunmetal. The intense, imperturbable focus he was known for fixed solely on her. "You taste *intoxicating*." He kissed the side of her mouth, her cheek, her jaw. His breath came in great gusts from his lips. "I would bottle the essence if I could."

Grinding his hips, he worked his length against her. She sighed at the pressure, foreign but so longed for. Anticipation danced along her skin. Her hand locked on his hip, nails biting into skin.

He whispered in a guttural admission that floated across her nipple, "I don't want...to hurt you."

She glanced down the minuscule space separating their bodies to see him touching himself, a long glide of curved fingers. Once and back again. *My*, how she wanted her hand there, her mouth, if he'd allow it. Another lesson she would negotiate. When she met his scorching gaze, something in hers must have transferred, because he swore roughly— his lids slipping low as he adjusted himself at her entrance.

"Slow...okay, Yank?" he rasped and began to fill her in the most minute increments when she wanted him to plunge to the hilt. Possess, *penetrate*. Crude desire when the physical overwhelmed the mental, caught in an uncontrollable frenzy of need. A jab of discomfort swept her as he slid forward, but the pain was carried away by increasing bursts of pleasured fullness.

It was as if he took a feather and stroked it across every sensitive inch of her; she was consumed from within, inflamed and reactive. Parts he claimed as his own. Lips at her breast; hand at the nape of her neck; at her hip, angling her pelvis high until he settled so thoroughly in her, and with such a feeling of completion, she experienced a second of unease.

A jolt of jealousy tore through her; he'd learned so much without her.

Going on instinct, she grasped his buttocks and met him as he slid deeper—and deeper still. It took mere moments to find the ideal fit and rhythm, the soft strike of their skin ringing through the moonlit room. This success led to an elemental parry and thrust, at first gentle, then increasing in urgency as they lunged together.

Groaning low in his throat, Julian's lips covered hers as he kissed her with reckless abandon, his sounds of gratification increasing her own. His scent mixed with hers, the combined fragrance falling like a blanket over them.

She gasped as he shifted his hips, hitting a hidden pleasure center. "Yes, *that*," she urged, the bliss so intense she could not maintain their kiss. She tucked her head in the crook of his neck and issued a plea against his damp skin. "*Again*." A moan broke free as he complied, her body rising off the mattress in response.

He lifted to his elbow, the muscles in his back jumping beneath her hands. His breath charged from his lips in a series of rapid pants. She scraped her nails lightly from shoulder to buttock and felt him shudder beneath the touch. Words were lost, thought abating like smoke in a fierce wind.

With almost cruel leisure, he withdrew to the tip —all the while staring at her with an expression of absolute intensity—then returned in a punishing glide. "Come with me," he said in a voice as hoarse as she'd ever heard it, "I'll be...right here."

Over and over, he stroked, never going as hard or as fast as she directed, begged for, but God in heaven, the way he moved, the way he used her body....

Redolent sighs. Friction. Slick skin.

Flesh entangled.

For as long as she could, she stared into his beautiful eyes, flecks of amber, stars immersed in solid bands of silver.

Adrift, boneless, untethered to everything in the world save for him.

Then it was simply too much, and she broke into pieces.

He swallowed her moan as he captured her lips, his lids sweeping low the last thing she saw before she crested, her body bowing off the bed and into him. Ecstasy rushed through her, as shocking as plunging in a chilled pond. Tantalizing and unparalleled. Pleasure—and intimacy—she'd not imagined existed. Incoherent, she clutched him as he broke into a harder rhythm, her body scooting up the bed with the force of his thrusts.

She realized he was close and that, with his slight withdrawal, he meant to leave her. "No," she uttered on a panicked breath as he leaned over her body, a savage groan ripping from his throat. Her hands rising to cup his face, she pleaded, "*Stay.*"

"Piper," he whispered as his eyes met hers, unfocused, his dark pupils swallowing the space.

She swept aside the damp hair hanging in his face. "Let go. I'm right here."

The words touched some part of him, and his

lashes fluttered, his body trembled. Then with a final thrust, he let his weight fall atop her, not fully, but with enough pressure to crowd her quite wonderfully into the thick bedding. His brow went to her shoulder, his lips a scalding press against her collarbone as he blew noisy breaths through them. She supported his broad body without issue, the feeling of entrapment exhilarating.

A gust of wind ripped through the window, dusting over her heated skin. In the distance, the sound of thunder rumbled. It had begun to rain, a steady cadence striking the panes. She had never felt more replete, as sure of, or in touch with, her body.

It was strange, lying there, naked limbs twisted about another's, visible as never before, but it also was quite...*natural*. Quite marvelous.

She could imagine no better way to see into one's soul.

Or expose your own.

This awareness brought a measure of trepidation.

As if he knew, Julian pressed a languid kiss to the hollow of her throat and rolled to his back. Hooking his arm under her shoulders, he brought her to his side and let his chin fall to the crown of her head. She nestled into the hard planes of his body, seeking his warmth against the sudden chill, listening to the patter of rain and their muted breaths.

Why, an entire world existed inside this small bedchamber.

"I have one question." She traced the scar on his shoulder. Her stitches had not been the most even, true, but the jagged mark only added to his masculine splendor. "A simple one."

A dark eyebrow swept high as his lips slid into a loose smile. His hand began a lazy caress at her waist. "What a surprise," he said in a satisfied voice. He was the epitome of the contented male, sprawled out there beside her.

"How many chapters did we complete?"

His lashes lifted, revealing smoky, intense regard. He turned the question over in his mind as his heartbeat skipped beneath her ear. "Some," he whispered, leaning in as his lips covered hers, "but not all."

CHAPTER 17

Who, being loved, is poor.
  ~Oscar Wilde

*T*he dream lingered at the fringe of her consciousness. Julian. Hands seeking, mouth demanding. His body atop hers, creating a molten web of whispered words and ardent cries.

Stretching, she encountered nothing but twisted sheets.

Alone. Blast it, she was *alone*.

Had it only been a dream?

Then, very faintly, she heard the sound of a pencil skating across paper.

She blinked, expelling the last vestiges of sleep from her mind to find Julian sprawled in a massive leather chair he'd pulled close to the window. The spill of light from the lamp perched on the ledge washed over him, throwing him into an intriguing mix of shadow and illumination. His aura shimmered, also an intriguing mix. Jagged spikes of joyous orange, red and blue, energy and happiness.

And…cautious, glaring yellow.

Oh, Julian, she thought and gave the counterpane a rough yank. Which only served to remind her how she'd nearly ripped the bedspread apart in her enthusiasm. Piper tussled with the sheet, pulling it to her chest and sliding high against a headboard Julian had gripped as he plunged into her.

Engrossed, he worked madly, head bowed, those incredible eyes trained on the sketch before him. She looked to the window, gauging the time to be an hour, maybe two, before dawn. The rain had ceased, but the curtains shook with the force of a fierce wind. A modest fire burned in the hearth, cutting the chill. Piper appreciated the time taken to compose herself if a battle was brewing. Preparation was essential with this man, and she was weakness personified. Imprisoned by desire, sensation still pulsing through her well-loved body.

Imprisoned by his bloody honor and her need to challenge it.

Time had, in actuality, changed little.

Paintings filled every spare inch of this room she noted for the first time, proving how crazed she'd been when she stumbled in hours ago. Leaning against the walls, the mahogany bureau, the velvet settee. Julian unleashed the chaos of his mind on his canvases.

The previous night, she had unleashed his passion.

The drapes danced with another gust, and she welcomed the frigid rush across her flushed skin. Her body throbbed as she recalled what they had done to each other.

Shocking *and* delicious.

"I knew it would be like this," he growled as if the words had been obtained at the end of a blade. His sketching intensified, his hand a blur across his sketchpad. His hair looked damp from bathing, curling with abandon, or conceivably—knowing Julian as she did—he'd stood in a ripping downpour and cursed the heavens. His spectacle lenses glittered, obscuring his eyes as he glanced up. Telling her little. A dark wash of stubble covered his jaw, calling her hand and, now, with more experience, her lips.

The notion sent a sweet zing racing between her thighs.

Holding her words until she figured out the best approach and was sure they would be steady, she instead took note of his bare chest, the wonderfully decadent line of hair trailing his flat belly and slipping into the paint-spattered trousers hanging low on his hips. She circled her arms about her knees and hugged them to her. He was long and lean, like an athlete, nothing like any man she'd ever encountered in the ton.

At least he wasn't fully dressed, set to deliver her to the main house as if nothing had occurred between them.

She'd rather endure a skirmish than that bit of hypocrisy.

So what if he wore a glower instead of a delighted smile? This was usually, as she imagined it, where the man offered his excuses and bolted from the bedchamber.

She wasn't distressed. *This* Julian she had loads of experience dealing with—lovingly resistant and a tad cross. He tended to react in this manner when something, or someone, didn't follow his blessed plan. As if life ever followed a plan. She held her smile because joy on her part would tilt his temper in the wrong direction.

But, oh lord, was he a gorgeous brooder.

"You have the look of a silk stocking found dangling from a chandelier," he muttered in a charmless tone.

Truthfully, she had never found Julian Alexander charming, nor had anyone else he'd run across. Honest, intelligent, principled, compassionate, so handsome it made her eyes burn, he made no effort to beguile—and she loved him more for it.

He was, quite simply, the least frivolous person she knew.

When she was the *most*.

She checked her sigh and smoothed her hair to find a jumbled mess she and Minnie would be unable to salvage. She blew a lock of it out of her eye with a gusty breath. Silk stocking, indeed. "If I do, you were the one who tossed me high enough to reach it."

"Inevitable," was all he said as if the word carried such consequence.

"Isn't it always?" she asked. Making love with him had been as instinctive as defending oneself from a blow.

"*No.*"

Leaning over the side of the bed, she rooted around for her shift but came up with his shirt instead. His eyes followed the movement, his back straightening as he retreated from his measured slouch. Lifting the wrinkled fabric to her nose, she inhaled the enticing scent she would *never* let slip from memory. Defenseless, her lids fluttered as his harsh exhalation settled like a barricade between them.

She had two options.

Make this easy on him by obeying his guidance.

Or follow her own counsel.

Decided, she let the sheet fall to her waist. With his gaze scorching every part of her it touched, his aura flooded fierce cobalt. While she—with the most leisurely undertaking unsteady hands could take— slipped his sleeve up one arm and then the other, the material dancing over her wrists, elbows, shoulders, trailing fingers of delight. An evocative caress. His scent enveloped her as she closed the buttons along the front, her nipples doing no one any kindness by pebbling beneath brushed linen in a way she couldn't hope to conceal.

Still, she covered them, thank you very much.

Her gaze shifted to the mahogany side table and the pistol resting there. She raised a brow. "Is this part of your plan to force me back to the house?"

The sketch lay forgotten on his lap, charcoal dangling from his fingers. A tiny crease she had never noticed before popped in between his brows. "I called off the guards for the night."

Ah, the reason for his uncertainty was becoming apparent.

His struggle was evident in his expression and his aura. Vulnerability and strength, apprehension and exultation. *Patience*, she told herself. He had to work out this shift in their relationship and what it might mean by himself.

He slid forward in the chair, and she found her eyes helplessly drawn to his thighs. Thin cotton did little to hide the taut muscle that had trapped her so effectively during the night. Or his hard length, which was rising to the occasion. "I seem to take things from you. Which is not my intent."

"My father was a spineless wastrel, Julian. His death left me beholden to a befuddled man more interested in ferreting out the details of my gift than assisting me with it." She laughed, pleating the sheet between her finger and thumb. "He expected a society marriage, can you imagine? With a meager dowry, an impossible reputation, *and* a frightening ability, he must have put great stock in my beauty."

"Your beauty has never been in question."

"This conversation is pointless—as I've told you more than once. I'm not marrying someone in the ton. I cannot. They wouldn't understand." She rolled the sleeves of his shirt high, ire pulsing fervently behind her eyes. Julian was not backing her into a marital corner out of a misplaced sense of propriety. And she couldn't tell him the truth; that she'd never love anyone else. That would go over like a boulder dropped upon them. "You *took* nothing. I *gave*."

Julian shook his head, a stock of dark hair tumbling in his face. He dragged his fingers through it with a sigh, creating further disorder.

"Think of who has cared for me in this world. You, Finn, Humphrey. You have been my savior."

He was out of the chair in two strides, his weight denting the mattress and sending her into him. "I don't want to be your bloody savior," he snapped, his hands going to her shoulders and giving her a gentle shake.

"What do you want?" she whispered, head tipping until their gazes locked. His eyes were turbulent storm clouds, a blustery, troubled slate. His aura bubbled around him, his breath rushing forth as he studied her. In the distance, a blackbird issued a countdown on the time they had left, and her heart squeezed. "What do you *want*?"

"Who cares what I want, Yank?"

She cupped his jaw, stubble dusting her palm. "I do."

Powerless, his gaze swept her as his lids lowered. "I want you to be safe. Safe with a partner who can love you and give you a family. We have a timeline, Yank. You're visiting a family friend this summer, fully chaperoned by a prostitute's daughter posing as the most experienced maid in England. A country tradition abided by all. But…after? The disgrace, even for Scandalous Scott, would be ruinous. We need a plan; you need a husband."

Tapping her finger on her bottom lip, she smiled as his gaze tracked the action like he was preparing for target practice. "I see how this goes. Oh, darling, your aura is a lovely shade of cerulean this morning. What is an aura? Gads, how long do you have?"

"Relationships are complicated, I agree, but your gift does not preclude you having one."

"Yet it does for you?"

He shoved off the bed. "I promised myself no child should suffer as I did. *Ever*. This gift could be inherited. And the first time, I didn't—"

"Withdraw, I know. I begged you not to." Her menses were regular, and she had a fair idea of safe timing, but she guessed this information would not be well taken. "Good news is, the other two times you did."

He kicked a canvas that had so impolitely gotten in his way as he strode back to the window, where he knocked aside the drape and peered into the darkness. "You have to be back before dawn. I realize the cat is out of the damned bag, but let's pretend for the lower house staff, at least."

"And then?" she asked and gave the sheet a hard twist. Their agreement had only been for one night, but she'd requested it include breakfast.

"And then I force myself to look at you as something other than a delectable treat I pour over my waffle."

A laugh burst from her. *"What?"*

He studied her without comment, the silence split only by a log in the hearth disintegrating with a snap.

Oh, those eyes of his; they were her absolute weakness. As she observed, his aura shifted in her favor. She tried to keep the delight from her face but, then, his lips curved. He pressed them together, but the smile grew, spreading across his face like the most recalcitrant ray of sunlight. "Idiocy," he whispered.

At last, he moved toward her, his expression a multi-faceted jewel, too many emotional edges to count. *This*. This revelation, this tenderness, was more intimate than anything they had shared. *This* was knowing him.

The enormity frightened her even as she ran toward it.

Julian reached hesitantly, his fingers sliding along her jaw and into her hair. The smell of his skin sent need surging through her body. Her lids drifted on a sigh of recognition.

He made no move to deepen the caress, only laid his lips on her brow as her mind teemed with impassioned images.

It was as if the kiss signaled a farewell.

And then she knew…

He didn't love her enough, and she loved him too much.

Julian survived fifty-two hours without a decision being forced on him.

Fifty-two hours comprised of two sleepless nights in the lodge, his *refuge*, where Piper lingered like one of Simon's ghosts. Her likeness resided on a hundred sketches and more than one incomplete canvas—as if the scent of her clinging to his sheets were not enough. The smell of lavender was making him wonder if he was losing his mind and his senses.

Consequently, when she burst into his study in

the main house two days later, it was no surprise he lost all thought.

She halted in the doorway, her cheeks gaining color in a rapid manner spelling disaster any way you read it. With a glance at the group assembled in the room, Julian struggled to compose a rationale for a meeting of the League, impromptu though it may be, without her. As he'd promised to alert her to the next one, etcetera, etcetera. But his voice departed, his throat going dry. Her hair was down, the ragged ends trailing her shoulder, and he could only recall brushing it for her before they'd left the lodge.

As intimate a thing as he'd ever done in his life.

The memory sent a blisteringly poignant rejoinder through him, one that burned any defense he might construct to a crisp.

Humphrey coughed beneath his breath, one brow winging high. Finn slouched in his chair until the cracked leather had to be pressed against his spine, his grin graceful and cunning.

Julian shook his head, clearing it. *Waffle*, he imagined them thinking.

"This isn't exactly what it looks like," he confessed, ignoring Humphrey's sigh and Finn's snort. Dear God, *that* isn't how he should have started.

Piper stepped into the study, and Julian swore the smell of cheroots and brandy disappeared to be replaced by the honeyed scent of lilacs. Cut grass. Earth. She'd been in the garden. He kept his gaze trained on her darkening-to-emerald eyes, ignoring the urge to check her skirt for stray bits of straw he could brush away for her.

She closed the door with a snap and leaned against it. "Your Grace," she said with a wispy curtsy for the Duke of Ashcroft, who'd requested the spontaneous meeting upon his arrival. Hence the damned gathering, thrown together in *minutes*, Julian would love to tell her.

Ashcroft turned from his study of the bookcase and a row of leather-bound volumes on the occult, popping the one in his hand back in its slot with a fragile smile. The dark slashes beneath his eyes attested to his inner turmoil, something Julian was sure Piper would notice. He hoped the sight of her did not elicit a ball of flame from the man's fingers.

As every breath in the room held suspended, the Duke bowed with all the crispness of his station, as if they stood in a crowded ballroom. "Lady Scott, again, a pleasure." Then he must have appreciated the ludicrousness of the entire episode as he threw himself in the lyre chair by the bookcase, the brass casters sending it into a wild spin.

Piper's gaze lit on her maid, sitting in the corner with a mildly abashed expression. Edward loomed next to Minnie, his regard wandering the room like an eager puppy trying to figure out who was taking him for a walk. Finally, Piper noticed Simon, on the floor by Finn's feet, managing a deck of cards like a sharper of the first order. The boy glanced to his side too frequently for it to mean anything other than one of his apparitions was with him. Even Henry was in the room, licking his privates without a hint of concern.

Julian tensed, preparing for the blow before it hit. Hmm, I really should have found the courage to round her up for this.

Fury darkened her eyes, her lips tightening to contain the vitriol that would have come spewing out if not for the oddity of a person one notch below a prince being in their presence. Julian rubbed at a streak of yellow paint on his wrist and sought to ignore the speaking glance *that* action got him.

Piper made a dismissive gesture with her hand. "Don't mind me. Please, continue."

"Where were we?" Julian asked, gaze shifting to Humphrey with desperation he knew said, *please save me.*

Humphrey rolled his eyes, his cheroot hanging so low it almost touched his collar. "Laundry cottage. Not fit for royalty, but it'll be hard to burn down."

All eyes turned to Ashcroft to gauge his reaction. Julian released an inward sigh of relief. At least Humphrey had not called him *fireball* again.

The Duke took the casualness of the entire scene —cheroots and open collars in front of ladies was not *de rigueur*—in with mildly arrested surprise. Studied the room like a painting hanging in the National Gallery, as if he struggled to find his place within the flowing lines. He rubbed fingertips together Julian would bet a hundred pounds had gotten hot. "It's more than adequate. Charming, in truth. And I'm sure," he added, struggling to conclude the account, "there are country amusements to be found. Hunting, fishing, the like."

Finn snorted, and Julian shot him a lethal look.

"We have a gamekeeper arriving any day." Julian fidgeted, trying to ignore Piper's gaze traveling from his crossed ankles to his face in a measured assessment. Tried to ignore the heat that swept his body just after.

"Next week," Minnie supplied with a little wiggle of her pinkie in Piper's direction, which possibly served as some sort of girlish apology.

Piper steepled her hands and rested her chin on her fingertips. Anyone else would consider the posture angelic, but he knew better. "A gamekeeper with no prior experience as a gamekeeper, am I correct?"

An unexpected burst of ire settled in Julian's gut.

He would apologize for mismanaging the situation if she'd allow a private arena in which to do so. But, no, she had to trot the League's baggage out for all to see. "The lad has years of experience managing a pack of stray dogs in Whitechapel. Is that sufficient?"

"And his gift?" Her probing gaze nailed him to the spot.

He raised his glass, letting brandy provide a moment's respite. As a healer, Piper deserved to know this and more. Bloody hell, her grandfather had created the League, in part, for *her*. Julian was letting his personal feelings impair his life's work, like he'd known he would if he became involved with her. "It appears he can communicate, send thoughts, without speaking."

"Any control?"

Julian shook his head. "He's *talking* to everyone. On the street. In the market. And when the thoughts point to being his, he's being savagely beaten for it. A family member of someone in the League let us know."

"Then he'll need me," she said, driving a splinter of guilt beneath his skin.

"Yes."

"Him, too," she added and nodded to Ashcroft, who followed the conversation with the zeal of one watching a vigorous fencing match. Julian hated to tell him, but these were the only *country amusements* to be had. "My roster is growing. Without my involvement. Or advisement."

Julian thumped his glass to the desk with a blatant display of impatience. "Should I provide a whip so you can draw blood from this interview?"

She exhaled on a whispered oath, which only sought to raise her breasts—marvelous ones, by the by—beneath her simple silk day dress. A lock of hair he knew was soft to the touch slipped loose from its clip to brush her face. *The woman would look stunning in a corn sack.* And this sour consideration, more than any other released since she stepped in the room, elevated his temper and his cock until he questioned if he'd be forced to hide behind the desk after all.

"I'm sorry," was all he managed. "I didn't think."

She palmed the door with a slap. "I'll see you tomorrow, Your Grace." A glance over her shoulder aimed like a dart at Julian. "With my chaperone and at least two guards in tow."

She exited the room as imposingly as she'd entered it, and he was halfway to the door himself before realizing he'd revealed his hand. He might have even surprised Humphrey and Finn this time. It was just too damn easy to forget his close connection to Piper.

Frightening, but with every day that passed, he felt less need to hide it.

How peculiar his obsession must look to others, he thought, as he went after her like a hound after a fox.

When it was entirely reasonable to him.

"Welcome to Harbingdon, Ashcroft," he heard Finn murmur as the study door clicked shut behind him.

CHAPTER 18

Speaking silence, dumb confession. Passion's birth and infants' play.
~Robert Burns

iper bolted down the arched hallway, her footfalls echoing off marble, the sting of tears a hot lick behind her lids. Sunlight shot through beveled panes in a brilliant display when she wished for rain and clouds the color of Julian's eyes.

Not here, not here, Piper.

She would not cry, she vowed and pressed her hand to her stomach. Her father had always said tears were to be hidden.

Tears are for commoners, for the weak.

Behind her, the study door closed, and Julian's heavy tread registered. *Oh, God.* She couldn't let him see her like this. He would never understand why such a simple gesture, or lack of one, had destroyed her. She passed a narrow door under the servants' staircase. A perfect place to hide until Julian left the house, as he surely thought she'd head to the gardens. She had to face him, of course.

Just not now. Not yet.

The door was unlocked, the darkness inside so complete it swallowed her whole. Reaching blindly, she encountered shelves, crisp sheets, cool plaster— the scent of lemon and starch. Pressing against the wall, she slid until her bottom hit pitted wood. *Please*, she prayed, dropping her brow to her drawn knees.

The silence in the confined chamber was absolute, the house in a peaceful lull between meals, not even the tick of a clock penetrating the space. She curled into herself, tears trailing her face and soaking her dress, an unattractive affair. As would likely be expected, she didn't cry with restraint. Gulping, airless breaths bringing the taste of salt to her mouth and stinging her cheeks.

Damn you, Julian.

The hair on the back of her neck lifted as the door opened. She peered through the fractured light to find him silhouetted by a circle of luminosity that made him look positively saintly. Her heartbeat skipped, and she recoiled, bumping her head on the wall.

"Hey, stop," he whispered, bringing the door within an inch of closing, the slender strip of light running over her slipper and his thigh as he kneeled before her. He approached as he would an animal in distress, cupping her chin and gently raising her face into the hushed glow. Mercifully, the pitch concealed his glorious eyes, though his scent was pointed and sweet, one she'd have known anywhere. His breath was coming quickly, and his hand trembled where it held her.

"Will you…leave me, please." The gasping halt in

the plea let him know precisely what shape she was in. "*Go.*"

He rocked back on his heels, striking the doorframe. "Have I hurt your feelings?" he asked, stunned. His hand went in and out of the light as he dragged his fingers through his hair.

Anger sliced through her, bringing with it a slight degree of control. "You don't think I have any? Is that it?"

"No, Piper, Jesus." He slid, too, until he rested against the doorframe. Silence hung like a specter between them. "I've just rarely seen you cry. And I didn't…I didn't mean to hurt you. I would never intentionally hurt you. I'm running from myself. Don't you see that? A mad scramble."

She swiped a knuckle beneath each eye and drew a shaky breath. "I'm on the outside looking in, Jules. That's what occurred to me when I walked in your study. I should have known, figured it out by being pressed into service with an aging aunt in Gloucestershire for three years, that you were never going to let me into the League *or* your heart. You've told me often enough. Been very honest and typically honorable. I have been warned. Repeatedly."

He jerked, his knee bumping hers. "You're mistaken. You've always been—"

"Don't make promises on top of promises you can't keep."

"Is that what you think I'm doing? Making a promise I won't keep?" he grit out, his censure lobbing around the closet like a ball.

When he reached, she shoved him back. "I allowed myself the luxury of taking what I *wanted* instead of what was prudent. So like Scandalous Scott, am I correct? Now I'm paying the price. Tomorrow, I will hold my head high and march on. But right now, right this minute, silly female that I am, I want to feel incensed and, yes, hurt." She dropped her head to her knees, drawing in air overwhelmed with the scent of him. "Truthfully, I want to feel nothing. For you—for the League. For all of it."

"Come here," he said, his appeal and the confined space leaving little room to refuse. "Fine, then I'll come there." He rose to a squat and braced his arms on the wall on either side of her. When she looked up, he was there, breath sweeping her cheek, broad shoulders blocking out the meager light streaming through the door. "I'm usually quite good at this—"

"Julian, you're *not* good at this."

His hand went to her jaw as he balanced before her. She tried to edge away, but she was firmly trapped. Her mind began to chant a powerful appeal, nipples pebbling, the area between her thighs pulsing in time to her heartbeat. *Oh, traitorous body.* The inability to see his reaction only made her arousal flare brighter.

"I don't know what to do with this, Piper. With *you.*" His fingers quivered against her cheek. "Finn's dreams are slicing a hole in our security, as he's giving away as much information as he's getting. It's torturing him, part of the reason he's shadowing you like a hound, afraid to let you out of his sight. And here we are, *us*, in the midst of this mess, involved as I've always suspected we someday would be, my fixation with you tearing me in two. My desires sit at the opposite ends of the galaxy. I want to shield you from danger while I spread you like butter over my body. And I can't find a way to combine those two with any judiciousness."

"Judiciousness, of course." She released a soft huff.

"The League is my destiny as well as yours. I'm coming to realize I need it more than I thought possible. It's finally providing a sense of place, of belonging. Providing a future. Healing others is healing *me*."

"I *know* that."

"Then why exclude me?"

"Sweetheart, men often need a moment to work things out in their sluggish brains. I'm not as quick on my feet as you are. Will it anger you if I admit I'm still thinking?"

She searched for his gaze in the darkness. "So, I'm to be included going forward, no matter the danger? This is your judicious pledge?"

"You underestimate the danger. When my fears are valid. Finn and Humphrey's fears—" She cut off his words with a crude kiss that landed on the side of his mouth. He groaned, his hands tangling in her hair as he corrected the fit. Her body spilled light from within. She hadn't touched him in two days, but it felt like weeks.

Months. Years.

"Piper," he whispered against her lips, "wait." He shifted, allowing just enough space between them to pass a sheet of parchment through. "If I agree to this, the League, complete involvement, you must promise me. You must give me your solemn vow." Giving her a gentle shake as if he sought to anchor his plea in her mind, he said, "If they come for you, for once in your life, play along. I'll need time to find you, and your gift will provide it. Do you understand? No rebellion."

She nodded as his fingertips dug into her shoulders, and he gave her another shake. "You are mine to protect. Deny me this, and you deny who I am, who I cannot help being."

"I belong to no one," she whispered, wishing it were so.

With a hissing rebuttal, he tugged her to her feet. An unsteady glide along cool plaster, breath tangling, skin heating. "You belong to *me*." Keeping one hand on her, he turned, kicking the door shut and throwing them into delicious blackness. "You always have."

That's true, she agreed, but you aren't going to keep me.

Concern vanished as he crowded into her, his hands crafting her like clay until fantasy and reality merged. Pulse points of pleasure and blind longing in the shadowed bliss. She bounced on the balls of her feet to get closer while whispering rough commands against his lips. In response, he caught her bottom and slid her high using the wall as a guide. Then he settled in, drawing her legs around his waist, the perfect solution to their height challenge. She moaned as his rigid shaft claimed its favored spot between her thighs, where he began stroking until thought vaporized like fog hit by a sunbeam.

"I'm ready," she whispered against his neck, then bit him gently beneath the ear to put an exclamation point on the announcement.

Testing her assertion, he worked his hand beneath her skirt, tunneling past the slit in her drawers, a swift entry into her moist, warm reach. Jamming his knee against the wall for leverage, he captured her lips beneath his as his fingers and tongue began to move in time. Not the easiest task, but she got a hand to his trouser close and started to flip buttons. He not only shifted to help, the sounds coming from him were *wildly* encouraging. What little restraint he had seemed lost.

While she'd never had any in the first place.

Buttons released, his cock sprang into her hand. She passed a thumb over the bulbous head, once, twice, as he broke the kiss and pressed his brow to hers, his breath a steady cadence across her cheek.

Heavens, she loved witnessing Julian Alexander going up in flames.

He caught her lips again as he worked her legs higher on his hip. Amazingly, he had her weight held entirely between his arm and the wall.

"I'm too…heavy," she whispered, head falling back as he inched the tip of his cock inside her. The feeling was so different than their previous encounters, a profound invasion, abrasive. She felt an animal caught in a trap, and the powerlessness was incredibly arousing.

He rocked into her, his hair catching between the damp press of their cheeks. "You're"—he groaned as he embedded himself fully, then with a twist of his hips, somehow gained deeper entry—"you're a dream."

Tilting her pelvis, he fell into a steady, pounding rhythm. Thoroughly entrenched, his hand rose to cradle her head as he thrust. Protective Julian. She fisted her fingers in his hair, drawing him to her. She wanted him closer when he could *be* no closer.

Julian palmed the wall, the muscles in his arms clenching. "Sweetheart, I can't…last much longer."

Again, he angled her hips, and she gasped. A brilliant burst exploded behind her lids, fireworks in a night sky. Words were impossible; she could only emit broken sounds of pleasure.

"Anyone could find us," he offered, his breath a molten wash. "My sliding into you. You dripping wet all over me."

His erotic words and the thrill of what they were doing and where they were doing it sent her over the abyss, her climax arriving so forcefully that for an instant, she felt faint. Spots colored her vision as she convulsed around him, her head dropping to his shoulder in defeat, her moan muffled against his lapel.

The final pulses shimmered through her as Julian stroked harder, persuading her body to give of itself fully, leaving nothing untold. Capturing her lips, his groan filled her throat as he crested. With a final stroke, he disengaged, releasing in a handkerchief she'd had no idea he held.

In the hallway, a clock struck a quarter-hour tone, which should have startled them, but they barely reacted. Finally, with a press of his lips to her brow, Julian slid her down his body. Leaning, he kissed her, his hands coming up to frame her face as if he couldn't—not quite yet—release her.

When skin was cool and breathing restored, they separated, arranging clothing without speaking.

Frankly, she had no clue what to say.

Again, please.

Standing up is as stimulating as lying down.

Julian turned, then turned back, threading his fingers through hers. Lifting their linked hands to his lips in a gesture of silence, he cracked the door and peeked into the hallway. A band of light splashed his face and one broad shoulder. Her gaze took him in hungrily. Hair disheveled, cravat a disaster. His cheeks held a detailed narrative of what had occurred behind a closed, *but not locked*, door. And his aura. *Ah.* She took a step back, her hand falling to her belly to calm her racing pulse.

Streaks of blue and bold bursts of lavender. Contentment and hope, though she suspected Julian would question the latter. *Trust your instincts*, she wanted to tell him.

However, with this man and this situation, patience was her friend.

If she were patient enough to let it be.

"It's clear," she said when she wanted to smooth the curl jutting past his ear. Place her mouth over the patch of stubble his morning shave had missed.

Ask him how many ways of making love he planned to show her. Or if this was the end of them. The end of *us*.

He glanced over his shoulder, and she got the first look at his eyes she'd had since he entered the closet. Pale, the hue of fog sliding over cobblestones. He raised a brow in question.

"Sometimes, I can feel auras, faintly." Lifting their links hands, she sketched a trivializing circle. "There's no one in the hallway."

Exiting the room, he pressed a swift kiss to her wrist and dropped her hand. He directed her to the front of the house while he started toward the back.

She only made it two steps before she turned to find he had halted before the bay window, sunlight a glorious waterfall over him. A flash of indecision crossed his face, so swift an alteration she almost missed it. He brought his hand to his temple, rubbing at either wanton thought or headache. Then he shook his head, hair falling in his face, a smile she felt sure he didn't want her to see tilting his lips. In four long strides, he made it back to her.

The kiss was impulsive and impassioned, right there in the open, so unlike Julian, her heart missed a beat. "Back door. Midnight," he whispered, then he was gone.

She climbed the stairs to her bedchamber with

half a mind on the steps she took. She stumbled on a wrinkle in the hallway runner she had meant to smooth out this morning.

Julian's aura had made the decision to deceive him much easier.

She was good for him. She *was*. His aura and the changes held within it when he was with her were proof.

He needed her, even if he didn't know it. Piper wondered if he even loved her, not the familial love he'd always carried, but passionate love a man felt for a woman. Love that made one forget idiotic promises made long ago, forget fear, forget *logic*. His account-ability for her had twisted him up inside until he wasn't sure where he belonged in her life.

Lover, friend, protector.

While she had always known.

If he did love her, it was going to take another of their raging battles to expose it. Unless she made love to him so often and so well, he gave up.

She flopped to her bed, her arms falling wide. She was not as honorable as Julian. *No one* was as honor-able as Julian.

As he'd told her on more than one occasion, she would make an excellent thief.

So, she'd steal his heart if he would not readily give it to her.

≈

They touched at every opportunity in the days that followed.

Even as Julian gave himself to her, strategically managing many of the encounters, she, serenely and unexpectedly, *seduced*. Whispered suggestions at the most inopportune times—*I think this might be fun to try*—when his hands were otherwise occupied but his mind all hers. At dinner, while passing in the village, across a lawn strewn with people, he had no time to fortify himself against her impassioned assault. From the simple brush of her hand when he reached for a breakfast scone to leading him into a shadowed nook for a heated kiss that stripped away thought, she kept him maddeningly off-balance as no woman ever had.

When she got that naughty, amused look on her face, he was lost.

The taste of her lived on his tongue, the feel of her on his fingertips. She laughed so easily, with a wicked wit he found not only utterly charming but bloody dangerous. He didn't understand her luminosity, considering the burden she carried. He couldn't create a painting with a hundredth of the intensity of her smile, let alone her *being* when the weight on his shoulders came out in dark slashes.

Julian had found a partner who matched him in agility, enthusiasm, and pluck. No location was off-limits for their trysts. The conservatory, which allowed for a beautiful view of the stars beneath the glass rooftop. The potter's shed, which had garnered Julian a splinter in a rather delicate location, one Piper had—with tears of hilarity streaming from her eyes—removed. They'd walked the estate before sunrise and made love on the dewy grass of the back lawn. Swam in the lake with moonlight shimmering across the surface of the water and their skin.

Darkness was their champion and their cloak.

Piper was pushing every other experience from his mind until she alone was his world. All he wanted or needed. But his trepidation remained. How could he trust his instincts when a blistering rush of desire took him down like a punch every time he saw the girl?

THE LADY IS TROUBLE

They had begun working on mastering control of his visions, although the images contained within continued to carve him up like daggers. Brought low, she stepped in and led him home.

Indeed, he feared their connection as he'd feared nothing in his life.

He was sharing parts of himself that had nothing to do with her luscious mouth and tantalizing body. He had even asked her opinion about a painting being shown at the next Royal Exhibition, something no one, not even Humphrey, knew about.

Cataloging her place in his life—healer, lover, friend—was a challenge with his promise to her grandfather held over his head like an ax set to swing. Marriage was not an option if he stuck to that promise; however, concern over her reputation, already dreadfully damaged due to her past escapades, was a thorn beneath his skin. He had never dishonored anyone in his life, and he didn't want to start with Piper.

Making things worse, like a lovesick fool, he'd outfitted the lodge with all the personal items she needed to stay there. Clothing, hairbrush, toothbrush. He was clearly intoxicated. Besotted. How to make rational choices when his heart was engaged, when she had become such an integral part of his life?

How could he protect her when the notion of not seeing her, touching her, made his heart stutter?

The answer to what he felt was clear if one spent but a moment considering the evidence. He let this morose certainty circle his mind for a full heartbeat before sending it away.

"You're getting that look again."

Startled, he glanced over, his paintbrush leaving an inadvertent streak on the canvas. Piper rested in her favorite spot before the settee, her research papers spread on the floor around her. He worked as close to her as he could without touching because touching brought more touching, and then all plans were mislaid, though he did find it necessary to brush his foot against hers occasionally. Remove a stray lock of hair from her cheek. Dab paint on her wrist, then promise to kiss it away later.

She was dressed in nothing but her shift, he in his paint trousers. The open windows of the lodge allowed for a ripping cross-breeze powered by an approaching storm. The night was peaceful, the call of an owl beyond the only sound. The evening sheltered them, once again. They had turned the hours of the day upside down, working into the night, returning her to the house before dawn, where they then showed up later than anyone for breakfast. Except for Finn, who'd slipped into the role of bastard son like he slipped on his drawers, one easy, elegant leg at a time. When, for the first time in Julian's life, he was keeping the indolent hours befitting a viscount.

"What look?" he asked, which was senseless when he knew *what look*.

Her gaze sparked at the edges, tinting the jade green that meant her mind was traveling to a place his body would soon follow. From his chest to his feet and back, he burned as she studied him. She enjoyed examination as much as he did, this coming from an artist who examined form as a matter of course.

She pressed her lips together, doing a little arse jiggle his cock recognized. His gaze fell to the dusky pink nipples hardening beneath her cotton shift. Couldn't hide his response, either, as he wore nothing but trousers—thin ones at that.

Laughing softly, she glanced at the sheet in her hand as she shook her head to clear it.

Julian leaned, righting the paper where she could properly read it. He loved that he seemed to confound her as much as she confounded him. Even though this time, he suspected she'd planned her attack. Weak fool that he was, he let her play her game.

He dabbled with his paints, searching for the exact shade of purple for her to record in her research. It was the color she alleged signified pregnancy, which he found a fascinating discovery. "Someone has to think about the future."

She dropped her head to the settee with a sigh. "Are we going to argue about this again? I don't know if I have the strength to consider your subsequent apology. But I will certainly give it my best."

He mixed the paint with more exuberance. Their arguments *had* led to one or two very intense encounters. "It's a lovely manor. The gardens are beautiful. And it's officially part of your trust. Nothing scandalous whatsoever."

"The earl's solicitor is awfully willing to take your money. I bet Freddie choked when told there is an asset, previously undiscovered, that is not legally his."

Julian made a dismissive motion with the brush. "London runs on bribes. At least you can presume a solicitor will keep the details to himself." He added white as the color needed to be closer to amethyst, not violet. "I'm only doing what your grandfather should have. Or better yet, your thoughtless father."

"That's part of the problem," she whispered, but loudly enough for him to hear.

"Don't push me, Yank."

She scooted high against the settee, and he tried to ignore the memory of his lips pressed to her thigh in just that spot two evenings prior. "Please

go on describing my life in the charming, unentailed country manor my dear grandpapa left to me.
It's near Viscount Beauchamp's country estate. A
close family friend, you see, as the departed earl
was a prudent man." She slapped the folio to the
carpet. "Will you sneak in there every night as
well?"

He removed his spectacles and rubbed his eyes.
"You'll be safe, you and your reputation. You and
your gift. I'll make it a goddamn fortress. And you'll
be close to the League, twenty minutes by carriage.
We can even have people come to you for healing." At
her look, his shoulders dropped. "It's not like I'm sug-
gesting Gloucestershire."

"And this summer?"

He tossed his spectacles atop a blank canvas at his
side. "A traditional house party. Chaperones, power
of levitation aside, aplenty. We even have a duke this
summer showcasing my heightened success. Ashcroft
can confirm, lying through his teeth, mind you, how
proper the goings-on. It actually may give your
rather unfortunate status a boost. But when the next
season starts, you *cannot* be here. The wolves will rip
you apart. I won't let that happen." He yanked his
hand through his hair when she failed to concur. No
way Piper Scott would immediately agree because
the proposal was too sensible. "Remember the plan?
To leave the door open for the bloody future, not
slam it shut in society's face."

She rose to her knees, her finger drilling into his
chest. It was pure helplessness on his part that even
indignant contact sent a spike of longing drumming
through his body. "What about what *I* want, Jules?"

"Ah, the narrative repeats itself."

She laid her finger over his lips. Her heat seared
him, and he just caught the swift inhalation before it

started. He removed her hand but drew her close. "That's not a fair fight."

"I prefer *this* narrative repeat itself," she whispered.

A hairsbreadth separated them. So close, her breath grazed his neck, the scent of lilac invading his senses and scattering the self-control he prized so much. He dove into the emerald pool of her eyes, fully submerged. "I know nothing of how to love," he murmured, "only how to survive. You have to take what I'm able, all I *know*, to give."

She swept her hand down his throat and along the path of hair trailing to his waistband. A part of his body she seemed overly fascinated by. During the slow, slow glide, his muscles contracted beneath her touch. He knew where she was headed, and although he should, he had no intention of stopping her. "I'm tempted to make you mine, no matter the cost," he said, his voice thick. If he did, his gift could destroy her. She'd enter the otherworld the visions thrust him into, following him out of love, not as a healer, and she might never return.

If she could help him as *only* a healer, with some degree of detachment, he might be more willing. But love was leading them both down a dangerous path, he feared.

And he wondered if he would survive the hurt of leaving her.

When he felt sure she was strong enough to.

Her gaze steady, confidence born of his impassioned teachings, she unbuttoned his trousers with practiced efficiency. She understood how to wreck him and began to stroke with the perfect mix of speed and strength—slowing when his hips rose in a plea for her to go faster, a whisper touch when he needed her to squeeze the life from him. With a groan, he fell back, bracing himself on his elbows, his head hanging low. If he watched her do this, he would explode in seconds.

When the silken ends of her hair grazed his thighs, he grasped her wrist. *"Piper,"* he breathed between his teeth. She batted his hand aside and set her lips to his shaft, her tongue circling the tip hesitantly, then with more vigor when he moaned his devotion. He found the clawfoot of the settee and wrapped his fingers around it to keep from dragging her over him. *Allow her, you fool.* The bite of pitted wood against his palm only marginally dimmed the feel of her teeth skimming, her mouth closing, sucking. Brilliant lover that she was, she recorded each gasp, each groan, documenting what he liked until he lay utterly broken before her.

He jerked the settee as his hips rose from the carpet, her papers a snowy spill around them. "Stop, love, I—"

But Piper being Piper, she followed her own course, her wicked mouth and coming-into-experience fingers driving him to the brink. He was *so* close. His hand rose to sink in her hair and guide her when she needed no guide. His skin felt like it was being stripped from him and reattached. How to finish, he wondered while his body turned against him.

This, he decided, and pulled her atop him. They tangled as she struggled and swore, rolling them over. She laughed as he yanked her shift high and slipped inside her with gentle splendor that stole both their breaths.

"Yes," she whispered against his nape.

He wanted to be tender, take it slow, make it last, but the feel of her mouth wrapped around him had left a fiery imprint that was only going to allow for modest sensation before pleasure overwhelmed him.

Already, he was lightheaded and gasping for oxygen. All body, little mind.

He shifted his hips, and she moaned, curving into him. "That? Okay." *Good.* She liked it. So, he did it again.

"There." Her words were an urgent caress. "Right *there.*"

He complied, plunging as determinedly as he dared. In response, she ground against him, having learned, *oh, God,* what drove them both mad.

She whimpered, and he urged: "Come with me, Yank. I may not be…able to wait…for you."

He gazed at her as she tossed her head, struggling to find her release. She was the most sensual vision he'd ever seen; her beauty astounded.

Her breath ripped from her, her cheeks flooding with color. "I can't—"

Reaching between their pumping bodies, he found the sensitive bud of her sex. "You can." One gentle manipulation, barely a touch really, and she shattered. Her cry reverberated as she clenched around him, ending any hope he had to prolong their pleasure. With a final, deep stroke, he ripped free and came in a wild gush in his hand.

Collapsing beside her, he groped for his shirt. With his vision graying at the edges and not enough air entering his lungs, he cleaned his hand, then turned to find her turning toward him, a rueful smile curving her lips. "You're going to kill me with this pace. I fell asleep during a meeting with Humphrey today," he said, drawing her to his side, where she fit like a piece of his puzzle. "Scrupulous opponent, Piper Scott is not."

"Every chance I get," she mumbled, gliding into slumber. Her lids drifted, lashes a dark sweep across her skin. His hand flexed around her hip, bringing her closer, the movement utterly possessive, conveying in action what he could not in word.

"I love your hair"—she twisted a strand around her finger, sending a blind rush through him—"most of all. So unruly when you're not."

Then she slipped into sleep.

Perhaps she was right. Perhaps he *had* been closed to her, fighting what they felt for each other. But they'd been so damn young, with so many impossible circumstances stacked against them. He could be persuaded by her clever hands, her winning smile, to refute his reservations and pitch his promise to the earl to hell.

But his gift had the power to destroy.

And not in the way of a broken love affair.

Even after all these years, he didn't understand his ability well enough to determine his level of risk, much less *hers*. If something happened when she sought to heal him, he would lose his mind.

He buried his face in her hair and drew a breath of what smelled like sunshine.

To let their relationship continue in this manner denied the man he was, the man who, in the end, did the *right* thing. It was too late to find the middle ground. Already, her touch was unbounded confusion. Ridiculous, but it seemed a personal strike against his honor that he needed her to light the dark corners inside him. Another man, one without a curse to bear, could have her in one way but not the other. Leave a part of her for herself.

To stay was life and death.

To leave was only the death of his heart.

As Piper sighed and snuggled into him, Julian felt the salty sting of tears and questioned how he thought to leave her when he'd begun to like the man he was when he was with her.

Like him as never before.

But, someday, and someday soon, he *must*.

When she'd made Harbingdon feel like home.

Because Piper Scott was *his*.

As he'd known the moment he stepped from the earl's carriage to find a locket on the ground and fallen in love the second he touched it.

CHAPTER 19

I hid my love to my despite, till I could not bear to look at light.
    ~John Clare

$\mathcal{T}$he collapse of her exquisite love affair began on an otherwise typical rainy English day.

After breakfast, she met with Edward, who had come along nicely in their weeks of working together. He still foretold the future, but he'd learned to manage his anxiety, in part, by keeping a journal. Some of his dreams were innocuous, the usual imaginings of a young man—a seamstress in the rookery he'd taken a fancy to—but some had more significant implications. Those she suggested he discuss with Julian and Humphrey. Only two instances made her breath catch. One, a dream about Finn as a grown man residing in a gaming hell.

The other about her.

In this one, Piper faced what Edward termed a challenger. A female with long, black hair. He compared the sight of them facing off to Finn and Julian fencing. A competition, charged and intense.

This dream she told Edward *she* would discuss with Julian.

Something she had yet to do.

Because, at certain times, the look on his face…

She might be winning the battle to secure his love.

If this woman was coming for her, Piper had a somewhat fatalistic view about her ability, anyone's ability, to correct the course. Her destiny may well be to face this test, but Julian would explode in a fury were she ever to voice this notion. Therefore, she kept quiet about Edward's intuition and docilely consented to having an armed guard shadow her every move.

She was only allowed to cut that protective cord while at the lodge. Where she and Julian had created an intimate domain separate from society, their responsibilities, the past *or* the future. They lived and loved in a world made of glass, a world capable of being shattered at any second.

Her mind was overflowing with thoughts of Julian that afternoon as she and Minnie left the Duke's cottage, what everyone on the estate had come to call the *stone fortress*. Ashcroft had brought a modest army with him, former soldiers he'd commanded, increasing protection not only at the fortress but Harbingdon's main gate and house. His Grace took training and weaponry seriously if the drills in the yard meant anything. She'd told Julian about the mock battles and glistening chests, and during her next visit, the men were buttoned-up like they were heading to a ball.

Controlling Ashcroft's gift *was* a challenge, as he wasn't sure of the trigger behind starting fires. To gain any jurisdiction, he had to understand where the impulse derived from. It was a peculiar healing experience as she didn't feel the heat, but an image of flames popped in her head every time she grasped his hands. Also, he and Piper had begun reviewing the detailed notes in his journals, the ones she and Julian had uncovered in Ashcroft House. It was tedious work, grueling at times, but he seemed comforted that he could, for the first time in his life, be honest about his situation.

As Julian advocated daily, there was strength in numbers.

If the Duke seemed lost in this strange world he'd stepped into, it was expected. Traveling from Mayfair to an Oxfordshire estate harboring orphans of the occult *did* take some getting used to. There was a new arrival each week, sometimes two, befuddled beings promptly placed in a position they were unsuited for. Consequently, Harbingdon operated like a carriage missing a wheel, with many bumps and spills. However, loyalty to Julian was absolute, as his compassion, protection, and dedication were unrelenting.

When she reached the main house, instead of going to freshen up for dinner, Piper went directly to Julian's study. She hadn't seen him in two agonizing days. A roof in the village had collapsed, and a group of men had volunteered to not only complete the repair but move the family to a new home.

His study door was open, but she hesitated to disturb as he stood lost in thought before the window, recording the night as it tilted from grey to black. He'd dressed in riding boots and breeches; waistcoat hanging loosely about his hips; shirtsleeves rolled high on his forearms. His hat and coat sat in a haphazard pile on the chair pulled close to his desk.

Piper took him in, skin flushing as it always did when he was near.

She'd expected to quench her passion with repeated effort, but this hadn't occurred.

She only wanted more.

Foolishly, she wanted everything.

"Are you coming in?" he asked and lifted a glass to his lips. Crystal glinted in the half-light from the sconce, reflecting off the pane and landing on the Aubusson at his feet. Across the short distance, she noted the tension holding his posture rigid. Her heart began to pound, and the words he'd whispered in bed the night before circled her mind.

You will lose this need for me. It will fade.

Making her want to weep with bewilderment. When she'd asked if his need for *her* would fade, he'd replied only by making love to her in a frenzy, as if it were the last time he'd be allowed to do so.

"Ashcroft?" he asked without turning, his gaze still fixed on the somber scene outside the window.

She stepped into the room, leaving the door ajar. "Nothing burned to a crisp yet." Her skirt did have a scorched hem, but Minnie had stamped the blaze out with her capable foot before it raced out of control.

He sipped, nodded. "Brilliant."

She halted at his desk, bracing her fingers on polished mahogany. His aura glowed the color of the blooming daffodils in her garden, measured caution. He stood only two paces from her, yet he seemed leagues away. Her gaze circled the room, seeking answers and finding them in the leather portmanteau sitting by the desk, packed and ready for travel. "Preparing for a journey?" Her query slid out without revealing a hint of the angst knotting her stomach, though she had to curl her hands in fists to keep them from shaking.

Julian turned, wedging his shoulder against the window frame, his steely gaze raking the length of her body in a blistering perusal. His eyes were shuttered behind his spectacle lenses.

He's foxed, was her first thought.

And already gone, was her second.

His aura sparked like one of Ashcroft's blazes, and she released the desk, taking a stumbling step back.

His hand flexed around the crystal tumbler as he brought it to his lips and polished off the amber liquid. "I would claim you," he finally said in a voice offering no opening to step inside and break the comment apart. "Take every part of you if I could." He thumped the glass to the desk and bracing his hands, leaned over it until he came so close his scent —citrus, sweat, brandy—circled her like she wished his arms would.

She swallowed, her throat clicking.

"Don't look so surprised. You've been a bloody obsession since I first laid eyes on you."

"You say that like that's *my* fault."

He laughed without a trace of humor. "Your persistence is not only legendary, Yank, it's also killing me."

"Remember our dance? You run"—she nodded to the portmanteau—"I chase." Sliding her hands next to his but not touching him, she added, "But I'm not going to chase forever."

She had not Finn's gift, but she read Julian's mind as easily as she could his flowing script on a page. Stepped straight through those astounding eyes and into his soul. Something had happened, and he was done with this, with *her*. A chill brought goosebumps to her skin, and she fought back the sting of tears. His bloody righteousness was going to win. From the grave, her grandfather was going to win. She'd be left adrift, brushed aside by the only man she would ever love.

A man who did not love her enough to keep her.

Julian's lids drifted low as he tilted his head. He was going to kiss her, that *bastard*. Thinking to leave her, but, no, he still wanted her. *Men*, she raged.

Could he not make up his blasted mind?

All at once, she wanted to consume him. Sweep everything from his desk and lay him upon it. Use her hands, lips, and teeth to drive him crazy while he did the same to her.

And...she wanted to bash him over the head with his ink blotter.

She was so distracted trying to decide between kissing and bashing that she shifted, sliding a brooch she had not noticed was lying there against his hand. A circle of sapphires, the ruby center glowed like a rabid eye.

She flinched as Julian groaned and brought his fist to his head.

She had thrown him into a vision with the touch of the brooch, one which appeared to be devouring him.

"Julian," she shouted and knocked the jewelry from the desk, where it hit the wall with a ping. His head dropped as if nothing but a thin string connected it to his body. A tortured inhalation lifted his shoulders.

Piper took a breath, covered his hand, and stepped into the vision with him.

It was evident from first sight that the woman in the otherworld was raving mad, her aura looking much like the floor of the lodge, spattered with random colors, a horrifying muddle. She stood before a window, her hair a sooty cascade down her back, searching but not appearing to see the horde of people and carriages passing in a blur of motion. She fingered the sapphire brooch at her neck, a sequence of aggravated repetition.

Unable to curb the compulsion, Piper pushed Julian aside. His anger ripped through her as he tried to stop her. But it was futile. In this, *she* governed.

When Piper got within reach, the woman's head spun like a child's toy toward her. Her eyes glowed, and Piper felt trapped, solidified like a bug in amber.

"You," she said, her heavily-accented threat crisping the air, "I seek *you*. And I'm close to gaining what I seek."

Piper's vision dimmed as the woman touched her, and she knew no more.

∾

"Leaving me to deal with Scamp again, is that it? I'm getting deuced sick of the two of you. You've ruined my thinking I might experience matrimonial serenity someday if this bedlam is what love is like. I'm telling you, if it is, I want no part of it. My widow friend in the village will do just fine. For the rest of my life, fine."

Christ, Julian thought and shoved a letter detailing the purchase of a gaming hell in his portmanteau. "How is she? Did Minnie give her the sleeping powder?"

"Cranky, mulish, and yes, finally sleeping. Thank the Lord. Rebellious chit threatened to find you herself, so here I am, doing her bidding. And dashed if you're not doing just what she thought..." Humphrey brushed aside the rest of the statement with an oath as he kicked the study door shut.

"I can't stay," Julian said, the most he could admit when what he meant was, *I can't breathe*. His chest was so constricted, he had yet to take a full mouthful in the twelve hours since Piper had fainted, striking her head hard enough on his desk to send blood *everywhere*. His hand shook as he fastened the portmanteau with a snap. "Tell her—"

"Hell, no. I'm not volunteering for *that* job."

"I can't. Not right now. Not when..." He shoved his hand in his pocket and fingered her hairclip, sending her lovely visage cascading through him. He'd known as he held her lifeless body in his arms what he was going to do. Not what he had to do, but what he *wanted* to do. With her blood streaking his skin, time had fluttered like the pages of a book until he was fifteen years old and stepping from the earl's carriage and into her life.

Remembrance of that moment had pierced his skin and let joy flow in. He wanted that feeling back, wanted it every morning when he woke next to her.

He'd been a fool to think he could deny her.

Deny himself.

Humphrey took one look at his face and threw himself to the settee, his large body overwhelming the tiny fixture. "She'll have my head on a platter when she finds you've hightailed it to London, and I didn't try to stop you."

"The storm won't last long because I'm going—" Julian thumped the portmanteau to the floor, swallowed, and tried again, "I'm going to ask her to marry me, but I need something from my safe in Mayfair to do it. Also, a brief meeting with my solicitor to secure a special license is in order. Keep her occupied; I'll be back before two days have passed. Call me a coward, but I need a moment to gather my resources before facing her."

Julian glanced over to find Humphrey—for the first time in memory—stunned to silence.

"Shocking, Rey, that you have no supplementary advice upon hearing this declaration."

Humphrey gave one hard blink, and then a slow smile cracked his lips. "If you'd followed my advice, you would've been married to Scamp for a while now. Can't ignore her healing when she's in your bed every night, now can you?"

Julian bumped back against his desk, this point the one compromise with himself he had yet to account for. He still thought his gift was ruinous, his future bleak.

But he loved her.

Too much to let them go on like this. In a quasi-state of inseparability, profound intimacy the likes of which he'd never imagined, even with her. He'd begun to think a balance may lie in the positive aspects of their union outweighing the negative.

She needed him, too, and if she weren't consumed with getting him to admit he loved her, maybe she'd start accepting his counsel.

Occasionally, anyway.

Was he insane to think marriage could settle down Scandalous Scott—without killing Julian Alexander in the process?

"You look like you're plotting a war campaign over there. It's downright frightening but makes me feel, sure to my bones, that you've found your match in that hellion."

Julian wrapped his hand around Piper's hairclip and released a breath that came out sounding horribly sentimental. "What if she says no? What will I do then?"

Humphrey threw his head back, laughter rolling from his throat. "You are one sad duck, Jule. It's tough to watch. I prefer Scamp's take-no-prisoners method."

Julian could only hang his head in agreement, hoping what was hidden away in his safe in Mayfair would convince Piper to share her future.

~

He had left for London without a word. A note. An explanation.

Piper digested this information as she rested against her bay's flank, the cottage Julian was forcing upon her sitting at the end of the pebbled footpath. Brook Cottage, to be exact. A bequest from the Earl of Montclaire to his cherished granddaughter, a delightful abode where she would follow expectation and live an undignified life with an undignified maid and ten screeching cats.

She kicked at a rock that had snuck beneath her boot. In truth, she was not overly fond of cats.

And, Julian might be surprised, but the damsel in distress was no longer up to the chase.

Drawing her ire like a shawl about her, she inhaled a breath scented with myrrh, musk, and tea rose. Regrettably, she understood Julian better than he understood himself. This insight allowed her to see both sides, even if she only wanted to see one.

Hers.

Julian tried to do the right thing, always—and she knew it. She supposed she loved him for his scrupulousness even when it got in her way.

Looping the reins around a fence post, she crossed to the babbling brook giving the cottage its name. The ivy-covered dwelling was constructed of the chalk brick in such favor in Oxfordshire; the window frames painted a splendidly contrasting blue. Gardens, modest but undeniably lovely, surrounded her. The manor was adorable, and she loved it on sight. Halting in a thicket of rose bushes, she popped a pale pink bloom from its stem, wondering what in heaven's name she was going to do now.

As she stood there, peeling the flower like an onion, at a home Julian had chosen for her, very personally now that she had a look at it, a feeling similar to being enfolded in his arms overtook her.

The gift of Brook Cottage was a loving embrace.

And a kick in the backside.

She and Humphrey had argued about this very topic at breakfast this morning, right before she snuck past her guards by telling them she was returning to her bedchamber with a *female complaint*.

For once in her life, she marveled with a humorless smile, Humphrey was on her side. *Agreed, Julian should not have left. You scared the life out of him*, and the like. He hadn't been able to look her directly in the eye, this bizarre occurrence making her wonder what he and Julian had up their sleeves.

Why did she have to love the noblest man in all of bloody England?

His motives were admirable, but she wanted more than saving.

She wanted to be *loved*.

When Julian was not capable. His fear too great. His affection too weak. His walls too high. She wrenched another rose off the bush, sick of trying to rationalize the situation.

Weary, perturbed, *finished*.

This time, the mess was his fault, his doing.

Although the episode in his study *had* been a disaster on every level.

Petals drifted from her fingers to the ground. That dashed brooch, she thought even as she dipped her hand in her pocket and curled her fingers around it. When the madwoman found her, and find her she would—and soon, Piper suspected with a spike of dread—she wanted the piece on her person. For reasons she could not define.

They had located the woman's London hotel from details contained in one of Finn's dreams, but she was gone when Julian's men searched her room. Nothing there except the brooch, tucked beneath a wrinkle in the carpet. It was delivered to Harbingdon for Julian to read, although he'd hesitated for days to touch it.

Until she'd forced him to.

When he was drinking and troubled, not in the best form. Too, Piper had forced her way into the otherworld, stepped right past him, then promptly fainted when the woman touched her. Humphrey didn't understand, and she couldn't properly explain how *powerless* Julian had felt, unable to reach her in the unsettling space between past and present. His aura had been clear on that score, flaring the color of a pearl freshly pulled from the sea.

It hadn't helped that she'd cracked her head. Blood a bright spill over her bodice, Julian's face matching his colorless aura when she awoke to find herself cradled in his arms. Neither Finn nor Humphrey could talk him out of his desolation.

Do you see? This is what her grandfather warned me about.

As soon as the doctor proclaimed her injury one she would fully recover from, he'd saddled his horse and left for London. Solicitors to meet. Papers to sign. Gaming hell to purchase.

Running, she'd shouted from her bedchamber window as he galloped down the drive, Minnie tearing at her sleeve to pull her inside.

Piper sighed and approached the cottage. The

door was unlocked and swung wide, the little-used hinge squealing.

Exposed beams, a lovely stone hearth. As charming inside as out.

She lost herself to the fantasy of walking the gardens with Julian before dawn, making love in the bedchamber she could see down the hall. Maybe he wouldn't be angry when he returned. Time usually restored an agreeable mood.

Then she heard the hinge's protest. And realized she should have let one of the Duke's soldiers accompany her after all. Stubborn, lovesick *fool*.

Sneaking out hadn't been wise.

The man blocking the door wore unfamiliar livery, a glorified mercenary similar to one of Ashcroft's soldiers. Pistol drawn, knife strapped to his hip, he fashioned an intimidating portrait. When another man joined him in the foyer, Julian's words shot like a bullet through her brain.

If they come for you, for once in our life, play along.

No tricks.

No rebellion.

He'd covered the possibilities more than once, often while their bodies were tangled and spent. So, she didn't resist when the brute crossed to her, when he took her wrist in a damaging grip.

She would follow through on her promise even as dread sent her skin tingling and her heart racing.

"The beautiful boy, the dreamer," the man whispered in accented English as he shook her so hard her hair whipped her cheeks. "*Where* is he?"

Finn. "I'll die first," she vowed.

With a violent shove, the brute sent her stumbling to the floor. "That can be arranged."

She gazed into the man's eyes, seeing only relentless brutality flashing back at her. *Your gift is your weapon*, Julian whispered. His sureness brought her strength. "Bring me to her," Piper directed, only a slight flutter bruising her words. "And take care, because a dead woman can't heal."

Julian said he would go to the ends of the earth to find her.

She believed him.

~

Simon peeked around the garden wall, watching as the men dragged Miss Piper to a waiting carriage. She staggered but caught her footing, and Simon's breath rattled in his throat. The rat bastards, he raged, his fists clenched. They were handling her very roughly, not like they should a proper lady. Simon had lived among vermin all his life and could pick out rats in a skinny second—no matter the flipping fancy attire.

Daft lass, going off on her own. Glad now he'd decided to follow her, but...

Lawks was Lord J going to be mad. Everyone knew he was near crazy about Miss Piper.

Simon wiped his hands on his trousers and danced from one foot to the other, trying to come up with a plan. *Think, Si, think.*

"See that platform at the rear?" the haunt at his side asked.

Simon nodded, not taking his eyes off Miss Piper as the men shoved her in the carriage. The annoying old gent had been following him for days and wasn't likely to leave anytime soon.

"Called a tiger's platform."

"Tiger. Like a cat?" Simon asked.

"Small footman."

Simon nodded. "Righty-ho."

"When they pull away, hop on the back. But you must jump off before the carriage stops."

"Then I go tell Finn." He could tell Finn anything, he thought with a spark of newfound adoration, when he'd yet to adore anyone in his life. Aye, he'd seen lads in livery attire, clinging like mud to the back of carriages. All over London, he'd watched them and marveled: what was *that* life like? Tigers. Blimey. He quite liked the name. But not the silly gig required for the job.

"They must not see you, boy. You understand?"

"You be one yappy ghost," Simon said. When the carriage rolled from the drive, he sprinted with it, and only when it gained speed did he hook his arm on the platform and swing himself up. Pressing his back to the outer wall, he crouched low and tight in the corner. His pulse pounded in his ears as the spot of cheese and bread he'd eaten on the walk rose in his throat. He actually felt a measure of calm when the old haunting gent settled in beside him.

Lord J talked a lot about destiny. Purpose. Goals, when Simon couldn't give a fig about them. He gave figs about a full belly and a soft bed, not having a knife pressed to his throat. The blunt he had secreted beneath his fancy mattress.

Only, he liked Miss Piper. She talked to him about the haunts without scooting away from him like he had the pox. She read him stories and had promised to let him plant rose bushes in the garden next week.

And he liked Finn, of course. He would follow Finn Alexander to the ends of the earth.

So, wot, just wot, if saving Miss Piper was *his* destiny?

CHAPTER 20

While we may, the sports of love; time will not be ours forever.
    ~Ben Johnson

In the past twenty-four hours, Julian had come to find he'd misconstrued life's signals.

Piper was his life; all he'd ever wanted once he let himself admit it. She had clawed her way into corners he hadn't exposed to light in years.

And he meant to have her.

Even if she entered the otherworld.

Even if what the earl had threatened was nothing *but* the painful truth.

Even if, and this idea nearly brought him to his knees, he and Piper created a child who carried his gift. Or hers.

A child he would love to the end of time.

He no longer cared. Or mayhap better to say, Piper was worth more than his concerns. She was worth more—and he could not, *would* not, live without her. The sun had gone behind a cloud, and it was never to reappear if she did not.

He dropped his head to his hands. *So, this is what dying feels like.*

"They want her alive. They want her to heal," Humphrey whispered and laid a fist on his shoulder.

Julian shook off the touch and paced Brook Cottage's lone drawing room. Once there and back before he was able to catch his breath. After Finn had intercepted him at the Cock and Bull, they'd tracked Piper to this dwelling and found her bay tied up outside. The sight of the horse waiting patiently for its rider made him question if he was losing his mind.

Ire was clouding his judgment, and all he could think was: *if they touch her, I'll rip out their hearts.* He would return to the savagery of the rookery without a second thought. As it was, he was holding himself back from unleashing his fury on the guards she'd slipped past.

"We'll find her, Jule."

"Piper has the brooch, Rey. I have nothing to read."

"They're not in London." This from Finn, who stood with a devastated expression by the stone fireplace Julian had known Piper would love the moment he saw it. It was one of the few times he recalled Finn looking anything other than bored. "The dream last night"—he held up his hand, then let it drop with a whispered oath—"they were in the country. They've taken her somewhere close. I can *feel* it."

Julian exhaled and let his head fall back. That crazy bitch was going to rue the day she messed with his family.

Ashcroft ducked inside as he, unbelievably, stood the tallest in the room. Two of his soldiers tramped in behind him. Truthfully, Julian was glad he was there because the man always looked as if he would joyfully tear someone apart. Like no duke Julian had ever seen. "There were two men. Easily fifteen stone. No sign of a struggle. Just one point in the yard where she stumbled. Their tracks were made from the cut of a French boot. I've seen it before." He scowled, chasing his hand down his coat to the knife holstered at his waist. An unconscious movement, Julian was sure. "A child's boot impression as well. By the garden wall and leading to the carriage. Fresh. The same time frame, from the dried mud."

Julian darted a glance at Finn. Finn's cheeks paled, bleeding parchment.

Simon, he mouthed.

As if they'd summoned him, Simon came through the doorway in a skidding burst, his face crimson, sweat streaking his skin. Finn was before him in two strides, tipping the boy's chin high. "Did you find her?"

Julian straightened, daring to breathe. His life flashed before his eyes—with and without Piper in it. The prick behind his lids had him blinking as he swallowed, his throat working furiously. "Where is she?"

Backing out of Finn's hold, Simon bolted for the door, making it as far as the rose bushes before he dropped to his knees and heaved. Finn yanked a handkerchief from his pocket and thrust it at the boy. "Calm down, Si. It's okay. We have you now."

Simon's head hung so low his hair skimmed the stalks of grass. As Julian reached him, a horrifying theory left him breathless. *What if they'd hurt her, and the boy hadn't the nerve to tell them?*

Julian kneeled. "Is she…"

The emotion in Julian's voice seemed to give

Simon courage. "I heard a floorboard outside my chamber creak. I've tested the entire hallway, for protection. It was the one by that stiff chair no one wants to sit in. She went out a window, first floor but still high up, like nothing I've seen a girl do. A lady most especially. Before dawn. Pitch-black. No guard. I don't much like the kind of *real* dark you find in the country, but I followed her anyway."

Finn grasped Simon's hand. "And?"

Simon sniffled and wiped his nose on his sleeve. "Two rat bastards shoved her into a carriage and the yappy haunt, the one been following me all week, said: jump on that tiger platform and hide. So, I did."

Julian rocked back on his heels, the relief coursing through him lethal enough to dim his vision. "You know—"

"Where Lady Piper is. She didn't fight, but..." A tear streaked Simon's cheek, and he turned his head to hide it. "The haunts. Godawful ones. Bloody horror the evil lady is."

Finn picked Simon up and cradled him to his chest. "My destiny," Julian heard him whimper.

Julian fisted his hands, wishing their gifts and the world it forced them to occupy to perdition.

"Mount up," Ashcroft instructed his men. They were armed, thankfully, to the teeth.

However, rescuing Piper wasn't precisely like fighting an opponent one knew well. A *sane* opponent. Adding an element of surprise to this campaign might deliver the superior approach, Julian decided as he swung his leg over the saddle of his black.

"Ashcroft, any chance your work with Piper has provided more control over those fires?"

"I met your grandfather many years ago. Were you aware of this?"

Piper brought her head up slowly. Too quick a movement, and she would lose consciousness. Leaving the present for even a moment could not happen again, as it had invoked her captor's rage, lunacy unlike any she'd ever experienced.

Sidonie.

The woman chasing her for weeks through Finn's dreams had a name. And a horrific past Piper had spent two days mired in. Being caged in Sidonie's mind was worse punishment than being beaten and tied to a chair—worse punishment than anything she could imagine. Healing was not the word for what she'd done, stitching together Sidonie's awareness with gossamer thread. The edges tattered and uneven, Piper had made a patchwork quilt of the mess but, impossibly, left gaping holes.

Gaping holes the woman's sanity was draining from like blood from a wound.

But what had Piper's skin stinging like a razor was being scraped across it: Sidonie had no aura. Only skin, bone, and madness. There was no way to save her, no matter the initial spark of hope Piper had held. No possibility for her to do anything but play this game until Julian found her.

Please, Jules, find me.

"My grandfather," she whispered from bruised lips. The room was overly warm. A fire raged in the stone hearth; the windows were closed to hold in the heat. Yet Piper shivered, tremors racking her body, the ropes binding her to the chair holding her up. The scent of Frankincense pressed, and her stomach heaved. "When?"

Sidonie paused in the middle of her trek across the room, a route she had repeated a thousand times without a hint of exhaustion slowing her. Her pupils were such a startling shade they appeared crimson in the firelight; her hair snarled, a black demon hanging down her back; her clothing well-made, speaking of affluence, but from another era. Piper shrank back helplessly as Sidonie leaned over her, the brooch she had relinquished in return for a sip of water glistening from its perch on the woman's collar.

Devil.

No more. *No more.*

Sidonie thumped her hand against her chest. *"Il y a longtemps.* You understand?"

Piper swallowed, her head beginning to pound. Her French was dreadful. That governess had only lasted a week. "A long time?"

"Long ago." Sidonie blew out a disgusted breath. "Senseless American."

"A good thing...my gift is from the English side, then."

Sidonie struck Piper across the cheek before she could prepare for the attack. With a snarl, the mad-woman drew her arm back to deliver another blow.

"I can't heal if you strike me senseless. Remember the last time?" Piper wiped the blood coursing down her chin on her shoulder, astounded her words were strong when she felt as feeble as a child. If Julian waited too long, Sidonie would kill her.

"Your grandfather was *known.*"

Piper gazed through the eye not swollen shut as Sidonie resumed her circuitous route. Blindfolded when they brought her in, Piper didn't know exactly where they were. A secluded manor. South, if her sense of direction was correct, less than an hour by carriage from Harbingdon. If Finn had enough time to dream, they would eventually find her. She simply needed to keep Sidonie from putting a knife through her neck as had been threatened multiple times.

In between impassioned demands to heal.

"Known?" Piper asked, directing Sidonie back to the conversation. Talking had proven effective at diminishing her wild ranting.

Sidonie turned in a fraught swirl of aged velvet. "Known! Even in Lyon. My father had contacts who requested a meeting with the Occult Earl. An ambassador. Or maybe it was the Baron who—*convoité moi* —wanted me." She waved this away as if her past were nothing. Her accent worsening with her agitation, Piper struggled to comprehend her speech. "Desperate, all of them, to keep me from an asylum. Imagine, a trip to England in the dead of winter. *Froid.*"

She halted, her gaze seeking Piper's. "Your grandmother tried to help me."

Piper straightened, gasping in pain. She had battled the knots securing her legs to the chair for hours with little success, leaving abraded, tender skin. "I was...too young to remember her."

Sidonie gestured frantically with each pass across the carpet. "Her eyes were kind. She didn't look at me like a, like a *monstre*. Like my family! Like everyone! Curse that I am, that I *have*, my thoughts stopped her heart." She dropped to her knees before Piper, her passionate gaze appealing for understanding. "I didn't mean to kill her. You must understand. You *must*."

Piper shuddered. Her lungs burned, her vision blacking at the edges.

Breathe, Piper. Defenseless if you faint.

Sidonie gripped Piper's knee, both of them trembling. "Before. Before she died, your grandfather told me there was another. Stronger. Someone to help me. *Un Americain*. I never forgot you were my savior. But years passed, and...your *amoureux* hid you well. Too, the beautiful boy. He distorted the communication traveling between us. He is not my friend."

I can't help you.

Sidonie took one look at the miserable validation on Piper's face and exploded. Bounding to her feet, she set about to *destroy*. Pages ripped from books; porcelain tossed to the floor; paintings ripped from the wall. The guards standing in each corner observed as indifferently as those at Buckingham Palace, apparently not the first time they had seen this feverish display.

A tear tracked Piper's cheek. She could not survive this encounter.

Then, miraculously, smoke slipped in and stung her nostrils.

She glanced frantically into each corner as a pop set the tassels of the carpet aflame. Another spark flickered near the drapes, not strong enough to hold. Then again, this one flaring to life.

Julian had found her.

And her lessons with Ashcroft were *working*.

The Duke of Ashcroft's imperfect, astounding gift was going to save her.

Chaos erupted as Sidonie's men scattered like croquet balls across a lawn. Sounds collided: Sidonie screaming; flames roaring up the exterior wall; stone splintering. Scents invaded: scorched fabric, wood, plaster. *Skin*.

Dash it, she thought and began a desperate struggle, the knots binding her unrelenting.

The room was an inferno.

A hand captured her wrist, in turns tender and insistent. Startled, she peered through the haze and into Julian's eyes, a deeper, darker grey than even the smoke. Her breath shot forth in a stunned gasp; he had the ferocious look of someone set to slay a dragon.

"Hold still." He slipped a knife from his boot and sliced through the ropes. Without another word, he yanked her from the chair as the ceiling rained plaster chunks like snow around them. When she stumbled, he lifted her into his arms and sprinted down the hallway, shouting orders that became a tonal blur. His heartbeat pounded beneath her cheek; a button on his waistcoat dug into her ribs as she tucked into him. Coughing, she gasped for air.

Above the smoldering scent of death, she smelled Julian.

Julian, she thought and collapsed against him.

"I have you," he whispered, "and I'm never letting you go."

CHAPTER 21

They that are rich in words, in words discover. That they are poor in that which makes a lover.
  ~Sir Walter Raleigh

The room she awoke in was remarkably crowded. Finn, his long body looking like it sought to escape the narrow confines of the chaise lounge, slept as soundly as a babe. Minnie hummed beneath her breath as she poured tea and arranged a tray Piper prayed contained something edible. Julian and Humphrey stood by the hearth, engaged in a heated exchange.

"She's my responsibility," she heard Julian say.

Piper grimaced, the word cutting through her lethargy. A grown woman, she didn't want to be anyone's *responsibility*. Making sure she was adequately covered, she inched off the bed. Pain shot through her ankle as she tried to stand. Wincing, she perched on the mattress. Each part of her body ached, right down to her toes. She reached to touch. Her eye was bandaged, her lips covered with an ointment that felt delightful but smelled dreadful.

She must look an absolute fright.

Minnie gasped and hurried to her. "Coo, Lady Piper, goodness no. No walking on that bum ankle. And, oh, your face. Mirrors are not going to be your friend for a bit, love." Turning, she glanced at the teacup she'd left too close to the edge of the tray, and it slid back with a gentle click.

Julian was there in seconds, tenderly cupping her cheek. His thumb brushed her lip, and she flinched, watching as his eyes darkened to the color of the ash that had blanketed them as they raced from Sidonie's horror chamber. "I would kill her if Ashcroft's fire had not taken care of that for us."

"I'm not your responsibility," she whispered. She wanted more. She'd meant it when she said she was finished chasing him.

His arm dropped, and he rocked back on his heels. Irritation wiped the soft smile from his face as his aura shimmered. "Yes. You *are*."

She rose with help from the mattress, a crooked lean, shaking off Julian's hand when he tried to assist. She wasn't going to debate her life, her *future,* while hiding beneath bedcovers.

"I'm willing to revoke any promise I made. Risk everything—"

"She killed my grandmother, Jules."

He stopped midstream, off-balance. "*What?*"

"Sidonie's father took her to see the earl. Years ago, before you and I were there. My grandmother tried to help her." She grasped the teacup Minnie offered, cradled it in her hands, and drank deeply. "Her heart gave out, maybe. I don't know. You see, the earl made you promise because of what Sidonie did to my grandmother. A frail, elderly woman, Julian. I spent two days inside her mind—and I survived. I can be a partner to you. Our relationship is not an exchange. Your honor for my love. And if you think it is…"

"Ah, a lover's quarrel," Finn drawled from the chaise lounge. "Brilliant."

Humphrey grunted, stoic sentry by the hearth.

Julian threw out his hand. "It's—"

"Don't you say it's not," Piper snapped. "This is our family, and if you can't admit to them what you feel, then how can we go on?"

Silent, Julian's jaw clenched. He hadn't shaved in days and was halfway to a full beard, giving him the look of a brigand. A serrated, rather angry scratch ran from his ear into the collar of his shirt. Yet he stood there in shirtsleeves and wrinkled trousers, hair askew, eyes flint, looking as formidable as a king. She should be frightened but was only vexed.

He braced his hand on the bedpost, effectively locking her in. "They bloody well know what I feel for you, Piper. *Everyone* knows."

"How about this for a novel idea? Tell *me*. Maybe I don't know."

"I've told you so many times in the past twenty-four hours, I'm hoarse with it."

"Care to try when I'm conscious?"

"Maybe you should start this discussion by apologizing for being reckless for the last time in your life, so help me God," he hissed between clenched teeth.

Caught in the crosshairs of her affection, she was rendered motionless, breathless.

Oh, she was over the moon for the blasted man.

"I love you, Lady Scott. Obsessively. Ardently. *Maddeningly*." He slapped the bedpost. "And you know it. You always have."

"You sound thrilled. No, make that resigned. La, the romance is killing me."

He looked away, lips pressed, a muscle in his jaw flexing. "Can we talk about this in private, please?"

"*No.*"

Julian exhaled, hand going to his temple in a bruising press.

She popped her teacup atop the table, tears stinging her eyes. She was irrational. Confused. Exhausted. Forcing his hand. They had played adversarial roles for so long, she slipped back into the Scott-Alexander groove without a moment's hesitation.

Julian had finally told her he loved her, and she was acting like an idiot!

When his gaze traveled back, his look was all intractable male. "I'm securing a special license."

She flopped to the bed with a sniff. "That's an abysmal proposal."

His aura rippled like a calm pond disturbed by a boulder.

As long as she'd known him, he had handled every hardship thrown his way with enviable composure. She didn't want to present another ordeal for a man who, truthfully, needed someone to soften the wild splash coloring his life.

But, this time, she needed him to fight for her, for *them.*

If she loved Julian in gross comparison, she would die a slow death.

When he realized she was not going to bend to his will, he growled to anyone willing to take on the job, "Reason with her, will you?" Then he exited her bedchamber, slamming the door behind him.

∾

He went to the lodge to hide.

Being surrounded by the scent of turpentine and paint used to bring relief. Now lilacs and lavender invaded the space, upending his equilibrium. Add to that a thousand lewd images, and you had complete unrest. The weight of her perfectly round breast balanced in the palm of his hand. Her lids fluttering as she glided into ecstasy. Their bodies colliding into every piece of furniture in the room—and draped languorously on the floor.

And the more deadly reminiscences.

Piper lounging on his bed, his shirt barely covering her pert bottom, a wicked grin on her face as she debated his repeated use of green in his paintings of late. Toe grazing his as they worked together on her research, her gaze so genuinely inquisitive he was conquered. Brushing his hair from his face as he labored over the pages of her grandfather's chronology deep into the night.

He hadn't told her why he strived for the exact shade of emerald in those paintings. A shade he only seemed able to recreate in his dreams.

Dammit.

He'd mucked it up, a foul effort. The Reluctant Viscount apparently could not propose with any delicacy.

Where was the romance?

Hidden deep in his heart, that's where.

He wasn't a poet, he lamented, drawing wrapping paper around a painting of Bond Street headed to a tobacconist he frequented, one who wished to modernize his shop. At Julian's core, he was an unpretentious man, caught up in managing the viscountcy, growing the League, working on his paintings. Protecting the motley assortment who were now his family.

He was somewhat staid, even slightly dull. He

THE LADY IS TROUBLE

wasn't vibrant enough for Piper, of that he was sure, but she was his, and he was *not* giving her up.

Helpless to fight his attraction, and with that atrocious promise standing between them, he'd mishandled the entire relationship. More than once sent them down the wrong path. Now he was willing to share every part of himself, yet, he was floundering.

Like most men, when it came down to it, he was simply a daft prick.

However, this time he might surprise her. When Beauchamp the Lionhearted made up his mind, he was as bloody stubborn as Scandalous Scott.

"She doesn't believe you."

Julian turned, having made a wager regarding whom he *least* wanted to provide counsel when counsel showed. Heartless Humphrey or chiding-with-a-smile Finn.

Obviously, the boy had lost the coin toss.

Finn closed the door with a soft snick and strolled in as if he owned the space. Sauntered from one side of the room to the other, inspecting canvases and toeing aside paintbrushes with a polished boot.

Julian tightened the noose knot around the painting and set it aside. The string had sent an image of a man loading spool through his mind. He blinked to clear it. "Did you come to review my latest work?" Grabbing another length of twine, he fashioned a piece long enough to secure the next bundle and slit his knife through it. "Make yourself useful then."

Finn hummed beneath his breath in agreement.

Julian nodded to a partial nude leaning against the settee. "That one, please."

Finn dropped to his haunches, tilted his head in assessment. "Naughty. Looks French." He whistled in appreciation. "Is it *de rigueur* for the artist to take the clothes off the model? If so, I may take up painting."

Julian flattened a square of paper with his palm. "Adam Davies can do anything he damn well pleases." The name he'd used in the rookery served as his *nom de plume*. It wouldn't do for a viscount to be associated with risqué artwork, which is likely why most days he felt more Mr. Davies than Viscount Beauchamp. "Out with it, will you?"

Finn brought the painting to Julian. "You're going to have to do better. A *lot* better. Groveling of the first order. Your proposal was dreadful. Remind me not to ask for tips should I ever decide to go that route."

"Astonishing observation." He secured the paper around the canvas with a snap.

Finn handed him the length of twine. "You create striking masterpieces, yet you can't charm the woman you love. This is where it's proven we are not, in truth, blood relations. It should be easy. If you meant what you said, that is."

Julian tied the knot, then gave it a vicious tug for good measure. "When have I ever *not* loved her?"

Finn huffed a laugh and settled his hip on the desk. "Give the hound a boon for having caught said fox."

"You may want to consider another analogy. Piper may not love being compared to a dog."

"Consider her predicament, then."

"Finn, my boy, I've been considering her *predicament* since I was fifteen years old. And rescued her from most of them." Finn had been too young to know the half of it. Did he think she'd gotten that blasted moniker for *nothing*?

Finn snapped his fingers. "Exactly. So, try a go at not being her minder. Court her, Jule. You can't expect her to trust you when she's always been the one on the hook. From a love standpoint, that is. I channeled no minds to gain this information, by the by. It's out there, ripe for the taking."

Julian froze, the twine sliding through his fingers. He'd never courted Piper. Never courted anyone. Never planned to court anyone.

Had he ever treated Piper like the woman he loved instead of the one he'd been asked to protect?

Show her you love her, Julian.

Finn clapped and peeled himself from the desk. "I see the wheels turning in the dusty equipment. My work is done."

At the door, he paused, sending Julian a look shaded with chagrin. "But, um, send the love notes to Brook Cottage. Piper, Minnie, and half of Ashcroft's army are heading there as we speak. I'm afraid...well, your woman has left you."

Julian tossed the twine to the floor as the door closed behind Finn. Brook Cottage had been a gift, a very personal one if Piper looked closely. She wasn't going to make it easy, and maybe he didn't deserve ease.

What had he expected from the most fascinating, bothersome, stunning creature he'd ever encountered?

Women, he grumbled and set about winning his.

CHAPTER 22

Whoever loved that loved not at first sight.
~Christopher Marlowe

A week passed before Piper concluded that her rejection of Julian's pitiable but heartfelt proposal might have been an unintentionally deceptive feminine ploy.

Minnie had located spare furniture in storage at Harbingdon and wonder of wonders established a comfortable home in short order. Brook Cottage was charming and agreeable, as Julian had known it would be. Ashcroft's men patrolled, but unobtrusively, as the threat had lessened with Sidonie's death. The gardens were beautiful and in need of just the right amount of attention to entice, not intimidate. Edward, Finn, and the Duke of Ashcroft visited daily, as did the new gamekeeper, a young man who delivered thoughts to her as steadily as bullets fired from a pistol without once opening his mouth. Simon had spent two nights on a pallet next to her bed, allowing them to continue reading *David Copperfield*. Henry had even begun to arrive in the afternoon, rolling about on his back among honeysuckle and a variety of wildflower Mr. Knotworth identified as enchanter's nightshade.

She should not be lonely, yet she was. A bone-crushing, soulless ache the likes of which she'd never encountered. Not even while sequestered in Gloucestershire.

Not surprising as two crucial elements were missing.

Julian. And her bay.

Julian the most critical, of course.

She'd ridden twice in the past week, feeling like she trespassed as she tiptoed into the stable, although Murphy hadn't blinked. Galloping along with her gaze fixed habitually over her shoulder, she'd finally deemed it unsafe to continue. Until Julian showed his face at Brook Cottage, she would walk. Or take a cart.

She admitted to being unsettled.

Because, for the first time in her life, Julian was pursuing *her*.

In an affectionate, persistent, patient, somewhat mysterious, oh-so-Julian way.

Every day for the past six, a gift arrived before dawn on her doorstep. Intimate selections chosen by a person who knew her better than she knew herself. The first a book on trees native to England wrapped in a sketch of the chapel in the wood and their picnic under the stars. The second a silver jewelry box decorated in tea roses, similar to the ones she had shown Julian on a clandestine, midnight walk, where she'd gushed over how well they'd blossomed under her tutelage. Inside, nestled among folds of royal blue silk, he'd left two things: the hairpin he'd been carrying with him for weeks and a brooch he'd given her

on her nineteenth birthday, one left behind in the
chaos surrounding her grandfather's death. It was Julian's mother's, one of the few items he had from her.
A treasured heirloom he'd not part with frivolously.

She scarcely drew a full breath upon opening the
door each morning, her heart expanding with every
present. A scandalous cobalt riding habit that would
allow her to ride astride. A lavender bush planted in
the corner of the yard, surrounded by river stones in
the shape of a heart. A telescope placed in the center
of the lawn, directed to Julian's beloved Canis Minor.
A handsome leather folio engraved with her initials
and filled with suggestions for her research, one that
brought to mind the partially-clothed investigative
sessions they'd conducted in the lodge.

This thought sent her mind down a treacherous
path littered with sensual images of stolen, breathless
moments. Lying atop his body as they made love
amidst the tall grass by the lake; standing in a heated
press against the potter's shed as he thrust inside her;
laughing as they rolled from his desk to the floor in a
tangle of arms and legs.

As if the gifts—a deliberate, chess-like advance—
were not enough, now *this*.

This offering not only weakened, it *slayed*.

Nay, it was not a gift but a statement. So ardent a
statement, she sank to the stone steps and pressed
her shaking hand to her chest to steady herself. Beneath the modest portico of Brook Cottage, the air
proclaiming the arrival of autumn, dew on the faded
pink Hydrangea petals sparkling in the sun, she
fought for composure.

Where in the world...?

He had kept it all this time.

She turned the tarnished locket—wrapped in a
cravat she recognized as one Julian had used to at-

tach her wrist to his bedpost—in her hand. Over and over in sluggish revolutions as if the movement could lessen the depth of emotion she experienced upon seeing it again.

As if she had *any* control over her love for the man.

Contain, ease, or rectify. She could do little.

As helpless as seaweed swept along by a strong tide.

The moment came back to her with the force of one of his kisses. Julian stumbling from her grandfather's carriage, his clothing tattered, his hair a scruffy mess hanging in his face. Lanky angles of a body in the midst of fulfilling a stunning promise, he'd looked a young ruffian being uncaged and set loose on the world. He'd paused on the drive, going to his knee to take this very locket in his hand. Turned it deliberately for inspection, as she did now. Then he'd glanced at the window where she stood gazing down upon him—had somehow known exactly where to look to find her. His smile had grown the longer they stared, until her future surrounded her.

He said his vision of her was the first time he didn't despise his gift.

And for her…

As trite as it seemed, love, formidable and ruthless, at first glance.

My, she thought, *what a fool I've been to deny him.*

To deny myself.

The shadow fell over her, and she jerked her head up. Curled her hand into a fist, the locket's clasp digging into her skin. Julian stood bathed in amber sunlight, dressed in nothing but shirtsleeves, trousers, and riding boots. He'd come to her directly upon waking if his tousled hair and shadowed jaw was any indication. Exhaling, his gaze found hers. His hands flexed at his side, something he only did when he was unsure. The scent of citrus and tobacco circled, over-taking her senses.

Motionless, he waited for her signal, her decision, his aura shimmering brighter than the light pouring over him.

She ducked her head, hiding a smile. She, Piper Scott, had rattled Julian Alexander—the most self-possessed man in all of England. The dart of pleasure this gave her surely meant she was headed for hell.

"What took you so long, you foolish man?" she asked and launched herself at him, pulling his mouth to hers. Their first contact in days sent a dizzying wave of lust streaking through her veins.

With a low groan and two short steps, Julian backed her into the door. "Don't ever leave me again," he whispered against her lips before sinking in deep. "You infuriating..."

Passion erased the rest of his diatribe. A storm that ravaged her willing, weak body. His skin a damp slide beneath her fingertips, pulse tripping, heart thumping. She fisted her hand in his hair and urged him closer.

She wanted the explosive magic they made to-gether. She wanted their inferno to scorch her like one of Ashcroft's fires.

Gasping, she fumbled behind her for the door-knob. Market day. Minnie was gone. They were alone. "Inside," she said and popped a button on his shirt with her free hand, deliciously trapped by the hard angles of the door and his body.

Sunlight speckled her lids when he released her.

"No," he said. Quite clearly, again: "*No*." His lips were slow to leave hers, however, lingering, drifting across her cheek and nipping her jaw.

She stumbled back, her shoulders lifting with her

unhinged breaths. He looked as bewildered, hair spiking around his head, his gaze tarnished silver. She raised her hand to shield her eyes from his gleaming aura. "*Why?*"

His lashes fluttered as his lids slipped low. He laughed and dropped his brow to the door, air gusting from his lungs. "No, unless *you* say yes."

Turning her head, she pressed her lips to the spot beneath his ear that never failed to elicit a response. Took a gentle bite. Smiled when he growled, his grip on her hips tightening. His proposal still needed a lot of work, damn the man. "Is my dragging you to my new bedchamber contingent on a positive response?"

He cradled her face, staring into her eyes as her heart stuttered. "I know I bungled everything. For years, a tangle. When you were there, waiting for me. Since that day on the earl's drive. I can only say I'm a fool. My intentions were honorable, my love constant, though not suitably directed. But I'm done. I'm *here*. I want you for myself. And I apologize, humbly, for not arriving sooner." Sighing, he moved to adjust spectacles that were doubtless in his waistcoat pocket. "I don't have all the answers. My fear of letting you help me, heal me, remains, so stout is my desire to protect you. I want you to be happy and secure and safe. But I want to be happy as well, so my promises now are only to you." He leaned in to kiss her brow. "Not one moment…not one moment from this day forward without you. I want you to be my wife. I'll beg if you require it, which maybe you do."

"The locket," she whispered, a tear streaking her face. It was still clutched in her fist because she couldn't bear to part with it. She would never again part with it.

He wiped the tear from her cheek. "Oh, love, I'd never let that go. Every time I held it, I saw *you*. It went with me to Rugby, Oxford. My good luck charm. Because you are the only treasure my gift has given me."

"Are you trying to break my heart, Julian Alexander?"

"No. I'm trying to win it."

She tucked her head against his chest, breathing him in. He was love, security, home. *Acceptance.* Everything she'd wanted and been so long denied. In the distance, the monotonous chirp of a humming-bird sounded, a light breeze tugged at her skirts. Typical occurrences on a typical morning when her life was changing forever. "I don't know how to be a vis-countess."

"It's quite easy once you get the hang of it, I'm sure."

Sniffing, she said, "We'll argue all the time. I'm trouble."

"Nothing *but* from the first day I met you."

Leaning back in his arms, she frowned.

"I don't care. You're worth the headaches. When Sidonie took you—" His eyes closed, and his grasp tightened, his strength, his certainty, his *anger*, flowing into her. "That would have been the death of me, Piper. You see, I don't wish to be free of you. I don't wish to live a day without you. Our world"—he caught her by the wrist, imploring—"I can't do it alone. My dreams for the League, Harbingdon. Man-aging the visions. I *need* you." A bemused expression crossed his face, his gaze going the color of the peb-bles he'd scattered around her lavender bush. "I want to share my life with you, Yank. I want children, *our* children. Love is stronger than fear on that score and so many others. If I look deeply, it's no comparison. I'm going to let my certitude guide me now."

This is what love returned feels like, she thought in wonder.

"Lady Elizabeth Piper Alexander, Viscountess Beauchamp. There is a certain something," he said with a tilt of his head. As if teacups in drawing rooms all over England were not rattling with the statement.

Tears blurred her vision; she dashed her hand across her eyes. "I love you, Jules. I always have. But I'll make an appalling viscountess. I wasn't even a passable granddaughter of an earl."

Cupping her jaw, he brought her face into the light, into his view. "Rather, love, you'll teach them how it's done."

"Hmm, perhaps," she murmured and began to think of ways to do just that.

Tipping his head, he laughed as her temper sparked. She could play dirty. Scandalous Scott was known for it. Bouncing on her toes, she set her lips to his, pressing against him in the way he liked, as close as she could get when she loved such a very tall man.

His smile vanished as he tumbled into the kiss, a ragged moan creeping from his throat. "Unfair," he said and reached to open the door and push her inside.

"Always."

He pulled back just enough to see her eyes. "Promise?"

"Yes, my lord, I do."

EPILOGUE

I have loved the stars too fondly to be fearful of the night.

> ~Sarah Williams

Oxfordshire, 1869

Julian lingered by the bassinette, listening to his son's whispery breaths, cut only by Piper's sturdier ones coming from the settee she slumbered on. Make no mistake, and he never would again: his entire world lay within the narrow confines of Harbingdon's nursery.

Walls he and Humphrey had painted an eye-stinging yellow because Piper had read bright colors comforted babes. Or encouraged intelligence or some such rot. He'd even gone so far as creating a whimsical series of landscapes featuring frolicking bears and romping unicorns, nonsensical apart from the smile that had lit Piper's face when she'd seen it.

He would do anything, *anything*, to be the reason behind that smile.

He slipped his finger into Lucien's curled fist and gave it a gentle waggle that had the boy cooing and shifting on the blankets. Then the baby smiled dreamily, a slight curve of his perfectly bowed lips, a tiny scrap of naught that shot an arrow straight through Julian's heart. *I'm going to paint a thousand paintings of you, my love.* He leaned in and gave the boy's silken cheek another caress, happiness as substantial a presence as the woolen coat warming his body.

Lost to love, he didn't hear her walk up behind him.

"If you wake him, I may have to kill you," she whispered as her arms circled his waist, her head settling on his back. Solace as necessary as the blood flowing through his veins, the oxygen entering his lungs. He released a tense sigh he hadn't realized he held—had been holding since he left them at dawn.

"You know how I am when I miss dinner with my two favorite people."

"Is that the reason for the pensive look? Isn't our darling boy enough to bring a smile to your face?"

He linked their fingers and pressed her hands against his belly. "A joy is what he is. An absolute terror and delight. With his mother's spirit—"

"And his father's eyes."

Julian released her and crossed to the window, ticked the drape aside to gaze into a night full of promise. The stars had agreed to create a remarkable show, bleeding light on the lawn and sparking off the blue-black waters of the lake. He located Canis Minor, his touchpoint, high in the heavens. Still bright, still there.

Piper fit herself onto the window seat, tucking her feet beneath her. "You're going to worry yourself sick until Lucien can tell us he touches things and doesn't see visions? Or until he tells he does? Just because he has your eyes…"

He let the drape fall and wiggled in beside her, pulling her against his body. This window seat wasn't large—but it was large enough. They'd made love on it more than once. Had made love in every room in the main house, the outbuildings, Brook Cottage. The conservatory. The stables. Every inch of his property presented delicious options. Piper loved leaving him notes telling him to meet her in said location. And like a dog on the hunt, he went. He never knew if he was going to find her naked and wearing only a wicked smile, or all those layers she expected him to peel from her luscious body.

Sexual games, bawdy negotiations, *laughter*.

She had punctured a hole in his life and let blissful contentment flood in. Let joy and fun flood in.

He placed a kiss on the crown of her head, trying for a carefree response. "Maybe. When do babies start talking again?"

She laughed, and he felt the pinch. Of wonder. Of ecstasy. Of disbelief. *He* made her happy. Amazingly, Julian Alexander made Piper Scott happy. This incredible, vibrant, generous woman. Almost daily, he wondered what he had done to deserve her.

"Are you worried about Ashcroft? Is that it?"

Julian let loose a sound falling somewhere between a snort and a sneer. "Come again?"

"It was in this morning's broadsheet. An opera singer this time. A slight skirmish, no flames whipping through Covent Garden or anything like that. I have to say, his control is remarkable, which it should be after years of diligent effort."

"Except when it's not. Remember the debacle at the Epsom Derby last year?"

"He's your friend. An essential part of the League's success. He can't continue like this, one woman after another. You could—"

"Love's going to sneak up and bite him on the ass just like it does the rest of us. We're going to have to ride his idiocy out, I fear. Someday, someone will mean enough to make him change his mind. And his ways. Make him understand he can share his gift, lighten the load."

"It's possible to have love and a mystical talent. We're proof of that." She sighed a heated breath against his neck. "I've told him this a thousand times. I only wish he believed me."

Julian wedged his shoulder against the wall and counted to twenty. He didn't want to seem too eager to ask the question. Broach the topic currently top of mind, the reason his mood was tinted as dark as the night at his back. "Anyone else in this family featured in the scandal sheets lately?"

"Oh, Julian."

He tipped his head back and closed his eyes. What was the use of artificiality when she knew him as well as she did? "We're losing Finn." He would have taken the words back—or never spoken them at all—if he knew they'd sound like shards of glass when they spilled out. Most days, he viewed Lucien and Finn with the same parental lens, which made Finn, a determined, confounding young man of twenty-three, viciously displeased. "The boy we couldn't save damaged him in a way I didn't expect. A crushing blow, when we can't possibly protect everyone. He's aimless, unable to recover. It's like he's cut the rope connecting us and set himself adrift. Living above that gaming hell I only bought as an investment, never thinking he would be involved. A graduate of

Oxford managing a gambling establishment? Is this his path?"

"I think he's trying to *find* his path. That's the point of rebellion. Learning from one's mistakes."

"First-rate insight from a master. What about that drunken scuffle with the Earl of Sandford five *blocks* from the rookery hellhole where he was born? Why would he want to step foot in that neighborhood again after we risked our very lives to get him out of it?"

Piper's fingers brushed his cheek and snaked into his hair. Her lips found his, her love and understanding flowing through him, giving him courage when he had little. "He'll be home next month, Jules. Simon's birthday is the thirteenth. Finn would never miss that."

"You'll talk to him? Because I'll get mad if I do."

Piper snuggled against him with one of those relaxed purrs that made the hairs on his nape stand on end. "I'll talk to him. Make him see a graduate of Oxford need not manage a gaming hell."

"Because I know what it's like to feel unworthy of happiness. So bewildered in this strange world we find ourselves thrust into. I don't want Finn to wait as long as I did to embrace love. A strong partner will help him navigate the chaos, find who he's meant to become."

"He's thought to be the most handsome man in England, Jules. Love is *plentiful*. He breaks hearts by doing nothing more than strolling down the street."

Julian smacked his head against the windowpane. "That doesn't make me feel better, Yank. What if he gets the pox?"

Smothering laughter Julian wouldn't appreciate, Piper lifted her nightdress to her shoulders and with a suggestive shimmy, let it drift to the floor. Then she climbed atop him as his breath left his body in a whoosh. "If you promise not to wake the babe, I have an interesting proposal, Viscount Beauchamp. A way to take your mind off your troubles."

A gorgeous, enthusiastic viscountess, naked and astride him?

He would promise anything.

~ END ~

THANKS!

Thanks for reading *The Lady is Trouble*. Look for Finn's supernatural romance, *The Rake is Taken*.

Continue reading for a sneak peek!

THE LEAGUE OF LORDS
SERIES

THE RAKE
IS
TAKEN

AWARD-WINNING AUTHOR
TRACY
SUMNER

ABOUT THE BOOK

A gorgeous psychic.
An unwanted betrothal.
A tantalizing compromise.

An independent hellion, a thief of time, and the only woman who can capture his heart...

Lady Victoria Hamilton has a supernatural gift, a fiancé, and a guardian angel. She just never expected her protector to be the most dazzling man in England, a devilish scoundrel they call the Blue Bastard. Victoria has agreed to marry for duty, not love, but her unforeseen desire for her mystical angel threatens to destroy not only her plans for the future but the armor surrounding her susceptible heart.

A confirmed scoundrel, a mind reader, and the only man she desires...

Illegitimate son of a viscount and reigning king of London's gossip sheets, Finn Alexander has spent a lifetime hiding his ability to read minds behind charming smiles and wicked behavior. No one knows the real man, and he likes it that way. Until he meets the lone woman who sees the man beneath the disguise—a blue-blooded temptress with the power to bring him to his knees.

As they embark on a journey of passion and friendship, Victoria and Finn must decide if they're willing to risk everything for the promise of true, magical love.

PROLOGUE

In a very loathsome part of the city...
London, 1855

Finn had two choices. Which wasn't dreadful, as he often had none.

Trust the word of the men waiting in the alley outside his lean-to. Or run. When he'd spent all nine years of his life running. Dodging misfortune, grasping hands, chaotic dreams, and thoughts not his own.

There'd been a life before. He had memories. A girl with flaxen hair clutching his hand as they raced through a field of some splendid purple flower, her smile wide, her gaze focused on him in a way no one's had since. But those memories were as out of reach as Queen Victoria's blooming crown, as murky as the rotten, throat-stinging stew hanging over the river outside his door.

Finn wiped his nose on his tattered sleeve and shivered, a frigid gust tearing inside his shack and sending the city's stench into his nostrils. A reminder of how close to the bone he lived. All he *didn't* have. Opportunities he couldn't *afford* to miss.

The men, their promises, could be a *good* thing.

Against the better judgment of a world trying to beat that belief out of him, Finn hadn't given up on good things.

He glanced around the dark, dank warren he'd constructed beneath the back staircase of the Cock and Bur with scraps of wood pilfered from the docks. It was a piss-poor rabbit hole in London's most despicable parish, but it was *his*. His when he had nothing but what he'd managed to steal. A silver fork, a cheap paste broach, a truly fine kid leather glove, a book, the stained pages nonetheless fascinating for what little he could read of the story.

Finn smiled, though it felt shaky around the edges. He was an incredibly good thief, of lots of things, and thank God for it, or he'd long ago be dead. Peering through a split in the timber, he inspected the two men conversing in low tones, their voices harmonizing with the howling wind. The posh bloke's words from moments ago returned to him. *Let me help you. I, too, have a supernatural gift I can't control. You can trust me.*

Trust.

Finn curled his hands into fists and slammed his eyes shut, tears pricking his lids. What he had—the ability to read minds—was no gift. It was a *curse*.

But he could use it. Would use it. Had used it every day to survive.

Calming himself, Finn let the men's thoughts ruthlessly worm their way through the ragged wood of his battered abode and into his mind. He couldn't always read a person without touching them...but sometimes, if they didn't put up a mental fuss, he could. One of the men, a giant the size one rarely saw outside a fighting ring, oh, his thoughts were there for the taking, a clear match for the pity shining in

344

his eyes. Humphrey. Well, nothing cross about Humphrey, even if he looked like he could smash you into the cobblestones with nothing more than a crook of his pinkie.

The fancy one, upon close inspection only a few years older than Finn, was a harder read. Troubled and angry, emotions Finn recognized right off. Slowing his breathing, Finn worked hard to grasp the man's name, needing it for some reason. Needing the connection.

Julian.

He would love to tell the spit-polished Julian, who spoke with an upmarket accent no one got while living in this hellhole, that if Finn touched him, he'd unlock every secret. Twist Lord High-Class inside out with what he could see, no matter how hard a brain-battle the man waged.

Finn caught his reflection in the mirror shard balanced on a crate, and his heart sank. Another curse. Another limiter of choices. Prettiness that had so far been nothing but a disaster. Eyes so bleeding blue that once seen, they were never forgotten. An unfortunate circumstance for a pickpocket—being unable to slink away without being identified as that *beautiful boy.*

"*Beau garçon,*" he whispered, the words coming to him in French like they always did. A language he dreamed in for no reason he could figure. Part of his blank slate of a past, when all he truly knew was the name—Finn—scribbled on the foolscap delivered to the orphanage with him.

Through a serrated gash in the wood, he watched Julian place his hand on the lean-to and shudder with comprehension. The word immediately tripped from the posh bloke's mind to his.

Family.

Finn's deepest desire, and the one phrase with the power to break him when nothing else had. Not the edge of a blade dug beneath his chin, not a flaming cheroot extinguished on his wrist. Not rough handling of the worst kind.

Pitch-black, nightmare handling one never, *ever* forgot.

Remembering, Finn released a cry that sounded like it had come from a distressed animal and dropped to the filthy cobblestones, hugging his knees to his chest. The hulking giant tore the lean-to's door aside and pulled Finn into his arms, making hushing sounds as if he were a babe. Finn sagged against the beast's rough woolen coat, appalled by his weakness, embarrassed, ashamed, but unable to find the courage to turn away.

To run.

In the end, he let them lead him down the alley and to the waiting hackney cab. Lead him to an uncertain future. Of course, he wouldn't have accepted the offer, *any* offer, without a fight if the men hadn't already visited his twilight musings on more than one wretched night.

Because he only dreamed about those who mattered.

In a very enchanting part of the city...

Her father was outraged. Again.

Victoria pressed her back against the nursery door and scrubbed her face free of tears. No use trying to leave the chamber when they'd locked her in. After the last incident, she'd gone two days without food. Now, there were crackers in the top drawer of her chest, secreted beneath her badly-embroidered handkerchiefs, and a slice of cheese wrapped in a linen napkin hidden underneath her pillow. Agnes, her companion, and lady's maid once Victoria was old enough to need one, always kept water in the room, just in case.

Victoria hadn't meant to ruin her father's party. She'd approached Lady Dane-Hawkins because the woman had whispered a rude comment about her to Lady Markem as they strolled from the dining room to the salon. Victoria *was* odd; she knew that. But she'd worked hard to appear normal, or as normal as a child could when they were, in fact, *not* normal. To have that gray-haired snipe say something that made her parents turn and look at her— as if to determine what precisely about their daughter was so strange—when Victoria tried valiantly to evaporate like morning mist when she was around them, was too much. Lady Dane-Hawkins had placed another crack in the cup that held their love, and Victoria felt it leaking away even faster.

She would have told them about her talent long ago if she wanted her parent's affection to wither like an aster bloom in the winter.

She'd only slipped her fingers around Lady Dane-Hawkins' wrist for one moment, long enough to erase whatever Victoria had done to make the woman think badly of her. A few minutes of the lady's memory obliterated. Maybe the entire night, but with a crowded social calendar, who needed another of those? Unfortunately, Lady Dane-Hawkins had fainted dead away, dropped right to the Aubusson carpet her mother loved, her glass of sherry going with her in a rosy-red spill.

Victoria's parlor trick, the ability to steal time,

was one she'd been employing since forever. Although it never worked out well for anyone.

A light knock sounded. A folded sheet of foolscap inched beneath the door.

Victoria opened the note, a tear rolling down her cheek and dropping to the parchment. She watched it bleed into the ink, fracturing the script into broken pieces. *You're not odd. You're unique.*

Charles.

Her brother, her protector. He and Agnes knew about her peculiarity when no one else did. No one else cared.

Her family was much smaller than it looked from the outside.

Dropping her head to her knees, she shivered. There would be no fire in the hearth tonight. No companion to read her a story. No food aside from the concealed cheese and crackers. No love, as expected.

She'd been told often enough that eccentric people usually grew to live solitary lives.

So often, she now believed it.

ABOUT TRACY

Tracy's story telling career began when she picked up a copy of LaVyrle Spencer's Vows on a college beach trip. A journalism degree and a thousand romance novels later, she decided to try her hand at writing a southern version of the perfect love story. With a great deal of luck and more than a bit of perseverance, she sold her first novel to Kensington Publishing.

When not writing sensual stories featuring complex characters and lush settings, Tracy can be found reading romance, snowboarding, watching college football and figuring out how she can get to 100 countries before she kicks. She lives in the south, but after spending a few years in NYC, considers herself a New Yorker at heart.

Tracy has been awarded the National Reader's Choice, the Write Touch and the Beacon—with finalist nominations in the HOLT Medallion, Heart of Romance, Rising Stars and Reader's Choice. Her books have been translated into German, Dutch, Portuguese and Spanish. She loves hearing from readers about why she tends to pit her hero and heroine against each other from the very first page or that great romance she simply must order in five seconds on her Kindle.

Connect with Tracy on http://www.tracy-sumner.com

Printed in Great Britain
by Amazon